PRAISE FOR

WATCH OUT FOR HER

"Relentlessly tense and incredibly twisty . . . I flew through the cinematic pages, riveted and completely immersed in this propulsive and original thriller. Everyone will be talking about this—do not miss it!"

Hank Phillippi Ryan, *USA TODAY* bestselling author of
Her Perfect Life

"An addictive read from start to finish . . . Will have you second-guessing everyone you meet and rooting for characters you don't trust—and there is nothing more fun than that. Absolutely riveting."

Jennifer Hillier, bestselling author of *Little Secrets* and the
award-winning *Jar of Hearts*

"Twisty and unpredictable, this deliciously creepy story full of deliciously creepy characters gave me goosebumps!"

Allie Reynolds, author of *Shiver*

"This insanely addictive, utterly propulsive, and unbelievably tense thriller will consume you. With intoxicating, scalpel-sharp prose and gasp-worthy twists, Bailey has crafted a fresh and deeply unsettling take on obsession and voyeurism."

May Cobb, author of *The Hunting Wives*

"A deep dive into a world of secrets, where no one is who you think they are and everyone has something to hide. Bailey's deft hand at ratcheting up tension makes this an exquisite read. It will suck you in and you'll love every moment of it!"

Amina Akhtar, author of *Kismet* and *#FashionVictim*

PRAISE FOR

WOMAN ON THE EDGE

"**A fast-moving thriller** with satisfying twists."

Toronto Star

"**Bailey has talent** and I, dear reader, am looking forward to her next novel."

The Globe and Mail

"An **explosive debut**. *Woman on the Edge* is **a white-knuckle read** that welcomes a bright new talent to the world of psychological suspense."

Mary Kubica, *New York Times* bestselling author of *Local Woman Missing*

"A shocking premise and two intriguingly damaged characters whose story lines hurtle toward each other, colliding in a powerful, moving climax. **A propulsive read!**"

Robyn Harding, bestselling author of *The Perfect Family*

"This is the page-turner you've been looking for! Bailey's writing is gripping and emotionally resonant at once."

Marissa Stapley, bestselling author of *Lucky*

"A propulsive beginning grabs the reader by the throat, but it's the unspooling of the plot and the layers of Bailey's characters that keep you turning the pages."

Lisa Unger, *New York Times*
bestselling author of *Confessions on the 7:45*

"[A] nail-biting debut . . . The tension becomes unrelenting. . . . Fans of psychological suspense are in for a treat."

Publishers Weekly (starred review)

"An impressive debut that will keep you reading until the final twist."

Samantha Downing, *USA TODAY*
bestselling author of *My Lovely Wife*

"A clever and addictive read from a bright new talent."

Kimberly Belle, *USA TODAY*
bestselling author of *Dear Wife*

"From the moment two women's lives collide on a subway platform to the shocking finale, you'll be dizzied by the twists and turns the story takes."

Amy Stuart, bestselling author of *Still Here*

"This masterful debut needs to be your next binge-read. A knockout page-turner."

Heather Gudenkauf, *New York Times*
bestselling author of *The Weight of Silence*

"Races towards its final destination with breakneck speed."

Chatelaine

ALSO BY SAMANTHA M. BAILEY

Woman on the Edge

WATCH
OUT FOR
HER

A NOVEL

SAMANTHA M. BAILEY

PUBLISHED BY SIMON & SCHUSTER

New York   London   Toronto   Sydney   New Delhi

Simon & Schuster Canada
A Division of Simon & Schuster, Inc.
166 King Street East, Suite 300
Toronto, Ontario M5A 1J3

This Simon & Schuster Canada edition April 2022

SIMON & SCHUSTER CANADA and colophon are
trademarks of Simon & Schuster, Inc.

For information about special discounts for bulk purchases,
please contact Simon & Schuster Special Sales at 1-800-268-3216
or CustomerService@simonandschuster.ca.

Manufactured in the United States of America

1 3 5 7 9 10 8 6 4 2

Library and Archives Canada Cataloguing in Publication
Title: Watch out for her / Samantha M. Bailey.
Names: Bailey, Samantha M., 1973– author.
Description: Simon & Schuster Canada edition.
Identifiers: Canadiana (print) 20210289546 | Canadiana (ebook) 20210289554 |
ISBN 9781982155193 (softcover) | ISBN 9781982155209 (ebook)
Classification: LCC PS8603.A44347 W38 2022 | DDC C813/.6—dc23

ISBN 978-1-9821-5519-3
ISBN 978-1-9821-5520-9 (ebook)

To Brent, Spencer, and Chloe,
I love you more.

Fear, indeed, is the mother of foresight.

—HENRY TAYLOR

CHAPTER ONE

SARAH

Now

I watch people.

With a voyeur's keen eyes, I peer out the window of our rental car as Daniel pulls up to our new house at 227 Lilac Lane. This is the house we'll be living in for the next six months until we find one we want to buy. I've seen only grainy pictures of the inside. The new consulting firm my husband will be working for found the home for us—an incentive to bring him on board. It makes this sudden move across the country easier. Easier but still hard.

At twilight, the detached two-story blends into the others on this quiet suburban Toronto street, like I hope we will. At the end of the block, there's a cul-de-sac, and a set of boxy town houses across from a ravine. I shiver, not from the bitter mid-September chill but because the woods feel too close. They remind me too much of everything we left behind in Vancouver.

Our son, Jacob, and I exit the car, sneakers squelching in the puddles from an overnight rain. The sound centers me in the present, far from Holly Monroe, our babysitter over the summer, and the reason I agreed to this unexpected move. Daniel is ahead of us, dragging a suitcase behind him. Every few seconds, he looks over his shoulder, smiling. I smile back, but inside I'm crying over everything I've hidden from him—and everything he might be hiding from me.

Jacob stops in front of the three-bedroom redbrick home looming before us.

"It has eyes," he says. His voice is flat, his body trembling through his thin coat. The wind is sharper in Toronto than North Vancouver, something else my son is now forced to get used to. "The windows are the eyes, and the door is the mouth. It has no nose, though."

I pull him close. A six-year-old's imagination, but still, his words haunt me.

Jacob isn't aware of the real reason we've left Vancouver. All he knows is that Daddy got an exciting new job as a business consultant in the city where he grew up, and Mommy supports Daddy. Neither my little boy nor my husband knows anything about the nights I hid in the thick cluster of trees outside our pool enclosure because it offered the perfect view of our babysitter's house.

I wanted to be her. Holly—young, beautiful, her whole life an exciting blank slate. But then I stopped trusting her. And in the end, I wanted only to protect what was mine.

I turn to my son as he slips his thumb into his mouth, a habit I thought he'd gotten over this summer. My heart constricts at how vividly the freckles dotting Jacob's nose stand out against his chalk-white skin. He looks terrible. We took the red-eye so he would sleep, but he was devastated about the move, about being uprooted so suddenly, that he cried for almost the entire flight. It's been said that you're only as happy as your unhappiest child. I have just one child, and he's shattered, so that's how I'm feeling, too. He's lost his home and left behind everyone he loves, except me and Daniel.

"Ready to see the house?" I ask, trying to sound upbeat.

Jacob pulls his wet thumb out of his mouth. The skin around the nail is ripped and chapped. "I want to go home."

Well, that's impossible, I think to myself, but I don't say it out loud. Two weeks ago, Daniel sold our beautiful cliffside home in Forest View to a private buyer from his exclusive golf club. Our home doesn't belong to us anymore. My husband has taken care of everything, for once, a far cry from the man who doesn't make his own lunches for work and who has left child-rearing our son mostly to me. All I have to do now, in this new place, is be Jacob's mother. I should have been content with that all along rather than yearning for more, for my own sense of self.

A porch light flicks on when Daniel gets to the front door. Jacob and I follow him up the three steep steps, and I peer through the decorative glass, our ghostly reflections staring back at me. Daniel rummages for the key in the lockbox, inserts it, and turns it. There's no click. The black oak door wasn't locked.

"Wow. The property manager forgot to lock it," Daniel says.

I feel eyes on me and spin around. Under the dim yellow glow of a streetlamp, a curtain twitches in the house across the street. A face appears, then disappears. I will not overreact. I refuse to give into the foreboding dread that's been pressing on my chest since the last time I saw Holly sixteen days ago.

I trail behind Daniel, pushing Jacob inside and locking the front door behind us. Before I can even look around the main floor, Jacob lets out a howl—a low, agonized wail that twists my insides. Daniel looks at me, shutting his eyes for a moment like he always does to try to make it all disappear.

I take over as usual. "What's wrong?" I ask Jacob as I kneel on the hardwood at his eye level.

"Mr. Blinkers! I can't live here without him!" He punches his fist over and over on his skinny thigh. I take his tiny hand and hold it between mine.

There's no pain greater than your child's pain. I've made so many mistakes that I can never undo. My sole focus now is making my son happy again. But I can't because we lost his favorite toy, Mr. Blinkers—the soft, gray stuffed bunny he slept with every night, all summer long. It disappeared while we were packing up the few items of clothing, toys, and electronics we brought with us. I blame myself. I probably threw it out by accident. It's my fault, like so many things that happened over the summer.

"Maybe we can find a new Mr. Blinkers at a store here, sweetheart."

Daniel drops our bags, and the house keys hit the small ebony table at the door. The clang makes me jump.

He crouches with me in front of Jacob. "Buddy, we'll get you a new bunny, and we'll take him to see the CN Tower. It has a restaurant at the top that spins."

Daniel's trying too hard, and Jacob sees right through it.

"I want the bunny Holly gave me!" He leans into my shoulder, and the tears come so fast and furious my coat is damp. I hug him fiercely and let him cry, my rainbow baby, my miracle after my miscarriage. Jacob is the only child I'll ever have.

Daniel locks eyes with me, his full of regret. Regret about what? How strained and distant our marriage has become? How invisible I've been to him for the last year? How friendly he and Holly were when they didn't know I was watching? No, I won't go there right now. He's reassured me—I had it wrong. It was all in my head.

Since the day Daniel suggested moving across the country to fix everything, he's been making such an effort to be more attentive, to make me feel like I matter, like when we got married fifteen years ago. I've chosen to believe him that nothing was going on between him and Holly. I've chosen to believe it, but do I actually?

I have to be rational, for once. Daniel is the man who massaged my feet every single night when I was pregnant with Jacob. Daniel

4

cried with me when we lost our first baby, our daughter, at sixteen weeks because her heart had stopped beating inside me.

I can't lose anyone else. It would break me.

Jacob keeps bringing up Holly, and every time, it puts my teeth on edge. Daniel is the first to answer him.

"Jacob, it's better we don't talk about Holly, okay? We need to move on."

There it is again: my husband is trying. I run my hand over his thick brown hair, just starting to gray at the temples. Of course the gray suits him, while my hair, which I dyed platinum at the end of July, is pulled back in a greasy ponytail, but the dark roots are already showing.

"I want everything the way it used to b-b-be," Jacob stutters.

"Honey," I say. "Change is hard, but everything's going to be okay. It will be even better than before."

My voice cracks. It was so hard to say goodbye to my mom, my brother, Nathan, sister-in-law, Pam, and nieces Sienna and Lily. Before this, I'd never left Vancouver for more than a couple of weeks. Now the mere idea of ever returning fills me with dread. I lost all control this summer. I saw things I should never have seen. I did things I should never have done.

I stroke Jacob's cheek before stepping out of the foyer toward the first doorway. There are two more doorways ahead, a creepy fairy-tale house of endless doors. The darkness immediately overwhelms me. Our old house boasted a large open-concept design with long windows, through which the morning light shone bright and happy. From our pool deck, we were mere steps from the forest of stately Douglas firs overlooking the Capilano River that swirled just beyond our backyard. Here the main floor is all dark molding and narrow windows. Eerie shadows spill onto the dusty, sable-colored hardwood.

I blow out a heavy breath and snuggle Jacob, whose teeth are chattering. "We should turn on the heat."

"Sure. Jacob, come with me. We'll find the thermostat. I forgot how much colder it is in Toronto. Even in September." My husband's skin is pallid. He looks as exhausted as I am. I feel another sharp pang of guilt, but I try to focus on Daniel, who seems happy to be back in Toronto, where he was raised, beginning a new consulting career after a decade as a COO in Vancouver, handcuffed to his desk.

I hold the black banister all the way up the curved staircase, leading to a spacious landing covered in brown hickory flooring. The master bedroom is large, with expensive, somber oak dressers and headboard. I itch to snoop in the nooks and crannies to discover who lived here before us and what skeletons they might have hidden in this house. Old habits die hard.

I close the door and glance in the full-length mirror on the back. My cheeks are hollow, and the circles under my eyes are a deep purple. I don't care. Here I can go back to being Sarah Goldman: just a mother and wife, no longer a photographer and a woman who was obsessed with her twenty-two-year-old babysitter.

My fatigue is debilitating. I've never slept well, but the frenzied rush to leave Vancouver has drained me.

With Daniel and Jacob downstairs working on the heat and hopefully bringing in the few boxes in the trunk, I lie back on the king-size bed, bare of sheets or a duvet. This maudlin house isn't to my taste, but at least it's furnished. I'm glad to see a smoke detector on the ceiling, but the tiny light in the middle isn't on. I should check the batteries. At only five foot one, I need to grab the black chaise next to the window that overlooks the street.

I drag it under the smoke detector, releasing dust motes into the air. I stand on it, sighing, because my fingers can't possibly reach high enough to take it down. But I can at least see it clearly now.

It's not a light in the middle, not a light at all. But there's something round in the center of the smoke detector.

It's a camera.

The house has eyes.

Someone is watching me.

CHAPTER TWO

HOLLY

Before

Holly's father sits across from her at the long mahogany dining room table. She woke up extra early this morning so she could have breakfast with him alone. She loves this time, only the two of them, when the sun hits the ornate crystal chandelier hanging from the vaulted ceiling, bathing them in a golden light. In these rare moments, he's just her dad, not John Monroe, scion of Health ProX.

Her University of British Columbia medical school transcripts, which have just come in the mail, rest next to his plate of fresh fruit. Her father doesn't eat heavy meals before work anymore. Holly's stepmother, Lisette, has him on a strict diet.

"Well done, Holly," her father says, taking a sip of coffee. "You passed all your exams, which is expected. Of course I still think your goal next term is to be top of your class, but an eighty-nine-percent average overall in your first year of med school is quite good." He taps the transcript with his index finger. "You should start thinking about choosing a supervisor for your pharmaceutical research project in third year."

She's not hungry anymore. Tears prick her eyes, but she hides them. Monroes can only be the best; everything else is deemed a failure. "Thank you, Daddy," she says as she tears a piece off her buttery croissant but puts it down. "Maybe we can have lunch today?"

If he says yes, she'll spend the morning working up the courage. Somehow, she'll spit it out, tell him that she doesn't want to go back to medical school in the fall. She doesn't want to be bound forever to Health ProX or bear the responsibility of carrying on the family legacy. She wants to be free to travel, maybe study psychology, exist as her own person aside from being a Monroe. But she doesn't want her father to ever be disappointed in her.

He shakes his head, his hair still thick at forty-seven. "Sorry, honey. I have a meeting with Charlie Lang. He wants to see the lab facilities and latest stats for Ritofan." Then he winks. "I think he might be close to investing. If we can bring in Charlie, this beta blocker could take Health ProX international. Lisette will set up a meeting with just you and him." He smiles at her then, and she feels like a princess. All her worries disappear under his gaze.

Still, Charlie Lang, owner of one of the largest Vancouver development firms and probably the wealthiest and most powerful man her father knows, is intimidating. Her father is counting on her. But what if she can't snag Charlie's investment? It's the most important one she's ever been tasked with. Failure is not an option. She's got this.

Holly doesn't remember a single meal when her father hasn't mentioned Health ProX, the leading national pharmaceutical company that is her birthright and, if her dad gets his way, will one day be her sole purpose in life. Her father wants the best for her. She knows that. He's devoted to his work, devoted to making the family name into a legend. But her heart sinks when she thinks of the summer ahead, spent wooing investors for Ritofan, her father's revolutionary heart drug, which in preliminary trials has produced fewer side effects than other such drugs on the market. It's the first product her father is seeking FDA approval for. But to begin the human clinical trials, the last and most expensive stage of the process before they can file the New Drug Application, they need to raise upward of forty million dollars. This is an epic time for their family.

Maybe she doesn't know exactly what she wants from life, but does she want this? Her mind is spinning today; she's out of sorts. She looks at her father as he smiles proudly at her. He doesn't get it. Every time she's approached the subject of her sales meetings, he veers away. He doesn't quite realize how much of Holly it takes to make these powerful men invest. When she manages to lure one in, it's the best thing in the world. Her father laughs and hugs her, lavishes her with praise and love, tells her he's the luckiest man in the world to have a daughter like her. So why isn't she happy? Why isn't it enough that she's his little girl, the apple of his eye?

Holly hears the *click-clack* of Lisette's heels echoing dangerously on the Italian hardwood in the atrium. Fuck. Here she comes. Holly smells her before she sees her. Lisette's expensive perfume clogs the air. Her stepmother's dressed for her day of ladies lunching in a floral sundress that hugs her gym-toned curves. She stands next to Holly, her blunt-cut black hair sprayed into a helmet.

"Your interview with the Goldmans is at nine," she says to Holly.

"Interview?" John asks as he pops a piece of mango in his mouth, smiling at his wife and daughter like they're his treasures. Or chattels.

Lisette grins, her face muscles barely twitching through the Botox. "Yes. Daniel Goldman is looking for a babysitter for their six-year-old son. They want someone all summer so his wife, Sarah, can have some time to herself." She reaches for a porcelain cup on the credenza and pours coffee from the silver French press. "Don't you remember him mentioning it at lunch last Sunday?"

"I don't think I heard that. But Holly babysitting for the Goldmans is an excellent idea. I like Daniel. He's done very well for himself as COO of Code Tek. He's moving up. Also, he's a smart investor, so I think there's potential there. For us, I mean." He does this sometimes, talks about Holly like she isn't there.

Lisette hovers next to her. She puts her hand on Holly's bare shoulder, but it's far from comforting. Holly looks at the woman who's a poor substitute for the mother she never knew. Her own mother, Caitlin, died giving birth to her. Holly isn't sure her father has ever forgiven her for killing his wife. To Holly, his marriage to Lisette is a punishment meant for her.

The fact that Lisette hasn't yet moved means she's waiting. She wants something. In the beginning, Holly tried to tell her father how sad Lisette made her, but he was so in love with the sultry beauty and truly believed Lisette loved Holly as much as she loved her own daughter, Alexis, and him. Men. They could be so dumb.

Holly has long given up on any kind of mother-daughter relationship with this woman. At least Holly has Alexis, her stepsister and best friend, the product of Lisette's first, short-lived marriage to a man whose name Lisette never utters.

Holly was six when she met eleven-year-old Alexis. They forged an immediate bond, making it easy for Lisette to place the responsibility of Holly's care on Alexis's capable shoulders. Holly knows she's blessed with her mother's natural beauty, whereas Alexis is big-boned and clumsy, not at all the kind of girl—then or now—who's the obvious glamour at a posh party or fancy event. The only time Lisette has ever showered attention on Holly is when she needs her, as she does now—for appearances, or for some kind of dirty work.

John pushes his chair back, then nods at Holly. "Babysitting would be a beneficial addition to your résumé if you want to specialize in pediatrics for your residency. The market for children's medicine is growing exponentially. It could be very useful. You should know that Daniel Goldman has friends in high places. I've seen him at the Canyon Club talking to Charlie. He's also golfed with me and Stan Fielding recently."

Useful. Holly doesn't want to babysit some whiny kid so his mother can get mani/pedis all summer long. Or hear about Stan Fielding, the CEO of a major oil company, her father's golf partner, and longtime investor in the family firm. But the way her father is looking at her, with adoration and pride, and the greedy glint in Lisette's eyes leaves her no choice. She's a Monroe. It's her job to help expand the empire. It's interesting, though, the double standard. Alexis has never been invited to work with Health ProX. And she's definitely not expected to woo clients. If anything, Holly's father and Lisette want her as far away from the business as possible.

Holly gets up from the table.

"Wait," Lisette says.

For a split second, Holly imagines her stepmother might say something encouraging. "Yes?" She hates the hope that leaps in her chest but can't stop it.

"Bring a bathing suit to the Goldman interview. They have a pool."

"Okay," she says. Even as she says it, she resents how sweet and obedient the word sounds as it leaves her mouth. It's a complete betrayal of everything in her heart.

Holly trudges up the spiral stairs to her wing in the massive Forest View house, passing Alexis's old bedroom, now Lisette's personal gym. It looks nothing like it did when Alexis lived here. Alexis moved out two years ago, because at twenty-five and a nursing school graduate, it was time to make her own way. It's what she wanted. Now she lives in Lynnmour, a ten-minute drive from here, in a basement apartment. It's a bare-bones one-bedroom because Alexis hasn't been able to find a nursing job. Caring and attentive, Alexis would be a wonderful nurse, but she doesn't interview well. She has no idea how to sell herself. That's Holly's domain.

Holly misses having Alexis in the house so much. She's good to the core, the most selfless, kindest person Holly has ever known. And yet only Holly seems to miss her. The PETA posters and colorful tapestries that adorned the blue walls have been replaced with floor-to-ceiling mirrors so Lisette can watch herself work out from every angle.

Holly pines for the days when Alexis flopped awkwardly on her bed every time she wanted to talk, which was always, and how she ordered sausage pizza, because it was Holly's favorite, on their movie nights in Holly's bedroom because she has the large-screen television. For her stepsister, Holly has always come first. Even when Alexis was thirteen and was invited to a sleepover at Sloane Perkins's, the coolest student in seventh grade, she chose Holly over the "it girl."

Alexis is the only person who fully accepts Holly. Of course, she only accepts her because she doesn't know everything. And she can never find out.

Holly sighs as she walks into her perfectly pink bedroom. She pushes the curtains apart and stares out her window, pressing her face to the glass. When her window's open, she can hear the water rush down the Capilano River below. To everyone else, this place is paradise; to Holly, it's a prison with a nice view.

She knows her relationship with her stepmother isn't normal, but she couldn't find the words to describe it until she took an elective in psychology this past year. Now she understands that Lisette is a classic narcissist; Alexis is her albatross, and Holly her pawn. The only lesson Lisette has imparted is that love is conditional. The professor of the course, Luke Phillips, taught Holly a lot about human behavior. She smiles to herself as she thinks about it. This is one relationship Lisette hasn't orchestrated.

Why didn't Holly tell her stepmother to go to hell? Why does Lisette have the right to tell Holly what job she has to take, how to behave, what to say? She's tired of being a Barbie, the trophy daughter.

Holly pulls on a navy one-piece, throws on her jean shorts, a tank top, and a hoodie, and grabs her backpack. On her way out the door, she spots Lisette's emerald earrings on the front hall table. She shoves them in her pocket, relishing the thrill that courses through her as she takes them just because she can.

Her irritation spikes when she gets to the circular driveway. "Damn it, Lisette." Like a child, she kicks the tire of her stepmother's Mercedes that blocks in the white Jeep her father gave Holly on her eighteenth birthday. She knows if she goes back inside and asks Lisette to move it, she'll only blame Holly and say that when she was young, she never had her own vehicle—"Girls these days are spoiled beyond belief. Not Alexis, of course, but others." She'll give Holly the silent treatment for at least a full day and complain about how even though one of her little birds has flown the nest, the house still feels too busy sometimes. Holly doesn't have the energy or the bandwidth for more guilt and blame to be piled on her shoulders today. The burden she carries right now is heavy enough.

She drags her bike from the back of the garage and decides to cycle the ten minutes to Cliffside Road, where the Goldmans live.

When she makes a right onto Montroyal Boulevard, her phone buzzes in her backpack. She stops, even though she might arrive at the Goldmans' a bit late.

"Hey, I can't talk," Holly tells Alexis when her round face fills the whole screen. She always holds the phone too close. She doesn't wear makeup anymore, not since she left home two years ago.

"You're all dewy under that helmet. Where are you going?"

"Biking to a babysitting interview. Your mother. Don't ask."

"*Babysitting?* I thought you were helping John with sales all summer."

"I am. Day job, night job."

Alexis shakes her head, then turns to someone behind her.

That's when Holly realizes where her stepsister is. She's at work. And behind her is Luke. When Alexis couldn't land a job in her field, Holly stepped in. She arranged for Alexis to work part-time over the summer, filing and researching for Holly's former psychology professor. Holly practically had to beg Luke—and more.

"Please. Alexis is amazing. A super hard worker, diligent. Totally different from me. She needs real work experience if she's ever going to get a job as a nurse."

"I'm not sure I can handle two Monroe women," he teased, kissing Holly's shoulder, because she'd snuck him into her bed while her dad and Lisette were in the opposite wing of the house, completely unaware he was there.

Holly shivers now, her stomach tightening with guilt. There are so many things she can only accomplish one way. Alexis still has no idea about Holly's relationship with Luke. No one does. So many secrets. But Holly's liaison with the professor is cooling. She got what she wanted. She's not into him at all anymore. He's a loose end she has no energy to tie up.

Holly refocuses on Alexis. "I've got to get to the Goldmans' house. Your mother wants me to take care of their kid. The dad's recently joined the Canyon Club."

"Ah," Alexis says. "I see."

"They have a pool at least. You good?"

"Yes. Want to come over after work? Or go out? Thai and a movie?"

Does she want to? She doesn't want to go home, where Lisette and her father will grill her about Daniel Goldman and coax her to ask him questions about his finances. And she should probably break up with Luke tonight, get that over with.

"Maybe. I'll text you when I'm done," Holly says.

"Okay. Drink water. Love you. Oh, Dr. Phillips says hello."

"Say hi back." Holly clears her throat. "Love you, too."

She clicks off, exhales a heavy breath, and cycles up Cliffside Road to an earth-colored detached home with aluminum siding and a porch with two white wicker chairs and a small wrought iron table. It's a nice, regular family house, unlike the gilded cage she lives in.

Leaving her bike propped up near the basketball net on the driveway, Holly pulls off her helmet, hangs it on one of the handlebars, then ties her hoodie around her waist. She grits her teeth as she lifts a hand to knock on the Goldmans' red door.

It bangs open, and a little boy in Iron Man pajamas hops over the basketball on the porch, hurtling past her, right into the street without checking for oncoming cars.

Instinctively, Holly runs and catches him around the waist. "Hey, speedy, the end of the driveway is the stop line, okay?"

The boy regards her with bright blue eyes, his shaggy blond hair falling in his face. He grins, and two dimples deepen his rosy cheeks. If she has to babysit, at least this kid is adorable.

He runs back to the open door where a woman appears, tugging a hand through her shoulder-length, limp blond hair. She looks shaky and tired, but her smile is friendly and warm. She wears no makeup and does not look like one of Lisette's society ladies. Holly can't imagine her lunching with Lisette's gaggle of shallow girlfriends.

"Hi, Holly. I'm Sarah, and this monkey is Jacob."

Jacob gives her an impish grin.

"Nice to meet you."

"Thank you. As you can see, Jacob needs to learn a few things, including how not to run out into the road." Sarah scolds her son, but it's accompanied with an affectionate head shake. "Or answer the door by himself before I can make it upstairs from the basement. I was in my red room just now."

"Red room?" Holly instantly thinks of "redrum" and shudders a little. She used to ask Alexis if they could watch *The Shining* when their parents went out. And Alexis would say, "Only if you promise to come to my room and not Mom and John's if you have a nightmare." Holly always had nightmares and always climbed into Alexis's bed.

She's so lost in her thoughts she fails to register what Sarah just said. She snaps her attention back to the woman in front of her.

"Anyway, I'm a photographer. The red room is my darkroom. Jacob calls it that because of the red lighting. I'll show you sometime, if you want. If you're into photography at all."

"I am into photography," Holly says. "I like travel shots."

"Nice," Sarah says. "I like travel shots, too, but these days, I stay pretty close to home. I shoot what I see around me." She looks at her son, who's pulling at her arm.

Sarah is the polar opposite of Lisette. Warm eyes rather than cold ones, her posture inviting rather than rigid. She's friendly and open, if a little tightly wound.

"Do you have an Instagram account I can follow?" Holly asks, then grins at Jacob, who's obviously desperate for her attention. "I'll bet you can jump really high."

"Watch this!" And he leaps into the air.

"Awesome!"

Sarah says, "Careful, Jacob," then turns back to Holly. "I don't know a thing about Instagram. I'm on Facebook, though." She shrugs. "But even that confuses me. Posts and tags and those emojicons."

Holly bites back a smile. "Emojis, yeah. It's all confusing at first." She already feels at ease with this down-to-earth mom with no social media sense. "If you're a photographer, Insta's the best platform for you. I can help you set up an account if you ever want."

Sarah touches her throat. "Oh, that's a very kind offer. Let's see how it goes. I haven't worked as a professional photographer since I got pregnant with Jacob. It's been such a long time. It's all just a lot right now, you know?"

"Of course. I totally understand," Holly says. She beams at the active little boy standing between them. He hasn't stopped moving through-out their entire conversation. "Can I see your basketball skills?"

"My dad says I'm the dribble master!" He runs to the other side of the porch, retrieves his basketball, and dribbles on the spot like a pro. He stops and waits for praise.

"Nice work!" Holly fist-bumps him and turns to Sarah. "My Insta-gram handle is 'HollyGoLightly99,' by the way. In case you ever want to check it out."

"Like from *Breakfast at Tiffany's*?" Sarah asks.

"Yes. One of my favorites."

"That's so funny. I love that movie, too," Sarah replies.

Holly takes out her phone and angles it toward Sarah so she can view her feed: the selfies Holly has taken at the beach, on campus, and her latest favorite—a shot of her holding *Becoming* by Michelle Obama, a book she hasn't yet read. Her picture-perfect life that looks great on this device but is a mess off-screen.

"Wow. You have a good eye. Shall we go in?"

Holly can't tell if Sarah's compliment is genuine. Sarah steers Jacob into the house, and Holly follows. Once inside, she puts her phone in her backpack. The interior is all light grays and creams, with splashes of orange and teal in accent pieces like pillows and end tables. It feels like a home, in contrast to her own house, which Lisette has designed to look like a special feature section in a magazine.

Jacob runs ahead, and while Holly and Sarah walk to the living room, they pass framed photos on the walls, stunning shots of Capilano River park, the Cleveland Dam, and the suspension bridge, candids of Jacob with his father, Daniel. He's a good-looking man—a full head of brown hair, a boyish face, brown eyes, and a strong jaw—but he definitely looks like all the other Forest View dads she knows—rich, busy, and bland.

"These are beautiful." Holly points to the photos of Daniel and Jacob, mid-leap in the Pacific Ocean at low tide. Sarah caught them at the perfect moment, the waves rolling under their bare feet, faces lit up with joy and freedom. Holly's heart twinges. What does that feel like?

"Oh, thank you," Sarah says, and looks over to the couch, where Jacob is now standing up, arms outstretched like he wants to fly. "Jacob, don't you dare." She blows out a breath and turns back to Holly. "Daniel thought it would be good for me to do something for myself this summer. I've been a stay-at-home mom for a long time." She walks to the couch and points to the floor. "Get down, please."

Holly stifles a smile at Jacob's fearless mischievousness. Then she looks out the large picture windows to the backyard, where an in-ground pool glitters under the sun.

Sarah gestures to the pool through the sliding glass door. "Lisette told me you're a certified lifeguard. Are you okay swimming with

17

Jacob?" She looks at Holly's shoulder. "I see you're wearing a bathing suit already."

Holly tucks the strap under her tank top and nods. She's more than okay. The water's her happy place. Her father and Lisette had insisted both she and her stepsister excel at swimming so they could join the swim team at York House, the prestigious private girls' school they'd attended as kids. Both skilled swimmers, they'd easily landed spots on the team and summer jobs as lifeguards. Alexis, of course, wanted to save lives, but for Holly, it was a great way to meet boys since she didn't go to school with them, not that she ever really dated them. Boys are for practicing. Men are for real life.

"Come. I'll show you the back."

Jacob yanks opens the door, racing out, and Holly follows Sarah to an enclosed deck with four turquoise lounge chairs surrounding a kidney-shaped pool and a round glass table with a red umbrella for shade. It's simple, unpretentious, like Sarah. Set to the right of the pool, there's a cedar cabana.

Sarah notices Holly looking at the cabana. "That's Daniel's man cave. Don't let Jacob play in there. Daniel's pretty protective of his space. He doesn't even like me to go in there." She rolls her eyes and laughs. "Men."

Holly smiles, shifting her attention to the spectacular view from the deck. She has to shield her eyes from the sun. "My house is just across the river. The concrete-and-glass one right in the middle there."

Sarah squints. "Oh, that's a gorgeous house. I didn't realize we lived so close to each other."

Holly moves her finger to the far left. "My bedroom is right there at the top." The river ripples, even without much wind, and the thick cluster of treetops in the woods, so close to the Goldmans' house, barely sway in the humidity. Through a small opening in the knotty branches, she sees her wide window, where she left her curtains open. No one understands what life is like for her in that house. It's so different on this side of the river.

Sarah gives a quick nod and leads Holly back inside to the living room. Jacob sticks close to Holly, and Sarah's eyes dart to her son. "Jacob, can you get in your bathing suit, please?"

Jacob ignores his mother, plopping onto the couch with a thud.

Sarah tenses up instantly but quickly covers her reaction by focusing on Holly. "Your stepmother told me you just finished your first year of medical school."

Holly coughs. "Yeah. I mean, yes. At UBC."

"What an accomplishment. Why medicine?"

Holly spouts the same lie she tells everyone. "To join my dad at Health ProX. We're one big, happy working family."

Holly wishes she wasn't a Monroe but just herself, whoever that might be. But her father made a stipulation to her trust fund, which she is to get when she turns twenty-five, that she has to graduate from medical school and represent Health ProX. It's his way of tethering her to Forest View—and him—forever.

How lucky Jacob is to have a mother who obviously loves him so much, who gives him the freedom to run and play. How lucky he is to have a mother at all.

Sarah looks expectantly at her. "So, what do you think? Are you up for the job? If you're okay doing a trial run today, maybe you can stay and we can see how things go with Jacob?"

"Yay!" Jacob squeals, grinning at Holly.

She grins back. "I'd love that." And she means it. Jacob seems to have taken an instant shine to her, Sarah's so nice, and this house is comfortable, definitely more comfortable than hers.

"Great. I'll be in my darkroom if you need me."

"I'll get my bathing suit!" Jacob speeds from the couch to the stairs in a blur.

Holly laughs. Taking care of this kid won't be so bad after all.

Sarah's eyes go wide. "Wow. He likes you. Usually he's much more . . . stubborn."

Holly feels her cheeks flush. "He won't be bored. I love swimming and biking, and I'll keep him busy."

Judging from the toys and electronics spilling out of a wicker basket in the corner of the living room and the easel pushed against one wall, Jacob has a lot to keep himself busy. Holly's dying to peek into the other rooms. It's something she does whenever she goes somewhere new: people's houses are a reflection of their true selves, but they keep their secrets hidden. There's so much one can learn by poking around. Luke taught her that. It's not about the possessions themselves but more about how people arrange them—what they display, what they hide. Everything tells a story. She wants to know what the Goldmans' story is.

Holly's phone pings, and she pulls it out of her backpack. She feels Sarah watching her. Does this look bad? Maybe she's not supposed to use her phone? After all, she's here to secure a job.

"It's my stepsister," she tells Sarah. "Do you mind if I quickly text her back?"

"Go ahead," Sarah says. "Then if you don't mind running up to hurry Jacob along and go for a swim?"

Holly smiles. "Definitely." Sarah turns on her heel and heads toward the basement stairs.

Alexis: How's it going?

> Holly: Mom nice. Kid cute.
> Haven't met the dad.

Alexis: He'll love you.

Holly winces.

> Holly: Gotta go.

She hears stomping from upstairs, so she puts her phone away to deal with Jacob. When she gets to the landing on the second floor,

Jacob's door is open. Still in his Iron Man pajamas, he's hopping from his bed to the floor and back again. He lands with a bang and his eyes widen when he sees Holly.

"I'm exercising."

Holly laughs. "Ready to go swimming?" She peels off her tank top to reveal her navy one-piece—tasteful but curve-hugging. It's important to always feel good on the outside even if she doesn't feel it on the inside. "Get into your swimsuit, and I'll teach you how to dive for pennies."

She tousles his hair and goes to the hall to wait while he changes. She's proud of herself for handling him so well. She wishes her dad could see how good she is with kids.

She looks down the hallway. Sarah's bedroom door is open. Holly creeps over and peers inside. It's a large but cozy space, with a mint-green armchair in the corner, draped with a fuzzy white blanket, where she imagines Sarah and Jacob cuddle and read together. It feels safe. Like the kind of bedroom she sees in family sitcoms. She wants to lie on the pretty sky-blue duvet, curl up with the fluffy cream pillows.

"Holly?" Jacob calls down the hallway.

She hurries back to his door. He's wearing a white swim shirt and blue swim trunks, leaving less skin exposed to the harsh rays of the sun. "Let's go!"

Together they walk downstairs, Jacob slipping his small hand in hers and tugging her toward the backyard pool. He jumps into the water before Holly can stop him. For a moment, she panics, but when she sees what a strong swimmer he is, she starts to breathe again.

"Watch this!" she calls out. Jacob's eyes pop as Holly performs a perfect-ten jackknife off the diving board.

"Wow! Will you teach me how to do that?"

"By the end of the summer, you'll do a killer dive!"

Jacob ducks under the water in the shallow end to do a gangly underwater cartwheel, which makes Holly giggle. But then she hears something behind her.

She turns, glances at the basement window at eye level. In the window, she sees Sarah, her face half-covered by a long lens. Sarah taps on the window, waves. Then she points the camera at Holly and clicks.

Holly smiles stiffly.

Jacob's in a far corner of the pool. He's not even in the frame.

The hairs on Holly's arms tingle. It feels like Sarah's looking right through her.

And Holly doesn't want anyone to know what she hides inside.

CHAPTER THREE

SARAH

Now

I'm frozen, staring up at the round eye of the camera in the smoke detector. I need to move. Fast. I slide off the chair I'm standing on and, in a panic, scan the room for other hidden dangers. But I don't even know what I'm looking for. It would be laughable if I weren't so frightened.

A hidden camera. That's exactly how it started with Holly.

It was innocent in the beginning. Nanny cams always are. It's what any good mother would do to check up on a stranger taking care of her child. But not every mother would take photos of their babysitter through her bedroom window when the babysitter had no idea she was being watched. The thought of it now makes me feel sick, both that I could sink so low and what I saw when I did.

I remember the day I hired Holly, how Jacob took to her

immediately. She was young, energetic, and playful—everything I'm not. My son listened to her, followed her around the house. It made me feel confident enough to leave them alone and shut myself away in my darkroom very soon after she arrived. Plus, I had two nanny cams in the living room: one hidden in a vase on the mantel and one in a wall clock.

Daniel knew nothing about the cameras. He would have told me I was losing it. He always thinks I overreact, that I believe the worst of everyone, especially him. He thinks I'm overprotective of Jacob, too. I didn't want to hear his complaints, so I hid the cameras from him until I had no choice but to show him what they'd recorded.

And I have to admit that the way Holly looked at me that first day, with admiration, it made me feel seen—seen for who I really am. Right from the moment she arrived in her jean shorts and black University of British Columbia hoodie tied around her tiny waist, all coltish legs and a delicate build, I had this heady feeling that we'd get along, that despite the huge age gap between us, we needed each other. I guess this masked my usually sharp instincts. Because I got everything wrong.

When I turned forty-one in January, I felt . . . lost. Without anything else to do, I found myself sticking to Jacob like glue, worrying about him constantly, overcome with bad thoughts about what would happen if I took my eyes off him for even a second. You hear stories of mothers whose children are taken or get hit by cars, who drown in the moments their mothers look away. Those scenarios played through my mind in horrifying freeze-framed images.

Daniel noticed the change in me, said I was hovering, that my constant stress about our son was verging on madness. His exact words: "Your mothering is smothering. You need a break."

At his insistence, I rediscovered my first love, photography. Still, I was torn. Wasn't it my job to be Jacob's mother? To protect him from danger, to spot it before he did and steer him away? I longed for some passion that was all my own, and deep down, I knew Daniel was right. There was guilt there, too, the guilt of wanting to be more than a mother, not even knowing what "more" was. Maybe that's what made me susceptible to the dewy-skinned young woman who took over my responsibilities like they were the easiest thing in the world.

I never meant for Holly to become the subject of my photography. Or my thoughts.

The first time I watched her was an accident. It was in the middle of the night, hours after she'd gone home from a successful trial day with Jacob.

"You're hired," I told her in the early afternoon, sure I was making the best decision, beaming with relief and appreciation for Daniel having the idea in the first place. He'd found her, after all.

"Really?" Holly asked, slightly unsure, the first indication I'd seen that she wasn't a hundred percent confident.

"Yes, you're fantastic with my son. Let's do nine until four, Monday to Friday. Does that work for you?"

"It's perfect," she said.

At 4:00 p.m., as she cycled away, Jacob turned to me, glowing, calmer than usual because Holly had swum with him for hours and then taken him to look for treasures around the front lawn. She seemed to know to stay close while also giving him space to explore.

"Is Holly coming back tomorrow?" he asked as she made her way back to her family mansion on the other side of the Capilano River.

"Every weekday," I told my happy boy.

I got an exhausted Jacob ready for bed around 8:00 p.m. I fell asleep at 10:00 p.m., and Daniel crawled into bed at 1:00 a.m. after a night out with Stan Fielding, one of his golf buddies, a former fraternity brother he's remained close with. I couldn't go back to sleep.

Finally, after two hours of tossing and turning, I grabbed my Leica and went out to the pool deck to take a few shots of the night sky. I've suffered on-and-off bouts of insomnia since Jacob was born. That night, though, it wasn't the sky or stars that caught my attention. It was a light across the river.

I don't know what compelled me to get a closer look by stepping onto the thickly tree-lined plateau outside the pool enclosure. Beyond the narrow ledge was a steep, dense forest, rife with gnarly branches and spiky tree roots, leading to the thrashing river. It was a beautiful view but dangerously precipitous.

Once on the ledge, I peered through a small opening in the cluster of trees. Then I sucked in a sharp breath because I realized where the light was coming from: Holly's bedroom window.

I couldn't stop myself from lifting my telephoto lens and aiming it at her sheer curtains. There she sat on her bed, her features not visible, but it was clear she wasn't clothed. I knew it was Holly because of her ponytail. The diaphanous curtains made only her dark silhouette discernable, her body an outline of youthful perfection but no specific feature completely clear. Someone else crossed the room. I couldn't see their face, either, but the figure had a muscular male frame. It didn't matter. It was Holly I wanted to see—this young woman in her prime, untouched by the ravages of time and responsibility. It's not like I could see anything—not overtly—and yet here she was with who I presumed was her boyfriend, completely unaware of what her life would become, going through this rite of passage in her bedroom.

Her boyfriend approached her on the bed, but she was the one who initiated the kiss. She took charge. This wasn't her first time—that much was clear—but it must have been fresh and new. And Holly was unaware that she was so lithe and lovely, that this moment was so fleeting, that age and experience would change everything. She also didn't know that anyone was watching her. I couldn't unsee the sight. I was mesmerized.

I clicked the shutter. There was something about her, something that made me nostalgic for days long gone when love and lust were so intoxicating and the whole world was mine, when I was young and naive, my skin didn't pucker and sag, and anxiety about my son's every move didn't hold me hostage. Sure, this wasn't a moment I was meant to see, but I felt happy for Holly, that she was a young woman experiencing life to the fullest. Maybe this was her first serious boyfriend. And he was allowed to sleep over. I was never allowed to have a boyfriend stay over even at her age.

Taking those photos was wrong. Yet I did it anyway, more than once. I was certain it was my secret alone, but now I'm not so sure.

I know I'm nervous about a lot of things. It's not like I have blinders on. Where other people seek adventure, I anticipate peril. I hate the jumpy anticipation in my chest whenever Jacob climbs too high in a tree or runs down the stairs too fast. Everywhere I look, I see danger; people I can't trust who might hurt us. The garbage collector is potentially stealing our personal information; Jacob's basketball coach is a pedophile; the customer service representative at the bank is going to drain my accounts. I have to corral my thoughts before they go wild. I'm staring into a round eye on my ceiling. There must be a reasonable explanation for a hidden camera being in my new bedroom. Holly is out of our lives.

It's all over and has been since her last day with us. No text or call, not even a note before she left Jacob alone in the house, waiting for her under his bed in a cruel game of hide-and-seek so she could walk out our door without having to say goodbye.

According to her father, she's off on some silent tropical retreat; according to her Instagram feed, she's "finding herself."

I leave the smoke detector with its ominous eye and head back down to the main floor, which is eerily quiet. Without any rugs to absorb the vibrations, my footsteps echo off the hardwood.

I get to the bottom, and I gasp.

A grinning blond woman in a hot-pink windbreaker is holding a plate of cookies in my dining room.

"Oh my gosh, I'm sorry. I didn't mean to scare you. Your husband let me through the back." She sticks out a hand. "I'm Tara Conroy. I live next door."

First, a hidden camera and now a stranger in my house? Where the hell are Daniel and Jacob?

"Oh, if you're looking for your husband and son, they're in the backyard playing with my boy, Cody."

I might be shaken up, but still, it's creepy that this woman has just waltzed into my house like it's the most normal thing in the world. I channel Daniel and try not to jump to conclusions. I've learned that can be dangerous. I walk toward the middle of the room, where she's standing next to the table.

I take her outstretched hand and shake it. "Sarah Goldman. Nice to meet you," I say.

"Same," she says.

I crane my neck to see over her shoulder, but every room in this house is so oppressively closed that I can't catch a glimpse of the backyard.

"These are for you." She hands me the plate of cookies. "I make them with carob instead of chocolate because Cody's allergic to peanuts. Does Jacob have any allergies?"

I stiffen but try to hide it. She's using my son's name as though we've been friends for years. "No, he doesn't. Thank you for these. They . . . look delicious. Why don't I take them to the kitchen? We can go out back, and I can meet Cody?"

She beams, her teeth so white she probably just bleached them. Her eyes don't crinkle in the corners like mine do. She must be younger than me.

I don't enjoy this envy, the part of me that always sizes up other women, comparing them, favorably or not, to myself. I never used to care so much, until the day I looked in the front hall mirror, and in the sunlight, I saw my mother's neck on my body. Aging happened so fast, I never noticed. Now it feels like it's all I ever notice. Of course my insecurities go deeper than that. It's not like I'm unaware. I'm just not sure what to do about them.

I lead Tara to the kitchen and through the sliding doors; I see Daniel near the sandbox where Jacob and a taller, towheaded boy are standing. Both kids are quiet; Jacob can't look at the other boy. He's kicking sand, his head down. My heart hurts. I don't know if it's losing Holly, his favorite person this past summer, or the move, but my rowdy, rambunctious son is a shell of his former self. Maybe it's good for him that a kid around his age lives right next door. Maybe this will all work out.

Tara stands close, too close, and opens her mouth, releasing a stream of breathless words. "I'm so happy you have a son. Cody is seven, and the other kids on this street are really young. He'll be thrilled to have a playmate. What school is Jacob going to? What grade is he in?"

Her rapid-fire questions are dizzying. I'm trying to keep up, to craft the best responses while maintaining some privacy. I won't fall into the trap of trusting someone's keen interest in me or my son ever again.

"Jacob is seven in November," I say. "He's starting second grade."

"Oh, where? Cody's at Blossom Court Elementary. Ms. Martin's class."

"Yes, Blossom Court Elementary," is all I confirm, though I'm uncomfortable giving her even that much detail. I definitely don't want to discuss how guilty I feel that Jacob's starting at a new school a week late, how unprepared I am for the transition. Normally, I'd have spent the last few days before the school year signing him up for sports, connecting with his teacher, who is indeed Ms. Martin, and the principal. So far, I've chatted with only the secretary at Blossom Court Elementary.

Tara claps her hands. "I hope they're in the same class. Ms. Martin is wonderful."

I don't have time to add a thing, because she speaks again.

"This is a rental, right? Staying long? Danny told me you're from Vancouver. I've never been."

Danny? Why would she call my husband Danny? He only ever introduces himself as Daniel, and the people who know him well call him Dan.

She continues after a second of silence. "Hopefully you'll want to stay in Blossom Court. It's a special neighborhood. Are you—" Tara is interrupted by Jacob, who bursts into loud tears. He breaks away from the sandbox and curls into Daniel's side, hiding his face.

They walk over to us. "Oh, good, you two met," Daniel says as Jacob shoves his head back into Daniel's waist.

"Everything okay?" I mouth to Daniel, who shrugs as though he has no idea what set our son off. I'll deal with that in a moment. "Tara was in our dining room." I smile, but I widen my eyes with a coded "What the fuck?"

Daniel either doesn't read me or thinks I'm overreacting again.

"I think I scared your wife with my cookies, Danny," Tara says, laughing. "I promise I know how to bake."

"You love cookies, right, Danny?" I grin at my husband, who coughs to cover what I assume is a laugh.

Jacob sniffles by his side.

"Is he okay?" Tara asks.

Jacob raises his head. "We lost Mr. Blinkers," he says, his voice quivering. "Holly gave him to me." He realizes his mistake the moment the words are out of his mouth. His head whips up, so his eyes meet mine. "Sorry, Mommy. I know I'm not supposed to talk about her."

My stomach corkscrews. I can't expect him never to mention the girl who became like a daughter to me and a big sister to him over just a few weeks. But hearing her name makes me feel ill.

Daniel and I exchange a look. "We lost his favorite stuffed animal," he explains.

Tara leans down so she and Jacob are eye to eye. "Do you like cookies? I made some for you."

I cringe. My plan was to toss them in the compost. Something about Tara makes me nervous. She's just . . . too much, too fast.

"Thank you, Tara. It's been a hectic night and morning. We should probably get settled in," Daniel says, finally reacting to my discomfort. "Lots of bags to unpack."

"Of course." She looks over at her son, who's playing by himself in the sandbox. "We're going home, Cody!" She touches my shoulder, and I jump. "Whenever you're ready, come on by for a coffee and a chat. I'm so glad to have a mom nearby. We need to watch out for each other, right?" She winks at me.

Watch out for each other.

I nod like an idiot. After she and Cody exit through our back gate, the three of us file through the kitchen door, sliding it behind us. I lock it immediately. Once we're alone, I bend in front of Jacob. "The tablet is in my purse in the front hall. Why don't you play Roblox?"

I thought he was too young for the game, but Daniel felt it was fine. I gave in. Jacob loves playing it, but he's so glum that he only shrugs when I offer this. Then he shuffles out of the kitchen. I close my eyes, wishing I could turn back time and have my happy little boy back.

Once Jacob is out of earshot, I toss the carob cookies in the garbage.

"What did you do that for?" Daniel asks.

"We don't even know her."

A patronizing smile curls on his lips, but he erases it before I pounce. "You're right," he says. He pulls me toward him, his hard chest soothing and warm against my cheek. I lean into him, reassured that we'll somehow find our way back to each other. Maybe I'll even find a way to recover the woman I was before I slammed headfirst into a midlife crisis.

I pull away from him and meet his eye. "I found a hidden camera," I say.

"What?" He scrunches his forehead, not understanding.

"In our bedroom. I'll show you."

We pop into the living room to tell Jacob we're going upstairs. I blow him a kiss, which he doesn't see because he's now face-first in Roblox. Upstairs, in our new bedroom, I gesture to the smoke detector in the ceiling.

"You think there's a camera there?" Daniel asks incredulously.

"Just take it down, please."

Daniel, at six feet tall, easily detaches the smoke detector, opens the back compartment, and pops out the lithium battery. He has a look at the device, then drops it on the bed. He doesn't speak. He signals for us to go out to the hall.

In the hallway, he presses his back against the banister.

"So?" I ask.

"It's not a smoke detector." He rubs his face with his hand. I notice a slight tremble, and it does nothing to quell my fears.

Seeing Daniel on edge immediately puts me in protective mode. "What the hell is going on?" I ask. "Why on earth would there be a camera in there?"

Daniel gathers me in his arms. "I'll call the property manager right now and ask what she knows about it. Probably left behind from past tenants."

I breathe a sigh of relief that Daniel isn't brushing this aside. For once, I'm not blowing things out of proportion. For once, I'm not the hysterical one.

He lets go of me and heads downstairs to make the call. I remain in the hallway by the stairs. My panic builds, invisible inside me. My chest tightens painfully with the weight of my secrets.

"What have I done?" I whisper.

A few moments later, Daniel's climbing the stairs and then standing beside me. "I left a message with Courtney, the property manager. And I got an email that the boxes of our clothes and stuff that we shipped will arrive on Monday."

"Good. I hope Courtney calls back soon," I say.

"Why don't you take a bit of time for yourself, okay? Maybe unpack, and I'll deal with Jacob? We'll get some fresh air and grab groceries. There's that strip mall we passed on the drive from the airport about fifteen minutes from here." He softly presses his lips to mine. "Don't worry," he says. "Don't jump to conclusions. I'm sure the camera can be explained. It's not a big deal."

My stomach fills with the butterflies he still gives me after sixteen years. I met Daniel when I was a twenty-five-year-old barista, and he'd complimented my photographs the coffee shop manager had let me display behind the counter. I'd flushed at the unexpected thrill of meeting a handsome man in an impeccable suit, who liked my work and seemed to like *me*. I'd done a fine arts degree, on full scholarship, at Emily Carr University of Art and Design, but my prestigious education wasn't getting me anywhere near the photography career I wanted. Daniel was twenty-six, an entry-level software engineer doing his MBA at night. In him, I found the stability I'd been missing since my father died of a stroke when I was thirteen, right before my bat mitzvah. The celebration was canceled, not just because we were sitting shiva but because we couldn't afford it anymore.

Yet, mixed with those butterflies is a gnawing, residual suspicion that he's keeping something from me. That the furtive whispering and odd looks I saw him exchange with Holly were, in fact, not my imagination. That he was sleeping with our babysitter, or was about to.

Daniel kisses me once more. "Everything's going to be okay," he says. "A new start."

He's right. The past is the past. It's buried deep. A new start will bring us closer. Everything *will* be okay if I can stop worry from consuming me.

But once Daniel grabs Jacob's hand and they head out the door, all I feel is a fizzing anxiety throughout my entire being. I want to scour the house for other cameras. If there are none, I'll know I'm being paranoid.

I walk from one large, impersonal room to another and search in the kitchen. I check inside the matte-black cabinetry and run my hand along the paneled walls. The only light comes from the sliding glass door leading to the small but tidy backyard. The Manitoba maple's long, fingerlike branches scrape the windows on the second floor. There's a smoke detector on the kitchen ceiling, and uneasiness swirls in my chest. I only breathe when I see that it's different from the one in the master bedroom. No eye.

I head to the living room next. I scan the ceiling. Nothing. I open the built-in wall cabinet. Something looks weird on the white electrical outlet attached to the wall. I lie down on the floor. There are six plugs, three in use. In the far-right corner of the outlet is an empty socket. Above it, right in the outlet, is a tiny eye.

My head pounds. I shoot up from the floor and head to the kitchen, yanking open the drawers. I find masking tape, tear off a piece with my teeth, and cover the strange outlet eye.

Next is the large, cold basement, decorated in lighter colors. I spot a tiny white cube that blends into the top of the white cabinet in the main room. I grab an armchair to stand on and tear it away, holding the two-inch-by-two-inch hidden camera in my palm.

I keep searching. There's nothing in the nanny suite. I head to the third floor. No cameras in two of the three rooms. I have one more place to check: Jacob's bedroom. Before I enter, though, I try to think rationally. Maybe the previous tenants have kids and installed nanny cams, like I did.

The door is open. There's something propped up against the wall on the bottom bunk bed. I walk closer. No. It can't be. It just can't.

But it is.

It's Mr. Blinkers, my son's lost stuffed toy.

Terror crawls under my skin. We left that toy behind. We couldn't find it anywhere.

Someone who knows how important Mr. Blinkers is to my son has followed us here to Blossom Court. And there's only one person it can be. Holly.

CHAPTER FOUR

HOLLY

Before

On Friday morning, like it has all week, Holly's alarm blares at seven thirty. Rolling over in bed, she smells vanilla and melted chocolate in her hair. She, Sarah, and Jacob made cookies the day before, laughing and joking the whole time just like in a movie. She never would have thought babysitting could be so fun, so rewarding. But these last five days, especially spending time with Sarah every morning on the porch, and sometimes at the end of the day, has already made this the best summer she can remember.

By Wednesday, they had a perfect routine. Holly shows up at nine, and she and Sarah have coffee on the porch for half an hour while Jacob plays basketball or rides his scooter up and down the driveway. Then Sarah goes to her darkroom, and Holly looks after Jacob all day. She still hasn't met Sarah's husband, Daniel, because he's already left for work when she arrives, and she leaves at 4:00 p.m., long before he gets home. Even after a few days, she fits right in. She feels like she has a place in this family, and a job to do.

Sometimes Holly pretends this is her house, too. The Goldmans' place is so different from hers. It's a home. Holly's allowed to eat anywhere she wants, and she's never worried about sharp edges and glass objets d'art that she'll break. Jacob loves everything they do together. Yesterday, he sat on Holly's lap, and she drew letters on his back.

When Sarah walked into the living room, she laughed. "That's a creative way to practice his spelling."

"I guess every letter right!" He turned and demanded, "Make it harder, Holly. I want to show my mom how good I'm getting."

She did, and the appreciation she saw on Sarah's face, the excitement Jacob felt over his accomplishment, meant more than all the money in the world.

Sarah is the mother she always imagines her own would have been like. Not that Sarah's perfect—she's not. She worries constantly about what Jacob eats—"You have to eat more veggies, Jacob. You need vitamins!" Whenever they go outside, Sarah runs after them—"Don't forget the sunscreen!" She kisses her son all the time, and even though Jacob sometimes pulls away from her, he knows she's always there for him. He knows Holly is, too.

No one has ever been as excited to see her as Jacob is, not even Alexis. He waits on the porch for her every morning, and when she cycles up the driveway, he races to meet her for their secret handshake. A complicated series of hand slaps and waves he made up just for them.

And Sarah seems interested in Holly, too. Throughout the day, she pops out of her darkroom to take photos of Holly and Jacob diving for pennies and making mud pies with soil from the garden of pink peonies to the right of the sliding doors.

"Don't look at the camera. Just pretend I'm not here," she says.

Yesterday, when Jacob banged his funny bone into the wall and started to cry, Sarah came running upstairs from the basement but left quickly because she saw that Holly had it under control. "I don't know what I'd do without you," Sarah said when she saw Jacob curled into Holly's lap.

Holly's beginning to feel the same about Sarah.

Before she gets out of bed to shower, she grabs her phone from the nightstand. There's a text from Alexis.

Alexis: What should I wear to the
party tonight?

Ugh, the Fielding engagement party. She'd forgotten, but it's tonight. Lisette has been dropping Charlie Lang's name into conversation all week: "Did you know that Lang Developments is building that large condo on Robson?" "Charlie likes to talk about politics, but he's conservative, so watch what you say." "Yellow is Charlie's favorite color."

Holly texts back.

Holly: Whatever you want.

Alexis: Jeans and a T-shirt it is.

Holly sends an LOL and then puts down her phone. She's just getting out of bed when Lisette opens her door without even knocking. She crosses the threshold uninvited.

"Be home by five today. Daniel and Sarah Goldman will be there tonight, by the way. I hope they're pleased with you? I guess we'll find out if they aren't. Also, remember that Charlie is our focus tonight. I don't need to tell you that with Charlie's investment in Ritofan, we can start phase three of the drug trials." Lisette hovers by her bed, her jade eyes—colored contacts—boring into Holly. "You should wear your lemon shift dress. Flattering but discreet." She smiles, which only Lisette can manage to do with no trace of affection.

Holly groans inwardly at the first event of many this summer where she'll be expected to flip her hair, smile, and make potential investors believe they're the most interesting men in the world. Last year, Stan Fielding was the focus at the children's hospital charity tournament at the Canyon Club. Oh, how proud her father was of her as she giggled and clinked glasses with Stan, his ruddy face red with excitement while her father beamed from across the room. The following Monday, Stan invested five hundred thousand dollars into Lenvotriq, their thyroid cancer drug.

And after she closed the deal, her father took her out for lunch at the oyster bar at Sutton Place, their favorite hotel, to celebrate his lucky charm, his daughter with extraordinary sales skills. If only all it took were smiles and clinking glasses. Thank goodness Alexis was at a nursing conference that weekend, trying to network for a job that never materialized.

So the Goldmans will be at the Fielding party. Interesting. Maybe that will make it easier to get through the night. At the very least, she'll meet the husband Sarah talks about and the father who Jacob mentions all the time: "Wait until Daddy sees me diving!" "Holly, remember Mommy said that we're never allowed in Daddy's cabana. It's his man cave."

Holly is curious. Very curious.

She already knows Alexis will hug the walls all night long, making awkward conversation that everyone will veer away from, waiting for Holly to finish making the rounds in the Canyon Club ballroom. Nothing is expected of Alexis. And yet she tries too hard and fails every time. Lisette will sweetly suggest to Alexis that she sit at the bar if she gets in the way, and she'll point her daughter to a quiet corner far from the glitterati and moneymongers, far from the power in the room.

Lisette has made her demand and her veiled threat. She leaves Holly's bedroom and closes the door gently behind her.

Holly lobs a silk pillow from her bed against her closed bedroom door. It lands with a hollow thump. That's how Holly feels in this house, in her family. Like no matter what she does, she makes no mark, leaves no impression at all.

She gets up and takes the stupid lemon dress out of her massive closet, laying it over her desk chair, scowling at it as she goes to her bathroom to shower. Once dressed in her swimsuit, a red one-piece this time, cutoffs, and a tank top, she heads outside to find once again that Lisette's car has prevented her from getting to her own. It's like she does this on purpose. A classic power play. Holly's going to be late.

As she walks her bike out of the garage and hops on, she looks up at the second-floor windows, hoping to see her father in his study so she can wave goodbye. She skipped breakfast because he wouldn't be there anyway. He has an early business call. But when she looks up, all she sees is Lisette at the window, arms crossed, glaring at her.

By the time Holly gets to the Goldmans', she's fifteen minutes late. She shakes off thoughts of her screwy family dynamics and races up the driveway, where Jacob hops on a pogo stick.

"Hi, Holly!" he yells, as if she isn't right next to him.

"Hi, Jakey!" she yells back as she takes off her helmet.

He stops so they can do their secret handshake while Sarah laughs from the porch, in her usual spot on the white wicker chair, sipping coffee and watching her son.

Holly brushes the sweat from the back of her neck, the baby hairs catching in her silver necklace. Sarah watches her struggle to remove the strands.

"Come here. Let me help."

Holly leaves her bike and helmet and walks up the porch steps, out of breath. Sarah gets up and gently separates the clasp from Holly's hair.

"Sorry I'm late. My car was blocked in. I biked as fast as I could."

"No worries. One of the perks of working from home is that I have no boss." She grins as Jacob bounces down the driveway. "Except for that little guy."

Holly closes her eyes, relishing the feeling of Sarah's warm fingers grazing her skin. She can't remember the last time she felt such a loving touch from anyone but Alexis.

Sarah pats her shoulders. "All fixed," she says as she walks in front of Holly. "That's such a pretty necklace. Cute snowflake logo. The pendant's a yin, right?"

Holly nods. "My stepsister gave it to me. She has the yang. It's from Unique, this cool boutique shop in Granville. Everything is one of a kind."

A year ago, on the fifteenth anniversary of the day they'd first come into each other's lives, her stepsister handed her a pale lavender box, where the delicate silver chain was nestled on a bed of cotton.

Alexis revealed the necklace she wore herself, a matching one with a similar pendant. "You're the yin to my yang." She grinned, her slightly crooked front tooth so endearing. "Matching sister necklaces."

Holly was so touched that she cried and hugged Alexis tightly. "You're the most important person in the world to me. Do you know that?"

"It's a really nice necklace," Sarah says now. "But it's way too cool for an old mom like me. May I?" she asks as she raises her hand to Holly's neck.

"Sure," Holly says. Sarah delicately holds the silver yin between two fingers and turns it over. "'H' for Holly. That's so nice. You and your stepsister must be close."

They would do anything for each other. It's always been that way. Alexis covered for her when she stayed out past her curfew; Holly sweet-talked a police officer into not pressing charges when Alexis and some friends chained themselves to a cedar tree so it wouldn't be cut down by a developer. Their bond is as strong as any blood sisters, maybe even more so.

The only thing that Alexis doesn't realize is how lucky she is. She doesn't realize the extra burden Holly carries, the expectations, the things she knows she has to do but are unspoken. If Alexis knew, she'd be disgusted, shocked. She wouldn't understand.

Holly nods, swallowing the lump in her throat. "Alexis has an 'A' on the back of her pendant. Do you have any siblings?"

"One." Sarah sits back down on the wicker chair, crossing her legs at the ankles. Her yoga pants are pilling, and she has a coffee stain on the bottom of her white T-shirt. "A younger brother. Nathan. I always wanted a sister." She shrugs. "And a daughter." Sarah glances wistfully at Jacob still hopping away on the driveway.

Holly sits in the other wicker chair and stays quiet. Over the last week, she's learned that Sarah sometimes needs time to express herself. So she leans back and waits.

"I—I miscarried when I was sixteen weeks pregnant. Sorry. That's probably too much information."

"Not at all," Holly says. "I'm so sorry. That must have been very hard." She notices heavy shadows under Sarah's eyes. "Are you okay?" she asks.

"Insomnia. But I'm fine." Her face flushes red.

"Holly! Come watch me! I can do a hundred bounces in one minute."

She moves to stand, but Sarah shakes her head. "You don't have to respond every time he wants something. It's okay to let him wait."

Holly appreciates this. She knows it's coming from a good place. "I'm just talking to your mom, Jakey," she calls out. "I'll be there in a minute." She turns back to Sarah after. "It's hard not to give him everything he wants. He's such a great kid."

"And demanding." Sarah laughs. "But thank you. He's completely enamored with you. He's just so happy these days."

Holly beams. "I hope you're getting a lot of work done. Are you planning to show your photography? Or sell it?"

Sarah picks up her coffee, taking a long sip. "I'm nowhere near that stage yet. Out of a hundred shots, maybe a few are good, and each film reel takes a long time to develop."

"Why don't you use digital?"

"I like the process of loading the film, mixing chemicals. Watching the transformation." She flinches as Jacob wobbles on the pogo stick. "And unlike parenting, it's something I can control."

Holly understands completely. She feels in her pocket for the Dior mascara she swiped from Lisette's bag before she left this morning.

"You know, it will only take me a couple of minutes to set up an Instagram account for you. You don't have to post every day or anything. But it's a good way to promote yourself."

Sarah bites her lip. "I don't know . . ." She looks down at herself, then up at Holly. She hands her the phone that's on the small table. "Do it before I change my mind."

Holly laughs, noticing Sarah has no lock screen. Then she downloads the app, and in minutes, Sarah has an Instagram account. She gives her the phone back and watches as a slow smile spreads across Sarah's face.

"Sarah Goldman Photography. I love it." She touches Holly's knee. "Thank you."

"The easiest thing to do would be to take some photos on your phone and share them."

"Oh my God, Holly, I've been waiting forever!" Jacob says from the driveway. "Please."

"That's my cue." Holly unzips her backpack. "I got him something." She removes the stuffed gray bunny and holds it out in front of Sarah.

Sarah smiles. "That's so sweet. He's really into superheroes right now, but I'm sure he'll appreciate it."

Holly's anticipation dims, but when Jacob spots the toy in her hand, he drops the pogo stick and comes running over. "For me?" He clutches the bunny to his chest. "I love him. I love him so much."

Sarah's eyes go wide with surprise. "What do you say to Holly, Jake?"

"Thank you!" he says, then throws his arms around her.

Holly laughs and hugs him back. "You're welcome."

"I'd better get moving," Sarah says. "I actually need to run some errands before I get to work. Text if you need me." Sarah pats Holly's shoulder, kisses Jacob on the head, picks up her phone and purse, then walks toward the garage.

She and Jacob both watch as Sarah backs her car out of the driveway and drives down the street. It's the first time since Holly started babysitting Jacob that Sarah has left them home alone.

Holly turns to Jacob. "Want to play hide-and-seek?"

As an answer, he runs into the house with the bunny. "You'll never find me and Mr. Blinkers!"

Holly follows him inside. "Mr. Blinkers?" Holly asks. "Is that what you're going to call him?"

"Yeah!" He giggles and runs up the stairs.

"Go hide, and I'll try to find you!"

Once he's gone, she heads to the living room and looks at the black vase on the mantel where she knows a nanny cam is hidden. She saw it her very first day, though she's never mentioned it to Sarah. Older people always think younger people don't know they're being watched, which is kind of funny given that old people barely have a grasp of technology.

Sarah seems shy about her photography, but now that she has an Instagram account, Holly can help her curate some photos to post. Sarah's never explicitly told her not to go in the darkroom, and with Jacob hiding, it will give her a few minutes to poke around. She won't take anything, of course. Just a quick look at Sarah's work.

She spins away from the nanny cam, calling, "I'll give you a bit longer to find a really good hiding spot," in case the camera picks up sound or Jacob's waiting for her, and tiptoes down the stairs to the basement, her pulse thumping. At the bottom of the steps, she looks past the bar, huge flat-screen television, and tan leather couch. She's never seen a camera down here, though it's not a space she and Jacob play in often. There's a bathroom right under the stairs, a guest room, and the darkroom she's never been inside. The door's always closed, and now she's desperate to open it.

Holly knows nothing about developing film. She doesn't want to ruin any photos, and she definitely doesn't want Sarah to know she's sneaking around. But the heady pull of seeing what Sarah creates is stronger than her worry.

Holly turns the knob. The room is pitch-black and windowless, and she quickly shuts the door behind her to block out any light. She's aware, at least, that light can damage photos, but she can't make out a thing in the dark. She can just make out the silhouette of a bulb hanging above her in the middle of the room, a white string hanging from it. She tugs the string. The room floods with red, and now she can see that it's divided into two spaces. One side houses a sink, above which a wire holds clips of negatives with images similar to the photos on the walls throughout the house. There's a shelf of bottles, a large tray, and a black-and-silver contraption that looks like a machine her eye doctor uses. Sarah's seriously old-school. Does she even know how to use a digital camera?

On the opposite side of the room in the back corner is a metal filing cabinet. Holly pulls on the cabinet handle. Locked.

She still has her backpack on. She hesitates for a moment, then quickly takes out the aquamarine key chain she found on Etsy, sliding out the mini knife, scissors, and nail file. Her heart bangs against her chest as she angles the nail file into the right spot in the lock and hears a satisfying click.

A loud crash from upstairs makes her jump.

Shit. Jacob. What has he done now? She relocks the drawer, leaves the darkroom, and runs back to the main floor. "Ready or not, here I come!"

No quiet giggle or heavy breathing. There's no noise at all.

Holly tosses her backpack on the couch and searches every room on the second floor. No Jacob. Her body is numb. She runs out to the pool deck, petrified about what she'll find. She heaves a huge sigh of relief when he's not in the pool. She hears something and runs to the door in the mudroom leading to the garage. Flinging it open, she sees Jacob in the garage, standing on the seat of his dirt bike, Mr. Blinkers dangling over the handlebars.

The bike wobbles, and Holly can't reach him before the bike falls to the concrete.

"Oh my God!"

Jacob lies on his side on the ground next to a red toolbox, which must have fallen from the metal shelf. His eyes are open, and he begins to quietly cry. "Ow," he says as tears streak down his face.

Holly shoves the toolbox and bike out of the way and rushes to him, running her fingers over his scalp to check for bumps and bleeding. His head is perfect, thank goodness. "What's your name?"

He pouts as he answers between sobs. "That's a dumb question. You know who I am."

Quickly, she examines him all over. Besides a large bruise blooming on his right knee, he seems okay. She wants to cry, too. "I'm trying to make sure you don't have a concussion."

"Ask me something harder."

What does your mom hide in her locked drawer? It's the first thing that springs to mind, though she doesn't say it out loud.

Holly helps Jacob sit up, and his little shoulders relax when he spots Mr. Blinkers, who fell from the handlebars. He seizes the bunny, inspecting him. "Is he hurt, Holly?"

He holds him out for her. She examines him as seriously as she would a real animal. "He's got a little rip in his bum. I'll sew him up for you." She bites her lip, hating herself for having left Jacob on his own. She knows it was wrong, that it's her fault he's hurt himself. "Just this once, maybe we tell your mom you tripped on the pool deck while we were swimming, okay? I don't think she'll like that you were in the garage by yourself."

Jacob nods. "Okay," he says.

Holly puts the toolbox back in the empty spot on the shelf. Once they go inside, she sets Jacob up on a chair in the kitchen and puts an ice pack on his bruised knee. Once he seems fine, she grabs a puzzle from the wicker basket in the living room, and they sit at the table together, away from the nanny cam, Jacob's leg resting on a pillow. A half hour later, the front door opens. Sarah, her hair piled into a lopsided bun, comes into the kitchen with grocery bags. She takes in the ice pack, Jacob's propped-up knee, and drops the bags instantly.

"What happened?"

"He fell, but he's fine. Just a bruised knee."

Sarah inspects Jacob's leg and pulls him to her, kissing his head. "Monkey. You have to be more careful."

"It was my fault," Holly says. "I was too far away from him to stop him from tripping." She waits for Sarah to get angry, but Sarah puts her warm hand on Holly's cold one.

"Not your fault. He's impulsive. You can't watch his every step."

Holly's stomach hurts. Sarah has been nothing but kind and generous to her, and she's not only violated her privacy, she's also just lied about her son's fall. Worse, she's shirked her responsibilities in looking after him and then taught Jacob how to lie to his own mother.

"Why don't I get our art supplies and you guys can make a rock garden or something creative?" Sarah asks.

Holly remembers the pet rocks she and Alexis made when Holly was seven that turned out to be expensive tanzanite worth thousands. Lisette was furious with them for painting her precious gemstones. She laughs out loud at the memory.

"What?" Sarah asks.

"Just thinking about the dumb things I did when I was a kid."

"You're lucky. That you got to do dumb things, I mean. My dad died when I was young. I was responsible for a lot at a young age." She shakes her head. "Maybe I should go easier on Jacob."

"You're a great mom," Holly says. "My mom died having me."

Sarah's mouth drops open. "Oh, honey, that's awful. I'm sorry."

"It's okay. You didn't know. I don't know anything about her because my dad never talks about her." It spills out of her mouth before she can stop it. She never talks about how much she misses her mother even though she's never known her. There are no photos of her around the house. The only picture she has of her mother was when she was six months pregnant with Holly. A flame-haired stunner with the prettiest amber eyes Holly has ever seen.

"It's just . . . it's so sad. But it must be great to have Lisette in your life."

They lock eyes. "It's not," Holly says. "I mean, it's not always great."

Sarah doesn't pry. She only nods. "Understood."

I wish you were my mom, Holly thinks to herself.

Sarah glances at the chunky Timex on her wrist. "I'd better get back to it. Call down if you need me?"

"Of course," Holly replies. "I just have to make sure I leave right at four to get ready for the party tonight."

Sarah grimaces. "Yes, the party."

"I know," Holly agrees, then worries she's said too much. "Lisette said you're going. I'm really glad you'll be there."

Sarah grins.

For the rest of the day, Holly works extra hard to keep Jacob busy with fun activities. She also sews up Mr. Blinkers, telling Jacob the bunny now has a cool scar. He likes that. By the time she sees Daniel Goldman in her peripheral vision through the living room window, walking around the pool and into the cabana, Jacob's beaten her twice at gin rummy. She glances at the clock on the wall to the right of the television. It's only 3:30 p.m. Maybe he's home early because of the party.

Holly expects Daniel to leave his cabana and come into the house any minute, but it's a full thirty minutes before he walks through the front door.

"Hey, kiddo," he says as he enters the living room, putting his brown leather satchel on the floor and holding out his arms for his son.

Jacob runs straight to him. "Daddy!" He launches himself at his father's leg, his injury forgotten, holding on while Daniel picks him up and swings him around the room, then puts him back down.

He extends his hand for Holly. "I'm Daniel. I've heard so much about you, Holly. Nice to meet you finally."

Holly shakes his hand and smiles reflexively.

Daniel looks down at his son. "Mommy and I are going out tonight. Nora from down the street is babysitting. You can order a pizza and watch *Avengers: Endgame.*" He looks at Holly and puts a finger to his lips. "Don't tell Sarah I said he could watch that." Daniel grins at her over Jacob's bouncing head, then turns to Holly. "Your father told me you're going to the engagement party, too."

"Yes."

Jacob gazes up at his dad. "I fell and got hurt. But I was brave."

"How did you fall?"

Jacob quickly shoots his eyes to Holly. "Tripped on the pool deck."

Holly feels sick all over again and avoids Daniel's eyes.

"We really appreciate your help with this dude. Sarah says you've been great with him. He's my number one." Daniel grins at Jacob.

Jacob flashes two fingers on each hand. "Because I was born on eleven eleven!"

"Eleven eleven. Your best numbers, and mine, too!"

It warms Holly's heart to see Jacob's easy, natural closeness with his dad.

"Is Sarah in her darkroom?" Daniel asks. "As usual?" There's definitely a tone to it.

"Your wife's really talented. I love her photos." Holly feels a need to defend Sarah, to justify her work.

"Photography is a good distraction for her, that's for sure."

Holly's hackles rise, but she says nothing. She leans over and ruffles Jacob's hair. "Have fun with your babysitter tonight, little man." She's surprised by the twinge of jealousy she feels that someone else will be in the house taking care of him. To Daniel she says, "See you at the Canyon Club later tonight."

She walks out of the living room, the sound of Jacob's excited chatter fading behind her. On her way, she bumps into Sarah, who's holding something out to her—her key chain, with the mini nail file.

Holly's heart stops. She swallows hard and takes it from Sarah's outstretched hand.

"It was on the basement steps. I'm assuming it's yours?"

"It is," Holly says, her voice strangled. She clears her throat. "Thank you. Jacob and I were playing. I guess it fell out of my pocket."

A look flashes across Sarah's face. She eyes Holly's shorts with their deep pockets. Just then, Daniel and Jacob come up behind her.

"Hey, my loves," Sarah says as she hugs her son and kisses her husband on the cheek. "Did you just get home?" she asks Daniel.

"Yup," he says. "Just walked in."

It's not true, though, not quite. Holly thinks about how long it took him to come in from the cabana. What was he doing in there—in the "man cave" Jacob's not allowed to enter?

"So you've met Holly?" Sarah says.

"Yes," Holly replies.

"I've been telling Dan how lucky we are to have you, how you already feel like part of the family. Trust is so important. You know?" As she says this, she puts an arm around her husband.

He's not paying attention. He's taken out his phone and is busy tapping on it.

"Oh, I almost forgot!" She grabs her keys from the front hall table and removes one, handing it to Holly. "I made you a key to the house. This way, you and Jacob can come and go as you please."

Holly takes the key, carefully holding it in her palm like it's a tiny pot of gold. "Thank you," Holly says. "I really appreciate this."

Trust is so important.

The words make Holly feel like retching. She was snooping on Sarah. She was breaking the trust. But only now does it occur to her that maybe she was snooping on the wrong person. And in the wrong place.

CHAPTER FIVE

SARAH

Now

Mr. Blinkers watches me from the bottom bunk, and I choke back the tears. How is this even possible? By yesterday morning, our house in Vancouver was almost empty. The movers had taken all the boxes we're having shipped, and we sold or gave away all the furniture. Jacob was quiet the whole day before we left for the airport last night to fly to Toronto, until he realized he couldn't find Mr. Blinkers. Then he fell apart. I soothed him while Daniel checked every single corner of the house, the cabana, the pool. The bunny was gone. Jacob was in pieces, and there was nothing we could do because we had to catch our flight.

Maybe Jacob left the bunny in the yard? But what if Holly took it from the house? She never did give her key back. She's the only person who knows how much Jacob loves this stuffed bunny, because she gave it to him. She made him love it. She made all of us love her.

With minimal makeup, beguiling hazel eyes, and those gorgeous auburn waves spilling over her tanned shoulders, she so effortlessly cajoled Jacob into adoring her. She carried a confidence that provoked both envy and awe in me. I'm not proud of it, but that's the truth. I'd never been carefree at her age, never allowed that privilege, and by twenty-two, I'd been working for seven years while studying. My only respite was photography. I had no boyfriends, no prom dress, no grand social events to attend with my father. I had no car given to me.

Still, I know I wasn't fair to Holly, not really. She may have exuded confidence, but she never exuded happiness. I knew she was vulnerable and lonely. I could tell by the way she hugged me, melting into me like I was . . . like I was her mother.

She needed love, and both Jacob and I were more than willing to lavish it on her. But there was something in her eyes, an emptiness, that scared me then. It still does. It made me wonder: To what lengths would she go to fill the void? And what was it she was looking for from us?

Now, as I stare down at the stuffed toy, I wish I'd followed my instincts more. I wish I didn't just brush my fears aside and blame my paranoia the way I always do.

I pick up the gray bunny and pat him down, checking for sharp edges, a camera, a wire.

There's nothing. The bunny is just a bunny.

This is what I've become.

Until I can talk to Daniel about Mr. Blinkers, I'll put him in a box in our bedroom closet where Jacob won't find him. I open the one with our passports and birth certificates inside and drop the toy in, my hands shaking as I slam the box flaps closed. The closet is dark, and I leave immediately, having trouble catching my breath because I'm so rattled.

And right then, I have a thought. If someone—or Holly—is watching me, trying to scare me, I'm going to watch them right back.

I know Daniel took the rental car to go shopping with Jacob.

They're still out, but I can walk. We passed a Best Buy close to here on our way from Pearson airport. The fresh air will be good for me, and I have to get out of this dark, oppressive house and its mysteries I can't unearth.

I leave the house, locking the door behind me, and survey the street. It's quiet. As I walk down the paved driveway, I spot a man, mug in hand, sitting on his porch at the gray-brick house across from ours. Like all the homes on this block, the porch is narrow. He doesn't even have room for a table. Just a white plastic rocking chair to the right of the brown front door.

He's staring at me without looking away. I clock him—thin, drawn, gaunt face; wispy sandy-blond hair; sharp, knobby knees that protrude from tan pants. Could he have put the cameras in our house? It's ridiculous, and I catch my overblown panic sneaking up on me again.

I should go over and introduce myself like a normal neighbor would, but I don't feel like it. And his stare looks rather unfriendly. Instead, I head to the end of Lilac Lane and spin around. He's still looking at me. I ignore him and make a left through the curlicue sign announcing the subdivision: WELCOME TO BLOSSOM COURT: YOUR COMMUNITY VILLAGE.

Thick gray clouds threaten rain. I don't know Toronto at all. We're far from the downtown core, and there are no breathtaking mountain ranges, no ocean, or a river view. Only a neighborhood that might be more dangerous than the one we left behind.

I'm sweaty and keyed up by the time I get to Best Buy twenty-five minutes later, but the fluorescent lights and familiar display in the store calm me as I head for the home-security aisle. My heart patters again when I pass the photography section, filled with Nikons and Leicas, tripods and light meters. But I don't stop to touch. I've given up photography because it's no longer good for me, or my family. It hurts, but I have to choose Daniel and Jacob.

I find light bulbs that are really wireless security cameras and pick one up, feeling that habitual tug of guilt when I spend anything, a holdover from growing up with overdue heating bills and eviction notices.

"May I help you?" I hear.

I whip my head around to find a boy, maybe in his early twenties, sporting a man bun and the Best Buy blue staff shirt.

"Yes. Are these any good?" I point to the light bulb cameras.

"Depends what you want them for."

"Just some extra security around the house."

"Outside only?"

I hesitate. How far am I willing to go? Someone's trying to frighten me, but I refuse to be a prisoner in my own home, the constant eye of a camera on us. Daniel and Jacob deserve their privacy, even if I don't.

I didn't stop watching Holly after that first night in the woods outside our pool deck. No, it became almost a nightly habit. I'd wait until I was sure Daniel was asleep, if he was even home, because he was so often out with the Canyon Club men he'd suddenly befriended. Then I'd creep to the backyard, holding my breath while sliding open the door leading to the pool, camera slung around my neck and sneakers with good treads on my feet so I wouldn't slip on the cliff and fall to my death.

The photos were art, not lurid in any way but provocative. My pictures of Holly through her window, and the man, or men—I wasn't sure if it was one or more. Part of the beauty of what I captured was the subtlety, the outlines just barely visible, the story they told not entirely clear, the viewer struggling to make sense of the image captured in the frame. Whoever Holly brought into her bedroom, I just knew it was done in secret. If John and Lisette were home, they didn't know.

But I knew that I had to hide those photos because of how it would have looked if anyone were to find them, a middle-aged woman taking pictures of her babysitter in her bedroom. But it wasn't like that. It wasn't illicit or explicit in any way. It was art that was just for me.

I kept the photos I took in my darkroom in Vancouver, in a locked drawer that Daniel never knew about. I never told him. It would have been further proof that I'm not as well-balanced as he is. That he's been right to downplay, even dismiss my fears as the neurotic, jealous tendencies of a mother who's afraid to lose control of her family.

I destroyed all the photos in our fireplace before we moved. Ash. That's what my passion, my photography, was reduced to. And after I had no choice but to show Daniel what I recorded of Holly in our home, I used a hammer to smash the two nanny cams to bits. I permanently deleted every video from the apps on my phone, then uninstalled them.

I left no evidence behind.

"Ma'am? Did you want the cameras for the inside or the outside only?"

I jerk back to the present and answer the salesperson's question. "Outside only."

"This one's a good choice. You can put one over your garage and the front door and windows to catch an intruder, if that's what you're worried about."

I'm worried someone will stand over our bed while we're sleeping, but I don't say that.

"Does it work as a motion detector?"

"Sure does. It sends you a notification if it senses any movement."

I mentally add up the windows on the main floor facing the front, plus the front door, and the passageway to the backyard. "I'll take four."

I also buy five smoke detectors to replace all the ones in the house and the fake one in our bedroom. I don't care if the rest of them work: I need to install our own. I exit the store and walk back along Dufferin Street, which seems to be the main road here, when I hear the drone of a car engine and tires rolling slowly along the asphalt.

I turn.

"Hi, Mommy!"

Relief makes my knees buckle a little. I hold on to the steel railing for a second and plaster a grin on my face. "Hi, guys!"

I open the passenger door and hop in. Jacob is smiling in his booster seat in the back, a new Blue Jays cap on his head, and Spider-Man sunglasses a size too big. Daniel, too, looks happy.

"We got food and clothes and stuff."

I gawk at Daniel, who doesn't even buy his own underwear. It's usually all up to me. I don't know what precipitated this change, what's finally made him really listen when I repeated yet again that I can't handle everything regarding childcare and housekeeping on my own. I hope it's not guilt. I hope it's that he now has time to give because he'll be making his own schedule at his new job, building his own list of clients whose businesses he'll help whip into shape. Plus, there's no country club or group of powerful men he's eager to befriend. I hope it stays that way.

He nods proudly, eyeing the Best Buy bags I put on the floor. "What's all that?"

"Later." I cock my head at the back seat.

Daniel glances in the rearview mirror. "Jake, tell Mom what we got her."

"Oh yeah!"

A plastic bag crinkles, and I shift in my seat to face a beaming Jacob, who holds up what looks like a watch. I'm confused.

"It's a Fitbit. So when you walk me to school and pick me up, you can count your steps!"

I take the bag from Jacob's outstretched hands, arranging a look of excitement and gratitude on my face. I already have my trusty Timex, which I prefer over learning some new technology. Daniel knows this. But I can't hurt Jacob. He looks so happy with this gift he's chosen for me.

"Thanks, guys. I guess Mommy needs to get in shape!" I laugh lightly, but I avoid Daniel's eyes.

He clears his throat. "Since you've given up photography, we thought this would be a good incentive."

"It's very thoughtful," I tell him, but really, without photography in my life, I don't know what I'll do with myself. I'm certainly not the socializing type, though I try. Last winter, when we were out for dinner with Stan Fielding and his wife, Gloria, I felt so out of place. We were dining at the Canyon Club, the exclusive, ridiculously overpriced golf club that Daniel suddenly seemed hell-bent on being invited to join. At that dinner, when Gloria mentioned a photography exhibit at the Audain Art Museum, I screwed up the nerve to ask if they were looking for more artists.

Daniel laughed and kissed my cheek. "They're professionals, honey. You have your hands full taking care of the house and Jacob."

I gripped my wineglass so hard I thought it might shatter. I imagined smashing it over his head. Instead, I nodded politely. But months later, he did an about-face, seeming to realize that I needed help and arranged for the interview with Holly.

Maybe Daniel was right at that dinner. Giving my child a stable home should have been enough for me.

And as we drive back to our new home together, I know that I'll never feel the same way about photography as I did this summer. It was exhilarating to reignite my passion for it, find a way to ensure our babysitter was good for our son, but in the end, everything I eventually saw through a lens only caused me fear and pain.

And as soon as Daniel pulls into the garage, my anxiety ramps up again. While Jacob runs upstairs to find places for all his new toys, and we're alone in the front hall, I tell Daniel about the other cameras I found, the light bulbs I bought, and Mr. Blinkers.

His face is pale. "Show me."

I gape at him. "Are you serious? You don't believe me?"

He rubs the back of his neck. "Of course I do. Some things you just need to see for yourself."

I lead him to the stairs. I feel instantly tired from the lack of light in here and the never-ending apprehension compressed deep in my chest. Daniel and I reach our cavernous bedroom closet, and I open the box. Then I hand him Mr. Blinkers.

Daniel blinks, visibly upset. "How is this possible?" he asks.

Before I can respond, Jacob spots us and runs into our room.

"You found him!" he shrieks, grabbing Mr. Blinkers from his father, hugging the bunny so close that if the toy were real, he'd be suffocating it.

Daniel looks at me, eyes wide.

"Buddy, did you maybe put him in a box or your bag by mistake when we packed in Vancouver?" Daniel asks, his voice higher pitched than normal.

He must be right. I don't know why I didn't think of this. In my panic, of course I neglected the obvious.

"Honey," I say as I bend on one knee in front of my son. "It's okay. You put him in a box, and you took him out earlier and left him on your bed, right?"

Jacob laughs. "That's silly. I'd never put Mr. Blinkers in a box." He holds out Mr. Blinkers at arm's length. "No running away again and leaving me alone," he says to the bunny, pure joy on his perfect face. "Wait until you see my new bunk beds!"

He runs out of the closet with the bunny, and I turn to my husband. "What the fuck is going on, Daniel? We looked everywhere. We checked every box."

"I know. But clearly, we must have missed one, okay? That's at least one mystery solved." He walks into our bedroom.

I follow. "This is fucked up. First the cameras, just like the nanny cams I had in the living room on Cliffside, and now the one thing Jacob loves more than anything shows up out of nowhere?" I touch my stomach, which is twisted with anxiety. I want Daniel to make it all better, tell me I'm letting my mind go wild. Instead, he strides to the window that overlooks Lilac Lane and stares through the glass at the quiet street below. He doesn't move for a long time.

This feels like some sort of cat-and-mouse game, and I don't know the rules. "I . . . I hate her. Holly," I say.

The instant I say the words, I know I shouldn't have. I know it's only going to make matters worse.

"It's over, Sarah. Forget her. Holly."

I move toward him and touch his arm until he turns my way. "What if she's followed us here?"

Shock appears on Daniel's face. "Sarah, come on. Why the hell would Holly follow us here? Yes, she's angry with us because we left with little warning, but she was just our babysitter. I told you that's all she ever was. I'm sure she has better things to do than hop on a plane and come after us in a Toronto suburb." His voice is weary.

"Of course," I reply. "I don't know what's gotten into me. Must be the stress of the move," I say, though I know it isn't. It's time to let it all go, but I don't know if I can.

I feel alone and untethered. I don't want to spend our first day in our new home upset and at odds. "I bought cameras for the outside of the house. And new smoke detectors."

He scrubs his face with those large hands I've always loved.

"You think I'm nuts," I say.

"You're not . . . nuts," he replies. "I think we're both wrung out from moving so quickly and . . . from everything that happened in Vancouver. And for the record, I don't think we have anything to be afraid of, but it's smart to be secure. I'm not trying to dismiss you." He sits heavily on the bed. "I'll install everything."

I sit next to him, resting my head on his shoulder. "Did you hear back from the property manager?"

"Not yet. I'll call her again right now." He stands and leaves the bedroom.

"Where are you going?"

"To get my phone."

"It's in your pocket." I point to the rectangular bulge in his sweat-pants pocket.

He sighs. "I'm exhausted, Sarah. Clearly. I'll call later, okay?"

"I'll make the bed up quickly, then you can nap."

"Sarah?" he mumbles.

"Yes?"

"If you want Jacob to adjust to the move, you have to forget the summer. It's over now. This is a new start."

I hope with everything in me that he's right. I stand up, walk over to him, and kiss his cheek. "It's nice out now. I'll take Jacob outside to play."

"I'll do it," Daniel offers groggily, but I know he's going to fall on the bed and crash the second I walk out of the room. I envy his ability to fall asleep anywhere at any time, his skill at shutting off.

After a quick lunch of boxed macaroni and cheese that Daniel bought, Jacob and I head to the front, where he dribbles his basketball that we brought from Vancouver, up and down the driveway. Mr. Blinkers watches from the porch. Jacob's moving so fast, and I force my lips together to stop myself from calling out a warning to be careful. The man across the street isn't on the porch; Tara's terracotta brick house to the left of us looks quiet. Our grass needs mowing, but there's a small garden of black-eyed Susans next to the porch. This really is a lovely neighborhood.

I tell my mother just that in a quick text. The three-hour time difference means it's just past 9:00 a.m. in Vancouver, and Saturday is the only day she can sleep in. She's up at the crack of dawn the rest of the week. I won't hear back until later.

"Mommy, a dog!" Jacob stops on the sidewalk as a woman in an army-green baseball cap walks a cute black-and-white fluffball up Lilac Lane toward us.

She stops in front of our house so Jacob can pet the dog. It jumps up with its paws on his legs. Jacob giggles, and it's the best sound I've ever heard.

"Roscoe, down," the woman chastises gently while Jacob reaches to scratch him behind his ears.

"It's fine. My son loves dogs. Your dog's very cute. I love his little boots." I point to the tiny red booties and extend a hand. "I'm Sarah."

She removes her baseball cap to reveal an electric-blue pageboy cut and rosy cheeks. She shakes my hand. "I'm Emily. And this is Roscoe, my rebel."

I laugh, and for once it feels genuine.

"What kind of dog is he?" Jacob asks, his eyes bright.

"Good question. He's a rescue, so I'm not really sure. What kind do you think he might be?"

Jacob cocks his head, a sign he's taking the question very seriously. "He might be a Westie. Or a poodle. Maybe a schnauzer."

I'm surprised by how many breeds he knows.

Emily grins. "You're a dog expert."

"I want one," Jacob says.

Another wave of guilt passes over me. Jacob has begged us to get him a dog, but I couldn't take on another responsibility, knowing full well I would be the one to walk and feed it.

"I live in the town houses at the end of the cul-de-sac," Emily says as she points toward the bottom of the lane across from the ravine, "so you're welcome to play with Roscoe anytime." Then she glances at our house. "Have you lived here long?"

"No. We just moved in." I jerk a little because the man across the street has now come onto his porch. He's wearing the same tan pants as this morning paired with a padded black jacket that's seen better days. I shift back to Emily and Roscoe, who strains at the leash.

"Sit, Roscoe." He does, and she gives the dog a treat.

Without asking, Jacob grabs the bag of treats from Emily's hand.

"Jake!" I say, embarrassed by his behavior.

Emily laughs. "It's no problem." She softly tells my son, "Break off a little piece and hold it in your hand for him to sniff."

Jacob does and grins when Roscoe gobbles it in a nanosecond.

"Good job!" Emily's compliment makes Jacob beam.

"I'd better go," she says. "I have a student coming to my place in a bit."

"You're a teacher?"

"Tutor. Math and reading, grades one to six."

"Well, it was great to meet you, Emily. And Roscoe."

"You, too. Welcome to the neighborhood." She grins again and continues her walk up the street until she makes a left and disappears.

"Wasn't that dog so cute, Mommy? I love his name. Do you think she'll let me walk him?"

I'm amazed at the abrupt change in him, all because of a stuffed bunny and now a dog. This talkative, energetic boy is the son I know, not the sad, apathetic kid he's been since Holly walked out on him without a goodbye. I hope we see Emily and Roscoe again soon.

"Why don't we order a pizza tonight?" I tell Jacob, and he lights up even more.

I head inside with him. Daniel comes down a minute later, still dazed from his nap, and asks Jacob to help him install the light bulbs and smoke detectors while I unpack as much as I can. After setting up Jacob's room so he feels at home at bedtime, we sit down at the functional, round kitchen table for a cozy dinner of pepperoni pizza for Jacob and one with hot peppers and feta for Daniel and me. I try not to think about any of the strangeness of the house, about whoever might be watching us—who had access to the cameras. It doesn't matter. The cameras have all been removed now anyway, and the new ones are in my control.

At 8:00 p.m., it's drizzling outside. I tuck Jacob under his new Avengers duvet that Daniel bought him and stay with him until he closes his eyes, enviably long lashes spidering over his delicate skin. Finally, I tiptoe into our room. I want to ask Daniel if he called the property manager again about the cameras, but he's conked out. I slide under the sheets and curl myself around him, the heat from his body warming me.

I don't know exactly what time it is when I hear a bang in the middle of the night. I jolt awake and reach over to shake Daniel, but he's sleeping so soundly. It might just have been a raccoon in the garbage can. Still, I walk to Jacob's room to check on him. He's sound asleep, his thumb in his mouth, Mr. Blinkers next to him on the pillow. Overcome with love, I sit on his floor and lean against the wall under the window, where the silver blinds are open, and the moon is so bright it illuminates the shadows under Jacob's eyes. I'm hopeful that he'll adapt to our new life here. I need to do the same.

I don't want the light to wake him up, so I stand, about to close the blinds, when I look outside.

Someone is there. In the backyard.

My heart seizes. I leave Jacob's room and quietly head to the back door off the kitchen. I peer through the glass, but the moon isn't at the right angle. It's pitch-black. The rain has stopped, but the clouds are covered by a thick, eerie mist.

I'm about to switch on the exterior light, but I don't need to. A light goes on in one of Tara's windows, allowing me to see the tidy bed of yellow mums; the small sandbox we should have covered with a tarp to ward off animals. But whoever was there is gone.

I slide the door open, shivering at the sudden chill through my thin pajamas. In bare feet, I walk through the wet grass toward the circle of dirt surrounding the large Manitoba maple. I know I'm probably seeing things. I've had a shock, and I'm not myself. I just need to make sure. If there's nothing in the yard, no signs of anything, I'll go upstairs, get under the covers, and try to sleep.

There's just one visible issue: two muddy footprints on the narrow path facing the house.

The light goes out in Tara's window.

I look up. I can see straight into Jacob's bedroom, where my innocent son lies fast asleep.

CHAPTER SIX

HOLLY

Before

Holly's purple lace cocktail dress itches, and she's dying for a drink, but she's driven to this stuffy engagement party separately from her dad and Lisette. Lisette is probably still tearing apart the house, looking for her Cartier diamond bracelet. It's missing. It's Lisette's most precious possession, not just because it's worth more than twenty thousand dollars. John had given it to her a little over a year ago when Jeff Hudson, whose family owns a large chain of grocery stores, finally committed to funding the penultimate research that put Broncotin on the market. The asthma drug is her father's most lucrative product to date. Her father still thinks Lisette clinched the investment, but he's wrong. That was Holly's first deal.

Now Ritofan could land Health ProX in the international pharmaceutical sphere. But final testing is impossible without a huge influx of cash, and Holly can't stop scratching because this stupid purple dress feels like sandpaper against her skin. She wishes she had worn the lemon dress like Lisette suggested. Her act of defiance is now giving her hives. No matter how uncomfortable she feels, nothing will stand in the way of her doing what she's meant to do at the party—schmooze, smile, and make the rounds among the Forest View elite, sandwiched between her father and Lisette.

And then, of course, at the end of the night, she'll approach Charlie Lang and secure the deal. Once he agrees to invest, that's when Holly will see her reward. Her father will beam at her and hug her tightly. "You're my best girl," he'll say, just like he used to before Lisette came along. If she imagines it, it will happen. Manifestation, it's called. And if the investment is big enough, maybe she'll never have to close a deal again.

She orders a Coke from the bar and looks around the expensively decorated ballroom for Alexis. She's supposed to be here already so they can all pretend they're the perfect blended family. She spots Nadia Fielding holding court at the head table set on a dais above the guests, next to her handsome fiancé, Stuart Lytton, oldest son of the real estate powerhouse family. The theme tonight is clearly opulence, from the silver candelabras on each blush toile tablecloth to the gaudy explosion of pastel flowers hanging from the ceiling. Holly's exhausted but forces herself to perk up when her dad and Lisette walk arm in arm into the ballroom. Lisette raises her eyebrows at Holly. It's go time.

She meets them in the middle of the ballroom and eyes Lisette's bare wrist. She smiles. Lissette looks impeccable in her flowing white dress, but Holly takes private enjoyment in thinking of her rushing around the house, swearing and searching for the bracelet she would never find.

Her father kisses her cheek and whispers, "Charlie Lang should be here somewhere. Make me proud, honey."

She takes a deep breath, then says something that surprises her as soon as it's out of her mouth. "Maybe Lisette can have lunch with Charlie next week? Now that I'm babysitting as my job?"

Her father laughs like she told the funniest joke. "You're my ace in the hole. I'm counting on you. And Lisette's already arranged for you to approach Charlie tonight."

Her heart sinks.

Lisette examines her. "That dress doesn't suit you."

Holly says nothing.

Lisette turns to the heavy oak door to the ballroom that's just opened, and Holly exhales with relief. Alexis is here, hunching her broad shoulders in an ill-fitting black maxi dress, her almost waist-length brown waves already frizzing. She looks around the room.

Lisette gives her daughter a little wave and mutters to Holly, "What is it with the two of you? Have I taught you nothing about style?"

Holly ignores her and grins at Alexis as she walks over and joins them, her espadrilles squeaking with every step on the shiny floor. Lisette cringes; Holly stifles a smile. Only Alexis would think flat canvas shoes are acceptable party wear at the Canyon Club.

Alexis hugs her mother first, then John, who stiffly embraces her back. Lisette brushes her hands over Alexis's hair. It's not about affection; she's trying to smooth the flyaways.

Holly hugs her stepsister. "You look happy, Lex."

"You look beautiful, like always."

Holly snorts. "I look like an eggplant."

They both laugh, the tension in the family circle melting, if only for a moment and only between them.

"There's Stan and Gloria. Let's go over." John taps Alexis's shoulder. "Let Holly do the talking."

Holly touches the yin pendant, her sign of solidarity with Alexis. Alexis touches her yang.

Forming a tight group, they head over to Stan and Gloria Fielding. Stan doesn't meet Holly's eyes, but Gloria flashes her a practiced smile.

"Ah, here's the beauty." Gloria air-kisses Holly, then realizes she's just insulted Alexis. "Alexis, my darling," she says. "Lovely to see you, too." She turns to John. "Two daughters. One a nurse, the other well on her way to becoming a doctor. Quite the family." She simpers.

Holly decides not to tell Gloria she has pink lipstick smeared across her front teeth.

Lisette releases a sparkling laugh and entwines her arm with John's. "I'm a lucky mother."

"Great to see you both," Holly says, getting into character under her father's proud gaze. "Mazel tov on Nadia's engagement," she congratulates the Fieldings, and herself for getting the Yiddish pronunciation correct.

"Thank you, dear," Gloria says. "Your dad tells me you scored very well in your first year of medical school. He's so proud of you. It won't be long before you're running Health ProX."

"And Holly's babysitting for Daniel Goldman's boy this summer," her father says, more to Stan than anyone else.

Holly notices Alexis wilting beside her. "Alexis has news, too. She's doing research for a psychology professor at UBC this summer. It's a prestigious project on mental health support for nurses."

It's too late. Her father's deep in conversation with Stan, and Lisette and Gloria are searching the room for their next social conquests. Out of nowhere, a picture appears in her mind—Daniel— a father who ruffles his son's hair and praises him for who he is. Nothing's ever a performance for an audience, not like this.

"Speaking of the Goldmans," Stan says. "They should be around here somewhere. And John, how about a round of golf on Sunday?"

"With you? I'd never miss a chance. Daniel will join us. Nine a.m. sharp."

Holly and Alexis exchange a look. Her father's friendships, if they could call them that, always have a purpose and a price.

"You must try the salmon," Gloria insists as a waitress passes by with a plate. "It has a gorgeous ginger glaze."

Both Holly and Alexis roll their eyes, and when Gloria has swanned off, Alexis whispers, "How many times do I have to tell her I'm a vegetarian?"

Holly laughs.

Lisette looks at them sharply. "Time to mingle, ladies." She waggles her fingers at someone across the room and says to John, "There's Chip and Lucy Rawlins. They have that organic candy company that's just gone public." To Holly she says, "Make the rounds, then come find us. Alexis, go with her but let Holly talk."

Once John and Lisette have left them, Holly links her arm with her stepsister's. They do a pass of the room, grabbing a plate of gourmet food from the buffet table—duck confit, roast beef, and pasta salad for Holly, and spinach quiche for Alexis. But after only one full circle of mingling, Alexis begs to stop. "I can't do this anymore. My cheeks hurt from fake smiling. I'm going to get some air," she announces. "Do you have to keep going in here?"

"You know I do. There will be hell to pay if I don't. I'll meet up with you later."

Alexis kisses her cheek. "Good luck. I wish I was as good at this as you are."

No, you don't, Holly thinks after Alexis has exited through the glass doors and is no longer visible on the wraparound balcony. She lets her eyes roam around the room but can't spot who she's looking for among the clusters of bedazzled and bejeweled power players.

She glances at her dad and Lisette. Lisette has her eye on Holly while she talks up the Rawlins. Chip is a portly man in his late fifties. Holly's stomach feels slick and oily. She gestures to the oak door leading out of the ballroom to the hallway, mouthing at Lisette, "Ladies' room."

Lisette nods and points to Holly's shoulders, her signal for her to stand straighter.

Holly walks down the long, elegant hallway where plaques boast the names of illustrious, long-standing members like her father and grandfather. The Monroes have a superb reputation in Vancouver, and Holly's sick of living up to it. It's all a lie anyway. Her grandfather, William, cheated his own brother out of the company they started together, leaving her great-uncle's family scrambling for scraps.

A few partygoers mill about the hallway, and she passes the alcove where, when she was little, she'd play hide-and-seek with Alexis, who was in charge of keeping an eye on her. Up ahead, she sees two men in well-tailored suits talking in hushed, tense whispers.

One of the men is Daniel. He seems so affable and in control at home, but right now, he looks scared. She's surprised that the other man is Charlie Lang, who's looming over Daniel like a dark cloud.

Holly presses herself in the alcove out of view and listens.

"I'm not playing games here."

"I'm working on it. It's not a problem. I just need a bit more time."

Charlie walks away then, going right past Holly without even noticing her. When he's gone, Daniel slides out a phone from inside his suit jacket and taps. She watches as he furiously presses keys, beads of sweat forming at his temples.

Whatever happened between these two men, Daniel looks so stressed. He works at a computer software firm, so maybe he and Charlie do business together and something's gone sour? Or it could even be about a stupid golf game. With these men, you never know. She can't believe how intense her father gets about his handicap.

Holly steps out of the alcove, and Daniel's face changes, recovering quickly. He slips the phone back into his suit jacket pocket, flashing her a grin. "Holly! So nice to see you."

"Is Sarah here?" Holly asks. "I mean it's nice to see you, too, but where's Sarah?"

Daniel laughs. "In the ballroom, I think. What a fun party. We wouldn't have missed it for the world. Stan's an old friend." He looks pleased with himself. "And your dad and I have started golfing this summer. Did you know that? It's been really great."

"He told me. He's glad you're playing with him and Stan."

Daniel doesn't acknowledge the phone or the tense conversation with Charlie. Instead, he says, "I needed a break from that crowded room and to check in with the babysitter." He runs his fingers through his thick hair, his eyes skimming her tight dress.

Holly never minds when men check her out. It's a primal reaction, and it gives her power. But Daniel's doing so makes her feel a twinge of something else. Something like disgust. She feels protective of Sarah.

There's no denying that Daniel's an attractive man—tall and slim, though with a slight dad stomach, and strong-looking hands. His suit is tailored, and his shoes shine. She's surprised how good he looks all dressed up. He's more put together than Sarah, who's heading down the hallway toward them.

"Holly! You look so beautiful." Sarah snakes an arm around Daniel's waist. Her black sheath dress has no shape, swallowing her generous curves, and she attempted an updo, but it isn't tight enough, so strands fall haphazardly around her face. Holly wants to brush them into place for her.

"Lisette insists on my glamour," Holly says, then immediately wants to slap her own hand over her mouth. She didn't mean to voice that so directly, but that's the way Sarah always makes her feel—like for once in her life, she can speak the truth.

Sarah chuckles and turns to Daniel. "Did you reach the sitter?" Before he can answer, she touches Holly's arm. "Jacob was really upset you weren't babysitting tonight. He seems to think you belong to him." She laughs.

Daniel turns to his wife. "I just talked to Nora. Everything's fine at home."

Interesting. He never made a call home, but Holly's not about to stir up trouble. At least Sarah is a proper mother, concerned about her son, talking about babysitters and worrying about Jacob because he's an important part of her life.

Daniel kisses Sarah's cheek. "I'm going to the men's room. I'll see you ladies back in the ballroom."

"Sure, honey." Sarah smiles at Holly. "I'm heading to the ladies' room."

"Me too." Holly follows her down the hall to the first door on the right, where a bloodred plush banquet chair and full-length mirror greet them. Her stomach cramps have passed now that she's with Sarah.

Holly points to Sarah's hair. "Can I fix that? It's coming loose."

Sarah looks in the mirror. "Is it? Sure. Thanks." She sighs, and Holly hears the weight of the world in her breath. "I wish I was young like you. It's so much harder to do this when you're my age. I wish I had hair like yours."

Holly's used to the compliment about her hair. Her long auburn waves always get a lot of attention. It's the one gift her mother gave her. She doesn't have to reach up because she's a good five inches taller than Sarah, so she leans down and removes the pins. She redoes Sarah's hair in a perfect, classic chignon. Then she rummages in her silver clutch and pulls out a highlighter makeup stick.

"May I?" she asks. "Just a little touch-up."

Sarah nods, and Holly adds a pink glow to her cheeks.

Sarah glances in the mirror. "I look terrible, I know. I was downplaying how upset Jacob was that you weren't babysitting tonight. He had a complete meltdown."

"Oh no. I'm sorry."

"Don't be sorry. You have to be with your family."

"I'd rather babysit, to be honest." Holly puts the highlighter back in her purse. "I pretty much count the minutes until these events are over."

Sarah smiles. "Really? Me too. But we do what we have to do."

Holly feels those words in her soul. "I wish . . ." She stops.

"You wish what?" Sarah asks.

"Nothing. Never mind." She fakes a grin. "I should get back before Lisette and my dad send a search party. Plus, my stepsister is on her own in there."

"I'd love to meet her," Sarah says.

Holly's chest tightens. She doesn't want to introduce Alexis to Sarah. She wants to keep Sarah to herself. At least for tonight.

She's in luck, because when they return to the ballroom, Alexis is nowhere in sight.

"I think I'm done for the night. I just want to go home and get back to Jacob. I don't like leaving him for long when he's upset. You know?"

"Of course," Holly says. "He's still young, and the last thing you want is for him to be traumatized when you go out."

"Exactly," she says. "Ugh, once I find Daniel, I'm out of here." Her eyes search for him. He doesn't seem to be in the ballroom. "At least I talked to Gloria and Stan, which is the main thing. And Daniel can just tell everyone Jacob was having a meltdown." She wraps Holly in a hug. "If I don't see you later, I'll see you on Monday."

Tears spring to Holly's eyes at the simple gesture. She hugs Sarah back, then Sarah exits the ballroom in search of Daniel. As soon as she's gone, Holly feels someone watching her. She swivels toward the bar. Charlie Lang catches her eye. It's time.

She walks over, touches his arm. She checks to make sure her father is paying attention. He is. He's standing with Stan at the buffet table and raises his martini glass to her.

She turns to her mission for the night. "Hello, Charlie."

"Ms. Monroe." His nearly black eyes roam the length of her body. "What's your poison?" He gestures to the bar. "I'm buying." He laughs like he's so clever.

She laughs back, hating herself the whole time. "Just a Coke, please. I'm driving."

He orders for her and sips from his highball of Macallan. She watches his strong fingers grip the glass, her own skin feeling hot and tight.

"Have you had a chance to tour the Ritofan lab? We're ready to start phase three of the clinical trials." She makes sure to hold his gaze, as though he's the only person in the room to whom she wants to talk.

"I have. It's impressive."

She's feeling off her game tonight, not quite sure what to say. Or is it the dress? It's a fine line to toe, between looking sexy yet sophisticated: the pious daughter on the one hand; on the other, a young and available ingenue eager for instruction. Maybe it's not the dress, though. Maybe it was seeing Sarah and Daniel here, her worlds colliding in a way she doesn't want them to.

Holly runs her finger around the rim of her glass. "I'm sure my father told you that he's seeking FDA approval of Ritofan now that importation to the US has been approved?" She twinkles her eyes at him. "It's very exciting."

"It's promising. And expensive." He raises his bushy eyebrows. He's looking at her mouth. "Tell me more."

She glances around the room. "Is your wife here?" she asks, knowing full well she's in Lake Louise with their teenagers. It's why Lisette keeps pressing the importance of tonight to clinch the deal.

He smiles slowly. "No. It's just me. All alone."

Holly suppresses a shudder. "Do you want to take a walk? It's a beautiful night, and it's too loud to talk about something so private here."

Charlie puts his glass on the bar and lets his hand fall to graze the small of her back. Holly scans the room again for Alexis and spots her with Lisette, chatting with Nadia and her fiancé. Lisette turns to Holly over her shoulder, nodding once with satisfaction. Then she puts her hand on Alexis's back and pivots her away to chat with another cluster of guests.

When Holly and Charlie exit the ballroom together, Holly glances behind her, hoping her father might see her, might either stop her from leaving the party or come along with her, but he's chatting with Daniel. He waves at her, then continues talking. Holly looks around for Sarah, but she's not with her husband. She probably went home alone.

She regains her focus on the task at hand. "Come," she says, as she fakes her enrapture with Charlie and leads him out of the club and toward the farthest parking lot, where Holly left her Jeep. It takes them about three long minutes to get from the crowded party to the remote and quiet lot, which is mostly empty and pitch-dark. She clicks open the locks. Holly slides into the front seat while Charlie's large, imposing frame fills the passenger seat like it's his car and he's letting Holly take it for a spin.

He reaches over, his meaty hand heavy on her neck. She grabs his hand, removes it from her body.

"You seem like an eager investor. Are you really?"

"Oh, I am," he says. "I promise you that I am."

Only then does Holly release his hand. It immediately wanders back to her neck, where she strokes her fingers across it. As she lowers her head, she looks out her windshield toward the bushes lining the far end of the parking lot. Her body jolts.

It's just for a moment before they disappear, but she could swear a pair of eyes were trained right on her.

CHAPTER SEVEN

SARAH

Now

It's Sunday morning, and when I open my eyes, I'm confused about why I'm smooshed next to Jacob in his bed, the bottoms of my pajamas cold and damp. Then I remember we're in Toronto, in our new house, and I saw someone in our backyard last night.

Jacob's still sleeping, with Mr. Blinkers in his arms. I hold him close, listening to him breathe. I used to be so worried about his defiance with his teachers, how easily he distracted his friends, disrupting every class he was in. Constant individual assessment plans, sports therapy—nothing worked to help him focus. Educational psychologists were convinced it wasn't attention-deficit or oppositional defiance disorder. Jacob simply enjoyed being the star of his own show.

I regret my impatience with his mischief and desperately hope the excitement of yesterday is here to stay, no more wallowing in sadness.

I stretch my sore muscles, extricate my arm from under Jacob's waist, and get out of the bed as quietly as possible.

I look through the slatted blinds. It rained heavily after I searched the backyard in the middle of the night, and the footsteps marked on the path are gone. Only pools of water remain. Sun dapples through the wet leaves of the Manitoba maple, and the grass looks lush. Even though the heat is on, I tug the window up, breathing in the fresh, clean air. Today is a new day.

"I smell bacon."

I startle at Jacob's croaky voice. He's lying on his side, looking at me.

I sniff the air and smile. "I think you're right."

He hops out of bed with more energy than I've seen from him in weeks. "I have to pee!" he calls out before running to his bathroom, taking the bunny with him.

I laugh, but it stings a little, too. We've gone from diapers and Pull-Ups to Jacob doing so much by himself. One day he won't need me. I both want that and don't want it.

I head to the kitchen, where there's a plate of fluffy pancakes stacked high, and bacon sizzling in a pan on the stove. I'm shocked. I didn't even know Daniel could make pancakes. The decor is dark, but light filters through the sliding doors, making everything feel safe. I feel silly for being so scared last night. Maybe I didn't really see someone out there. I know my imagination plays tricks on me.

"New skill you've picked up?" I joke and kiss Daniel's cheek.

He kisses me on the mouth, and I drift into it, grateful for his attention and newfound willingness to share the household responsibilities. Maybe it's real that he does want to change, wants to regain the closeness we once had.

He turns back to the stove, his muscles stretching across the white T-shirt he sleeps in. "When I was little, my mom taught me to make pancakes. I don't know why I never did this for you guys before."

Because I took on that role and you were happy enough to just be served. I think it but don't say it because we're finally in a better place in our marriage, better than a month ago at least.

"From now on, you're the breakfast maker," I say. A weight lifts from my shoulders. It's that easy to cede control. To accept help. I catch irritation on his face before it morphs into a consenting nod.

While Jacob is still upstairs, I fix myself a cup of coffee from the pot on the counter. It's weird trying to find mugs and spoons in my own house. I take a few sips, then tell Daniel about the bang I heard in the night, the person and footsteps I think I saw in our yard.

He sighs and puts down the spatula. "Just one day. That's all I want," he mutters under his breath.

I flinch. "What's that supposed to mean?"

He faces me. "I'm sorry, Sarah. But we just got here yesterday, and it's been one thing after another. I'd like to enjoy the day for even a minute before there's some incident that scares you."

I glare at him. "That's so unfair. There were hidden cameras when we got here and—"

"I heard back from Courtney. She thinks the previous residents probably put those cameras inside the house," he replies.

I frown. "Why didn't you tell me right away?"

Daniel grabs a plate from the cupboard, placing it next to the stove. "I didn't get a chance, Sarah. Jeez, you just got down here."

He's right. I have to give him a chance, stop second-guessing him all the time. "So . . . Courtney. She's sure the cameras belonged to the previous tenants?"

"It's the only thing that makes any sense. Who else could they belong to?" I hear a sharpness to his voice, and I know I'm being dismissed. "Also," Daniel adds, "I installed the security cameras outside yesterday, so let's just let it be."

"About that," I say. "Let's check the cameras. I wasn't thinking straight last night. Maybe I didn't really see anyone in the yard, but can we look at the security app to be sure? The footprints were right under Jacob's window, Dan." I cock my chin at his phone on the island.

"I didn't put a camera in the backyard, but there's one at the side of the house leading to the gate." He turns off the stove, moving the pan of bacon to another element, and grabs his phone. Then he punches into an app and angles the screen so we can both view it.

I gasp as someone, head down in a bulky hoodie pulled tightly around their face, skulks through the narrow passage between our house and Tara's. He or she walks carefully, quickly, toward the back-yard, I assume, and disappears off camera, not appearing again.

"Holy shit. You're right," Daniel says, drawing away from me and bringing the phone closer to his eyes. "I don't get it. Where did they go?"

I move closer, feeling him flex and unflex his bicep. He's nervous, which worries me even more. And I'm already having trouble control-ling my distress. I didn't want to be right. I feel like crying. "Maybe they hopped the back fence. I can't identify a single feature. Can you?"

He shakes his head.

Fear skitters up my chest. "I think we should call the police about this backyard prowler," I decide. "Maybe I'll mention the inside cam-eras, too."

"I'll do it," he says, and puts his phone on the counter. "I'll call them." Then he takes my hands in his. His palms are sweaty. "It's not that I didn't believe you saw someone out there last night." Water rushes through the pipes from upstairs, and he glances at the ceil-ing. "Jacob will be down any minute, and he needs to feel good here. Happy. We all do."

"I'm trying, Dan. I'm trying."

He nods. "I know. But listen, I grew up here. People prowl. Some-times it's teens goofing around; sometimes it's just petty criminals looking for something quick to steal and sell."

I jerk, but he doesn't notice and continues. "There are porch pirates who steal packages and people who sneak into backyards to take stuff, Sarah. Shit happens. It's not the end of the world."

I want to believe Daniel, but he's not always right. He likes to think the worst won't happen. I ignore the sick ripple in the pit of my stomach and smile brightly when Jacob finally comes downstairs in his Avengers pajamas, Mr. Blinkers dangling from one hand. Jacob's blue eyes are so big, and his shaggy blond hair falls in his beautiful face. My first thought is I want to tether him to me and never let him out of my sight. But I know I can't do that. It's wrong. And futile.

"First family breakfast in our new house!" I make Jacob a plate of pancakes and bacon and hand it to him, swallowing my usual words of caution not to drop the plate. What does it matter if it breaks?

We sit at the kitchen table and all laugh as a squirrel looks inside from the door in the yard. It's a perfect tableau I wish I could capture and hold forever. But I've left that part of me behind, so I force myself to simply be present, enjoy this moment until Daniel can call the police.

"I think if we get a dog, I'll like it here even more," Jacob says, then shovels bacon into his mouth.

"Small pieces, buddy," Daniel tells him, and we exchange a smile. "I don't think now's the right time for a dog."

Jacob's face falls.

"I'll bet that Emily woman we met yesterday would let you pet Roscoe again."

He brightens. "Today? Right now?"

"No, not right this second," I say, realizing I'm making matters worse.

Just then, the doorbell rings.

"Are you expecting anyone?" I ask Daniel.

"Nope." He shrugs. "Could be one of the neighbors."

I get up to check the security app on my phone, charging next to the coffee maker. Daniel is right. On our porch are Tara and Cody. She's got another plate of something in her hands. She's a one-woman welcome wagon.

I'm still in my pajamas, my teeth unbrushed. "It's Tara and Cody. Can you get the door?" I ask Daniel. "I need to make myself more presentable."

"I'll go!" Jacob says as he gets up so fast that he knocks his chair over.

I hear Jacob squeal with delight, and I imagine Daniel's tossed him over his shoulder to carry him to the door. I go upstairs to our bathroom, wash my face, brush my teeth, and yank a comb through my tangled hair. It still looks like shit, so I opt for my usual ponytail. I swipe on a bit of concealer and lip gloss before heading downstairs.

Cody and Jacob are sitting in the living room, close together, heads bent over a tablet on the couch, plates of untouched pancakes on the table in front of them. It's amazing how quickly little kids bond. I smile at the scene and follow the adult voices I hear to the kitchen, where Tara's pouring herself a mug of coffee and Daniel's clearing the table. It's cozy and neighborly, and I don't understand how Daniel can be so comfortable with a stranger in our kitchen. I've always been hesitant around new people, and even more so now.

"Morning! I brought you muffins!" Tara chirps. Her blond hair is glossy, pulled off her face with a headband, a look I would never dare attempt, and she's decked out in head-to-toe tight yoga gear. On the island is a plate of what look like blueberry muffins. "How was your first night here?" She opens the fridge to get milk, then grabs a spoon from the cutlery drawer in the island.

I goggle at her. She catches my surprise.

"Oh! Sorry," she says. "Wild guess at where you keep your cutlery." She gives a pert shrug. "I'm an interior designer, so I'm pretty used to home layouts. I have a small business. Designs by Tara."

"We could definitely use your help with this place," Daniel says while loading the dishwasher. "Too bad it's a rental, and we're stuck with the haunted house theme."

She laughs again, but I recoil. Why would he say that when she's coming on so fast and furious?

I get another cup of coffee for myself with the dregs of what's left in the pot and steer the conversation to what I saw in the yard. "So, someone was in our backyard late last night. Maybe Daniel told you?" I glance at my husband, who shakes his head.

Alarm flits across Tara's eyes and her hand jerks. She puts her coffee down on the counter. "That's scary! Danny didn't tell me. Thank you for letting me know. Did they take anything?"

I brush aside the "Danny." I'll let that go, for now. "No, nothing was taken. I went out there, though, and saw a light on in your house. You didn't see anything?"

She stiffens. "No. I was up late because Cody had a nightmare, but I never looked out the window. Did you call the police?"

Daniel pushes the dishwasher door closed. "I'm going to call them today."

I wait for him to mention the security camera at the side of our house between Tara's place and ours, but he doesn't. I don't, either. The less she knows, the better.

"Keep me posted. I have a lock on our gate, but still." She shivers. "Someone creeping around our properties is worrisome." Her fingers tap on her thigh. "Do you know if it was a man or a woman?"

"They concealed their face with a hoodie." I look carefully at her expression for any sign it might have been her in our yard. She's already made herself quite at home here. "We'll get a lock on our back gate, too."

"Good." She smooths her perfect-fitting yoga pants. "I actually came over to invite Jacob for a playdate. You must have so much to get done, and since the boys will be at the same school starting tomorrow, I thought it might be nice for them to hang out."

I turn my head toward the living room, where the boys are

laughing. I feel such relief that Jacob seems back to his usually social self that I almost agree. Then I get my wits together. "How about the boys play here?" I suggest. I haven't met Cody's father, and I don't want my boy in this woman's house. I don't know enough about her yet. I don't trust her.

Tara flicks her eyes to the boys and back at me. I see the hesitation. Daniel pipes in, "Does Cody like basketball?"

Tara grins. "Loves it."

"Great. So does Jacob. Is there a court close by? I'm happy to take the boys for a couple of hours."

I watch our new next-door neighbor the way I would through my lens: how she's trying to hold herself casually, but her left hand makes a quick fist. She's scared to let Daniel take her son. Beneath her shiny surface, Tara's hiding something.

"Do you mind if a boring woman who sucks at basketball tags along?" she asks. "There's a net at the boys' school. I can show you where it is."

Daniel glances at me. "Sarah? Do you want to come, too?"

I don't, but I'm not sure Daniel's picking up on how odd Tara is. Maybe I'm not being fair to him, though. He's always protected us, always tries to make me feel safe when my worry overtakes logic. If Daniel's going to be with Jacob, everything will be fine. I need to decompress, unpack, get Jacob's backpack ready for school tomorrow.

"I should take care of stuff here," I say. "But have fun." I'm about to remind Daniel to take sunscreen, water, and a sweater in case it gets cooler out, but I decide against it.

"Jake, go get changed, buddy!" Daniel shouts into the living room. "We're going to play basketball with Cody at your new school!" He runs his hand through his hair. "I'll just take a quick shower and get dressed. Be down in five."

"Come on, Cody. You can see my room!" I hear Jacob's feet thud on the floor, and he speeds out of the living room, Cody's long legs trailing behind him as he races up the stairs. It reminds me of how he

84

used to listen so well to Holly. She rarely had to ask him twice to do something. When will I get her out of my head?

"Sarah?"

I snap my attention back to Tara. "Sorry." I laugh. "Letting my mom brain wander there for a minute."

"I do that, too."

We stand there, looking at each other, both smiling, both hiding things. This woman is giving me emotional whiplash. On the one hand, she's overly friendly, but on the other, she seems nervous and cautious, an anxious mom just like me.

I didn't have a lot of friends in Vancouver because I was so busy catering to Daniel's and Jacob's needs. And the other moms at his private school engaged in a passive-aggressive competition I had no interest in joining, so I kept my distance.

Jacob and Cody have come back downstairs, giggling and saying "bum" to each other. I can't help but laugh, too, until I realize why. Jacob pushes Mr. Blinkers's tail in Cody's face, where just underneath Holly sewed a small tear.

"Jake, stop shoving the bunny at Cody."

Tara grins. "I don't think Cody minds. Is that the stuffed animal he was so upset about?" she asks.

"Yes. It turned up."

"Funny how things work out, isn't it?"

Hilarious, I think.

We all shuffle to the front door, where Daniel says, "I'll text on our way home. Take it easy, too, okay? Don't do everything around here without me."

"And the police?"

"I'll call right after our game. Promise." He kisses me on the cheek.

I hug Jacob, who squeezes me back, and the four of them head out into the crisp air and bright sunshine. Tara flutters her fingers at me as they turn left from Lilac Lane onto Daisy Drive.

I'm about to close the door when I notice the man across the street on his porch again. Same tan pants paired with a plaid flannel button-down. He's rocking in his chair, eyes locked on mine. I venture a wave. He nods back.

Is it just me or is something off in this neighborhood? Some neighbors get too close; some stay too far away.

I close the door behind me, leaning against it, letting myself breathe in the quiet for a moment. The silence is short-lived, though, because I hear my phone buzz from the kitchen. My initial thought is something's already happened on the walk to the basketball court, then I berate myself for being ridiculous.

I walk to the kitchen, where my phone flashes with a text notification. Expecting it to be my mother or Nathan, I'm surprised to see it's come from a private caller. My surprise quickly turns to terror when I open the message to find three chilling words.

Unknown: I see you.

CHAPTER EIGHT

HOLLY

Before

Holly's meeting with Charlie in her Jeep seems interminable. But finally, it's over. He adjusts the crisp crease in his suit pants and opens the passenger door, a satisfied smirk on his craggy face. He turns his leonine head and says to Holly, "I hope we can arrange another discussion to finalize the details of my investment. I'm pleased to contribute to Ritofan."

The door closes. He walks away. The light in the car goes out. And Holly lays her head against the steering wheel in relief. She's done it.

Her father is going to be so happy. His dream of building an internationally successful pharmaceutical conglomerate is coming true. Why? Because of her. A thrill courses through her when she visualizes the pride on his face, his strong arms around her. He'll spin her around and tell her how much he loves her.

She wipes her face. She can still smell Charlie's thick cologne in her car. She peers out the windows to make sure that Charlie has left the parking lot before popping the gold Dunhill pen she slipped from his suit jacket pocket into the console between the front seats. Something for him; something for her.

She flicks on the light and angles the rearview mirror to check her makeup. She fixes her pale pink lipstick, which is smudged above her top lip. She wants to look perfect when she gets home and tells her father the meeting was a success. She needs to get her story straight— they spoke in the parking lot; he was interested in product details and extremely eager to invest. He'll be reaching out to John on Monday.

Holly scans the bushes again for the eyes she saw glowing in the dark. Nothing. She probably imagined it, but still, she wants to check. She steps out of the car with her phone. It's midnight already. She's a grown woman, not a child. She's not afraid to be alone in the dark parking lot. She hears a rustle. Her bravado slips. There *is* someone out here. She presses the flashlight on the phone and almost drops it when a tall, broadly built woman emerges from the brush. Alexis.

Shit. What did her stepsister see? *Think fast*, she tells herself as Alexis comes closer.

Alexis holds up her hands to protect her eyes from the light. Holly clicks off the flashlight. She doesn't say a word.

"Holly, who was that man?"

She gulps, blood roaring in her ears. Why didn't she insist they go elsewhere? It was so stupid to do this right in the parking lot when all the guests at the Fielding party were on the other side of the golf course. She knows exactly why, of course. Because men like Charlie love the danger of being inches away from their own doom. But she should have insisted.

"The man?" Holly repeats, buying herself time. "He was just a guest at the party."

"Why was he in your car all the way out here?" Alexis asks.

"Why are *you* all the way out here?" Holly deflects.

"I was looking for you. We can go. John and my mom went home already." She points to the black backpack at her feet. "I'm staying at the house tonight. Remember?"

"Of course I remember. Sorry. I can give you a ride."

"Who was it?"

She isn't relenting.

"Just some friend of the Fieldings. He was helping me with my car. It wouldn't start." Holly's face burns, and she's grateful it's dark out.

"I saw you, Holly," Alexis says, her tone softer, and sad. She steps closer to the Jeep, putting her hand on Holly's shoulder.

Holly's insides turn to ice, but she laughs, hoping it doesn't sound as fake to Alexis as it does to her. "I was just having some fun. Blowing off steam."

Laughter from the balcony drifts across the golf course behind them. Holly wonders if Charlie's gone back inside, if he's speaking to someone else's daughter by now.

"Is that the man whose son you babysit?"

Holly lurches. "No! Why would you even think that?"

"He looked . . . older," she says.

"No way. He's not." She wills a deep breath into her lungs.

She can't see Alexis's expression, but she can feel the worry when Alexis squeezes her shoulder. "You can tell me anything. You know that, right? I won't judge you."

But she will, Holly knows. Alexis is selfless, generous, and thoroughly good. She'd never understand why Holly does what she does. It's not as though anyone is forcing her, and her dad doesn't even know. Holly barely understands herself why she does it. But a worse thought occurs to her—what if Alexis tells their parents? She can't bear the thought, and she knows that Lisette will play dumb, pretend she hasn't known all along.

Holly laughs lightly and gently removes Alexis's hand. "You're making a big deal out of nothing, Lex. I'm young and free and sowing some wild oats. It's totally normal." She walks away from Alexis and opens the driver's side door. "Get in. Let's go home."

Alexis's espadrilles slap the pavement as she approaches the Jeep. She gets in and closes the door. "Having sex with some older man in your car isn't normal, you know." Alexis sighs. "Sex doesn't mean anything to you?"

Holly doesn't even know how to answer that. Sex is obligation, and power. It's a way to get what she needs. How is she supposed to explain that to her stepsister? "It's a summer fling, Lex. A one-off."

"But why him? Is he married?"

"Maybe? But I'm not."

"Holly." Her tone is firm.

"You're judging me, Alexis. You said you wouldn't."

Holly feels sick as Alexis looks at her now, waiting for answers. "Can we please drop it? If it's so important to you, I promise I won't do it again."

"Really? You promise?"

"Yes. I do. As long as you promise you won't tell my dad or Lisette." Holly's dealings are a deck of cards, carefully arranged. One false move, wrong word, and everything will collapse around her.

"I won't tell. I would never betray you like that."

Guilt and self-loathing nearly make her breathless, but Holly holds out her finger. "Pinky swear."

That earns her a grin, because it's their thing, their private sign of a secret kept from their parents.

Holly tugs at the purple lace dress she can't wait to take off and toss in the trash. She starts the car and puts on her seat belt. Alexis does the same. But when she does, she sees the gold pen in the cup-holder between their two seats.

Alexis reaches and grabs it. "This is nice." She holds the pen out to inspect it.

Holly's heart hammers. She doesn't make eye contact. "Thanks. It was a gift from . . . my dad."

"It's engraved. What's 'CL'?"

Holly closes her eyes. She just wants this night to end. "'Caitlin's love,'" she says. She clears her throat. "My dad gave it to me on my mom's birthday." This is the problem with lies. They're like fire. They start as a spark and become a five-alarm inferno in no time at all.

Alexis smiles. Thank God she buys it. Her stepsister has a beautiful smile, but her face is always hidden under the same curtain of brown waves she's had since she was a teenager. Holly brushes a strand from Alexis's cheek. Alexis holds her hand there for a moment, then touches the yang necklace at the base of her throat.

Holly touches hers back. Then she puts both hands on the steering wheel, shifts the Jeep into drive, and turns onto the highway.

They're quiet on their way home, or her stepsister is, at least. Holly's chattering senselessly about anything she can think of.

By the time she pulls up behind her dad's Porsche in the circular driveway of the mansion, she yearns for sleep and yawns hugely.

Alexis laughs. "What's happened to my party-animal stepsister who can stay up all night?"

"Babysitting a little kid every day is exhausting."

"You're the last person I ever imagined taking care of a little kid for the summer."

That stings. "Why?"

"I didn't mean it in a bad way. You're usually all about your dad's business or attending all the galas."

Holly stomach rolls. "I actually like babysitting better. Sarah, the kid's mom, is super nice, and Jacob is really sweet."

Holly turns off the car. The interior light goes on. She moves her hair from her shoulder, and Alexis's eyes narrow in on her neck. Instinctively, Holly puts her hand there. "What?"

"You have a mark."

Holly flips down the mirror, and her cheeks blaze when she sees it—a dime-size hickey on her collarbone. Cringing, she doesn't say anything to Alexis, just pulls her hair over her shoulder to cover it as they both jump out of the car.

The house is dark. It looks like her dad and Lisette have already gone to bed. Tomorrow, she'll update them on her progress with sealing an investment from Charlie. But a light from the living room window flicks on. Damn it, her father and Lisette probably heard her drive up in the Jeep. She has no choice but to see them, talk to them, and she can't really mention Charlie until Alexis has gone to sleep. This will be the longest night ever.

They walk together up the two wide stairs to the slate-gray pivot door that's always a struggle to open, as though it wants to keep the secrets of the house inside.

A rush of frigid air greets her as they step inside the expansive foyer. Lisette always keeps the temperature at morgue-level cold, likely to preserve herself. But when she and Alexis head to the living room, the cold is the least of Holly's worries. Her father and stepmother sit stone-faced on the couch, staring at her. The taste of Charlie coats the back of her throat, and she thinks she might throw up all over Lisette's precious hardwood.

Lisette's diamond bracelet twinkles on the coffee table, the one Holly stole from her a week ago and hid at the very back of her desk drawer, after Lisette informed her that Charlie was their next investment target.

They found it.

They know.

CHAPTER NINE

SARAH

Now

I see you.

Words Holly and I said to each other all the time.

Words someone who's watching me might send in an anonymous text.

Words someone who knows I watched Holly might threaten me with.

I can barely think over the blood thrashing in my ears. I count to ten, like I've taught Jacob to do to slow his impulsive reactions. Then I run to the door in the kitchen, scanning every corner of the backyard for anyone who might have gotten in again. There's no shed to hide in. It's an open space, enclosed with a six-foot fence on both sides, perfect for my young son to run and play, for me to feel safe letting him go outside on his own while I cook, do dishes, sit for one second. It's not safe anymore. We're not safe.

"I see you, Sarah. I know you're tired and fed up. I'm here to help you," Holly told me about ten days after Nadia Fielding's engagement party, when Daniel had sent me home in an Uber because he wanted to keep partying it up with the Canyon Club men while I was more concerned with Jacob's raging meltdown. Those men in their high-end three-piece suits, smarmy charm, and an interest, for some reason, in my nerdy husband. I tried asking him why he was so eager to fit in with the designer clan in Forest View.

"I'm the COO of a successful software firm, Sarah. Jacob's in private school. We live in a house overlooking the Capilano River. We belong at the Canyon Club, and we need to do what's best for Jacob's future."

I rolled my eyes. "Jacob is six. His future is learning subtraction and how to write a paragraph."

I couldn't understand the importance of being included with the elite. It's not something I ever longed for, but Daniel did. He knew I was ill at ease with the socialites, which is probably why he golfed. It meant he could schmooze on his own, with just "the guys," leaving me at home to look after Jacob. This offered an extra advantage for him, too. He could avoid my nagging, my unhappiness. Anyone was better at navigating the Canyon Club gentry than I was, even a young girl like Holly.

I should have paid more attention to how they acted when they were together, right from the beginning. I was so happy to see Holly in the hallway at the engagement party that I failed to notice if she and Daniel were standing too close, touching, or there was a frisson of anything inappropriate between my son's babysitter and my husband. She seemed so excited to see me, too. We bonded over feeling like outcasts, with the one difference that Holly never let it show. She flitted around like a butterfly. Lisette demanded it, according to Holly. No one asked this of me, not even my own husband. So I went home early that night.

I've asked Daniel more than a few times over the last six weeks to be honest with me about Holly. Was there something between them or not? He's always laughed it off.

"Why would a young woman want a middle-aged man with a wife, a kid, and a paunch?"

I didn't know, and I wasn't sure I believed him.

I see you. Perhaps Holly knows I watched her, photographed her in her bedroom. Maybe she spotted me. I thought I'd concealed myself in the close-packed trees and crooked branches that jutted out of the muddy ground choked with leaves. But I could be wrong. Maybe she holds a grudge for that, for other things, too.

I can't help but think about the very first time I started to wonder about Holly, to question whether she really was who I thought she was. It was the first time I left her for the day with Jacob alone in the house. When I'd gotten home, I found her keys on the basement stairs. She and Jacob played down there sometimes, so it was possible she'd dropped them, like she'd told me. It wasn't her words that alerted me to a possible lie, it was her eyes, hooded and shocked, like an animal in headlights.

Maybe she was snooping. I do that, too, when I'm in someone else's house. It's fun, a little risky. But the photos of Holly I hid in that basement, in the locked drawer in my darkroom, weren't for anyone's eyes but mine. To this day, I don't know if she ever found them. She would have had to break into the drawer, and there were no signs that she had.

I didn't listen to my gut, and now I regret it.

"I see you, too, Holly," I say aloud in the empty room. "But what are you after?"

And why wouldn't she send me texts that are clearly from her? Why all of this "private caller" subterfuge? She's not shy. She's a calculating snake who slithered into my family. The problem is, I don't know what she wants. And come to think of it, maybe I never did.

I head upstairs and grab my laptop from our bedroom closet,

where I tucked it in my carry-on. Holly posted photos of herself all the time on social media, right up until seventeen days ago, when everything came to a head, and I told her we were moving to Toronto, leaving her behind in Vancouver. We rejected a girl desperate for love and attention. How dangerous might that be?

I didn't even want to consider moving when Daniel first told me that he'd been headhunted, that he really wanted to take the consulting job so he could be with me and Jacob more, try something new. Why would we move when Jacob was doing so well with Holly, and I, too, was blossoming in ways I hadn't for years? Why would Daniel want to leave his golf buddies, the Canyon Club, his cushy job for the unknown?

Not long after, that all changed, and I wanted to be as far from Forest View and Holly as I could get.

I plug the computer into the outlet behind the nightstand and settle on the bed. I'm going to creep her, hunt her down. Maybe she's leaving clues about what she wants from me. I deactivated my Instagram account right before we left Vancouver. It was meant to promote my photography, but that's not part of my life anymore. I gave it up the minute we decided to move halfway across the country. So I shut down my Instagram, too, since I'd have nothing to post on it.

I google "Holly Monroe Instagram," and her feed pops up— HollyGoLightly99. I'd been amused when she'd told me her handle, but at the time, I didn't cue to the fact that she'd named herself after a character who slept with rich, older men for their money.

There's nothing new on her feed since her last post on September 1, proclaiming she's off social media, a day after the last time I saw her. It's not even a photo, just a moving picture, a GIF I think it's called, or maybe it's a meme, of a woman, who's not Holly, doing yoga on a beach at sunset. The caption reads: "Finding myself." There are two hashtags: "#selfcare #goingoffthegrid." The post doesn't tell me anything I don't already know.

I scroll back through her older photos, Holly's carefully curated posts—her practiced smile, beautiful life of galas and parties, a few candid shots of her on the university campus with girlfriends she never once mentioned. The Holly I finally saw does not appear in these posts: the conniving one, off-kilter and cunning. The Holly who would do anything for male attention. There's no evidence of that here. None at all.

There's no way I'm reaching out to her by text or on social media, not until I understand what her game is.

Google is my only hope. I type "Holly Monroe; Forest View; Vancouver" into the search engine, not for the first time, of course, because what mother wouldn't research her son's babysitter? I find the same links I did when I checked her out after Daniel had suggested hiring her.

Write-ups about Ritofan and Health ProX. Society photos, including a link to one from almost fifteen years ago. John and Lisette's wedding, held at the Canyon Club, a very young Holly, dressed in pink silk, hand in hand down the aisle, led by an older girl in yellow, with frizzy, out-of-control brown waves, beaming at the child next to her.

The caption reads: "Widower John Monroe, who helms Health ProX, marries in splashy ceremony. Also pictured are his daughter, Holly, six, and stepdaughter, Alexis, eleven."

There's nothing helpful there. Her stepmother sounded like a monster, but then again, can I trust anything Holly told me? I've seen Lisette only a couple of times in person—once at a lunch at the Canyon Club Daniel dragged me to right after he joined, and then again at the Fielding party, when we waved at each other across a room. Daniel was the one who'd asked John if his daughter did any babysitting. They'd just started playing golf together, and John mentioned Holly had recently finished her first year of medical school. Who better than a young, responsible doctor-to-be to help out with Jacob?

All polished exterior and very little substance—that was always my feeling about Holly's stepmother. At lunch, we engaged in perfectly pleasant conversations about her kids and mine, but our interests are so vastly different we didn't have much to say to each other. Also, in her eyes, I saw greed and hunger, never a good combination. It wasn't a leap to understand why Holly hooked herself to me so quickly.

I scroll through the Health ProX website, which I also did right after I hired Holly. I glance at the same landing page emphasizing that it's a family company built on ethics and integrity. I click quickly through the funding and corporate partnership opportunities, various preclinical and clinical trials for different drugs. There's a page about the company's future as a leading international manufacturer of lifesaving medications. I pull the laptop closer, looking for the family photo that was there two months ago, a professional shot of Holly, Lisette, and John, proudly standing side by side in a pristine white lab, but it's not there. In its place is a photo of John and Lisette in a corporate office.

Of course I knew Holly had been disowned. She cried to me about it, confessed that she didn't want to carry on the family legacy. I was dismayed her father and Lisette had kicked her out for wanting to follow her own path, and over some argument about jewelry. Now I wonder if that was the whole truth. Is there another reason they let her go so easily? Did they want to eject her from their lives as much as I do? Was she a threat to her own family?

Despite my search, I still don't know anything concrete about Holly. Disowned, she's gone on a retreat at an unknown location. That's all. She's out there somewhere, trying to find herself, trying to figure things out, things that have nothing to do with me or Daniel. There has to be some other explanation; something I'm missing about what's going on here and now.

I close the laptop and pick up my phone to watch last night's footage from the camera app one more time. The image is in black and white, and the light bulb only turns on when it detects motion. The hooded figure enters the frame, then disappears, leaving no more than a grainy view of the side of Tara's house and the grass between our walls. I play the few seconds over and over, studying the figure for evidence of it being Holly—her long waves peeking out from the hoodie, her slim build in the dark clothes—but there's nothing. I can't even tell if it's a man or a woman. I have to let it go. I'm ramping up again. I can feel it. Daniel will call the police today. He'll take care of this. Why do I always feel it's my job to resolve everything?

Being intimidated by our twenty-two-year-old babysitter is ridiculous. There's an easy solution. I go into the contacts on my cell and press her number. *Be calm*, I tell myself, but my hands are shaking as I hold the phone to my ear.

I'll talk to her softly, like I used to, explain once more that we appreciate everything she did for us over the summer. This time I'll be explicit. "We didn't leave because of you," I'll say. Basically, I'll lie through my teeth. But I get voice mail and stutter out a message that's nothing like I planned.

"Holly, it's Sarah. I just want to— Can we talk? Please? I know you're upset with how things ended, but you need to get on with your life. Okay?"

I hang up, wondering what it is I've done, if anything. I've wasted an hour on an internet search, and I've just reached out to a young woman I don't want in my life. What is wrong with me?

It will stop. All of this. I know it will. If it's she who's stalking me, she'll soon give up, move on, and everything can return to normal—for her and for us. Now, what I really need to do is something productive. Tomorrow Jacob starts second grade at Blossom Court Elementary, and Daniel begins a consulting career at Strategic Solutions. Me? I'm back to being a cleaner, cook, chauffeur without a car, because until we buy one, the only vehicle we have is the rental car Daniel will need for his job. I'm happy for him to start a new adventure, and jealous, too. I don't have a passion that's all my own. Everything I had before is gone.

I get off the bed and head to the closet, making five trips in and out to put our clothes in the heavy wood drawers, arranging the piles into seasons, wondering where we'll be once our six-month lease is up here. What next summer might be like.

My phone pings, and my pulse ratchets up, but it's the camera app alerting me to a presence in our driveway. I check the feed: it's Daniel and Tara. They stroll together to our porch steps, the boys trailing behind, bouncing the basketball between them as they walk. Jacob and Cody look happy together, and I'm thrilled my son's found a friend so quickly. Daniel, too, seems far more relaxed than he has in weeks. He's laughing at something Tara said, flipping his hand through his hair. Something in me twinges. I feel like I swallowed a rock.

I hear the front door close. I look again at the camera, but I can't tell if Tara and Cody have gone home. No one's on the screen.

I run downstairs. There's Tara, surprising me in my house once again. This time, she's right at the bottom of the stairs.

I sigh. "Hello, Tara. Where are the boys and Daniel?"

"Cody and Jacob are in the living room playing video games, and Danny's in the kitchen." She grins. "I feel like we haven't had a chance to get to know each other. I'm really hoping we can be friends." There's a lovely sheen on her pretty face, and she looks pleased with herself for being so forthright.

For my part, I'm suffocating. I'd like some breathing room.

I step forward, hoping she'll step back, but she barely moves an inch.

"Did you get a lot done here while we were gone?" she asks, looking around the main floor.

Is she checking to see if the hidden cameras are in working order?

"A bit." I maneuver around her so there's more space between us.

I hear clattering from the kitchen. From the opening and closing of cupboards, I can tell my husband is unloading the dishwasher. I appreciate it, but why now? And why did he let Tara in again?

"We had a wonderful time at the basketball court. The boys are very similar. I mean, Jacob's more outgoing than Cody, who's a bit shy, but they have a lot of interests in common. Basketball, video games . . ." She peers closely at me. "I think Jacob's a lot like Danny."

I narrow my eyes. "You mean my husband? How so?"

"Oh, I just mean Danny's very friendly."

And I'm not, is the not-so-subtle subtext.

"Did you need something?" I ask, trying to keep my voice steady and my face amiable. It's hard, though, because Tara's busy looking around the room, sharp eyes taking in the utilitarian design and who knows what else. "Oh, yes! I wanted to invite you all for a barbecue later this afternoon."

Is everyone on Lilac Lane this "welcoming"? On Cliffside, we waved at our neighbors on either side and watered each other's plants when anyone was away, but that was it. Everyone kept to themselves, maintained an appropriate distance.

"That sounds . . . nice," I say, though it's not what I feel at all.

She claps her hands. "Great! Four o'clock okay?"

Since I can't get out of it, I decide I'll get what I want from it. "Yes. Can we bring anything?"

"Just those two lovely men of yours."

I cringe. "Will Cody's father be there, too?" I ask.

Her demeanor shifts instantly. "He's away," she says, her voice clipped.

The temperature in the room drops a few degrees. "Oh?" I respond, waiting for more. But she just stands there, mute.

It's uncomfortable until she shakes her head as though ridding herself of a thought, then brightens. "Well, I'd better say goodbye to Danny and grab Cody."

Together we walk to the kitchen, where Daniel's finishing unstacking the clean dishes from the dishwasher. His hair is mussed, and his blue T-shirt sticks to his back with sweat from playing with the boys. I go to him and possessively put my hand between his shoulder blades. "Looks like you got a workout," I say as I lean in for a performative kiss.

Tara watches, which is exactly the point.

"You two are so cute," she says. "Such a perfect couple. Anyway,

I'd better get Cody home for lunch." She smiles at Daniel, then at me. Tara gathers Cody, and with Jacob still in the living room, Daniel and I head to the porch to wave them off.

"See you at four!" she calls before I lead us back inside the house and shut the door.

"What are we doing at four?" Daniel asks after the door is closed.

"Barbecue at her place. Tara didn't tell you?"

"Nope," he says. "I've kind of had enough of her for one day. She's . . . a lot."

I smile. "I'll say. And maybe next time don't leave her alone in the house while you empty the dishwasher?"

"She told me she'd see herself out."

"Well, she didn't. And now we have to go to her place for dinner because I didn't know what to say."

He sighs. "Sorry."

"Let's just make the best of it, okay?" I say, resigned.

He nods. "I'm going up to shower in a sec," he says, fanning his damp shirt. "Did you get a lot done?"

"Some." Now would be the time to tell him about the text, but I don't. He'll just tell me it's spam and that I'm inventing worries because I don't know how to relax.

"Mommy, I'm hungry!" Jacob skids in his socks toward us.

"Go to the kitchen and help your mom make lunch," Daniel says. And he heads upstairs to shower.

"You could have made him lunch," I mutter to myself. But then I remember he did make breakfast and took Jacob to play basketball. It's far more than Daniel ever did on a Sunday in Vancouver, because he usually golfed and worked all weekend.

"What did you say, Mommy?" Jacob asks.

"Nothing, honey. What do you want to eat?"

Jacob's eyes are bright. I've noticed he hasn't sucked his thumb today at all.

He grins. "Your famous grilled cheese?"

I put my arm around his small shoulders. "You got it. You can help me butter the bread."

As we walk together through the living room, we pass the window that faces Tara's kitchen. The filmy curtains, dotted with pale blue and gray flowers, are open.

She stands at her window, looking straight inside our house. When she sees me, she quickly turns and reaches for something on the counter. The hairs on the back of my neck spike. I hurry to catch up to Jacob.

Maybe the person I really need to worry about isn't Holly. Maybe the threat is much closer than I think.

CHAPTER TEN

HOLLY

Before

Lisette's diamond bracelet sparkles on the table in front of her father and Lisette. Holly feels the urge to run, but she can't just turn and race out the front door. It's too late now. There's no escape. Her heart pounds so rapidly she's light-headed. How is it possible? She hid the bracelet so well, tucking it under essays and study guides at the very back of her desk drawer. Why would Lisette or her father ever look in there?

She can't speak. She can't move. Alexis's eyes toggle between the bracelet on the table, Holly, and their parents. She takes one step closer to Holly, a subtle choosing of sides before the showdown has even begun.

"Alexis, go upstairs to your old wing, please," John says in a steely tone. His eyes are rigid and hard. He's sitting like a statue in the middle of the couch, his hands gripping his thighs. Lisette is pressed against him.

"I think I should stay," Alexis says.

"Honey, this doesn't concern you," Lisette replies. Her eyes are swollen, and her helmet of black hair is a mess.

"Go hang out in my room, Alexis. I'll come up after. It's okay." Holly's mind scrambles to invent an explanation that will wipe away the horrible, disappointed frown etched into her father's face.

Alexis shakes her head. "I'm staying right here."

"Suit yourself," her father says, then he turns to Holly.

"Why?" he asks. He's staring at her like she's a stranger.

She stands there dumbly, unable to look at Alexis, afraid of what's going to happen next.

Holly can't explain any of it. There's no answer to why. She doesn't even understand it herself—why she needs to steal things that matter to Lisette, relishes making her feel loss.

"I don't know," she says, hating how weak and small her voice sounds. "I'm sorry."

"You're sorry? That's it? Do you have anything else to say for yourself?" her father demands through clenched teeth.

Lisette moves closer to John. She looks shocked. And victorious.

Holly does have something to say, but she's terrified to say it. Maybe, just maybe, her father will understand. She'll finally unburden herself of the sick feeling constantly churning inside her. "I don't want to continue medical school or work at Health ProX."

The fury contorting her father's face instantly alerts her that she's made a huge mistake.

"You're a thief. And a liar," her father says. "You've disappointed me beyond all measure. You've betrayed my wife and the integrity of our family name. And all you can say is you don't want the education that we've generously been giving you?" His eyes travel to the hickey on her collarbone. His face screws up in disgust.

Holly almost chokes. Integrity? She digs her nails into her palms to stop herself from touching the hickey. Acknowledging that her father saw it will make everything worse. He has no idea how much she's given just to belong to this family, to have his approval. She's about to speak, but he's not finished and holds out his hand.

"I want you gone now. You'll give me the keys to the house, the office, and your Jeep."

Alexis gasps beside her. "Mom—" she starts to say.

"No, Alexis," Lisette answers her daughter sternly. "Holly can't commit a crime, steal from me, and think it's okay. Actions have consequences. Perhaps you shouldn't be spending so much time together, either. I hate to say it, but she's a bad influence."

Alexis shifts from foot to foot. "Why don't you let Holly explain?" She turns to Holly. "Were you just borrowing it and forgot to return it?" She's trying to save Holly, like she always does.

"No," Holly says. She's done lying, She's done pretending. The shame is too much to bear. It's too confusing and heavy.

Holly takes her key chain out of her clutch and unhooks the keys her father has asked for. She hands them to him. When their fingers touch, his are ice-cold. He slides the keys inside his suit jacket pocket. Lisette puts a bony hand on her father's shoulder, and he lays his hand on hers. His wife over his daughter. It's always been this way. Why should she be surprised? He's clearly made his choice. He made it long ago.

Holly looks around the elaborate living room with the beige silk furniture, the high-and-mighty ten-foot ceiling. She doesn't belong here. She hates this house, but she didn't realize it until she met the Goldmans.

She looks straight at the two people who should love her unconditionally. "I'm sorry I can't be who you want me to be," she says. "I'll pack my things."

"No!" Alexis cries.

But Holly shakes her head. "It's okay," she says to her stepsister. Then she exits the room and walks to her wing, climbs the stairs, and goes to her bedroom for possibly the last time. How can it be? How did everything implode so quickly? It's all her fault.

Up in her room, she sits on her bed, taking in the suffocating pale pink palette and Lisette's stale, lifeless art on every wall. She pushes aside her thin curtains and peers out the window across the black, churning river. From here, she can see the Goldmans' house. In the moonlight, she can just make out the top of their gabled roof.

She yanks the curtains closed and stuffs a duffel bag with clothes, toiletries, electronics, and the only keepsake she wants to take—the photo of her mother. In the hallway, she listens to make sure everyone is still in the living room. It sounds like they are. She can't stop herself, doesn't want to stop herself as she crosses the landing to the other wing of the house, tiptoes to her father and Lisette's bedroom, and turns the brass knob on their bedroom door. Once inside she goes to the display shelf in their walk-in closet, where she plucks Lisette's orange, gold-studded Valentino purse, worth thousands. She shoves it in her duffel bag like it's dirty laundry.

She walks back down the spiral stairs and into the living room, where only Lisette is seated on the couch, with a fresh cocktail in front of her like she's celebrating.

"Where are my dad and Alexis?" Holly asks.

"Alexis is waiting in the foyer for you. Your father is in his study. He can't even bear to look at you. I can't believe you'd hurt him like this. And me—the only mother you have."

Holly lets out a sharp laugh. "You're not my mother. You've never been my mother."

Lisette narrows her eyes and whispers so only the two of them can hear, "You ungrateful, spoiled girl. After all I've done for you."

"All you've done for me? Do you think it's normal, what I do for this company, for this family?" Holly blurts.

Lisette leans back. "I don't know what you're talking about."

"Maybe my father deserves to know everything," Holly says, her voice shaky.

Lisette only laughs. "You're a drama queen, Holly, and a klepto-maniac. Get out."

Holly spins before Lisette can see her face burn. When she gets to the front door, Alexis is waiting, her phone in her hand, black back-pack at her feet. "I'll call an Uber. You'll stay with me."

Holly considers it, staying in Alexis's one-bedroom basement apartment, her stepsister's constant fussing and hovering. She appre-ciates how much Alexis wants to help, but she can think of only one place where she'll be seen and appreciated the way she wants to be. "I don't want to get you involved, Lex. I'll be okay. I have a place to stay."

"Where?"

"The Goldmans'."

Alexis's shoulders droop slightly. "You sure?"

"I'm sure." As she says it, she really is sure. She knows Sarah will take her in. Sarah will understand. The hollow crater in her stomach eases a little when she imagines waking up in the Goldmans' house tomorrow morning. Jacob will be so happy. She doesn't know how Daniel will react, but Sarah will smooth things over. She'll open her arms wide and embrace her. That's what a good mother does.

Alexis nods. "Okay, for tonight that's fine. But call or text if you need me. We'll figure this out. Together."

Holly tries to smile, but the truth is that she's alone. Alexis can't help her with this one. She's been kicked out of the family. She's a disgrace. There's no way back.

"Text when you arrive at the Goldmans', okay?"

"I will." She kisses her stepsister on the cheek, touches her yin pen-dant with a trembling hand, and Alexis repeats the gesture back.

Then, leaving Alexis behind with Holly's mess, Holly opens the heavy pivot door, hearing it slowly thwack closed behind her for the very last time.

She goes to the garage and grabs her bike, walking it to the end of the circular driveway. She hops on and starts to ride in the dark. She leaves the Canopy Crescent house she's lived in all her life and cycles toward her new house and her new family.

CHAPTER ELEVEN

SARAH

Now

Before we go to Tara's, Daniel wants to call the police about last night's intruder, so Jacob and I head out on a mother-son tour of the neighborhood. The houses are all large, new models in various shades of gray, terra-cotta, and sand; the streets, wide and tree-lined. It feels like nothing bad can happen here.

Jacob holds my hand and points out the frozen yogurt shop, community center with an indoor and outdoor pool, and the tennis courts he saw when he went to play basketball this morning. I'm impressed with his sense of direction, and my heart warms at how proud he is to take me around our new neighborhood.

"There's my school, Mommy!" He pulls away from me, racing to the front of the brown-brick building. "They have monkey bars!" He vibrates with excitement as we stand outside the gates of the Blossom

Court Elementary School playground. "Wait until I show Cody how high I can climb on the net."

I hug him close. "I think we're going to be really happy here."

He grins, his dimples so delicious I have to kiss them.

"Ew, stop eating my face." But he's giggling.

On the way home, we get some daisies for Tara at a small grocery store and meet Daniel, who's waiting for us on the front porch.

"So?" I ask.

"The police can't really do anything."

I look at Jacob. "Want to play in the sandbox for a bit? We have about fifteen minutes before we go to Tara and Cody's."

He nods, and we walk in the house together. I blink from the contrast of the sunshine outside to the pervading darkness in here. Once we're in the kitchen, and Jacob's building a fortress in the sandbox, I drop the flowers on the kitchen table and sit on the chair closest to the sliding doors.

"What do you mean the police can't really do anything? Why not?" I ask.

"They took a report over the phone, but thieves break into yards and steal stuff off porches all the time. The police can't take someone trespassing too seriously. Especially when there's no theft."

"What about the security video? Can they at least look at it?" I splutter, helpless.

He sips from a glass of water. "There's no point. You can't see anything distinctive about the person."

"Did you tell them everything, Dan? About Holly?"

His jaw clenches. "What was I supposed to say? That our babysitter is a little desperate for attention? That my wife thinks she wanted to get me into bed with her? That we moved halfway across the country, so it's not like she even lives near us?"

He puts the glass on the table. The water left is filmy and unclear, much like what's happening in my house.

"What do we do now? Just sit here and wait for the next time? I don't like it," I say.

"I don't like it, either, but it is what it is. And it's probably nothing." Two of the most frustrating statements ever uttered.

Still, I can't do anything about it, but before we go to Tara's, I try talking to Daniel about canceling this barbecue, at least until we've been here for more than two days.

I take his glass and put it in the dishwasher, then turn to him. "Don't you want a relaxing, early night just the three of us before you start a new job tomorrow?"

"It's a bit late to cancel now, isn't it? And it's great for Jacob to have a friend right away." He peers closely at me. "Don't you want friends here? A social life?"

Of course I do. Eventually. But Tara is not exactly my first choice for a new mom friend. She's weird. Off, somehow. She barges her way in, gets too close too fast. But I have a plan for keeping an eye on her.

"You're right," I say. "Best to be social. For Jacob's sake."

Daniel nods and kisses my cheek.

Before we leave for the overfamiliar neighbor's house, I make sure the outdoor cameras are on and working—the one over the front door; the garage; the backyard; and at the side of the house in the narrow passageway between our house and Tara's. I lock everything up tight, while Daniel and Jacob gape at me like I'm nuts. I stop checking everything. It's exhausting to let my worst self get the better of me. A house is just a house; not everyone is waiting to invade or trespass or steal. Besides, I have the two most important people in my life with me anyway. It's up to me to watch out for them because the police won't.

So as Daniel, Jacob, and I walk up the three wide steps to Tara's porch at 4:00 p.m., seeing her for the second time in one day, I arrange a pleasant, approachable smile on my face. I glance once over my shoulder to see if that strange man across the street is rocking in his chair. He's not, though. His porch is empty.

My sweet boy clutches the bouquet of daisies, and I ring the door-bell. Wind chimes hanging on the brick sway in the wind, calling out a song when the door opens.

Cody, dressed in a T-shirt and sweatpants similar to Jacob's, smiles shyly at us. "Hi."

"These are for your mom." Jacob shoves the flowers at him.

Cody flinches, an odd look crossing his face before he takes the flowers. An old soul, my mother would say about this boy, quieter and more self-contained than Jacob, who's always thrown himself into the center of every play circle, is slow to understand taking his turn, and interrupts his teachers to correct them. Still, my son has a huge heart. His happiness and safety are all I care about.

Tara comes up behind Cody in a gorgeous burnt-orange sweater and tight black pants. I wish I'd worn something nicer than black leggings and a roomy blue-and-white pin-striped button-down. At least I brushed my hair.

"Hello! Welcome!" She opens the door wider. Her skin is smooth, even in the bright sunshine. I wonder how much younger than me she is.

She touches Cody's shoulder. For a second, he leans his cheek against her hand. No matter what darkness lies beneath Tara's ebullient exterior, she appears to be a loving mom.

She sees the flowers Cody is holding. "Are those for me?"

He nods. "From Jacob."

"Oh, thank you, Jacob. That's very thoughtful." She sticks her nose in the daisies to smell them. "Why don't you two go play in the backyard? We have a trampoline," Tara suggests. Then she quickly checks with me. "I mean, if that's okay with you."

"Sure." I don't want to ruin Jacob's fun, and even though I worry he could break his neck if he lands the wrong way, I smile, my cheeks already hurting because I'm grinding my teeth at the same time.

"Awesome!" Jacob shouts, and he and Cody run to the back while Daniel and I follow her through the enviably open-concept house to the kitchen. The interior of our houses are so different. Hers is one long room, sunny and spacious, with elegantly simple rustic furniture from the ladder bookcase in the living room to the white distressed hutch in the dining room.

"Your house is lovely," I say.

Daniel murmurs agreement beside me.

"Thank you. I refinished a lot of the furniture myself." Tara opens the fridge. "What would you like to drink? I have beer, white, red, and rosé."

I'm not sure I should let my defenses down, but the bottle dripping condensation in the fridge makes my mouth water. "Rosé would be great. Thank you."

"Beer for me." Daniel leans against the granite island, shoulders loose, relaxed.

While Tara retrieves a beer for Daniel, I sweep my eyes around the kitchen. It looks like mine does at the beginning of every school year. A fridge covered with what I assume is Cody's colorful artwork, a calendar filled with activities and appointments: basketball, track, a few different doctors' names. One square catches my attention more than the others—September twenty-third, a week from now, has a big red "X" through it. Mentally filing away the date, I notice a pink flyer for "Emily Lawrence Tutoring."

I point to the flyer with a photo of a smiling blue-haired woman. "That's the woman with the dog, right? She introduced herself yesterday."

Tara pours me a generous glass of rosé. "Yes, Emily. She's lovely. She told me she's lived in Blossom Court for a while." She smiles. "We might hire her. She tutors a lot of kids in the neighborhood. Cody struggles with reading."

"Jacob has trouble with math," I reply, and bring the glass to my lips. My first sip is glorious. It warms my chest and relaxes me, as does the late-afternoon sunshine flowing in through the wide kitchen windows, from where I can see Jacob and Cody laughing and jumping wildly. I've been so frantic I didn't realize how much I've missed the simple pleasure of a glass of wine.

"Maybe Jacob will catch on faster this year," Daniel says, taking a deep swallow of his beer.

"And you'll have time to help him with his homework now that you're working fewer hours." I smile to show I'm not being passive-aggressive, but his eyes cloud with uncertainty.

Tara tracks our every move. "Are you okay eating outside tonight?" she asks, cocking her sharp chin at the backyard. "I can barbecue, and we can watch the kids and chat. It's supposed to get chilly in an hour or so, but there's a firepit on the patio."

Daniel perks up. "I'm happy to help with the barbecue," he says. "I'm a damn good griller, if I do say so myself."

This is true. I did all the oven and stove-top cooking, the bake sale cupcakes, and even Jacob's birthday cakes until he was five, but I don't know how to barbecue. The propane, lighter, flames shooting out of the grill—all of it makes me nervous.

"That would be wonderful!" Tara glances at the clock on the stove. "Is it too early to start grilling?"

Daniel's stomach grumbles. He laughs. "I didn't eat lunch, so anytime is good for me."

Tara laughs, too, opens the fridge, and hands him a plate of thick rib eyes and four hamburger patties. "Since it's just me at the moment, you can be the grill master."

I'm hoping she'll reveal more about why it's just her, but she stops right there, turning around to close the fridge.

Daniel holds the plate. "Tongs?"

"Right." Tara rummages in a drawer next to the farmhouse sink.

I glance outside at the boys so happy together, wrestling and bouncing with unbridled glee. "Jacob does have Ms. Martin as his teacher. I'm so glad the kids will be in the same class." For once, the words that spill out of my mouth are true. I *am* happy that Jacob's starting class tomorrow with a friend. What I'm not happy about is that his friend's mother is Tara.

Tara nods while giving Daniel the tongs. "I know. And Valerie's excited to meet Jacob. That's Ms. Martin," she explains. "I emailed her right after the boys played basketball today to ask if Jacob's in Cody's class."

I stiffen. She was talking to my son's teacher about my child, a teacher whom I've never met?

"How well do you know Valerie?" Daniel asks. And I'm grateful that he does.

Tara grabs cutlery from the drawer next to the stove. I notice she doesn't keep silverware in the island, where ours is, yet she "guessed" where to find it in our home.

"Me and Valerie? I chatted with her quite a bit at parents' welcome night the first week of school. So sorry you missed it." She smiles at us. "When she confirmed Jacob's in her class, I asked if Cody and Jacob could sit at the same table. I think it would be nice for them. And to be honest, Cody doesn't always have the easiest time making friends."

I blink to give myself time to figure out the appropriate reaction. I don't like her commandeering Jacob's seating plan and stepping on my toes. I'm annoyed and disturbed, but I look to Daniel to gauge his reaction, because I don't trust my own.

He nods placidly. Clearly, he's unaware that this woman is trespassing on my turf. Still, I won't overreact. Not yet.

"That's kind of you," I say with a forced smile. "I'm looking forward to talking to Ms. Martin myself." Yes, that's the right response.

"Oh, it's my pleasure." She reaches for a phone on the counter and aims it at the backyard. "Smile for the camera!" she calls through the open window.

Both boys duck out of view, giggling.

"You can't hide from me! I see you!" Tara singsongs.

My wineglass slips from my hand and shatters on the kitchen tiles.

"I'm so sorry." I bend down to start picking up the pieces. "Shit," I say as a sharp piece of glass slices my skin. A bloom of blood appears on my finger.

"You okay, honey?" Daniel asks, but Tara's faster.

She grabs my hand and inspects the wound. "Thank goodness. It's not deep. Let me get you a Band-Aid."

"I'm fine. It's nothing. Don't worry about it. I'll just wash it off. May I use your bathroom?"

"Of course! It's to the right of the front door." She looks at the floor. "I'll get a broom and sweep this up in a heartbeat." She walks over to a closet off the kitchen.

Daniel examines my finger, too. "Sure you're okay?"

Do I hear judgment? Or is it concern? "I'm fine. Just clumsy." I shrug.

"Accidents happen," he says.

They do, of course, but my gut churns with the worry he's dismissed all of the strange things that have happened since we've arrived as simple accidents and misfortunes. Whether it's because he's an analytical, not an emotional thinker, or because he's afraid, I don't know. To him, the cameras, Mr. Blinkers's sudden appearance, someone lurking in our backyard, are unconnected events. And the fact that Tara just said, "I see you!" to the boys, well, he'd think nothing of it. I know better.

"I'm going to head to the yard and heat up the barbecue." He grins. "And maybe leap around with the boys on the trampoline."

Tara laughs. "Their energy is contagious. I'll come out, too." She looks at me. "You sure you're all right?"

"Yes," I say. "Surface cut. Nothing to worry about."

She nods and slides the door open, lets Daniel go out with the plate first, then grabs his beer for him, closing the door behind them both.

Holding my throbbing finger, I wait for them to be distracted before I pretend I'm walking to the powder room. A quick peek over my shoulder and when I see they're not watching me, I dart up the stairs.

Her second floor is entirely pink—pink paint with a fluffy rose-colored chair and an ottoman at the top of the stairs. The bathroom between two other rooms with their doors closed is also done in a pale blush, save for the white toilet and bath. Even the candles and a jar of sea glass are pink. I remember the sea glass Jacob collected a few years ago on a weekend trip to Victoria with Daniel and me. There's no sea glass in Toronto because Lake Ontario is fresh water, not salt. I'm hit with a pang for the tangy air of home.

I don't have time to think any further on the weird design choice. I have to find her bedroom fast. If she's just pushy and overbearing, maybe we can be friends—or at least friendly. I'll point my conjecture elsewhere if that's the case. But first, I have to know who she really is.

I turn the silver knob on the door to the right of the bathroom. It's a boy's dream room. I quickly take in the race-car-shaped bed and superhero decals on the white walls and shut the door. I move to the last room on this floor and turn the knob as silently as possible. It smells of a light floral perfume, and it's as neat as a pin. There are no photos of Cody's father, or Tara with anyone, just a pastel print of a waterfall on the wall above her bed.

I'm not even sure what I'm looking for, but that's never stopped me before. A camera feed into my house? Proof she was in my backyard? Family photos? A connection to Holly? My pulse races as I slide open the drawers of the tall white dresser across from her bed to find Marie Kondo rolled T-shirts, socks, bras, and underwear. I check under her bed and in her walk-in closet for a hoodie that resembles the one our backyard prowler wore. Nothing. Time is running out.

I spin to leave her room. I zero in on the white-gold jewelry tree where five necklaces hang on delicate branches. I feel a jolt in my stomach.

My eyes are drawn to one necklace in particular, a rose-gold chain with a ring pendant. It's stunning, but that's not why I can't look away. It's the clasp, stamped with a tiny swirly logo that I instantly recognize—a snowflake, and just above it is the name of the one-of-a-kind jewelry boutique on Granville Street where Holly's yin necklace came from: Unique.

CHAPTER TWELVE

HOLLY

Before

Holly opens her eyes, and at first, she isn't sure whose bed she's in. It's a cream-colored upholstered queen, draped with a blue-and-white polka-dot duvet. Then last night floods back. Alexis seeing her with Charlie Lang in the parking lot. Lisette's bracelet on the coffee table. Her father's fury and disappointment. Jumping on her bike, duffel bag on her back, a thin sheen of sweat on her skin as she pumped her legs as hard as she could in the pitch-black night toward the Goldmans' and away from the only home she has ever known.

She curls into a ball under the covers, feeling a complicated mix of pain and relief. It's the first time in her life that her future isn't mapped out for her. She's free, but with that freedom comes the exhilarating and also frightening possibility of choice. What comes next? No matter what, everything will be okay. She has a place to stay, people who've let her in, who value her for who she is.

When she arrived at the Goldmans' last night, it was after 2:00 a.m. She stopped right before she turned onto Cliffside Road, breathing hard from the frantic cycle and nervousness. There, alone in the dark and quiet, trees towering over her, it occurred to her: What was she thinking coming here? Had she made a huge mistake? What if she rang the bell, woke the whole family up, and then, after spilling all her news, Sarah wouldn't let her stay? What if Sarah abandoned her the way everyone seemed to, even her own father and stepmother?

She contemplated calling Alexis, going to her place for the night, but it wasn't her stepsister's comfort she wanted.

She got back on her bike and, under a blanket of stars, rode the last leg to the Goldmans'. Leaving her bike next to the basketball net on the driveway, she looked up at the house, which was dark, of course. Holly didn't want to scare anyone by using her key and walking inside.

She unlatched the back gate and almost jumped out of her skin when she realized she wasn't alone. The lights around the pool cast just enough of a glow to reveal that Sarah was in her backyard. She had her camera in her hands and was taking pictures on the embankment outside the pool deck. The night was clear and cloudless, and Sarah pointed the lens at the last quarter moon suspended in the black sky above the river. She looked so small in the dense clump of imposing trees.

"Sarah," Holly said softly. The cliff was steep, and the last thing she wanted was to startle her and send her plummeting over the edge into the river below.

Sarah gasped and whirled around. "What the hell!" she squeaked, her brow scrunched up, one hand on her heart, camera in the other.

"I'm so sorry. I didn't mean to scare you."

Sarah, in oversize cotton pajamas, held on to tree roots to walk up the embankment and onto the pool deck. "Holly, what on earth? It's two in the morning. What are you doing here?"

Sarah's face was pale, and her hands were shaking. Holly had scared the hell out of her. Now she somehow had to say something, to explain things not even she herself fully understood. How much of the truth could she tell Sarah? Not about the bracelet she stole, for sure, because Sarah wouldn't accept a thief in her house, and definitely not about Charlie. The very thought of Sarah finding out about that filled her with shame. So, after Sarah invited her inside and made them both cups of chamomile tea, they sat together on the couch, where Holly gave her a semblance of the truth: that she finally admitted to her father and Lisette what she's kept inside for so long—she doesn't want to work at her father's company anymore; she wants to make her own way, like Alexis. In exchange for her honesty, they'd kicked her out.

Sarah sat cross-legged facing her, cup of tea forgotten on the coffee table. "What do you mean they kicked you out? Just because you don't want to go to med school?"

"Not only that. Health ProX is like my father's firstborn child. It means everything to him. If I don't graduate from med school and ultimately take over the family firm, I get cut off completely."

"But that's crazy. I don't know your parents that well, but I can't believe they would do that. I'm sure it will blow over in the morning."

"No," Holly choked out, tears streaming down her cheeks. "You don't understand them, Sarah. They're not like you. Lisette isn't my birth mother. And my dad—well, he's set in his ways. They don't want me back unless I fit their mold. I'm not who they raised me to be." Another sob broke free.

Sarah scooted closer to her and pulled Holly into her arms. "I don't understand any parent who lets their child walk out the door in the middle of the night. But I do understand what it's like when people don't get who you really are."

"You do?" Holly asked in a small voice.

"I do."

Sarah's face closed then, so Holly didn't push. And she was so tired. All Holly asked was: "Can I stay here tonight?"

Sarah was quiet for a moment. Then she nodded. "I'll make up the guest room for you." She stood and held out her hand. "Come. I'll call your parents in the morning. Maybe I can help smooth things over."

"No!" Holly realized how sharp she sounded. "Sorry, this is my problem, not yours. I appreciate the help, but you don't have to make everything all right." She sighed. "And who knows . . . maybe it's for the best."

"If that's what you want. But if you change your mind, I'll speak with them."

What she wanted was the reassurance that she had a place to stay, not just for tonight but for the long term. But of course she couldn't ask that. Not yet.

Now in the morning light the day after, Holly burrows under sheets that smell like sunshine and Sarah's sweet scent of vanilla. She wraps herself in the softness, looking around her basement bedroom across from Sarah's darkroom. A pine dresser sits opposite the window well, the only window in the small room, but the white walls make it seem bright and spacious.

On the wall next to the door hang five of Sarah's gorgeous photos in a circle montage. The theme is motherhood, each frame holding a single object in focus: a baby bottle; small shoe; schedule of activities; laundry basket; a glass of wine.

Everything is perfect. Holly can't stop smiling, even as a residual ache throbs in her chest.

She picks up her phone to find seven texts, all from Alexis. Five missed calls. Shit. She completely forgot to text her when she arrived last night, like she promised.

Alexis: Are you okay? Are you there?
Alexis: Holly, it's four in the morning. Are you
okay??
Alexis: Text me!!!

Every message after is increasingly frantic. Holly FaceTimes her stepsister immediately.

"Oh my God!" Alexis exclaims when she answers after the first ring. "I've been so worried about you! Why didn't you text? Are you okay?"

Alexis looks terrible. Her hair is a bird's nest of tangles, and she has black circles dug deep under her eyes.

"I'm so sorry. Please forgive me. I got here, talked to Sarah, then went right to sleep. It was such a brutal night." Shame at everything Alexis witnessed last night floods over her. Holly bites her lip. Should she ask how things are at the house this morning? She can't tell if Alexis is there or not because her face fills the whole screen, as usual.

"I was really worried something happened to you." She lowers her voice. "Mom and John just left for the Whistler house until tomorrow, so I'll be here on my own today if you want to come back and hang out. You could even stay overnight."

Holly knows Alexis is purposely avoiding the obvious question—whether she'll ever be allowed back. It doesn't matter. Holly knows she won't. Once their minds are set, no change is ever possible. Just another part of being a Monroe.

"Thanks. I don't want to go back. But we could hike the trail later?" She glances at the clock on the nightstand. It's seven forty-five. "We can meet at the trailhead at two?"

Holly means the Capilano River park trail that leads deep into the forest to the canyon.

Alexis beams. "I'd love that. I'm doing some work for Professor Phillips this morning, but I'm free all day after that."

Professor Phillips, a.k.a. Luke. Holly's former professor, and then some. Holly's ghosted him. She never got the courage to formally end things after they slept together several times. Instead, she's simply ignored his texts about how Alexis is fitting in at the office. It's pretty clear what he's after, and she doesn't feel like giving it to him anymore. Alexis still has no idea she was seeing Luke, and Holly resolves that she'll never find out. It was all a big mistake anyhow—sleeping with her forty-year-old professor, like some kind of bad porn. It was exciting, though, for a while—illicit—screwing in his office in the first semester, sneaking him into her bedroom in the second.

Transference. That's what Luke taught her in psychology class. Holly's self-aware enough to name it, to know that her attraction to older men is about her father, but that doesn't really change the feelings. Or make them go away.

But she doesn't need that kind of thrill to soothe her soul anymore. She knows better now. She's matured. Plus, now she has Sarah in her life, and she'd never want to disappoint her.

"I'll text you before I leave," Holly says to her sister. "And I love you." She reaches to click off, but Alexis opens her mouth.

"Wait! How long are you planning on staying with the Goldmans?"

Forever. But she can't tell Alexis that.

"I'll keep you posted."

They end the call. Holly pads to the kitchen, which is empty, but there's half a pot of coffee in the machine. She doesn't hear Jacob jumping around, and the house is silent. Maybe Daniel or Sarah made the coffee and then climbed back into bed together before Jacob woke up. She imagines Jacob leaping in bed between them, everyone laughing.

She smiles at the happy image as she helps herself to a cup, adds cream and sugar, then sits at the kitchen table, gazing at the aquamarine water sparkling under the sun, reveling in the peace of no expectations placed on her.

"Oh, thank God there's coffee." Sarah walks in a few minutes later and yawns, pulling her fraying yellow robe tighter.

She looks exhausted, as usual, but now Holly understands why. She takes pictures at night.

Holly jumps up, pours Sarah a cup of coffee, and opens the fridge. "I can't take credit for the coffee. One cream, one sugar?"

"You pay attention." Sarah takes the cup and sips, moaning with pleasure. "It's so good. Thank you. Daniel must have brewed a pot before he left to play golf." She smiles at Holly over the rim of her cup. "How did you sleep?"

"Like a baby. I'm really grateful you're letting me stay here."

Sarah gapes at her. "I wasn't about to turn you away in the middle of the night. I'm not a monster." She puts her cup on the counter. "You're welcome to stay here tonight, too."

Holly tries to look happy. But one more night isn't enough for her. Yet, she has to approach this the same way she has all her sales deals—one step at a time.

Sarah pulls out a frying pan and the eggs from the fridge while Holly rests her back against the quartz island.

"Does Daniel know I'm here?"

"He was gone by the time I woke up. I'm sure he'll be fine with it. I'll explain the situation. Anyhow, he's barely here these days. Work has been insane for him." She cracks one of the eggs. "Omelet okay?" Sarah glances to the ceiling. "Jacob's brushing his teeth. He'll be down soon. He's going to be ecstatic to see you here. And it's nice for me to have another woman around."

Woman. Not a girl under anyone's thumb.

Without warning, Holly starts to cry.

"Oh, gosh. I'm sorry, Holly. I'm trying to act like things are normal, but I know they're not for you. I know you're suffering." Sarah drops the whisk on the counter and focuses her full attention on Holly.

Seeing this nurturing woman in front of her, a woman who can read her moves and actually cares what she thinks and feels, bursts open a dam inside Holly. She lets herself go completely.

"I've disappointed my father. He hates me. I'm his only child, and now he doesn't want anything to do with me. I don't matter at all." Holly's voice breaks. Her limbs feel limp and numb.

"Have they called or texted since you walked out last night?"

Holly shakes her head.

Sarah exhales. "I don't want to disrespect your father and Lisette, but I'd never do that to a daughter of mine. Never." She squeezes

Holly's hand. "You're really wise for your age, you know that? Your parents are so lucky to have a daughter like you. And as for your dreams, they're important. Trust me on that. I wish I'd spent more time on mine instead of always putting myself last."

Holly sniffles, wiping her nose with the back of her hand. "What do you mean?"

Sarah hands her a tissue from the box on the counter. "I didn't have a stable childhood, so it was all I wanted for Jacob. Me at home for him all the time, available for everything he needs." She peers out of the room for a second and lowers her voice. "But I hit a point this winter when I realized I have needs, too. Which is why I'm so glad you're here to help out with Jacob." She reaches over to wipe Holly's tears from her cheeks. "You're not alone. You have us."

Holly launches herself at Sarah, hugging her so tightly that she can feel Sarah's surprise. "Thank you. I wish Lisette was as easy to talk to as you are."

They stay entwined for a moment, then Sarah pulls away. "Shit. I think the eggs are burning."

Holly's heart expands. She's never once experienced a surge of love for Lisette, and with her father, of course she loves him to her very core, but understanding him is always an effort. She loves Alexis with her whole being, but this love she's experiencing for Sarah is different. For the first time in her life, Holly feels sheltered. Safe.

Jacob comes downstairs then, his mouth open with delight when he lays eyes on Holly in the kitchen on a Saturday morning.

"Holly!" He leaps on her, squeezing so hard she almost can't breathe. "You're here early!"

"Jake, give her some space. Holly's our guest for the weekend, just like when your cousins, Sienna and Lily, sleep over."

"Really?" he says. "Your parents need a break like Uncle Nathan and Auntie Pam do?" he asks innocently.

She and Sarah lock eyes. "Something like that," Holly replies, tousling his hair.

After a delicious breakfast at the round kitchen table, scratched with wear and stained with raspberry jam, Jacob hops up and sits on Holly's lap, putting his thumb in his mouth. She runs her fingers through his hair, like she might if she had a younger sibling. It hits her then—taking care of Jacob isn't just a job to her; he's like the little brother she always wanted.

Sarah glances at Jacob. "Honey, remember what the dentist said about sucking your thumb? It's not good for your teeth." To Holly she says, "We need to get him to stop before school starts in less than two months."

Holly winks at her. "Hey, Jakey?"

He turns to look at her.

"If you don't suck your thumb, you'll get an even better grip on your basketball. Imagine your dribbles if your thumb isn't all wet." She tickles him.

He giggles and immediately pops his thumb out. "We're still going to the beach today, right, Mommy?" Jacob unfolds himself from Holly's arms and runs circles around the kitchen. "And because Holly's here, she's coming, too?"

"You don't own Holly, you know, Jacob. You have to ask her if she has plans." Then she mouths to Holly, "Thank you."

Jacob plops on the chair next to her. "Do you have plans?"

Holly thinks about Alexis. Guilt jabs her in the gut, but she says, "No plans. I'd love to come."

At the same time, both Sarah and Jacob say, "Yay!"

The rush Holly feels is potent.

In her room later, she types a quick text.

> Holly: Can't go to the trail today. Sorry.
> Babysitting all day. Maybe tomorrow?

Her stepsister responds immediately: *K.*

Holly knows Alexis is hurt, but she pushes that away the moment she, Sarah, and Jacob pile into the black Highlander. Thirty minutes later, after sing-alongs, snacks, and Jacob's never-ending chatter, they're nearing Kitsilano Beach.

Jacob yells, "I spy something red!"

"I think we're done with the games now, Jake," Sarah says as she pulls into the parking lot, stops, and pops the trunk.

"Just one more. I spy something red. It's your turn to guess, Holly."

From the front seat, she grins at him through the mirror facing the back, where he's firmly strapped in his booster seat. She points at one of the beachfront stores. "The shop over there?"

Jacob giggles. "Nope. Closer."

Holly hears him unbuckle the belt before his hands reach around her neck.

"Are you done guessing?" He taps Holly's collarbone.

Oh no.

Sarah looks like she's trying not to laugh. "It's not polite to point, honey." She grins at Holly. "Don't be embarrassed. It's part of being young, right?"

Holly puts her hand over the hickey, fuming that she was so worked up over last night that she forgot about it, forgot to cover it up with makeup. Men. How she hates them and their need to mark their territory.

She doesn't say anything when they exit the car. Holly doesn't want to talk about this with Sarah at all. She slides her pendant across the chain and busies herself grabbing the bag of towels and sand toys from the trunk.

Sarah comes beside her, a camera bag slung over her shoulder, and reaches for the water and sunscreen. "You have a boyfriend? Or girl-friend? Someone special?" Sarah asks as she slams the trunk closed.

"Are you married, Holly?" Jacob asks, gazing up at her with his dazzling blue eyes.

"No," Holly replies with a laugh, transferring the bag to her other hand so she can hold Jacob's as they cross the busy parking lot, past the bicycle path to the beach. "I'm kind of young to get all serious." She grins at Jacob. "Are *you* married?"

He giggles. "I'd marry you."

A sad film crosses Sarah's eyes for a quick second, but she blinks and says to Holly, "I was twenty-six when Daniel and I got married. Very young." Her voice is wistful.

"I guess you just knew he was the one?"

Sarah nods. "Something like that. He made me feel safe. I knew he'd never break my heart."

Sarah doesn't ask or say anything else, and they laugh when they reach the beach, and Jacob drops Holly's hand, grabs the bucket and shovel, and speeds across the sand toward the frothy waves, plopping down at the water's edge.

Holly's about to go play with Jacob, but Sarah touches her arm. "He's fine on his own for a bit. Come sit with me." She smiles as she takes her camera out of the black leather bag, snaps a photo of Jacob pouring water into the moat he's dug, then quickly aims the lens at Holly.

Holly grins for the photo. She can't remember the last time she had a family beach day. Maybe Sarah will frame it for the wall at home.

Their towels are side by side, and Holly's arm brushes against Sarah's as she leans back on her elbows. It's a perfect morning. The air is balmy with a cool breeze coming off the water, and the grainy sand under her feet is better than any pumice stone. Holly pulls her hair from its ponytail and begins to braid it.

Sarah watches. She places her camera back in the bag. "Can I?" she asks.

"Braid my hair? Sure."

Sarah comes closer and takes Holly's hair in her hands. Only Alexis has ever braided her hair, and whenever she does, Holly imagines the mother she never knew in her place. She shuts her eyes as Sarah gently works on her hair.

Jacob, just up ahead on the beach, shrieks as the waves tickle his legs, and Holly, heart pounding, with her back still to Sarah, says, "I stole Lisette's bracelet. That's really why they kicked me out."

Sarah's hands stop, and Holly feels a gentle tug on her hair. In the beat of silence, she regrets confessing. But then Sarah drops her braid and suddenly wraps her arms around her.

"That's a heavy burden to carry," she says as she releases her hold. "Why did you steal it?"

Holly shifts around so she's facing her. "I'm not sure. Because I could?" Tears slip down her cheeks. Mortified, she ducks her head.

Sarah lifts her chin, so they're eye to eye. "We all make mistakes."

"I don't know who I am. I really don't," Holly replies.

"You're not supposed to. I'm forty-one, and I still don't. That's why I take pictures. I point my lens at other people in the hopes of finding out who I am and what I want." She snorts then and looks away at her son playing on the sandy shoreline. "That must sound so weird."

"I get it," Holly says. "I didn't need her bracelet. But it made me feel like I have control, even though I know I don't. My dad and Lisette control everything. Nothing I do is ever good enough." She points at Sarah's camera. "You decide what you look at, what you shoot. Must be nice."

Sarah nods. "Yes, I guess so. But I'm still trying to figure out who I want to be. I'll get there. You will, too." Sarah looks out at the shore. "Be careful!" she yells out to Jacob. "Stay right at the edge! Don't go into the water!"

A flash of Holly's childhood comes to her, she and Alexis running on the beach, laughing. Yin to her yang. But Holly *can* exist without Alexis. She's proving it, just by being here with Sarah. She sighs and pulls her knees to her chest.

Sarah mirrors her posture, tugging her faded black bathing suit up. "Have you stolen only from Lisette?"

Holly's chest constricts thinking of Charlie's gold pen, suddenly remembering it's still in the console of the Jeep. She forces that whole encounter out of her mind. "Only Lisette," she says as she clears her throat. "I'd never take anything from you. Or anyone else."

Sarah nods. "Then listen, Holly, I think you should tell your father and Lisette what you've just told me. About how they make you feel."

Holly pictures it, telling them everything. How she feels about the "sales meetings," how they've used her without ever asking what she wants, how she's sure Lisette knows how she seals the deals, yet her own stepmother doesn't seem to care. No, it's her little secret. And it doesn't matter anymore. If they don't need her, she'll just have to not need them.

"I'll think about that," Holly says and exhales. "You're really incredible. I feel like I can tell you anything."

Sarah gives her hand a quick squeeze. "Me too."

They both laugh when Jacob comes running, landing on top of them, getting sand everywhere. "Group hug!"

An hour later, they pack up, sun-soaked and sand-filled, and head home.

Daniel saunters in at two o'clock, golf bag slung over his shoulder just as Holly walks up from the basement after taking a shower.

He looks shocked to see her. "Oh, hey, Holly." He takes in her wet hair. "Uh, is Sarah in her darkroom? I didn't know you were babysitting today. It's Saturday." He looks around the room. "Where's Jacob?"

She wishes Sarah could have been the one to tell him. She smiles uncertainly. "I stayed here last night in the guest room in the basement. I, um, well, I'm . . ." She has to speak carefully, because Daniel and her father know each other. "I had a little tiff with my dad and stepmom."

His eyes widen as Sarah appears over the second-floor railing, her skin glowing from her time at the beach. "Hi, honey!"

He looks up at her. "I hear we have an overnight guest." He gives Holly an affable, charming smile, but she catches the flash of irritation on his face.

"Yes, Holly's staying in the guest room for a couple of nights. Jacob's thrilled." She grins. "I am, too. Anyway, we can talk about that later. You missed such a nice day at the beach. How was golf with Stan?"

At the same time that Holly feels a spark of hope that Sarah might invite her to stay longer than the weekend, she also narrows her eyes. Daniel is lying. He couldn't have played golf with Stan Fielding because it's Saturday, Shabbat. Stan's not the most devout Jew, but there's no way he would have missed synagogue. Not a chance.

"It was great. We had lunch at the club after, which is why I'm so late."

"Jacob would love to play basketball with you, if you're up for it," Sarah says.

Jacob bounds down the steps toward his dad, as though he doesn't have a care in the world. Holly, however, is suddenly weighted down.

"Who won? You or Stan?" Holly asks, but she can't keep the edge out of her voice.

He twitches slightly. "Stan."

It doesn't bother Holly that he's deceiving her, but it enrages her to watch him deceive Sarah.

Why? she wonders. Why is he lying?

Holly doesn't know. But she's going to find out.

CHAPTER THIRTEEN

SARAH

Now

A dog barks outside, and I drop Tara's necklace from Unique to the floor. Shit. With trembling fingers, I get on my hands and knees to pick it up. I have to get back downstairs before she or Daniel comes looking for me. He'll think I'm nuts to snoop around her bedroom, and I definitely don't feel good doing it. But her behavior is weird. I've known her for only two days, and most of that time she's been hovering around us. Why? That's beyond what a friendly neighbor does with the newest residents. There has to be a reason she's so interested in us. Is the necklace from Vancouver a clue?

I don't have any more time to think about it right now. I replace the necklace on the tree and tiptoe down the stairs, eyes peeled. I make a mad dash to the powder room to wash my finger of the blood. Blood. Oh no. Did it drip in Tara's bedroom?

"Sarah?"

Daniel walks toward me from the kitchen as I emerge from the powder room. He's alone.

He puts his hands on my shoulders. "You're white as a sheet."

I'm debating telling Daniel about the necklace, but Tara comes up behind him.

"There you are! I know the house is big, but I thought we'd have to call a search team for you." Tara laughs, but it's flat. She hands me a Band-Aid.

I titter nervously and apply it, feeling sweat drip down the back of my neck.

"Dinner's ready. The temperature's dropped, so I thought the boys could eat and watch a movie in the living room and the grown-ups can eat in the kitchen."

"Sounds good. I'm just going to check on Jacob," I say, leaving Tara and Daniel in the kitchen, and walking across the room to where Jacob and Cody are on the floor right in front of the television, watching *Phineas and Ferb*.

"No *Avengers*?" I ask Jacob, kissing him on the head.

Cody shakes his head. "Tara doesn't let me watch movies with a lot of fighting."

Tara? Not Mom? I can't imagine Jacob calling me Sarah, but I won't judge her, not for that at least. Every family has its own dynamics.

"Well, it looks really funny." I hesitate but can't help myself. "Maybe, though, you guys should move back a bit? You're awfully close to the screen."

Both boys scoot back an inch. I smile and leave them be to join Tara and Daniel at the white farmhouse table, groaning with platters of steak and corn and a bowl of Mediterranean salad in the middle.

"So, tell me about Vancouver. I've always wanted to go." Tara passes the salad bowl to me.

The fresh vegetables look delicious, but my throat closes. Here she goes, prying again, all the while making it seem like she's never been.

Is she lying? I can't tell. I glance at Daniel and take a serving, plus put a steak on my plate, even though I don't know how I'm going to choke down a bite. Blood oozes from it, pooling in the center of the plate.

"It's beautiful. Forest View, where we lived, is very outdoorsy, so we hiked a lot, went to the beach, skiing," Daniel answers her, then forks a huge piece of steak in his mouth.

"If you like hiking, there's a really nice trail just at the end of the cul-de-sac." Tara smiles at Daniel and spoons a heaping serving of salad on her plate. She doesn't touch the steak. She catches me looking. "I'm a vegetarian," she says. "I don't mind cooking meat, but I prefer not to eat it."

"Good for you," Daniel says. "I think about doing it from time to time, but I like meat too much." To prove it, Daniel rams another chunk in his mouth.

When has he ever mentioned wanting to be a vegetarian? Maybe it's another facet of the new Daniel he became over the last year, the one who all but disappeared from our marriage. I look at him, the salt-and-pepper stubble on his jaw now, instead of the clean-shaven face; the T-shirt and sweats, not the expensive suits and ties that replaced his chinos and button-downs in our closet on Cliffside. Will he be happy here in Toronto, no one to impress but our next-door neighbor?

I realize it's my turn to start asking questions. "How long have you lived on Lilac Lane?"

"Just a month, actually." Tara stabs a cherry tomato but doesn't lift it from her plate.

"Oh, that's all?"

She nods. "That's why I'm so happy you guys are here. I haven't met a lot of other people yet. Parents, at least."

I finally swallow a bit of steak. "Where did you and Cody move from?" I ask.

"Here and there. We've bounced around a bit."

I take a sip of wine. She has no problem prying into our lives, asking a ton of personal questions, but now, when it's my turn, she offers nothing. If she thinks that's going to stop me, she's wrong.

"What does Cody's father do?" I ask, smiling as I chew the gristly bit of meat in my mouth.

Tara looks down at her plate, pushing her salad around on it. "This and that," she says.

"Does he travel a lot?" I venture again, knowing from the way her lips are mashed together that I'm pushing. Still, it's an ordinary question for an ordinary chat with a neighbor I'm getting to know, a neighbor with an inordinate interest in my life.

"Aren't you a curious one?" Tara says, grinning.

But my body goes cold.

I give up. It's clear she doesn't want to talk about Cody's father. If I want to get to the bottom of that hole, I'll have to dig it myself.

"Well, it'll be great to meet him when he comes back home." Daniel breezily drinks his beer as though all is normal. "What's his name?" he asks.

I send him a small smile of gratitude even though I have no idea if he's pressing her purposely.

"His name's Nick," Tara responds tightly. She glances into the living room where the boys are giggling. "We should probably talk about something else," she says quietly. "Cody has separation anxiety. He gets triggered when we discuss Nick. I hope you understand."

Now I feel terrible. I'd never want to hurt Cody. And I know something about having a kid with separation anxiety. Though he hasn't brought Mr. Blinkers here tonight or mentioned Holly even once today, Jacob's made sure his bunny is safely tucked away under the covers in his bedroom. I think he's so eager to spend time with Cody because he misses a connection with someone who's not me or Daniel.

The conversation moves to the news, books, and television, and it's as companionable as it can be when three people are all tiptoeing around their pasts for different reasons. After homemade sugar-free cheesecake, which is surprisingly delicious, we say our goodbyes at the front door.

While Jacob shoves his feet into his laced-up sneakers—the laces are in a neat bow, and he's still learning to tie his shoes on his own—I smile at Tara. "Thank you for dinner. You've been very welcoming."

"It's my pleasure. We'd love to have you over again anytime. Remember, I'm just next door."

It's my cue to repeat the offer, but I don't. I'd like some space for even a day.

She opens the door to the chilly air, and we step onto the porch. It's just after 7:00 p.m., and the sun is starting to set above the treetops in the ravine at the end of the cul-de-sac, a brilliant blaze of pink and orange streaks. It's beautiful, but I look away, because the woods remind me of what I've given up—my home in Vancouver, photography—and everything that's humming beneath the surface between Daniel and me. There's still a chasm; we're not being completely honest with each other. I've done things no good mother or wife would do.

And Tara? What is she all about? She's parenting alone, yet she has her own design business, an uncluttered home, a well-behaved child, and the energy to keep up with him? Something doesn't jive. Or maybe it's just me who can't do it all.

Cody and Jacob fist-bump each other, grinning.

"Say thank you to Tara, Jake."

"Thank you, Tara," Jacob parrots, then jumps straight over the three steps from the top of the porch to the walkway.

I breathe when he hits the bottom safely. I follow, taking each step carefully.

"I'll be watching you," I hear behind me.

I turn so sharply to look at Tara that the base of my skull stings with heat. "What?"

She looks taken aback at my abrupt response. "I said I'll be watching for you. In the morning, we can walk the boys to school together."

I nod, trembling but trying to hide it. "Sounds good."

Daniel whistles cheerily while I'm silent as we cross the narrow strip of lawn connecting the two houses. Jacob's already run ahead to our front door. I get to our porch and look up at Tara's bedroom window. A light goes on, and behind the sheer white cloth, I see her shadow. She doesn't move from the window, and I'm jumpy to get inside. I don't know if she sees me looking up. I don't know if she's discovered that I went through her things.

I feel different as we enter the house, but I can't put my finger on what. Nothing looks out of place. Nothing is gone. But there's an anxious knot in my stomach.

Daniel closes the door behind us and locks it. "Buddy, go get in your pj's."

Jacob's wired and flings his shoes off in the middle of the hall, running down the never-ending hallway, vanishing from sight, then running back. He does it again, yelling, "I get to go to school with Cody in the morning!" Finally, he stops, barely out of breath. "We're going to sit next to each other and play together at recess. Can he come over here tomorrow after school, Mommy? Can we get a trampoline?"

I laugh. "One step at a time, honey. Let's start with a bath, okay?"

"Want me to do it?" Daniel asks.

I smile. "Thank you, but it's okay."

Once Jacob is in the large tub in my bathroom, surrounded by a couple of action figures he brought from Vancouver, and a Tupperware container from the kitchen, I sit on the steps. I don't love that there's nothing covering the window right above the bath. I grab a large, fluffy towel and hook the ends over each corner of the frame.

Jacob doesn't seem to notice because he's so busy chattering about the trampoline, where he and Cody will sit at lunchtime, and when he's going to see Roscoe again. He takes a breath for a second, then grabs the shampoo bottle, dumps way too much into his hand, and scrubs it into his hair. He's so beautiful that I have to catch my breath.

He takes one of the action figures and puts it in the Tupperware, then turns the container over. "Now you're trapped in jail."

I don't think anything of it at first. But then he says, "Look, Cody, the daddy's in jail."

My heart taps faster. "Why is the daddy in jail?" I ask, trying to keep my voice even.

"He's a criminal," Jacob responds, nonchalantly.

I measure my words precisely. "What crime did he commit?"

He shrugs his small shoulders. "Dunno. Bad stuff, so he can't go home for a long time."

Is he talking about Cody's dad, Nick? Is that where he is and why Tara's so reticent to talk about him? I let Jacob play out the scene for a minute while I gently rinse the shampoo from his hair.

As I run a comb through it, I ask, "Does Cody talk about his dad?"

"I just told you. His dad's in jail like bad guys."

And there it is. Even though I knew that's what Jacob was saying with his game, I'm shocked to hear the words when they come out bluntly. I soften my tone. "Do you know why he's in jail?"

He shakes his head.

"That's so sad. It must be hard for Cody." I hand my son a towel to wipe the water from his eyes.

Different emotions are at war inside me while Jacob gets out of the tub and towels himself down. Fear that Cody's dad is a criminal, that Tara knows more about me than I've told her, that she's hiding something even worse than a convict husband. I'm also curious what crime Cody's dad committed.

I tuck Jacob in with Mr. Blinkers, make sure the blinds are completely closed, then I lay next to him, scratching the perfectly smooth skin on his narrow back, a flood of love rushing through me. My darling boy, who has so much turmoil inside, because of me, Holly, and now his new friend whose father is a criminal, something that Jacob has only ever experienced through a television screen. My innocent child, like me, is learning far too young that life is hard and messy.

I head back downstairs so I can talk to Daniel about what Jacob's told me and how we should approach it. But he's not here. I find a torn piece of paper on the coffee table and a handwritten note.

Have to meet my boss to sign some paperwork before tomorrow. Back soon. Love you, D.

No. Is it happening again? Daniel disappearing to take care of his own needs, leaving me to deal with everything at home, leaving me to question if he's telling the truth or lies? *Stop it*, I tell myself. He offered to bathe Jacob. I should have accepted. He's been here, right beside me, for the two days we've been here. He's trying; he really is. Surely, this is the truth. He has a new career and wants to make a good first impression. Still, I wish he'd taken five seconds to come upstairs to let me know.

While he's out, and I'm alone with Jacob in this mausoleum of a house, I decide to check the security cameras. I open the security app, but something's wrong with the camera at the side of the house. I can't see the passageway or Tara's wall. There's only grass and dirt in the frame.

I go back through the footage on all the cameras from 4:00 p.m., when we left for Tara's. At around 4:15 p.m., the camera over the garage records Emily and Roscoe passing by the front of our house, which was when I must have been in Tara's bedroom and heard a dog bark. For the next hour, cars drive by, and a couple of mothers holding coffee cups push strollers up Lilac Lane. At 6 p.m., the strange man across the street comes out of his house dragging a hose and proceeds to water the dead brown shrub on his lawn. That's weird enough, but then he moves, so the hose is watering the sidewalk, and stares at our house for the next two minutes without looking away.

I shudder. Finally, he pulls the hose back to the side of his house, drops it, and heads inside. The camera in the passageway shows no activity at all until 6:15 p.m., when it jostles, and the image shakes like someone is moving the camera, but they're not in the frame. Then all I see is the ground. Grass and dirt for the rest of the video.

The light bulb is at about a seven-foot height off the ground. Daniel's the only one of the three of us tall enough to reach it with his hands, and he's not home. Someone moved that camera. Someone who's at least half a foot taller than me.

Is it Tara? Did she somehow sneak out while we were at her house, maybe when she went to the bathroom after dinner and the boys were occupied with their movie? Or was it the creepy man across the street?

Whoever it is knows where the camera is and didn't want to be seen.

Whoever it is, they're an even better watcher than me.

CHAPTER FOURTEEN

HOLLY

Before

It's Sunday evening, nine days since Holly showed up on her bike in the middle of the night at the Goldmans' and Sarah invited her in. It's amazing how much can change in less than two weeks. Holly herself has changed a lot over the course of these days spent living with a new and better family. Here she feels accepted for who she is, or who she wants to be. No longer stifled by business obligations, she's free to become a better person, for Jacob, and mostly for Sarah. She wants to be the woman Sarah sees in her.

Now the four of them are sitting in their chairs at the table on the backyard deck, birds chirping in the woods behind them. They're laughing at the blueberries smeared around Jacob's mouth. The pie Sarah had picked up at the Lonsdale Quay Market, just like the ribs Daniel grilled, and the avocado salad Sarah made, was perfect.

Holly leans over and swipes at Jacob's mouth, lips, nose, and forehead. "You have a little something on your face."

Sarah and Daniel laugh, exchanging a look that Holly deciphers as gratitude. She doesn't know if their family dinners were as much fun before she joined the family, but she wants to make sure they see how well she fits in. Holly doesn't ever want to leave this house. She has no plans whatsoever to vacate her basement bedroom at the Goldmans'. If Sarah asked her right now to change her last name from Monroe to Goldman, she'd do it. She'd do it in a heartbeat.

Still, she fears her days living here are numbered. Yesterday Sarah asked what her plans are, and Holly had to ask if she could stay a few more days. Sarah agreed, but then right before dinner tonight, through the air duct in her bedroom closet, Holly overheard Sarah and Daniel discussing her.

"Should I call John? At least let him know she's been here the whole time?" Daniel asked.

"Not yet. Let's wait a bit. Holly's not a child, and we shouldn't treat her like one. But I can't believe he hasn't even texted her. And Lisette? I know she's not technically her mother, but really, not even a phone call? They're not good parents, Dan. The way they've treated her is appalling."

There was some indistinct mumbling, then Daniel said, "We probably shouldn't get involved."

Holly couldn't catch Sarah's response because the pipes upstairs whooshed with water, then light footsteps creaked down the basement stairs. She flew to her bed so Daniel and Sarah wouldn't know she was eavesdropping.

"Dinner!" Sarah said, and knocked on her door.

Now, after dinner, Holly helps Sarah clean up and Jacob comes back downstairs in his pajamas, all clean from the bath Daniel gave him. "I can put Jacob to bed," Holly says.

Jacob's face lights up. "Holly, will you read me a story?"

"Of course I will," Holly replies. "I'll read you three if you run up and choose them for me."

He takes off immediately, and Sarah smiles. "What did I ever do without you? But listen, you don't have to read to him if you want to beg off for the night and do your own thing."

"I want to do it." She looks around the kitchen. "Where's Daniel?"

Sarah rolls her eyes and points out the window to the backyard. "If he's not out, he's in the cabana. Even I'm not allowed in his man cave."

Holly nods, but she wonders if it bothers Sarah that he spends so much time away from the house and home. Does she ever worry about why he needs his own space, his little man cave? "Um, after I put Jacob to bed, do you want to watch a movie?" Holly asks Sarah, feeling insecure all of a sudden. "I've never seen *Pretty Woman*, and I saw that you actually have the DVD in the living room."

"Have you ever watched a DVD?" Sarah teases.

Holly laughs. "When I was little."

"I'd love to. Dan's actually going out later with Stan Fielding and some other frat brothers for drinks."

At the mention of Stan, Holly's chest heats up. "Is that how he and Stan know each other? Through a fraternity?"

"Yes, they met at the University of Toronto during undergrad, and both ended up here together at the same time." She shrugs. "I don't know Stan and Gloria as well as he does, but Stan's one of Daniel's closest friends."

Holly wants to ask if Daniel's also friends with Charlie Lang, but the light in the cabana goes out, then Daniel comes inside to say goodbye before leaving for his boys' night out.

Once Holly's read Jacob three stories and his eyelids have fluttered shut, she gently closes his door behind her and joins Sarah on the couch. It's pure bliss to sit with Sarah eating ice cream and watching a movie. But the entire night she's thinking about Daniel and the stupid cabana. What does he need it for? Why does a father need a man cave that no one else in his family is allowed to enter?

We'll see if you can keep me out, she thinks to herself. And a plan starts to form in her mind. It's impossible, though, to do it tonight, but that's okay. She can be very patient, when she wants to be.

At 11:00 p.m., Sarah's curled at the end of the couch, asleep. She crashed in the middle of the movie. Not wanting to wake Sarah when she looks so comfortable, Holly drapes a throw blanket over her and tiptoes down to her basement bedroom, where she gets in bed and closes her eyes. She's thinking about *Pretty Woman*. She couldn't help rooting for Vivian, who sold her body for money but did it on her own terms. She had agency. Holly gets that. More than gets it. It's what she wants, too.

———

The next day at 1:00 p.m., once Holly has settled Jacob in his room for his hour of quiet time—which usually consists of him playing with LEGO bricks or making a pillow fort out of all his bedding—she heads straight for the living room couch. After a morning of swimming and lunch on the pool deck, she needs a quick break. That kid has endless energy. Daniel's at work, and Sarah's left to run errands, so, she has until 2:00 p.m. to be downstairs on her own.

Right when Holly sits down, her phone jitters across the glass coffee table with another text from Alexis.

Alexis: Can we please have dinner this
week? I miss you.

Holly: Of course! Name the place and time.

Alexis: How about tomorrow night at 8?
There's a new vegan place close to me.

Holly: LOL. Whatever you want.
Text me the address tomorrow.

She puts down her phone. She hates vegan restaurants, but she owes Alexis for bailing on her.

Restless, she can't stop looking out the sliding doors at Daniel's cabana, empty. Now is the perfect time to check it out.

Her eyes track the nanny cam in the black vase on the mantel facing the couch. It's been in the living room since the day she came for her babysitting interview. She can't tell if it's even on, so to be safe, she pretends she's looking up at the ceiling before going out to the backyard.

The ravine overlooking the yard stretches as far as the eye can see, and she breathes in the sharp pine scent of the woods outside the pool enclosure. If she has her way, this will be her house, her pool, her family. Sarah said herself that she thinks Holly should be treated better, that she deserves more. She doesn't know if she should ask Sarah directly exactly how long she can stay, or not say a word and hope Sarah and Daniel don't tell her it's time to go.

She turns her gaze to the cabana and glances up at Jacob's open window. She can hear him singing to himself. Perfect. He's distracted. Sarah's been gone about half an hour and said she'd be out until the late afternoon, so Holly still has plenty of time to take a quick peek inside Daniel's man cave. It's wrong for sure, but as long as she doesn't get caught, no one ever has to know.

It's clear Jacob adores his father. Holly doesn't have a healthy parental relationship to judge by, because her father and Lisette are completely codependent, but though Daniel's a bit dismissive with Sarah, he's loving toward her when he's not engrossed in his phone. He's been nothing but kind and welcoming to Holly, but twice now, that she knows of, he's lied to Sarah's face. First at the Fielding party when Holly saw the tense argument between him and Charlie Lang and Daniel pretended he'd called the babysitter, then when he told Sarah and Holly he golfed with Stan. If he wasn't with Stan the Saturday morning that she, Sarah, and Jacob went to Kitsilano Beach, where was he? Maybe the cabana will give her a hint.

She has her nail file ready to pick the crappy lock on the cabana door, but when she gets outside and tries the handle, she realizes it's open. She turns the handle, steps in, and shuts the door behind her. It's a simple, elegant cedar shed with a light beige couch and a few of Sarah's sepia family photos on the walls. Two medium-size windows, one at the side facing the woods and one facing the pool, give it a cottage-like feel. Holly isn't as nervous snooping here as she was in Sarah's red room. Sarah's intuitive, but Daniel's a business guy in tech. He seems a little clueless about what goes on in his own home.

Holly's not sure how often Sarah goes out to the woods to take photos at night, and she doesn't know if Daniel's even aware. Surely, he's interested in his wife's art, but she's never heard him ask Sarah about her work. While Sarah pays attention to every detail, Daniel seems oblivious of pretty much everything.

Holly hones in on a small wooden desk to the right of the couch. She opens the bottom drawer first, finding old high school yearbooks when Daniel was a gangly, awkward teenager in Toronto. He was a member of the computer science and Dungeons & Dragons clubs. She stifles a laugh. It's exactly how she pictured him as a teenager. The other drawers hold innocuous papers and spreadsheets, odd souvenirs like a snow globe and poker chips. There's a yellow Post-it with a line of numbers stuck to the right side of one of the drawers: "1-1-1-1-5-2-3-4-2." A password? For what? So far this snooping mission is a bust. It's just a boring middle-aged man's locker.

She peeks quickly out the front window. No Jacob. She should leave, but some instinct compels her to get on her knees and stick her hand under the couch cushions. She's found great things in couches before, like the time when she pocketed a Gucci cuff link from the divan at the Canyon Club. She slides her hand around under the pillows, finds loose quarters, lint, and something rectangular. She pulls it out. It's the palm-size phone Daniel slid into his pocket as she watched him from the alcove at the Canyon Club. And it's locked.

"Holly! Where are you? I'm ready!" she hears from outside the cabana. She shoves the phone into her shorts' pocket, heart racing, and opens the door.

Jacob stands with his head cocked to one side, squinting at her. "I found you!" he says. "Why are you in Daddy's cabana? Are we playing hide-and-seek?"

"I was looking for Mr. Blinkers so we could give him a bath."

"He's in my room, silly. I'm not allowed in the cabana. I told you that."

Because Daddy is hiding something, she thinks to herself.

"You're supposed to be in your swimsuit. Go up and change, then wait for me in the kitchen. We can make smoothies and have them with dinner tonight." She grins, waits until he's run off, and races back into the cabana.

She slides Daniel's phone out of her pocket. If he's gone to the trouble of concealing it under couch cushions in a space he knows Sarah won't go into, he's hiding something. She hopes for Sarah's sake that she finds nothing, but she wants to be sure.

There's a password. Damn. But then she remembers the Post-it. She runs over and yanks open the top drawer, looking at the numbers carefully.

1-1-1-1-5-2-3-4-2.

With jittery fingers, Holly keys in the series of numbers.

She's in. She closes her eyes for a second. Does she want to do this? Invade Daniel's privacy? This is clearly a burner phone. If he finds out she's been in the cabana, then discovers she's broken into his secret phone, he'll kick her out. She'll have nothing left.

Taking a deep breath, Holly swipes through the only two apps she sees on the screen: Monero and CoverMe, neither of which Holly has ever heard of. She taps on each one, but they require another password to open and there are no other passwords or Post-its around. There are no regular text messages or email accounts on the phone. Just the apps.

If he were having an affair, she'd expect to find sexts. Porn addiction? His web history just has the names of different bars and restaurants in Vancouver, totally clean. Still, her skin tingles. She has no clue what this phone is all about, but something feels very wrong.

"Holly! I'm waiting in the kitchen! Where are you?"

She almost screams from the sudden interruption, her heart thrashing against her rib cage. How long has she been in the cabana? It felt like just a moment. Sarah could be home any minute. Holly lifts the small window facing the woods, not the house, and yells, "I'll be there in just a second!"

Then she shuts the window, pulls her own phone out of her pocket, and takes screenshots of the apps on Daniel's phone. Later, when she's alone in her bedroom, she'll research what the hell Monero and CoverMe are. She only has a few minutes left. Quickly, she installs an undetectable tracking app she's seen on TikTok onto Daniel's phone. It's supposed to be able to follow his every move without him knowing it's there.

If Daniel is up to no good, Holly has to find out exactly what kind of no good. She finishes and slides the phone back under the couch cushions.

When she exits the cabana, she hears rustling in the woods. She shields her eyes from the sun to look through the thicket of trees and sharp branches, the clumps of leaves covering the ground. She thinks she sees something, or someone, take cover behind a Douglas fir. Holly squints in the distance, holding her breath to listen for any movement. Except for the chirping birds and the leaves swaying in the breeze, there's silence.

She tiptoes to the side of the cabana, facing away from the pool, to get a different angle of the woods. In her peripheral vision, she catches a flash of something moving so fast it's a blur.

When she looks again, whatever—or whoever—it was is gone.

CHAPTER FIFTEEN

SARAH

Now

It's almost 9:30 p.m., and Daniel's been at his meeting with his boss for more than an hour already. I'm sitting on the couch in the living room with my phone in my hand, exposed and vulnerable, alone with Jacob asleep upstairs. I don't like that the camera at the side of the house is now facing the ground and won't catch anyone who might try to get in the backyard again.

I don't want to interrupt Daniel's business meeting, but it's Sunday night, our son starts at a new school tomorrow, and Daniel knows I'm already scared in this house. What the hell is he doing? He's not being fair to me. I text him, trying to keep my tone light and breezy because I don't want to start a fight. I don't want things to escalate and blow up the way they did in Vancouver.

Sarah: Can you let me know when
to expect you home?

I hear a faint buzz, and it's not from my phone. I walk to the kitchen, where I think I heard the noise come from. Daniel's phone is charging on the counter. What the hell? He left his phone here? It's not like him to be so forgetful.

Anxious, I run upstairs to check on Jacob, who's sleeping soundly on top of his duvet. Mr. Blinkers is on the floor. I sigh, walking back downstairs to the living room. It's early to go to bed, but I'm so tired. I don't know if I should wait for Daniel so I can tell him off and also report that someone moved the camera or go to sleep and hash it out in the morning. Tomorrow's a big day. I'll be meeting Jacob's new teacher, gearing up for the school year, filling out forms, learning the school rules, and trying to find a place for myself in our new neighborhood. I don't want to be lonely the way I was before, with no real friends to speak of, pretending I was just like the other mothers happily handing their kids over for playdates while really, I worried incessantly that something bad would happen to Jacob if I wasn't there. I want a community. I want other women whom I feel safe with. The very thought makes me long for a genuine connection.

There's no way I can sleep now. I'll watch TV. Read a book. Anything to distract myself because I'm panicking. I head to the kitchen to get a drink of water and turn on the backyard light. No prowlers, thank goodness.

Even with all the lights on, the house is so dark. I step back into the living room. Through the curtains over the single-hung window, I feel a breeze. Did Daniel open it while I was upstairs bathing Jacob and forget to close it before he left? I haul myself over, and right before I pull down the sash, I hear footsteps squelching on the grass in the passageway. A very faint light goes on.

Then a shadow appears in the window behind the curtain. I cry out.

"Sarah?" a female voice whispers.

I separate the curtains and squint through the screen.

It's her. Again. Tara, her blond hair pushed back in a terry-cloth headband, her face moist, gives me a little wave. "I remembered I left the grass shears leaning against the side of my house, and I didn't want one of the boys to trip on them and get hurt." She holds up the sharp gardening tool.

I don't believe for a second that's why she's outside my house in the dark. I don't know what's up with this woman. Did she move the camera? And if so, why?

"Glad you remembered," I say, watching how she assesses me, her eyes roaming my face then darting to the left so she can see behind me into the living room.

She makes an apologetic face. "Sorry to bug you. Still good to meet out front in the morning?"

She's standing under the pool of light the security camera casts on the grass. "Did you happen to knock into that bulb? It's a motion detector for the passageway. It's facing the wrong way." I focus on her eyes, searching them for answers.

She shrugs. "Maybe? Do you want me to move it back for you?"

"That's okay. Daniel can do it later." I wait a few moments. "So," I say, as though just thinking of it, "will Nick be back in town soon?"

"I don't know, Sarah," she snaps.

"Oh?" I answer, not letting it go. At least I didn't call her husband "Nicky."

"Listen, I don't really want to talk about Nick. Is that okay?" Her mouth is one tight, thin line.

"Sure," I say in my best singsong voice. "Totally fine. And sorry to pry. Have a good night, then."

With that, she turns and heads down the passageway. I can hear her footsteps whisper across the grass back to her house.

I listen for the sound of her front door closing before I lock the window and close the curtains. What the fuck is Tara's game? And who is this Nick of hers? Is it just that she's embarrassed that her husband is in jail, or is it more sinister than that? God, him being in jail is sinister enough. I flop on the couch, eyes on the window in case she comes back again, because she always seems to. She's like a bad rash.

I'm too wired, and Daniel's still not home. I pick up my phone and search for Cody's father, Nick Conroy, the mysterious criminal husband and dad.

I find a rock musician in Missouri, a plumber in Atlanta, and a villain character in *Smallville*. Nothing nefarious comes up, not an arrest nor a conviction for anyone I can locate. That doesn't mean he doesn't have a record. I widen my search to "Nick Conroy; Toronto" and just in case, "Nick Conroy; Vancouver." There are way too many hits, and without any idea of what he looks like, I don't know where to begin. I'm swimming through sludge here.

I keep listening for the front door to open and Daniel to walk in. I hold my phone in my hand, staring again at the threatening text.

Unknown: I see you.

Before I lose my nerve, I set my phone to vibrate, slide it into the waistband pocket of my leggings, grab the keys from the small table at the front door, and exit the house. The moon is hiding behind the clouds, and the stars aren't as visible here as in Forest View because there's too much light pollution, even north of Toronto.

I lock the front door, praying Jacob won't wake up and come looking for me. I'll just be outside, but I don't want to alert any of the neighbors that I'm out here fiddling with our security camera. The second I hit the first porch step, the light bulb in the camera over the front door turns on, making me visible to everyone. Well, at least that camera works.

I creep to the passageway. The light bulb, attached to the brick wall, has a rotating bracket that should be aimed at around a forty-five-degree angle to capture as much of the passageway as possible.

Now it's pointing straight down to the ground. It's plausible a bird flew into it, jostling it, but my gut says it's been moved by human hands.

I know it's wrong, and Daniel will be furious with me for what I'm about to do. But he's not here. It's up to me to find out what Tara doesn't want us to know about Nick and why we're the object of her insane attention.

I open the side door to our garage, a large space for two cars, a concrete floor, and wooden shelving along the back wall that holds a toolbox, gardening necessities like gloves, a spade, shears, and electrical cords. Nothing I can stand on to reach the light bulb. Then I spot a towering set of brown milk crates right under the shelf at the opposite side of the garage. As quietly as I can, I take two, keeping an ear out for Jacob. The house seems quiet.

I prop open the side door with my foot, lift the two crates outside, and shut the door. Then I place the crates on top of each other, take a breath because I'm afraid to fall, and stand on them to reach the bulb. And I angle the security camera right into Tara's kitchen window. Then, on my phone, I turn off the motion detector for only that camera. It will still record. It just won't flash a light at her every time she moves around the room.

Carefully, I get off the milk crates, put them back in the garage, and wipe my leggings. I justify what I've done by reassuring myself that I haven't aimed the camera at Tara's bedroom or anywhere near Cody's room. I'm about to go back when a telltale finger of fear runs up my spine. I'm not alone out here.

I turn. The man across the street is sitting on his porch in the dark, wearing a beige turtleneck and the same tan pants he always wears. In all probability, he saw everything I did. I prefer he stopped seeing at all. If I could, I'd board up his entire porch so he couldn't stare at anyone. I give him my best menacing look before heading inside. I run upstairs and press my ear against Jacob's door.

He's still asleep, unaware his mother is starting to lose it and that his father is in some ultra-important meeting at almost ten on a Sunday night.

Now I regret not confronting the man across the street. Why am I always the one to walk away? To accept fear instead of challenging the source? Not anymore. I go back outside, lock the door behind me, and march to the man's house. It's gotten frigid, and I'm just in a thin button-down, so I wrap my arms around myself when I get to the bottom of his porch.

He visibly stiffens before standing and approaching me. Under the dim porch light, his ice-blue eyes are cold and searching. His hand trembles on the porch railing, from the nighttime chill maybe, or nervousness.

I decide being pleasant is my best course of action. "Hi. You must have wanted some fresh air, too. I'm Sarah Goldman, your new neighbor." I reach out my hand, and he looks at it like he doesn't know what to do with it.

"I'm Ezra. I'm on neighborhood watch."

I drop my hand. I can't tell if he's serious or if this is a joke. His face betrays no emotion at all. His cheekbones are so sharp they could cut glass; his eyes are hollow—he's a lonely, strange man who's probably off-kilter.

"I'm glad we have a neighborhood watch," I say. "We just moved in yesterday, and I saw someone in our yard late last night. I thought I heard something outside again earlier," I lie, "so I came out to check." I'm rambling because the only indication he's listening is the muscle jumping in his sharp jaw. "Have you seen anyone go into my yard or into the passageway?" I point across the street.

He shakes his head. "Do you keep a close eye on Jacob?"

My blood runs cold. How does he know my son's name? Before I can say anything, though, he speaks again. "Be careful. You never know who your neighbors really are." Then he turns and goes into his house. I hear the grate of the lock closing on the other side.

I'm left on his porch, gaping. I want to bang on his door and demand that he explain, but I'm not sure it's even safe to be here by myself. I run back to our house, lock the door behind me, and fall onto the couch. Suddenly, a new worry forms in my mind. Daniel's still not home, and this creepy man probably watched him leave. What if . . .

No. I won't let my mind go there. I have to stop jumping to conclusions, writing horror stories in my head. He's probably a reclusive man with nothing to do. Looks aren't always what they seem.

The next thing I know, someone's shaking me awake. How is it even possible? How can I have fallen asleep?

"Sarah."

"What?!" I shout. I'm groggy and confused. I squint at Daniel, whose face is blanched and filled with terror as he peers down at me.

"I can't find Jacob."

CHAPTER SIXTEEN

HOLLY

Before

Holly holds her breath, leaning against the side of the cabana, peering into the woods to see who's hiding in the trees. She's sure she spotted a person running through there a minute ago. What if someone's trying to sneak onto the property? And they saw her go in Daniel's cabana? She was definitely in there for at least fifteen minutes breaking into his phone and installing the tracker on it. She's not sure what time it is now, but it's got to be close to 2:30 p.m. Oh God. Jacob's stopped calling for her from the kitchen. Could he have figured out how to scale the enclosure and gone into the ravine to look for her?

She edges back around the cabana to the front, and with her heart in her throat, she unlatches the gate leading to the plateau and steps onto the grassy ledge, a dizzying drop to the Capilano River below.

She looks everywhere for Jacob's small frame, or anyone else lurking. There's no one.

Sarah must not have a fear of heights to take photos from here. Holly doesn't, either, but still, the steep, forested incline is tangled with sharp branches, hard to navigate without holding on to tree trunks for balance, and she doesn't exhale until she reaches the top again. She scans the forest once more. She can't go far with Jacob inside the house alone and finally gives up when there's no hint that anyone was there.

"Weird," she says as she walks back onto the pool deck.

"What's weird?"

She shrieks. Daniel and Jacob are coming out of the sliding doors from the living room. Her stomach plunges, and she breaks out in a cold sweat. Daniel shouldn't be home from work for a few more hours. At least Sarah's been out a long time today, so she didn't catch Holly near the cabana. She can't take stupid risks like she just did. Sarah and Daniel will never let her live with them if they think they can't trust her.

Letting out a quivery breath, she tells the truth, or at least part of it. "I thought I saw someone run through the woods toward the gate, so I wanted to check. I was worried someone was trying to get on the property or into the pool."

Daniel's eyebrows lift. "And you left Jacob alone in the house?"

Her face flames. "Jacob was supposed to be in the kitchen waiting for me. I was only in the woods for a minute." She's terrified he's going to fire her and kick her out. She makes as contrite an expression as she can. "I'm so sorry."

"It's okay. Maybe next time, though, wait for me to get home to check it out. It was probably just a raccoon." He shrugs, sliding the door closed, and smiles. His forgiveness makes Holly feel like an idiot. Then his face becomes serious. "Sarah texted me to come home because she couldn't reach you."

Fear grips Holly's throat. She's royally screwed up this time. But she's also confused. "I never got any messages." Slowly, she slides her phone out of her shorts' pocket. She can't remember if she left the tab open with the screenshots she took of Daniel's apps. Fuck. She did leave it open. She taps until all her tabs are closed then flips to her main screen. Now she sees that Sarah tried to contact her three times. Damn it.

Immediately, she texts Sarah to explain and apologize.

Sarah writes back only: *It's okay.*

It's not okay, though, and she knows it.

"Tell Holly your joke, Daddy!" Jacob interrupts, bouncing on his feet at the edge of the pool.

"Careful, Jakey," she warns.

"You sound like Sarah." Daniel laughs, but it's tinged with subtle judgment.

He takes a seat at the patio table. He's in a navy suit today, and the powder-blue shirt looks good against his lightly tanned skin. He doesn't have the same powerful presence her father does, but he definitely carries himself with ease. Maybe because he believes he's getting away with what he's doing on the phone he's squirreled away under couch cushions mere steps away. He wouldn't be so dismissive if he knew Holly was onto him.

"Where is Sarah?" she asks, joining him at the table because she doesn't know what else to do.

"Hair salon." His lips compress. "I was in a meeting."

"I'm really sorry you got pulled out of your meeting. I didn't realize my sound was off. I must have pushed the button by mistake."

"Joke, Dad!" Jacob repeats and runs to sit on his father's lap.

"Right. Okay, what did the slow tomato say to the other tomatoes?"

Jacob and Holly both ask, "What?"

"Don't worry. I'll ketchup."

Holly pretends to laugh, but inside she's a mess of conflicting emotions.

The sliding glass door whooshes open, and Sarah steps onto the deck. "What's so funny?"

Holly's jaw almost crashes to the ground. Daniel, too, seems speechless by what he sees.

Sarah's lackluster dark blond hair has been transformed into platinum beachy waves, much like Holly's own lustrous locks.

Holly watches Sarah's face go from excited to crushed in seconds. Only Holly walks over to stand in front of Sarah.

"You look gorgeous!" she says, though in fact she prefers the way Sarah looked before, more like a mom than one of Lisette's overly polished society friends.

"Yeah? I'm still not sure . . ."

Before she can finish speaking, Jacob bursts into tears.

Sarah rushes to her son. "What's wrong, honey?" she asks.

"You don't look like you. I hate it!" With that, he storms into the house.

"Well, that wasn't the reaction I was expecting," Sarah says into the void of silence. She looks to her husband, waiting for him to acknowledge her. "So? What do you think?"

Finally, Daniel stands and moves toward his wife. "You look . . . different. It's nice. I just . . . I think we need a little time to get used to the change."

Sarah's face falls, and she turns away and mutters, "It's always about the two of you," but Holly hears it. She hears it clearly. The cracks in this marriage are starting to show, and it makes her stomach cramp.

Daniel pulls his wife into his arms. "I'm sorry. I'm an idiot. Really, honey. You're a knockout. I wish I could whisk you away right now."

Sarah beams. It's Holly's turn to look away.

"What's stopping you? Dinner out tonight?" Sarah suggests. "Just the two of us? Maybe Holly can babysit?" She looks hopefully at Holly.

"Of course!" Holly says, because there's nothing else she can say.

Daniel's face changes. "I'm so sorry, honey. I totally want to, but

I've got a late meeting at the office. I just came home to check on Jacob like you wanted, but I've got to run back."

Holly wants to hide, because it's her fault he had to come home early, and it hurts to witness Sarah being humiliated like this by a man who's supposed to love her. Wherever Daniel is going, Holly suspects that it's *not* back to his office.

"Sarah, I'm really sorry I didn't answer your texts. I feel awful. It will never happen again."

Sarah's pale and looks upset. She touches her hair self-consciously, and Holly wants to hug her. So she does. Sarah's stiff at first, but then Holly feels her limbs relax.

She makes a vow to herself then and there. She'll find out where Daniel is spending all his time and where he's going tonight. What the apps on his phone mean. She'll do this for Sarah's sake, for Jacob, and for this family she loves.

They all head inside, and when Jacob's in the living room for his one hour of screen time, Holly says, "I'm going to my room, if that's okay."

Looking distracted, Sarah nods. Daniel doesn't say anything and goes upstairs.

Once in her basement bedroom—the first space she's called her own that Lisette hasn't touched, a room she's already planned to decorate with funky wall art—Holly sits cross-legged on the bed and looks at the screenshots of Daniel's apps. She starts with Monero.

As she types it into the search bar, she hears the front door close. Daniel's leaving for "work." The house is quiet. Holly goes back to her research. According to Google, Monero is a private, secure form of cryptocurrency, like Bitcoin. It isn't controlled by the government. It uses stealth addresses, so the sender and receiver of the funds are untraceable. She knows very little about cryptocurrency. It's plausible Daniel uses it in his role as COO of Code Tek. But why on a secret phone?

Next, she searches CoverMe, which is more suspicious. It's a message app with "military-grade encryption." *Military-grade?*

Daniel's covering his digital tracks. Which means he's hiding something. What the fuck is he up to?

Light footsteps tap on the floor above her. She'd better go upstairs and help Sarah get dinner ready. Before she does, though, she checks the app she secretly downloaded onto Daniel's phone. She lets out a little squeal when a red dot shows that Daniel is indeed at Code Tek. He was telling the truth about that, at least. Maybe Holly's wrong about him? Maybe there are logical explanations for everything? She hopes so, but those apps on his phone are worrisome.

In the kitchen, Sarah's standing at the stove, pushing chicken and broccoli around a sizzling pan. Holly joins her, noticing that Sarah has swept her fancy new hairstyle into a messy ponytail. Her eyes are red-rimmed. The television is blaring from the living room, and Jacob's glued to the screen well past his hour limit.

Holly grabs three plates from the cupboard and says, "I really do love your hair."

Sarah smiles sadly. "I guess everyone likes me looking the same all the time. There's no room for change." There's a noticeable tremor in her hands. "It was a mistake. I don't know what I was thinking. Trying to be young and hip, I guess."

Holly shakes her head. "It doesn't matter what anyone else thinks. It only matters if you like it. Do you?"

Sarah looks directly at her, steely determination in her eyes. "You know what? I love it. I don't care if anyone else does. It's high time I do one single thing for myself."

Holly touches Sarah's shoulder. "I see you, Sarah. You do so much and don't get enough in return. You're tired and fed up. You deserve a break. That's what I'm here for."

Sarah brightens, appreciation filling her blue eyes. Then she squints. "Why didn't you answer my texts earlier?"

Holly has to fight the panic that surges through her. "I'm so sorry. I shut off my sound without realizing and didn't see any notifications. I'll be more careful."

Sarah puts down the spatula and turns off the stove. "It's okay. Mistakes happen. And for once, Daniel had to deal with the frantic call and rush out the door, like I do whenever Jacob's school calls me because he's gotten hit in the head or there's been an incident in class." She bites her lip, then laughs. "That sounds bad."

"No, I get it. You want help from your partner. Makes sense."

Jacob wanders happily into the kitchen, recovered from his earlier meltdown about his mother's new hairdo, and they sit down to eat. Sarah is quiet as she ladles some vegetables and chicken onto Jacob's plate, moving her mouth like she's trying not to cry. It's clear she's still deeply hurt. Holly will do anything to prevent her from experiencing any more pain. She just has to figure out exactly what Daniel's up to.

Jacob makes a face at his plate. "Broccoli is gross."

"Are you kidding?" Holly says. "This is what all the famous athletes and superheroes eat."

Jacob laughs. "I know you're trying to make me eat it."

"Just eat it, please," Sarah says, her voice unusually sharp.

Jacob pouts and ignores her.

Sarah looks at him. "If you're done pushing the broccoli around your plate, can you please empty it in the compost and put the plate in the dishwasher?"

Jacob's mouth forms an "O." "I'm only six."

Holly pushes her chair back. "I'll show you how. Six-year-olds need to learn how to help their moms, you know." She stands and shows Jacob what to do. While he loads his plate and cutlery, as subtly as she can, she pulls out her phone and checks the tracker. It's almost 7:30 p.m. Daniel's left his office. Holly hopes it doesn't show on her face when she sees where he is now: a strip club on Seymour Street. She *knew* he was lying. But she feels no vindication, only disappointment. And disgust.

Sarah gets up from the table and kisses Jacob on the head. "You did a great cleaning job. You can go to the living room to color or do a puzzle."

167

"I want to stay with Holly."

"Actually, Jakey, I'm going out. My stepsister wants me to meet her and some friends at the beach for a bonfire." She looks at Sarah. "If that's okay?"

"You're off the clock. Of course it's okay." She touches Holly's arm. "Why don't you invite Alexis here for dinner sometime this week? I'd love to meet her."

"Sure!" Holly answers, but she knows that isn't going to happen. She doesn't want it to happen.

"Can I come with you to the beach?" Jacob asks, eyes wide with hope.

Holly's heart pinches. "Sorry, Jakey. It's big kids only. But tomorrow maybe we can go to the beach just you and me."

Jacob pouts but kisses Holly's hand before running to the living room.

"I'll finish cleaning the kitchen, Sarah," Holly says.

"I'll do it with you." Sarah rinses a dish and hands it to Holly. "Will your guy be there? At the beach?" Sarah asks. "Or . . . girl?"

Holly thinks of Luke, who's probably in another student's bed tonight and has forgotten all about her. And none of her father's investors would be caught dead at a beach bonfire. "That guy was nothing. Just some fun," Holly says. "I don't want to be tied down."

"Must be nice to be so independent." Sarah holds up a hand. "Sorry. Not quite myself. I'll have a pity party with a rom-com and some ice cream once Jacob's in bed."

At close to 8:30 p.m., after the kitchen is clean and Holly's put Jacob to bed because she couldn't refuse when he begged her, she's itching to go. She doesn't have time to change out of her jean shorts and white tank top. She's afraid Daniel will leave before she shows up at the strip joint.

Sarah walks her to the door. They hug, and Holly can't resist pressing her face into Sarah's hair. It smells like strawberries. "If you need me to do more, just ask. You should know that this has been the best summer of my life."

Sarah does a double take. "It's not over yet," she jokes. "There's a whole month left." But her face turns serious when she looks up at Holly. "You mean a lot to us. To me." She squeezes Holly's hand.

Holly's body, infused with warmth, suddenly goes cold when Sarah asks, "Have you talked to your dad and Lisette about going home?"

I am home, Holly thinks, but she shakes her head. "I'll never be welcome there again." Her heart flutters. "I'm so thankful you're letting me stay here while I figure out what I'm going to do next."

Sarah smiles, and Holly opens the front door, grabs her bike from the garage, and waves to Sarah, who watches her go from the porch.

How could she ever think Daniel was the perfect husband and father? While Sarah's feeding and caring for Jacob, he's getting lap dances and maybe more. *Men are sick as fuck*, she thinks to herself.

Holly has to put a stop to it, for all their sakes.

CHAPTER SEVENTEEN

SARAH

Now

"What do mean you can't find Jacob?" I've vaulted off the couch, fully awake.

Daniel's fists are clenched, and his face is ashen. He's in flat-front pants and a wrinkled navy dress shirt that looks like he's slept in it. I don't know what time he got in from his meeting with his boss last night or what time it is now.

"He's not in his bed or downstairs. I just checked."

"How can he not be in bed?" I look at the clock on the TV console. "It's only seven fifteen in the morning." My insides liquefy with blind terror. I push past Daniel, shouting our son's name as loudly as I can.

I snatch my phone from the coffee table, then run up the stairs two at a time to Jacob's room, my heart dropping straight to my stomach when I see his empty bed, the covers pushed to the bottom, and Mr. Blinkers on the floor. I tear off his sheets and look under the bed and in the closet for any clues where he might have gone. I don't see his pajamas or anything that tells me where my little boy is.

"Jacob!" I scream again, running back downstairs to the main floor where Daniel's racing around, opening closets and shouting for our son into the ghastly silence of an empty house.

"I'll check the basement. You check the backyard." He flies down the stairs.

I pull so hard on the sliding door to the yard that I almost crack it before racing out back, shrieking, "Jacob!" over and over, to no avail.

Breaking out in a cold sweat, I fling open the gate and bolt barefoot to the front of the house, twigs digging into the soles of my feet, but I feel no pain. I stand in the middle of the street, crying for Jacob.

I hear a door slam, but it's Daniel running toward me, fear in his eyes. "I can't find him anywhere!"

My phone buzzes in my hand.

There's a text from a private caller on the home screen.

Unknown: Missing something?

I fall into Daniel, noisy sobs rushing from me, so strong I can barely breathe. Then I show him the text.

He looks at the screen, then at me, his mouth puckered in confusion. "What does it mean?"

"I'm calling the police!" I press "9" on my phone when I hear sharp barks and see Roscoe and Emily trotting up the road three houses away. I fiercely hope to see Jacob following the dog, but he's nowhere in sight.

Emily rushes over. "Sarah, what's wrong? I was walking Roscoe and heard a scream."

"Jacob's missing! He wasn't in his bed, and we can't find him!"

Ezra comes out onto his porch, shielding his eyes from the sun. I grab Daniel's arm. "That guy knows Jacob's name. I spoke to him last night while you were out. I'm going over there right now. Call the police!" I thrust my phone at Daniel.

"I'm coming with you," Emily says, but as she steps forward, Roscoe pulls hard at the leash, heading for something behind us.

"Mommy?" I hear.

I whip around. Tara and Cody are on her front porch. Jacob is beside them.

My son takes in my face, streaming with tears, and his mouth falls open. Daniel and I both run to him. Roscoe's barking intensifies, and he drags Emily onto Tara's lawn as I gather Jacob in my arms, squeezing so hard he yelps.

"Mommy, what's wrong?" he says. I loosen my grip on him, but not much.

"I thought you were missing!" Fresh tears fall from my eyes. I can't stop the flow.

Daniel wraps his arms around the both of us, and against my cheek, I feel his heartbeat race.

"I'm so glad everything is okay," Emily says, trying unsuccessfully to stop Roscoe from jumping on Jacob, who brings the dog into our family hug.

"Oh my gosh, I'm so sorry." Tara covers her mouth with her hand.

Jacob pulls away from us. "I got ready by myself, Mommy. You were asleep on the couch, and I didn't want to wake you." Now, my beautiful son starts to cry. "I did something good. I thought you'd be happy."

I grab his hand. "Honey, you can't just go off without telling Daddy and me where you are. Never ever. Do you understand?"

He nods solemnly, and Daniel also gives him a stern admonition. "You really scared us, Jake. Always tell us where you're going, even if we're sleeping."

Tara has both hands on her chest. She's pale and looks about to cry. "He knocked on our door. I thought you knew he was here. I don't even know what to say, Sarah. I'm so, so sorry."

I study Tara, looking for some crack in her veneer, some evidence that she's done this on purpose, but all I see in front of me is a mother truly horrified by what she's inadvertently caused.

It doesn't matter. I don't care what she's feeling right now. Right now, all I care about is that Jacob's safe. I stroke his face and look down at his outfit. He's wearing mismatched socks and his T-shirt is on inside out. "You scared me so much. But I'm very proud of you for getting dressed and ready for school." I fight to keep my tone even, because I'm still howling inside, thinking that life as I know it was over. "Where did you put your pajamas?"

"In the laundry room downstairs, so they can get washed."

My strong, sweet boy is trying to be helpful, to be more independent and thoughtful.

Emily comes closer and hands Jacob and Cody a treat each. Cody looks as shocked by everything as Jacob.

"Can you boys get Roscoe to sit?" Emily asks.

"Sit, Roscoe," they say in unison. The dog obeys, and the boys giggle. For them, this trauma is over. For me, I may never forget it.

Daniel puts his arm around me. "All's well that ends well."

I stiffen, remembering the taunting text. How can he say that? Why is he always so cavalier?

Missing something?

Yes, I'm missing something. I'm missing a lot. Why did he leave his phone at home last night? What time did he get home? I can't exactly mention it right at this moment, in front of our neighbors and the kids. But I remove his hand from my shoulder.

"Did you text me this morning?" I ask Tara, my voice coming out sharp and accusatory. I'm angry at everyone and I can't hide it.

She squints. "No. I don't have your number. We should probably exchange numbers, now that I think about it. Anyhow, I would have knocked on your door immediately if I'd known you didn't send Jacob over." Her face is a convincing mask of guilt. "I'm so, so sorry. I . . . I can't even imagine. If it were me, I would have reacted exactly the same way. A mom's worst nightmare." She can barely get the last words out, and she starts sniffling.

I'm coming off as cold and vicious. It's not even eight and it's already been a hell of a morning.

Emily extends Roscoe's leash and walks over to us. "Are you okay, Sarah?" she asks quietly. "I know it's not the same, but after Roscoe ran out the front door of my place and took off for the woods, it was a good few hours before I could breathe again."

I nod. That's exactly it. I'm holding my breath. I'm replaying everything in my mind. Not just the terror that I could have lost my son, but every menacing occurrence since we arrived on Saturday—the hidden cameras, Mr. Blinkers, the intruder in our yard, the camera at the side of the house being moved, the texts.

Daniel's walked over to Jacob and Cody. His large hand cups our son's head. I feel nauseated and need a moment to collect myself. Adrenaline is still coursing through me.

I look around. At Tara, Emily, Ezra's porch across the street, where he's no longer observing us, and at my husband who is brushing aside my every worry and disappearing again like he did in Vancouver. Who can I trust in Blossom Court? And if I can't trust my husband, what then?

It occurs to me that we have the cameras in front of the house, which I should have checked the second I knew Jacob was gone. I would have seen him leave the house. I panicked and assumed the worst, like I always do.

I see you.

There's a threat here, thrumming beneath the surface. I'm going to start by talking to Daniel the minute we're inside.

Thankfully, I'm in bare feet, so I have an excuse to hang back. "You guys head off to school, okay? I'll go put on shoes and Jacob and I will catch up to you."

Tara nods and with Emily, Roscoe, and Cody, they set out. I see Emily put an arm around Tara's shoulders, probably reassuring her this was all just an accident and not her fault.

I turn to Jacob, who still looks nervous and guilty. "Come on, honey. Let's go inside and you can butter some bread for yourself in the kitchen. Then I'll take you to school."

"With a knife?" His eyes pop out.

Daniel smiles. "A butter knife, buddy. They're in the top drawer on the kitchen island."

The sharp knives are safely tucked away in a wooden block too high on the counter for Jacob to reach, so I'm not worried when he runs to the kitchen, his little shoulders pulled back with pride. Even one small step toward independence makes him stand taller.

Daniel shuts the front door behind us. "That was intense."

"Daniel. Something terrible could have happened just now. I know it didn't, but still. And that man across the street, Ezra, is creepy. He knows our son's name. But that's not what I want to talk to you about."

Uneasiness flashes in his eyes. "That weird text you got? 'Missing something?'"

"Do you know what it means? Who sent it?" I look at him carefully.

He shrugs. "No clue. The timing is odd, but it was probably spam. Have you signed up for any loyalty programs or anything like that?"

"No." The text isn't the only thing that's bothering me. "You look like you slept in your clothes. What time did your meeting with your boss end?"

"I got in really late. Around one. I'm sorry. Steve, my boss, and I hit it off and talked for a long time. We went to one of those Fox and Fiddle-type places." He tugs his hand through his hair. "You can call him yourself if you don't believe me."

I want to believe him. Where else could he have been? He doesn't know anyone here.

"I'm not calling your boss." I sigh, but I'm not letting him off the hook that easily. "But I'm pissed, Dan. Not only did you leave us here for hours, and forgot your phone, but why did your boss even need to meet you on a Sunday night?"

He reaches for me, but I shrink back. Blowing out a breath, he says, "I have my first client meeting with an aerospace engineering firm this afternoon, and Steve is out of the office today. He wanted to meet me in person and give me the background on them. I'm an idiot for leaving my phone here."

"Why didn't you borrow Steve's phone to get in touch with me? At least tell me you were going to be home so late."

"I wasn't thinking. I was distracted."

I glare at him. "You weren't thinking about me. As usual. Only about yourself."

He shakes his head. "It wasn't intentional, Sarah. I'm sorry. I'm just . . . I'm focused on a new beginning. And I messed up."

"Moving here was supposed to change all that. You promised not to get overly caught up in work."

"I know. It will change. Promise. It won't happen again." Once more he tries to hug me, but I sidestep him.

I don't have the energy to talk in circles with him, but we're not finished yet. I have to tell him what happened last night. "Someone moved the camera at the side of the house."

"I'll check it right now."

Damn it. "It's fine. I took care of it." I don't want him to know I've angled the camera into Tara's house.

He nods. "I'm really sorry about last night, honey." He brushes his hair back from his forehead. "Please give me a chance to do better. You won't be sorry." He checks his watch and cringes. "I'd better go change. I shouldn't be late on my first day." He leans in to kiss me.

I hesitate and look at him, my husband of fifteen years, the idealistic man who got down on one knee at the coffee shop where we'd first met and told me he wanted to take care of me forever. Does he still feel the same? Do I? I don't know anything anymore. But I let him kiss me, then he runs up the stairs.

After I brush my teeth, not bothering to change out of the leggings and button-down I fell asleep in, I encourage Jacob to put on matching socks, a clean pair of sweatpants, and to turn his shirt the right way. Then I wait as patiently as I can at the front door. Jacob's decided now's the time to loosen the laces on his shoes to try to tie them, his little fingers fumbling. Finally, we make it outside, where Daniel's just pulling out of the driveway and waving. Jacob and I jog up Lilac Lane, turn left onto Daisy Drive, and make it to Blossom Court Elementary right as the first bell rings. It's unseasonably warm, and the humid air sticks to my skin, which itches with uneasiness.

Tara bites her lip when we join her, Cody, Emily, and Roscoe at the front gates. I guess Emily walked with them all the way to the school. In my panic earlier, I didn't notice that Tara's wearing the damn ring pendant necklace from Unique I saw in her bedroom last night. Did she do that on purpose? I wonder.

"Feeling better?" Emily asks kindly.

I sigh. "I guess. I'm just glad Jacob is okay."

Tara looks at me, her eyes puffy from crying. "I'm so sorry. That will never happen again."

No, it won't, I think, but I just nod.

Kids and parents stream past us, and Emily says, "I'd better go prep for my student this afternoon. I've had an influx of kids this year. Have a great day, boys!" She waves and continues down the sidewalk with Roscoe.

Tara and I bring the boys to the back of the school so they can line up with their class. Other parents mill about. I'd like to break away from Tara for a moment and meet some of the other parents, but she's firmly glued to my side.

"There's Valerie." She gestures to a small Black woman with a clipboard in her hand, standing at the front of a line of little kids. "Come. I'll introduce you."

I don't want Jacob's teacher to think Tara and I are best friends, that she can talk to Tara about Jacob, but she's already at the teacher's side, so I have no choice but to join them.

"Valerie, this is Sarah Goldman, Jacob's mother."

"Nice to meet you," I say, and extend my hand. "Jacob's very excited to be in your class." I debate filling her in on his past rambunctious behavior and attention issues, but when I see him and Cody jostling each other in line, and he looks so happy, I decide to let him have the fresh start he needs.

"We're thrilled to have him." Valerie smiles at me, then claps her hands. "Okay, friends, time to say good morning to the person in front of you and behind you."

I like her energy immediately. After we kiss our boys goodbye and watch their class go inside, Tara and I walk together to the front of the school.

I point to the necklace. "That's pretty," I say.

She looks down at it. "Thanks."

"Where did you get it?"

She narrows her eyes for a quick second, but then she shrugs. "Don't remember."

Right. I shuffle my feet and look around the yard, as though I'm taking in the scene before I say, "I wish Daniel could have come for Jacob's first day. It's nice for a kid to have his father participate in the big moments, don't you think?"

"Mmm" is all I get in response, but if she thinks that's going to stop me, she's deluded.

"Is Nick involved with the school?" I ask. "Must be difficult with him away." I smile to show I'm not being intrusive, rather I'm looking for solidarity. You'd think she'd be more forthcoming after the debacle this morning. Can she not give me just this one thing?

She turns to face me, her eyes wide and neutral. "Actually, Nick and I are separated."

"Separated?" It's an interesting choice of words. Separated because her husband is in jail.

She doesn't respond at first, only adjusts her purse on her shoulder. Finally, she says, "I have to run. I have another appointment this morning." In her eyes, I catch a darkness, the kind I'm trained to see and capture in photos.

"Everything okay?" I ask.

"Yes, for sure," Tara says, but I spot it—the quick grimace that turns her lips down.

"Before you go, can we exchange numbers? Just in case?" I ask.

"Of course," she replies. "Give me your number, and I'll text you mine."

I reel off the digits, which she plugs into her phone, then she quickly walks away like I've been holding her back. For once, she's trying to get away from me. Fast.

When I get home and I have the whole house to myself, I realize I haven't had breakfast. I prepare some cheese and crackers and sit on the couch with my phone. My eyes fall on the app for the security cameras. The light bulb on the side of the house is still angled into Tara's kitchen. I hate that she knows more about me than I know about her. It's time to remedy that.

The video is quite grainy, but I can see her bright kitchen, which is empty, and a laptop resting open on the table. I get an idea. I rarely go on Facebook, haven't even checked it since we arrived. I mostly used it to communicate with the moms at Jacob's former private school, where parental involvement was intense. I send Tara a friend request. A minute later, she accepts.

Then my phone buzzes with a text. Unknown number.

Dread twists in my gut. I open the message.

Unknown: It's Tara. ☺ I hope Jakey's first day
is wonderful. Have a great day!

Sarah: Thanks! You too.

But then it hits me like an electric charge. Only one person has ever called my son "Jakey," and that person is Holly.

CHAPTER EIGHTEEN

HOLLY

Before

As Holly rides her bike away from the Goldmans' and heads to the dot on the map where Daniel's at, she second-guesses herself. Is it so bad if Daniel's getting lap dances in some seedy bar? What if Sarah knows and is fine with it? But what's all this about the cryptocurrency and undercover-message apps? All password protected. Are the two things linked? Holly's determined to find out.

The surge of protectiveness she feels toward Sarah keeps her cycling the forty minutes through myriad rights and lefts on residential streets, the thick fog obscuring the road in front of her until she reaches the busy highway. The cars zip past her, and her hair that's not covered by her helmet whips her in the face. Finally, at almost 9:30 p.m., she makes a right onto Seymour Street from Robson and walks her bike up the sidewalk until she sees a neon magenta sign blazing PINKY'S across the entrance.

She takes off her helmet, shakes out her hair, and locks up her bike outside the club, where a burly bouncer blocks the door, barely glancing at her when she stands right in front of him.

"How much is it to get in?" she asks, trying to sound like she does this all the time.

He examines her from head to toe. "What are you doing here?"

"I want to go to the club. What's the problem?" Realizing he might think she's underage, Holly reaches into her backpack for her wallet. "I have my ID."

"I don't give a shit about your ID. Why don't you get on your little bike and pedal back to the fancy suburb you came from?"

Totally confused and mad, Holly doesn't move. She has every right to go to a strip club if she wants to. She tells him so.

"It's not your kind of club."

What an asshole. But there's nothing she can do, since his brawny frame prevents her from accessing the entrance. Maybe if she'd shoved chicken cutlets into her bra and worn stilettos, it would be her kind of club.

She walks back to her bike and checks the tracker on her phone, where the red dot shows that Daniel is definitely still here. Sighing, she's about to unlock her bike and give up for the night when she notices two stocky men turn into the alley next to Pinky's. Craning her neck, she sees them walk to an entrance at the back. Then she checks to see if the prick of a bouncer is watching her. He's not. He's distracted by someone walking into the club, a tall man in a finely cut black suit.

Holly runs into the alley, straight for the back door, where there's another bigger bouncer guarding the entrance. It seems like over-the-top security for a run-of-the-mill strip club.

It's dark back here, so she can barely make out the man, even more intimidating than the bouncer at the front, who eyes her with disgust like she's a piece of meat stuck in someone's teeth.

"What are you looking for?" he asks, crossing his thick arms and glaring at her.

"I'm trying to find the service entrance. I'm the new hire. Starting today."

"Yeah?" the man says, checking her out from top to bottom again. "Wrong door."

She cocks her head at the door. "This is the entrance, right?"

"The strip club's up front, honey. This is the entrance to the other club."

Holly raises her eyebrows. "The other club?"

"Look," the man answers. "Who's your boss? That's all I need to know. Who are you here to see?"

She pauses, considers, then says, "Daniel Goldman," while meeting his eye.

"Wait here."

He opens the door and goes inside. She puts her foot in the door to stop it from closing. Looking in, she sees a cloud of smoke hovering above a round table where five men sit playing cards. Ashtrays, poker chips, and money litter the center. All the men turn in her direction, each in an expensive suit, with serious expressions on their bronzed faces. It's straight out of a scene from a bad Mafia movie, so cliché she almost laughs out loud.

But when Daniel comes out from a room off the side, all her mirth vanishes.

His eyes are so wide she thinks they might pop out of his head. "Holly? What the hell are you doing here?"

Every muscle in her body tenses. Daniel looks more terrified than angry.

"I—I—" Everything she wants to say sounds foolish.

"You can't be here." He scrubs his hands over his face. "Just go."

His tone is harsh. He's speaking to her the way her dad does whenever she's supposed to shut up, whenever she's dismissed. This time, though, she's not going to let a man tell her what to do. She stands her ground in the doorway. "Why are you playing cards in the back room of a strip club?"

"It's not what it looks like," he says as his eyes dart to the smoky room.

"Oh yeah? Maybe Sarah can explain it to me?" she says.

He sighs, his shoulders slumping. "Look, come with me somewhere we can talk more privately, okay?"

She nods and follows him farther into the alley, right next to a dumpster. The rank odor makes her gag, but she holds back the impulse. She feels her pulse quicken.

He turns to her, ire in his eyes. "I don't understand why you're here. How did you even know where to find me?" The headlights of a car driving past on Seymour Street flash into the alley for a second. Alarm is written all over Daniel's face. "Does Sarah know where you are?" he asks.

"No. Does Sarah know where *you* are?" she retorts.

He looks at her with fury, his jaw set with anger. "You will destroy Sarah and Jacob if you say anything about this. This is adult stuff. You're a child."

Her blood boils. How dare he belittle her. Does he really think that's all it takes to scare her off? An insult? He's wrong. He's just another pathetic guy who thinks his three-piece suit puts him on a pedestal, who thinks he can get away with living a double life.

"I'm smarter than you think, Daniel," she says, crossing her arms. "Which is it? Are you pimping girls or illegally gambling? Or is it both? I just want to get the details right when I tell your wife." She moves close enough to see sweat start to bead on his forehead.

He bows his head. "Don't do that," he whispers. "Please. Promise me you won't tell her anything." He lifts his head, his face completely wracked with guilt. "Promise me right now."

She can't help but feel a twinge of sympathy. Still, whatever he's doing is wrong and probably dangerous. Worse—it's a secret.

"If you want me to even think about staying quiet, you're going to have to explain," she says. "If you don't, Sarah finds out."

His fists clench at his sides.

"I saw an argument between you and Charlie Lang at the Fieldings' party. Is he involved with your little side hustle here?"

His eyes bug out. "How long have you been following me?"

"Long enough to know you're not who your wife thinks you are."

To her shock, he puts his face in his hands. He's crying. She's reduced this grown man to tears.

"I'm not hustling girls," he says through his fingers. "I just want to be clear about that. This is a business for men. No women are involved. I wouldn't do that."

"Well, that's great. I'm sure Sarah will be delighted to hear that." But secretly, Holly is relieved that it's gambling over the other possibility. She starts to put the pieces together, beginning with the argument she heard in the alcove at the Canyon Club, when Daniel told Charlie he was working on something and just needed a bit more time, the cryptocurrency and secret-messaging apps on his hidden phone.

"Here's what I think," she says. "You're in this illicit business with Charlie Lang."

She waits while he pulls himself together and stands straight.

"How do you know Charlie Lang?"

"Through my dad. He's a Health ProX investor." It's only then that it occurs to her. This might stretch deeper than she thought. "Is my dad involved?" she asks before she can even think it through. Holly isn't sure she wants to hear the answer, but it's too late now.

Thankfully, Daniel shakes his head. He looks around the dumpster and lowers his voice. "Holly. I have debts. A lot of them. I'm in too deep now to get out, and I can't ruin Sarah and Jacob's lives. I just have to finish what I started, and they don't ever need to know. Once I'm out, I'll never go back. You need to stay out of this. You can't possibly understand."

But she can. She's done terrible things, too. Things she'd never want her father or Sarah to find out about.

Just then, something at the end of the alley catches her eye. A flash of long brown waves brushing past the brick wall of the tattoo parlor next to Pinky's. No, it's impossible. It can't be.

Holly focuses her attention back to the broken man in front of her. "Look, Daniel," she says. "The one with choices right now isn't you. It's me. So you'd better start talking."

CHAPTER NINETEEN

SARAH

Now

Tara called my son Jakey, like only Holly ever has. Who is this woman? And what is she after?

I continue investigating Tara's life. I scroll through her scant list of friends on Facebook, no names that I recognize, and her photos, none of which are of Cody. The bulk of them are of furniture she's refinished and workouts. Her posts are innocuous and sparse: books, movies, and vegetarian recipes. Next, I look at her groups: yoga, cooking, and home decor. At the bottom, though, is a group we're both members of—Mother Knows Best, a hugely popular parenting group almost every mom I know is in.

I've never posted, but I used to lurk, reading every post I could find about high-spirited boys to get strategies and a sense of camaraderie. I type Tara's name in the search bar and a few posts pop up. Most advertise her small business—Designs by Tara—and ask for recommendations for pediatricians and dentists in Blossom Court. But one stops me in my tracks. She's responding to a mother who also has a son with allergies.

> My nephew has a severe peanut allergy, so we avoid candy and most processed sugar altogether. We really like carob instead of chocolate. Give it a try!

Nephew, not son. My instincts are dead-on. Tara is lying about who she is. She's Cody's aunt, not his mother. So, who are his parents? And where are they? And why is she lying about how she's related to the boy?

I search all of her posts and photos again for any clue she might have been in Vancouver, knows Holly somehow. I find nothing, but there's a notification on my feed. When I click it, it's a post from my brother, Nathan, a Shabbat dinner with my mom and his family at his house in Burnaby.

"Missing my older sis," he's commented, tagging me.

I miss him, too. I wish our relationship was one in which I could ask him for advice, but it's never been like that between us. We never show our weaknesses to each other. We hide everything, from each other and sometimes from ourselves.

The doorbell rings. I freeze, then check the security app to see who's at the front door. It's just the moving company with the rest of our stuff from Vancouver.

The truck is huge, and as two brawny men pop open the back doors and release a ramp, I'm not sure I want all of our things from Vancouver here. They're part of a life I've left behind, or desperately want to. Because our rental is furnished, we sold all of our couches, chairs, beds, and dressers from the Cliffside house, so these boxes contain our memories, keepsakes, clothes, Jacob's toys, and all the photographs I've ever taken, except the ones of Holly.

I prop the front door open for them, then stand on the far end of the porch, out of the movers' way but keeping an eye on them, as they haul things into the house.

Across the street, Ezra's plain white curtains part, and I know he's watching me. I just don't know why. I glance at Tara's house, which stands empty because she hasn't been home all day.

Then I spot Emily, who's walking Roscoe down the sidewalk toward the ravine. Her tutoring flyer said her last name is Lawrence. I might as well check her out, too. I lean against the wall on my porch and take out my phone, flicking my attention between the movers carrying boxes into the front hall and a quick search on Emily. Her website is clean and simple, detailing her teaching degree from Bishop's University, and glowing testimonials from three very satisfied parents, who rave about Emily's patience and creativity with their children. Maybe her kind, friendly nature is truly genuine.

I don't know how long I've been standing on the porch, thinking and getting nowhere, as the men walk in and out of the house, when one of the movers approaches and says, "Mrs. Goldman? We're done."

I thank them and then watch them slam the doors, get into the truck, and drive off. I head back inside, where the boxes are piled against the walls in the front hall. I don't have the energy to unpack anything. I just sit in the kitchen, my phone quiet beside me, wondering what I'm supposed to do now that Jacob's in school all day and Daniel's at his new job.

I can't make any decisions about it right this moment because somehow it's after 3:00 p.m. I need to get to Blossom Court Elementary so I'm waiting for Jacob when he's dismissed, and I can chat with his teacher about his day. It feels odd that Tara hasn't texted or called to ask to walk over with me or tell me she'll meet me at the school after spending so much of the last couple of days by my side. Daniel, too, has texted me only once to check in.

At first, it's lonely walking by myself past the manicured lawns and large brick houses that all look so similar. But as I stroll on streets named Willow Way and Magnolia Road, I marvel at how safe and pristine everything feels. I've got to stop worrying. Maybe there's a logical explanation for everything. And besides, nothing's really happened. We haven't been robbed or assaulted or . . . worse.

Daniel and the police are right. I'm overblowing everything, reading signs of danger that aren't real. This realization calms me, and I breathe in the crisp, cool air as I head toward Blossom Court Boulevard. I make a right. There are flashing red lights up ahead.

I run toward the school, where an ambulance is parked out front. Someone is being carried out of the building on a stretcher.

CHAPTER TWENTY

HOLLY

Before

"Morning," Sarah murmurs, yawning, when she walks into the kitchen on Tuesday morning. Her beautiful new hair is a big tangle of knots, and black circles are deeply etched under her eyes. "Did you have a good time at the bonfire last night with your friends?" she asks, and pours coffee from the pot Daniel made before he left for work.

Holly's surprised he didn't drink the whole pot. She hardly slept after tiptoeing in at 12:30 a.m., about twenty minutes after Daniel. Once she encouraged him to reveal the huge secret he's keeping from Sarah, they left the alley behind the strip club and went to another regular bar close by, a hole-in-the-wall where no one would know them. They both ordered Cokes, but Holly could barely drink hers. She listened to Daniel's story, riveted and horrified. He explained how he went from being a hardworking family man intent on rising through the ranks at work to a man seduced into being involved in running a high-stakes illegal gambling ring.

He'd met Charlie at a casino, where they immediately hit it off. Charlie was the one who recommended Daniel to the Canyon Club membership committee. Daniel didn't realize why. Now he's caught in Charlie Lang's twisted net of illegal games for the wealthiest, most powerful Canyon Club members. And there's no way out of his debts to Charlie.

"I'm fucked unless I can pay Charlie over half a million dollars or recruit more members into his gambling scheme." He fell back against the scratched black leather seat. "You can't tell anyone, Holly. I'm begging you."

"You can't tell me what to do, Daniel. I have the advantage here. I don't know what I'm going to do yet. I need to think about it."

He looked at his wedding ring, his face twisted with guilt and worry. "I love my family more than anything, but I'm in too deep. There's no way out except doing what Charlie wants. If I can just see things through with Charlie, I'll find an off-ramp. And then I'll never get involved with him again. I swear."

"You swear? So your promises still mean something?"

He sighed. "Yes, they do. What is it you want from me, Holly?"

"What I want is for you to find every fucking way—and I mean that—to make Sarah feel better about herself, because you're living a lie and you've ruined her life."

"Of course I will. But why is this any of your business?"

How could he not understand? "Because I'm part of your family now."

He kneaded the space between his eyebrows. "No, you're not. You shouldn't get involved. Please just pretend you never heard any of this."

"I can't, Daniel." She couldn't possibly let another dark, shameful secret ruin her life. The Goldmans were her only chance to have a real family. And that knowledge was her trump card. "You need to do something for me."

He looked scared and pressed himself further against the booth.

Holly leaned over the table until there were only a few inches of space between them. "You have to convince Sarah to hire me as your live-in nanny. Not just for the summer. I want to stay for the long term."

He balked. "How long?"

"Forever."

"Holly—" He held up his hands in protest.

"If you don't, I'll tell Sarah and the police everything you're doing with Charlie. You'll lose Sarah, and you'll go to jail." She tried to maintain her composure, but her pulse was racing. Both from the ultimatum she issued, and her future in the house that was so close she could almost touch it.

His face drained of color. "You wouldn't."

"I would." She wasn't sure she could ever hurt Sarah that deeply, but he didn't need to know that.

It worked, because he closed his eyes and nodded. "Okay. I'll do it."

As angry as she is this morning over Daniel's deceit and stupidity, he's still a dad, a man who loves his wife and his son. And that revelation makes Holly feel torn about the threat she delivered last night. When they were finished talking, he tossed her bike in his trunk and drove her back to Cliffside Road because he didn't want her riding alone in the dark. They timed it so they wouldn't walk in the door at the same moment if Sarah was up and could see them.

Then this morning Alexis sent her a terse text.

Alexis: Going camping with friends
at Roberts Creek. If you care.

There's so much to keep track of, too much Holly feels bad about to know what to do first. She texted Alexis back, but it isn't enough to make up for flaking on her so many times lately.

Holly: Have fun! Love you. I promise
to see you when you get back.

There was no response. And she doesn't want to outright lie to Sarah now about the bonfire she was supposedly at last night, but how can she answer that question honestly? All she says is "Mmm."

She feels sick and confused about what to do next. If Daniel keeps his promise to her, she gets exactly what she wants: to stay with the Goldmans. But she also has to help Daniel before he tears his family apart. He can't escape Charlie until he brings more men into the gambling scheme or pays off the almost seven figures he owes Charlie. It's an impossible situation . . . unless Holly can fix it.

Now, though, she has to focus on Sarah. Everything Holly does is for her. She's lost one family; she's not about to sit around watching while her new family gets slowly dismantled.

"I made some plans for us." Holly grins, excited to see the look on Sarah's face when she finds out the surprise Holly's arranged for today. She did it before Sarah got up. "Jacob's brushing his teeth. I went up a few minutes ago."

"Plans? I promised Jacob I'd take him to the Granville Island Water Park this afternoon. We go every year." Sarah joins her at the kitchen table, where Holly's been staring into her cereal. "I thought we could all go together."

"I have another idea." She smiles. "Jacob's going to his friend Leo's house for a playdate today."

Sarah's eyes snap to her. "How did you even get Leo's mom's number?"

Sarah looks a little annoyed. Maybe Holly's overstepped?

"Oh, I ran into them out front over the weekend. Karen introduced herself and told me Jacob and Leo are good friends, so we made plans for today." This isn't exactly how it happened, though. She got the phone number of Leo's mom by snooping in Sarah's phone this morning. It was easy. The phone was just sitting on the kitchen counter. Sarah doesn't even have a lock screen.

Sarah stares at her, not speaking.

Holly can't stop talking. "I booked us a mani/pedi. I wanted to do something nice for you because you're always taking care of everyone else. Even me."

Sarah looks like she's about to say something, then stops. She flops back in the chair and rubs her eyes. Holly wants to hug her, to tell her everything's going to be okay, but she has to tread carefully. All she wants is for everything to be okay.

"That's . . . that's really nice of you, Holly. And you're right. I'm completely depleted. I'm tired of keeping this family together on my own, and you're the only one who seems to notice that I need a break."

Holly takes her hand. "I don't know what it's like to be a mom, and I definitely never had a real role model for one. But just so you know—you're an amazing mother."

Sarah squeezes her hand, then releases it and gets up. "Did you tell Jacob about going to Leo's? He was really excited about the water park, and I don't want to disappoint him."

Holly nods. "He's happy to see Leo. I told him not to say anything about their playdate until I told you."

Sarah's mouth turns down. "You told my son to lie?"

Holly feels awful. Her plan to make Sarah feel better is a disaster. "No, I would never do that. I meant for it to be a nice surprise for you."

Sarah sighs. "Of course you did. God. I don't know what's wrong with me. Thank you, Holly. I mean it."

Holly's shoulders relax in relief. "You're welcome. This summer is supposed to be about you and your photography, remember? That's why I'm here. You've posted only two pictures to Instagram, and those are shots from before the summer. I haven't seen anything you've done since I started babysitting."

She doesn't say anymore, not for now. She has to stay close to

Sarah, keep her on her side. If she ever found out the risks Daniel's taking with their lives, she'd be completely undone. Holly will protect her.

———

Sarah's and Holly's feet are in tubs of hot, soapy water, and they're reclining in massage chairs. Sarah drove, and when they dropped Jacob off at Leo's, Holly was relieved that his mom, Karen, just waved from the porch. Holly didn't want to get caught in the lie that she'd met Karen over the weekend. She's never met her in person at all. She texted Karen from her phone.

Holly and Sarah were comfortably silent on the drive to the salon, and after Sarah parked outside and they entered the cool, serene space that smelled like lavender, Sarah visibly relaxed. Holly almost heard her bones sigh. Now two nail technicians sit on small stools in front of them and begin massaging their feet. Sarah keeps reaching into her bag beside her on the arm rest.

"Leo's mom has my number if she needs to get in touch, you know."

"How did I ever survive without you?" Sarah moans as the technician eases her fingers into the soles of her feet. "You got in late last night."

Holly's pulse quickens. "Did I wake you?"

Sarah shakes her head. "Barely. For once, I went right back to sleep. My comment was just an observation, not a judgment."

If she had a mother, Holly assumes this is what the conversation would be like. Gentle, continuous reminders that she's open to listen, but without pressure to spill everything. So she gives Sarah what she wants. "It was nice to see some friends again."

"And Alexis? You said she was going, too."

"Yeah," Holly says. She counts to three, so the next question won't be obvious. "I guess it was good to have an escape for a night and not worry where I'm going to live in the future."

Holly looks down and waits for this to sink in, for Sarah to tell her that she and Daniel were discussing just that before he went to work this morning.

"Oh, Holly. I know you're going through a lot. So much uncertainty."

Holly looks up to see Sarah, who seems mortified, biting her lip.

"Do you need money? If you do, you can tell me."

"No!" Holly says. "You're more than generous with my babysitting pay. But I can't stay rent-free and eat your food for too long. I don't want to wear out my welcome." She sips from the cucumber water on the small table next to her chair. "And you've got your own family to look after. I'm sure it's hard on one income."

She stops there, hoping this will prompt where she wants the conversation to go, but Sarah merely closes her eyes as the technician lathers a salt scrub on her legs, making it hard to gauge how Holly's comment has landed.

Sarah opens her eyes, turning to Holly. "Do you know what you want to do in the fall?" she asks.

What she wants is never to leave the Goldmans' house. Now that she's made that clear to Daniel, all he has to do is make it happen. But clearly Daniel hasn't broached the subject yet, so she makes something up. "I might talk to my psychology professor about working for him and getting a master's in clinical psych," she says. It's a total lie, but it shows initiative.

"You'd make a wonderful psychologist," Sarah says. "You see into people so well."

"I see you," Holly says.

Sarah meets her eye. She clears her throat. "I see you, too."

Holly swallows hard.

An hour later, their fingers and toes glitter with matching hot-pink polish. At the cashier, Holly takes out her wallet, but Sarah tosses her credit card on the counter. "My treat."

"But I booked this for you. I'm sure you have enough expenses of your own, no?" Holly says, hoping this time she'll take the cue.

"Don't you worry about that," she says. "Daniel and I are doing just fine. More than fine, actually." Sarah smiles. "If Daniel can afford the Canyon Club, I can certainly pay for our mani/pedis."

This is not the behavior of a wife who suspects her husband has plunged them into financial ruin. Sarah really has no clue.

On their drive to pick up Jacob, Sarah sings along to some nineties song on the radio; Holly yearns for the day to end. An idea tickles her mind about how she can help Daniel get out of his debt to Charlie Lang, but it's not quite fully formed yet. She's so lost in thought that Sarah's opened the door, one foot out of the car to head up Leo's porch steps before Holly realizes. She can't let Sarah speak to Karen, so she jumps out. "I'll get Jacob. You stay here."

"Thanks," Sarah says, shutting the door and drumming her newly painted nails on the steering wheel.

Holly gets Jacob, waves goodbye to Karen and the sturdy little boy next to her, and takes Jacob's hand to lead him to the back of the Highlander, where she buckles him into his booster seat.

"Hi, Mommy!"

"Hi, sweetie. How was Leo's?"

"We made ice cream sundaes!" He licks his lips where chocolate still remains. "I was going to bring some home, but I had to eat it all."

Sarah chuckles. "Of course you did."

They drive the three minutes from Leo's back to the Cliffside house, and when Sarah pulls into the garage, Holly's both surprised and relieved to see that Daniel's Audi is already parked there.

Sarah furrows her brow. "That's weird." She glances at her watch. "It's only four fifteen."

Entering the mudroom from the garage, Sarah calls, "Dan? You here?"

He calls back, "Yeah!" He joins them in the mudroom, and Jacob tackle hugs him. "There's a golf thing at the Canyon Club tonight, so I ducked out of work early."

Holly stares at him, but he refuses to meet her eye.

"Daddy! I got chocolate sundaes at Leo's!"

Daniel kisses Jacob above his top lip. "Yum!"

Jacob giggles. "Can I watch TV?"

"Go ahead, honey," Sarah says. Once Jacob's run off, she holds up her fingers to Daniel. "Holly and I got our nails done."

"Nice."

He's still avoiding Holly's eyes, but that doesn't stop her from saying, "Sarah and I had a great day. Very relaxing. And we had a good chat."

Daniel blanches. "What did you chat about?"

Sarah winks at Holly, then says to Daniel, "You wouldn't understand."

Holly laughs. "You know, just girly stuff."

He swallows, and Holly sees how hard he's working to smile, but a line of sweat has appeared above his lip. She turns to Sarah. "Thanks again for paying for everything today, Sarah," Holly says pointedly, while looking at Daniel. "You really didn't have to."

Daniel winces.

"It was absolutely my pleasure." Sarah touches Daniel's arm. "Are you home for dinner?"

"I can't. The event is a dinner, too. A networking thing."

"I thought you said it was a golf thing," Sarah says.

His neck, right above the collar, reddens slightly. "Yes, a networking event for all the newest members of the golf club."

"Okay, well, can you at least unload the dishwasher before you leave? I wouldn't mind lying down for a little bit."

Daniel looks like he's about to refuse, but Holly catches his eye, gives a little nod.

"Sure." He kisses her cheek. "Love you."

"Love you, too." And Sarah disappears up the stairs, leaving Holly and Daniel alone.

"I'll help you unload," Holly says loudly, in case Sarah's listening. Together they head for the kitchen, where Daniel opens the dishwasher, then leans against the counter. "I can't talk to you about last night, Holly," he whispers roughly.

"But you have to. I'm the only person you can talk to about it."

He shakes his head. "No. I'm begging you to stop involving yourself."

Holly steps closer. "You need me, Daniel. I'll make everything better for you."

He eyes her warily. "What are you talking about?"

She's still formulating her strategy. "All in good time. I just need you to understand that I belong here, Daniel."

He looks speechless, so she makes it clear. "I'm making a plan."

"To do what?"

"To get you out of debt."

The footsteps are right behind her before she has a chance to move back from Daniel, for him to clear the nervous shock on his face.

"Hey," says Sarah as she walks into the room. "What are you two whispering about in here?"

Holly and Daniel jump apart. What has Sarah heard? Her head cocks to the side as she looks from her husband to Holly and back again.

No, Holly thinks to herself as she takes in the suspicion on Sarah's face. *It's not what you think. I swear.*

CHAPTER TWENTY-ONE

SARAH

Now

I run so fast down Blossom Court Boulevard toward the ambulance parked at the curb in front of Jacob's school that I nearly trip over a crack in the sidewalk. The ominous children's rhyme about a mother's broken back rings through my head as I look frantically for Jacob, my heart beating so rapidly I'm gasping for breath. A cacophonous swarm of parents and kids surround the ambulance. I can't see through the crush of people to find out if the stretcher carries a child or an adult; male or female.

Jacob's not with his class, who are in a line against the brick wall opposite the playground. Valerie Martin, his teacher, is not with them, either.

The worst scenarios flash in my mind—Jacob hit his head; he fell off the climber; he tumbled down the stairs—when I'm sure I see someone lurk in the large cluster of trees adjacent to the school.

I catch a flash of tan, like Ezra's omnipresent pants.

I push through the crowd of parents to get to the ambulance when someone touches my back.

"Mrs. Goldman?"

I whirl around. Valerie stands there, with Jacob next to her, quivering.

"Are you hurt?" I drop to my knees to inspect him.

"No. It's C-Cody." He sobs, his body shaking, and I look questioningly at his teacher, then at the ambulance just as Tara climbs into the back of it.

Before the doors close, Tara locks eyes with me. Her face hardens like stone, and the ambulance shrieks away.

"I didn't kill Cody!" Jacob presses his face into my knit sweater, wailing uncontrollably.

My mouth opens in horror. But Valerie shakes her head and touches Jacob's shoulder. "Cody will be fine. That's what the EpiPen is for, remember? I gave him medicine, so he'll be okay." She straightens and gives me a wan smile. She looks frightened but is trying to hide it for the benefit of my son. "Apparently, Cody ate a chocolate bar that contained peanuts," Valerie says.

"Oh God. How did it happen? Tara is so careful."

Jacob is ghostly pale, whispering, "Is he going to die? Is Cody going to die?"

I pull Jacob closer to me. "Honey, he's going to be fine. We'll call Tara later to check on him, okay? But they'll take good care of him at the hospital." I look again at his poor teacher, who nods.

The stress of everything, how quickly a life-changing threat can occur, undoes me, and I put my face in my hands for a moment. Jacob peels them away, his face pale with fear at my reaction. Valerie kindly, gently, puts her hand on my arm. "It was an accident. Another student gave Cody a piece of a chocolate bar that contained nuts."

"Mommy, I should have told Cody not to eat it. I'm supposed to be his friend." Jacob's tears spill down his cheeks. Valerie pats his back then mouths, "Everything will be okay," to me before she goes off to talk to other anxious parents.

Jacob's tears only stop when Emily and Roscoe walk up to the front of the school. Jacob runs and flings himself at the dog, burying his face in his fur.

"What's going on?" Emily asks, her voice soft with concern. "I came to meet a student for tutoring, and it's total chaos here."

I fill her in quickly.

"Oh, that's awful," she says. "Tara must be a mess."

"She was with him in the ambulance," I say.

"Will Cody be all right?" my son asks as he looks up at Emily.

"Of course he will," Emily says. "Right, Roscoe?"

Roscoe wags his tail as if on cue, and at long last my son's tears stop falling.

"Can I walk Roscoe?" Jacob asks in a small voice.

"He'd love that. Why don't you take him up and down the grass right here?" Emily hands him the leash and points to a neat square of space off school property but not right near the road. Once he's walking away, she hugs me, quick and firm. "Thought you might need a moment."

I lower my shoulders and some of the tension I've been holding loosens. Emily's embrace is a comfort to me. I exhale. "What a fucking day."

She nods. "It sounds like the teacher did all the right things."

"Yes." I bring my hands together and hold them to my mouth for a moment, as if in prayer. Then I realize Emily's looking for someone among the crowd. "Go if you need to. I know you have a student to see."

"I haven't spotted him yet. He's in sixth grade and wanders out slowly." She smiles. "But you and Jacob probably want to get home. Just have him pass back the leash. It's all good."

I do need to get home. There are boxes piled in my front hall, but I don't know how I can focus on any of that now. All I can think about is the chilling look Tara gave me as she climbed into the back of the ambulance. Plus the fact that I swear I saw Ezra here somewhere. I can't wait to be inside my house, safe and secure. Then I shudder. Nothing feels safe anymore. But at least Jacob's not crying now that he's been given the responsibility of walking Roscoe around. He's focused on the dog, who's sniffing a patch of grass outside the school fence.

"Thank you, Emily. Roscoe's like magic. That dog makes Jacob feel better every time he sees him. I really appreciate you sharing him."

She smiles. "It's not all selfless. Roscoe's a bit hyper, so having the boys' attention on him helps me catch a break, too." She waves at someone. "There's my student. Listen, Jacob's welcome to play with Roscoe anytime. And if you're ever looking for a tutor for your son, keep me in mind."

"You know what? I just might take you up on that. Let me talk to Daniel."

"Great. I'd better go. Take it easy, all right?"

I call out for Jacob to bring Roscoe to us, and he and the dog trot over. Jacob leans down to kiss the dog on the head, then hands the leash back to Emily.

"You're very responsible, Jacob."

He looks happier, his face calmer despite the tear streaks. I can see why Emily has such glowing reviews as a tutor. She's wonderful with kids.

Emily and Roscoe head into the cluster of students until all I see is blue hair bobbing up and down.

Jacob shuffles to my side. "Will Cody really be okay?"

I tuck his hand in mine. "He'll be fine. Let's go home."

Jacob is quiet all the way to Lilac Lane. I know he's deep in thought, worried about his friend. I can't fix this for him, and it kills me. I run my fingers through his silky hair. If anything happened to my son, I'd never survive.

With my hand on his bony shoulder, we enter the house, where I expect Jacob to make a mad dash for the boxes with his name on them lined up against the walls. But he stands there at the front door, thumb in his mouth.

"Do you think Cody would like some cookies once he gets home from the hospital?" I ask.

He nods, and I find a recipe for sugar-free, nut-free lemon cookies, gather the ingredients, bowls, and spoons, and put everything on the counter in front of us.

"Okay, sweetie, can you scoop out a cup of flour and put it in the silver bowl, please?"

While he's distracted with that, I say, "It wasn't your fault that Cody ate the chocolate bar. I know that, and so does he."

He pours the flour in the bowl, spilling half of it on the counter. I say nothing and give him the cup for the baking soda. He doesn't look at me when he says, "Some friends never forgive each other. Some friends never get to see each other again."

I know he's not talking about Cody anymore. I've avoided mentioning Holly because it's a discussion I don't want to have. There's so much I can't explain because Jacob's too young to grasp how deceiving appearances can be, and it's a lesson he can't learn yet.

I gently take the cup and place it on the counter. I bend down and hold his face in my hands. "Some friendships need to end if they're not good for you. But Cody is a kind friend, and so are you."

"I want to forgive you," he says quietly.

The statement is a gut punch. "Forgive me for what?"

"For fighting with Holly and making her leave. You never came to find me under the bed. You left me there all alone."

My heart cracks. Holly left him all alone in the house the day she quit. She didn't even send a text or call, but of course his anger at being abandoned is directed at me.

"I never meant to hurt you, baby. I wasn't the one to leave you alone. There were a few things that Holly did—" I stop and regroup.

"She should never have left you on your own. It was irresponsible. I just wanted to go for a long walk to get some space after Holly and I talked. It was her job to take care of you while I was gone. Do you understand?"

He nods, but I can tell he's only doing so to please me. I've never been sure what Jacob heard that end of August morning two weeks ago on the pool deck, the last time I spoke to Holly. I wanted to believe he only caught the tail end of our horrible argument, but it's clear he heard something. I watched Holly from the kitchen window as she nonchalantly skimmed my pool, her lean legs so long in her cutoff jean shorts, no makeup needed on her lightly tanned skin. I'd fumed. Who the hell was this lying sneak I'd trusted with my son and my deepest feelings?

This was after I'd discovered that she'd been hiding things, doing terrible things in my home when I wasn't there. And yet there she was, acting as innocent as ever, a graceful nymph cleaning my pool. I wanted to hold her down under the water until she begged for mercy, that's how angry I was.

I stalked toward her, unable to control the fury and hurt that steamed off my skin. I was always just a stepping-stone to fulfill her bottomless need for male attention and approval. I'd seen the proof through my cameras.

I stood in front of her on the pool deck. She stopped skimming immediately. "What's going on?" she asked. "Please, I don't know what's made you so upset."

I had to stop myself from grabbing and shaking her. "You know exactly what's making me so upset."

She fiddled with that yin necklace she always wore. How could she just stand there and play dumb?

I laced into her. "I want the truth. You owe me that after everything I've done for you, all the support I've given you." I came closer and growled, "What is it you're doing here anyhow? What game are you playing?"

She pretended to be confused by my question. I knew, though, what a good actress she was. She stopped for a moment, nodded, then said, "It's not *my* games you should be worried about." Then she stepped back right to the edge of the pool.

Was this deceitful young girl gaslighting me? "Who exactly should I be pointing fingers at, then, if you're not responsible for doing what you did in my house?"

"Ask your husband."

I was enraged and got right in Holly's face. "Stay away from my husband. Do you understand?"

"No, I don't. What are you implying?"

"Shut up and listen," I said. "Here's what's going to happen. You'll finish the day and then you're gone. Pack your bags and don't mention anything to my son. You've found another place to live. That's it. You're moving on."

It felt so good to take control, even as her face crumpled. She started to cry big, fat crocodile tears. I didn't believe them, not for a second. She wiped the tears with the palms of her hands and stood taller, a power play over my diminutive height. "What did Daniel tell you?" she asked.

I sucked in a sharp breath. What was she trying to say? I didn't want my husband's name in her mouth. "Don't speak his name ever again," I said.

Holly pretended to be stunned. "Why would you do this, Sarah? I've never done a single thing to hurt you."

I was onto her, and I wasn't done. "Except lie. Deceive. Betray my trust. You're a manipulator and a conniver, and I don't want you anywhere near us anymore. You don't belong in this family, Holly." I leaned in very close. "We've sold the house. We're moving to Toronto."

It wasn't technically true. We hadn't sold the house, but Daniel was working on it. I'd only just agreed to leaving Vancouver the day before, and Daniel accepted the position with Strategic Solutions. They offered to find him a furnished rental for six months, but he still had to give notice at Code Tek and confirm the private sale of our home with the interested buyer from the Canyon Club. We had decided to tell Holly only once the house was sold, but now, it didn't matter. I needed her gone. Away from me, from my son, from us. Immediately.

"I saw what you did," I said.

Holly responded, but I don't know what she said because I heard a squeaking noise behind me and turned around. Jacob was on the deck, his head swiveling from me to his favorite babysitter, both of us arguing at the edge of the pool.

"Why are you two fighting?" he asked.

I gave him a wobbly smile. I had to come up with a lie—fast. "We're not fighting, sweetie. Just grown-up talking. There's a difference." I pointed to the patio table and asked him to raise the umbrella. I was desperate to distract him from the tension between Holly and me. But Jacob wouldn't move until Holly repeated my request to him.

"Listen to your mom, Jakey."

Jealousy pricked my heart. My son was under her spell, too.

"Mommy, I did it!" Jacob said a minute later, standing proudly next to the opened umbrella.

I smiled at my son while my chest flamed with anger toward Holly. I didn't know what to do. If I stayed on that deck any longer, I'd explode. I either had to fire Holly right there in front of Jacob or leave them alone and calm down. It was clear she was a danger around men, but I still believed then that she truly loved my son and would never intentionally cause him harm, despite betraying me so deeply. I'd damage Jacob more if I didn't walk away. "Awesome job, honey! I'm going for a walk, okay?" To Holly, I warned, "Take care of him. Tell him exactly what we agreed to and nothing else. I'll be back soon."

I turned my back on her. The last thing I heard her say was: "You won't get away with this."

At the time I thought they were merely empty, resentful words.

I figured she'd just tell my son she was leaving while I stomped in circles around Forest View and figured out what to do next. I had to get my anger in check. When I was halfway to Capilano River park, I called Daniel and told him about the confrontation with Holly.

"I'll go home as soon as I can. I'll deal with her, Sarah, okay? Leave it with me." I was relieved because I was done engaging with Holly.

But when Daniel texted me an hour later to come home immediately, I was terrified that something had happened to Jacob. My fears were founded because I could hear him sobbing the second I opened our front door. I raced up the stairs to his room, where Daniel cradled our son in his arms.

"She left. No text. No call. She told Jacob to go in the house for hide-and-seek, and she'd come and find him. She never came."

I dropped beside them and gathered Jacob to me. He was crying so hard that he was almost hyperventilating. Once I'd rubbed his back enough to calm him down, he told me, "I was under my bed for hours! I was so scared. Where's Holly? Where did she go?"

I never should have left him alone with her. It was another terrible judgment call I regret. Now I know that our leaving was the beginning of her terrorizing me, and I still don't know how far she's prepared to go.

I can't explain all of this to Jacob, and it doesn't matter anyhow. She's supposed to be gone. Daniel overheard John Monroe at the Canyon Club telling someone that she'd left on a long, tropical retreat of some kind, confirmed by her last Instagram post.

I won't let Holly hurt Jacob or my family anymore. I keep it simple, focus it back on Cody and the present tense. "Baby, Holly doesn't care about our family the way we thought she did, but Cody does."

Jacob looks up at me, his eyes bright with hope. "But, Mommy, Holly does care. She for sure cares about you. She told me right before hide-and-seek, when you went for a walk after you got angry."

I grip the edge of the counter. "What did she say exactly?"

"She said, 'Tell your mommy to watch out for herself.' See? She cares about you, Mommy. She does."

No, I think, she's coming after me, and a chill runs through my bones.

CHAPTER TWENTY-TWO

HOLLY

Before

Sarah eyes Daniel and Holly warily as they stand there, complicit, in the middle of the kitchen. Holly wants the ground to swallow her whole. How could she be so stupid to talk to Daniel in the kitchen of his home? She should have waited, followed him wherever he's going tonight to talk to him alone.

The two bright spots of color mottling Sarah's cheeks are evidence of her surprise and suspicion—the babysitter and her husband jumping apart right when she comes into the room? Such a cliché, and so easy to misread. Now Holly has to think of something fast because Daniel's standing there like an idiot. How this man has gotten away with his secret for so long is shocking.

"We were whispering about the tooth fairy," Holly says, the words spilling off her tongue before she has a chance to think about them.

"Jacob has a loose tooth, and we were scheming about how to sneak some money under his pillow when the tooth falls out."

"Yeah," Daniel says, unconvincingly, adding not a single detail.

Still, Sarah's relief is evident. "That's so cute," she says. "Daniel and I can handle this, though." She smiles and joins Daniel, planting a kiss on his cheek.

"I thought you were going for a nap," Daniel says, his voice finally at a normal pitch.

"I was, but then Nathan called. He invited the three of us for dinner tonight." She looks hopefully at Holly. "I've raved about you so much that they'd love for you to join us."

Her heart swells. Sarah wants her to meet the family. "I'd love that! Can I bring anything? Maybe something for his daughters?"

"That's so thoughtful, but I'll just grab a bottle of wine on the way. We'll leave here at five thirty. Sound good?"

"Great."

Daniel makes a sad face. "I'm sorry I'm missing it, honey."

"Well, that golf networking event at the club sounds too exciting to skip," Sarah teases, but Holly detects her frustration because Sarah clenches her hand into a quick fist.

"Actually, Sarah, I was thinking that it might be a good idea for Holly to stay here longer, in the fall." He looks at Holly, then back to Sarah. "It's been working out so well, and you'll have more time to work on photography. Maybe hire her as our live-in nanny."

Holly looks down at her feet. Leave it to an idiot man not to read the room and realize now might not be the right time. Sarah's irritation flushes red on her neck. "I wish you'd thought about talking to me about this first privately," she says, not even trying to hide her anger.

An uncomfortable, extended silence hangs in the room. Finally, Daniel nods. "You're right. Sorry. I was getting ahead of myself. Anyway, we can discuss it later."

"I think Daniel's just really happy you're helping us," Sarah says to Holly, trying to smooth over the tension. But it's only a thin coat.

Before anyone can say anything else, Holly's phone rings. She takes it out of her pocket. It's Alexis FaceTiming her. Thank God. Her stepsister is saving her, yet again.

"I'd better take this. I'll be ready to go to your brother's at five thirty." She practically runs out of the kitchen, knowing as soon as she's gone that Sarah will tear into Daniel for inviting her to move in without consulting her.

In her bedroom, she accepts the call. Alexis's face appears, and Holly instantly relaxes. She feels it in the pit of her stomach, suddenly and forcefully, just how much she misses her stepsister.

"Hey!" she says. "Are you calling me from a campground?" She can't see the area behind Alexis's mass of brown waves.

Alexis nods. "Well, sort of. We ran out of propane, so I'm waiting near the truck while my friends grab some."

"Who are you with?"

"Just some girls from the nursing program." She touches her yang pendant. "Look, I'm sorry if I was curt in my text this morning. I miss you."

Holly slumps. "No, I'm sorry. It's just been busy here with Jacob and trying to make sure I earn my keep." She laughs.

Alexis doesn't.

"We'll talk about it more when I get home. I'm worried about you, Holly."

"Worried about me? Why?"

"Oh, I don't know. You stole my mom's bracelet, decided you don't want to stay in med school or work at your family's company, and got kicked out. Plus . . . the stuff in the car? And you never want to see me anymore." She shakes her head and changes track. "Look, it's weird that you're living with complete strangers instead of with me. You've been . . . different this summer."

Holly digs her nails into her palms to keep the defensiveness out of her voice. She doesn't want to fight with Alexis. "Different how?"

"Sketchy."

"*Sketchy?*" She laughs again.

"It's not the right word. Not exactly. But you know what I mean. You're doing things that . . . seem out of character. And I'm not sure that family is good for you."

Right then, a crack of thunder bursts through the audio. "You'd better go if you're standing outside," Holly says.

Alexis's eyes shift. "Yeah. Okay, we'll talk more when I'm home on Friday."

They both click off, and Holly hears murmurs through the air duct, then her name. She presses her ear to the cold metal tube.

"It's not why we hired her—to clean, to cook. She's here for him. And he'll be in school come fall."

Holly lies on the floor of her closet, a wave of sadness rolling through her. Doesn't Sarah want to be with her? Wouldn't she miss her if she were gone? A terrible feeling starts to sink into Holly's chest, like she's unwanted, like she doesn't really belong.

"Holly will be in university, too, even if it's not med school. She won't be here all the time." Daniel's voice is soft and encouraging. He's trying hard. "You're much happier this summer than you've been in months. Calmer."

Is she? Holly's worked hard to make Sarah feel important and give her the time and space to create, but Daniel doesn't seem to understand that it's his attention Sarah wants most.

"It's not good for us or Jacob, Daniel, to always be relying on . . ."

That's the last thing she hears before the conversation gets muffled, and she loses the flow. Then it's Daniel she hears, announcing how he has to fly to Calgary tomorrow for a conference. "I'll be back Thursday night, but I'd feel better knowing Holly's here, that you're not alone in the house."

"I can take care of myself, Dan," Sarah shoots back.

"Of course you can. But you know how you get."

Holly hears rustling. Something creaks.

"Fine. For now," she hears Sarah say. Holly fist-pumps the air and leaves her post by the vent to sit on her bed. Daniel's kept up his end of the bargain, so she'll keep her mouth shut. For now. And her plans are gelling in her mind. She's been thinking a lot about how to convince Charlie to let Daniel out of his debts. There's no way Daniel can pay back nearly a million dollars, not without taking the whole family down with him. And Holly won't let that happen. But she needs leverage.

Information is power, and Holly doesn't know enough about the scheme Charlie has going with the Canyon Club, how many members are involved, how dangerous it might be. She also doesn't want Daniel to know anything about the nature of her relationship with Charlie.

She waits until 4:30 p.m., an hour before they're supposed to go to Nathan's, then walks upstairs. Jacob and Daniel are watching a movie in the living room. Over Jacob's head, Daniel nods at her once; she nods back.

"Where's Sarah?" she asks.

"Our bedroom."

Holly heads upstairs and knocks on the bedroom door.

"It's me," she says quietly.

"Come in."

She enters Sarah's bedroom. "Oh, what a pretty room," she says, like it's the first time she's seen it.

"Thanks. Once Jacob stopped coming into our bed in the middle of the night, when he was five, I redid it so it was more of an adult space." She blushes. "I mean—"

Holly laughs. "I know what you meant." Then she clutches her stomach in a fake wince.

"You okay?"

"Cramps. They came out of nowhere," she says.

"Do you want to take something? Have a bath? That sometimes helps me."

"I think I should lie down until we leave for dinner."

"You don't have to come. I hate to see you suffer through a long family affair, especially when it's not even your own family." She points to the bed. "Lie down. I'll get you a heating pad."

The care Sarah offers both pleases and sickens her. Her stomach really is cramping now. The bed is so inviting, and Holly lays back, leaning against the soft pillows, while Sarah goes to the bathroom and comes back with the heating pad. She plugs it in and sits next to Holly.

"I'm so sorry," Holly says. "I've had brutal cramps since I was thirteen. It usually passes after the first day."

Not true. It's Alexis who gets debilitating cramps. Holly barely bleeds.

"Listen," Sarah says. "I'm sorry I was rude in the kitchen earlier when Daniel suggested you work as our live-in nanny. It's just that I'm tired of him making decisions without consulting me first." She sighs. "But I don't want you to think I don't want you here, because I do."

Holly nods, all warm inside. "I get it. It's okay. You want to have a say in what happens in the house because you're the one responsible for it."

"That's it. That's it exactly," Sarah says, and she gives Holly's hand a squeeze.

Daniel appears in the doorway, brown eyes slitting at the sight of Holly on his bed.

"She's going to stay home tonight," Sarah tells him. "She's not feeling well." She looks at Holly. "I know you need to mend things with your family, and we're happy to help with that if you need us. And I also worry that you shouldn't be investing so much time and energy into us, and Jacob, because you have your own life." Sarah glances at Daniel, then smiles. "But, well, like Daniel mentioned before, if you're interested, for the short term at least, we'd love to keep you employed as our live-in babysitter."

Employed—Holly doesn't like how that word sounds, but she loves everything else.

Forgetting she's supposed to be in pain, Holly throws her arms around Sarah. "Yes! I'd love that so much! Oh my God, thank you."

Sarah laughs and hugs her back. "We'll make it work with whatever schedule you have at school."

I love you, Holly almost says but stops herself just in time. "I love being here. It feels like home."

Sarah grins. "That's settled, then. We can tell Jacob tomorrow. We should talk about the logistics first like pay, your responsibilities, and then I think it's time Daniel and I speak to your father and Lisette."

"I can speak to John," Daniel offers, catching Holly's eye.

Maybe he's not a total idiot after all. There's no way either of them wants her dad involved.

"That sounds great," Holly says, another total lie.

"Great!" Sarah gets off the bed. "Feel free to stay here until Jacob and I get back. Sleep. Watch a little TV." She gestures to the cabinet across from the bed, opens it, and swings out a flat-screen. Then she drops the remote on the bed.

This is what heaven what must feel like, Holly thinks, once Sarah and Daniel leave the room. She waits until she hears Jacob's feet pound the floor below and the front door close. She doesn't ever want to leave this cozy bedroom, but when half an hour's passed, and she's sure everyone is gone—Sarah and Jacob to Nathan's; Daniel to a probably fictional golf event—she gets up and tiptoes outside to the cabana.

All she has are screenshots of the password-protected Monero and CoverMe apps and Daniel's word about the illegal gambling dens Charlie's organized. If she's going to help Daniel escape his debt and get out of Charlie's clutches, she needs more details.

It's 6:00 p.m., and the sun is still strong as she quickly scans the woods for anyone out there. Seeing nothing, Holly pushes down the handle on the cabana door, leaving it a tiny bit ajar so she can hear anything worrisome outside.

This time she looks more carefully at the papers in Daniel's drawers for any that might hold the password to the CoverMe app and Daniel's messages, or information about which other Canyon Club members are indebted to Charlie. She's so focused on the job at hand that she doesn't hear the door open until it's too late.

"What are you doing in here?"

She turns around. Sarah stands in front of her, her eyes wide with disbelief.

CHAPTER TWENTY-THREE

SARAH

Now

Tell your mommy to watch out for herself.

Holly used Jacob to deliver a message to me, a message that arrived later than she thought, but arrive it did. Whether it's a threat or a warning is still unclear, but what is clear is that she used my son as a messenger, and I hate her for it. I also hate her for callously walking out on him, leaving a young boy completely alone and unattended. Anything could have happened to him. Anything.

My face must reflect the abject fear I feel, because Jacob asks, "What did I say, Mommy? What's wrong?"

"Nothing, honey. Everything's fine. Why don't you watch a show, and I'll finish making the cookies?" I hug him quickly. "I love you more than anything."

Once I hear the TV on, I go back to the kitchen, bending my head to halt the sudden dizziness making the room spin. A door slams shut from inside the house.

I jump but realize it's five o'clock, and Daniel must have entered through the mudroom.

"I'm home!" he calls out, and five seconds later, he joins me in the kitchen and plugs his phone into the charger. Then he loosens his tie and kisses me. "I got your text about Cody. What a strange first day at school. How is everyone?"

"Jacob is okay. Worried about his friend."

"Do you know how he is?"

I shake my head. "I haven't texted Tara yet. I will. How was work?"

He smiles. "Really good. I met some of the other consultants on my team, and we went to the aerospace firm for a first strategy session." He kisses me on the lips. "You okay?"

I nod even though I'm still rattled from what Jacob told me Holly said. I can't broach it now because Jacob runs toward Daniel.

"Come watch cartoons with me, Daddy." He starts dragging his father toward the living room.

Daniel mouths to me, "We'll talk after," and follows his son out of the kitchen.

I give them a minute, then peer into the living room, where they're snuggling on the couch. Sometimes I'm jealous that Daniel's obviously Jacob's hero and a cuddle from him does so much more than my clumsy attempts at armchair therapy. And I feel guilty for being envious because I know how important a strong male role model is for a young boy.

I turn away and focus on finishing the cookies. I pop them into the oven before venturing back into the living room, where I sit between my two males and gather Jacob in my arms.

"Can we bring Cody the cookies after they're done?" he asks, looking up at me with hope.

"If they're back from the hospital and Cody's feeling better. We'll have to see."

Daniel strokes my thigh; I squeeze his hand. The silent communication of parents trying to shield their child from adult problems. He looks so handsome in his charcoal suit, his wavy brown hair mussed from Jacob's hands, a thin layer of afternoon stubble covering his strong jaw. My husband, who's a better person than I am. Or he's led me to believe he is.

Tell your mommy to watch out for herself.

After twenty minutes, Daniel tousles Jacob's hair. "I'm going to take a quick shower." He looks at me and says, "Let me know if Tara and Cody get home." He leaves to go upstairs.

I kiss Jacob on the cheek. "You can watch a bit more TV. I'm going to check on the cookies."

I head back to the kitchen and lean against the counter to stare at the oven timer. Daniel's phone rings.

I peek quickly at the screen, where "Blossom Court Properties" flashes before the call goes to voice mail.

Could that be about the cameras? I don't know Daniel's password. Is it strange he's never given it to me? I'd tell him mine, if I had one. And I wouldn't go so far as to listen to his messages.

I would like to talk to the property manager myself, though. To ask about the cameras and who exactly had access to our house before we moved in. I decide to google the company and call. The shower's still running when I sit at the kitchen table and dial.

"Blossom Court Properties. Courtney Pham speaking," I hear.

"Hi, Courtney. This is Sarah Goldman, Daniel's wife. We're the renters at 227 Lilac Lane. I saw that you called my husband, but he's not available right now so I thought I'd call you back myself."

"Hi, Sarah," Courtney says. "Yes, I just called him to follow up on first and last months' rental deposit. The check bounced."

This surprises me because Daniel's on top of all our finances, always has been. He handles the bills and accounts himself.

"Sorry about that," I reply. "It must be a mistake. I'll ask Daniel to reissue the check."

"Good. Thank you."

Before she hangs up, I say, "Oh, I know you spoke to Daniel about this, but you're pretty sure the cameras inside the house were put in by the previous residents?"

There's an awkward pause. "Pardon?"

I'm not sure why her voice rises in a question. "Yes. Daniel asked you about them on Saturday, when we moved in?"

"I've never spoken to Daniel before on the phone. Until now, we've only communicated through email. What kinds of cameras did you find?"

"H-hidden cameras," I stammer, because I'm not sure what's going on.

"The last tenants didn't have cameras, and we definitely haven't engaged a security company."

"Really? Okay. Well, I think there's been some kind of miscommunication between Daniel and me."

"Well, call me back after you speak with your husband, but we definitely didn't put security in your house."

"Okay," I say. "Thanks." The water upstairs stops running. "Just one thing: Did anyone have access to this house after the last tenants left and before we moved in? Anyone who wasn't related to your property management group?"

"Just those who viewed it. And there was only one person interested besides you, a man."

A man. Ezra across the street? Nick, Tara's criminal husband?

"Do you know his name?"

She huffs. "Even if I did," she says, "it's not like I'd be able to give it to you. I don't think it's anything to worry about."

"Thank you," I say. "Goodbye." I'm disoriented when I hang up, the phone still in my hand when Daniel strolls into the kitchen in a gray tracksuit, his hair wet.

"The rent deposits bounced." My tone is flat.

He pinches the bridge of his nose. "Fuck," he says. "It's been so nuts that I must have sent the check from the wrong account. I'll fix it right now." He peers at me. "What? It was a mistake."

"Did you really call the property manager about the hidden cameras?"

"Sarah, of course I called."

"Courtney said you didn't."

"Well, maybe it wasn't Courtney I spoke to, but someone called me back late Saturday and she told me the previous residents might have placed cameras inside for security. She apologized for not knowing. She offered to have someone come to remove them, but I said we'd taken care of it." His neck tenses. "I'm trying to do everything you ask of me. I can't help take care of things if you try to micromanage it all."

He's right, but I'm still apprehensive about that call, even though it's possible it wasn't Courtney he spoke to.

"Can I go to Cody's now?" Jacob yells from the living room.

"It's only been five minutes since the last time you asked," I say, irritation rising in my voice.

"I can text Tara if you want," Daniel offers.

"No, I should do it." I'm nervous as I type and delete, not sure what I want my message to say. Finally, I keep it simple.

Sarah: So sorry about Cody. Jacob wants to
see Cody when and if he's up for it.

I press send.

Thirty minutes goes by with no response. Jacob and Daniel go to the backyard to play. Finally, my phone buzzes.

It's not Tara. It's the private caller again.

Unknown: I know everything. Do you?

And there's a video attached.

CHAPTER TWENTY-FOUR

HOLLY

Before

Holly, suddenly ice-cold with fear, shivers in front of Sarah, who's standing inside the cabana she was never supposed to enter.

"Why are you in here?" Sarah repeats.

Holly can't think of an excuse fast enough. "I—I saw a light. I came in to turn it off," she stammers, hoping her face isn't as red as it feels.

Sarah's eyes don't leave hers. "Daniel doesn't want you in his cabana."

Holly's whole body quakes, and she holds herself as tightly as possible to stop it. It doesn't work. "I know. Sorry." It's all she can think to say.

Sarah's head tilts. "You're feeling better, then?"

"A bit." The words catch in Holly's throat.

"Cramps all gone, I guess?"

"Yes. I'm really sorry if I did anything wrong."

Sarah glances around the cabana. "I haven't been in here in ages."

Holly, too, looks around as if she's never done so before. "It's great that you have your darkroom and Daniel has his own space, too."

Sarah looks at her sharply.

"Not that I've seen your darkroom. I just mean—"

"Is there something you want to tell me, Holly?"

Holly's heart beats so loudly she's sure Sarah can hear it. Then she has an idea. "I'm the worst at keeping secrets," she says.

Sarah's eyes narrow to slits. "What do you mean?"

Holly doesn't want to be in the claustrophobic cabana anymore and needs a minute to formulate exactly what she's going to say. "Can we talk about this inside?"

"I already drove twenty minutes back here because Jacob left Mr. Blinkers in his room, and he wants to show his cousins the toy." She gives Holly a pointed look. "He loves that bunny almost as much as he loves you."

"I love him, too." She does, and she'd better think of something right away or she's going to lose everything.

She follows Sarah into the kitchen, where Sarah stands in front of her and crosses her arms. She looks scared and angry.

"What do you need to tell me?" She pulls at the skin on her neck.

"Daniel wanted it to be a surprise." Holly lifts her shoulders sheepishly, like she does when Alexis is mad at her and she's trying to be cute. "He's taking you away to a hotel overnight this week. Just the two of you."

Sarah drops her hand and exhales. Her eyes sparkle. "That's the big secret?"

"Yup. We arranged it all. I'll stay with Jacob, and you two can go have a romantic dinner, get a massage, go shopping, whatever you wish." She giggles, and for a second, she almost believes her lie is true.

Sarah squints. "What does that have to do with the cabana?"

She swallows. "I needed the reservation number to check the

details for Daniel while you were out. That's all." She hopes to hell Sarah doesn't ask to see that number.

"And the cramps?"

"Those are real. But much better now."

Sarah shakes her head. Holly can see her relaxing by the moment. It's working. She's back on track. "Was the hotel your idea or Daniel's?" Sarah asks. There's an edge to it, though.

Holly clears her throat and says, "Daniel's. Totally his idea."

Sarah's face breaks into a grin. "I doubt that. But thank you. We haven't been anywhere alone since Jacob was born, and I wouldn't have even considered it if you weren't living here. Or if I didn't trust you."

Sarah eyes her carefully. Is she forgiven? Holly can't tell, but she's proud of herself for coming up with a brilliant lie, and fast. A night away with her husband so they can reconnect—ingenious. Now she'll just have to inform Daniel.

"Let Daniel tell you his own way, okay? Don't mention it. He's really excited. And Sarah? I'm so lucky to have you. I'd never do anything to jeopardize that."

Sarah nods and reaches out a hand. "Sorry for jumping to the wrong conclusions. It's a bad habit of mine."

"No worries. I know what it looked like. But that's not it. That's not it at all. You can trust me."

"I know that," Sarah says. "And I'm grateful, more than you can possibly know."

———

"Are you sure this is okay? Daniel and I can cancel," Sarah says nervously late Friday afternoon, half an hour before she and Daniel are set to leave for the Pacific Rim hotel. "He's probably too tired from his conference anyway. He got back so late from Calgary last night, and he's still working in the cabana now."

Holly's stomach drops. Sarah and Daniel *have* to leave the house.

And even though she's not exactly sure where Daniel was last night because he turned off his secret phone, she highly doubts he was at a conference in Calgary. "It's fine. He needs this as much as you do. Jacob and I will have a blast, and you deserve a night away."

It's been two days since Holly set up this romantic getaway. Daniel had no choice but to get on board once she told him he was taking Sarah away or she'd tell her everything. Luckily, Sarah never said a thing to Daniel about finding her in the cabana.

Daniel was not eager to leave Forest View or Holly alone in the house. He clearly doesn't trust her, doesn't like that she has information that could hurt him. But he's kept his promise to let her stay indefinitely, so she'll maintain her end of their deal and stay quiet about his illegal gambling activities. For now.

It doesn't solve his debts to Charlie, though. But tonight, she'll put her plan into action; this night alone in the house is the perfect time to execute it. She can turn the tables if Sarah and Daniel get on the road already.

So, while Sarah's face lights up with pleasure as she spoons home-made chili for Jacob's dinner into Tupperware, Daniel texts Holly from his secret phone for the third time today.

Unknown: Please don't do anything
stupid. Stay out of it.

Holly writes back quickly: *Give me some credit.*

The less Daniel knows, the less he has to lie about. Alexis, though, is an issue. She's already invited herself over after Jacob's in bed. Holly had to tell her the Goldmans were going away for the night because her stepsister wanted to have dinner. Holly can't say no to her again. So, she has to get the timing of both her visitors right tonight. Not that Charlie has any idea yet that he's coming over. But soon, he will. And if Holly knows anything about this creep, it's that he won't be able to resist her spontaneous invitation.

Sarah looks so happy. Her platinum hair flows over her shoulders and the coral sundress Holly suggested she buy hugs her curves. She seems like a different woman. But she's still the same Sarah because a drop of chili drips on the dress, and she doesn't notice.

"Daniel and I haven't had a romantic getaway in years." Sarah puts the Tupperware on the counter next to the five other ones, as though she's leaving for a week, and glances at her watch. "Ugh. Daniel's got to finish up his work. I don't want to get stuck in traffic."

Holly nods, but outrage burns a path up her chest. What's he up to in there?

Just then, he strolls into the kitchen like he's king of the castle. But Holly notices how his hair stands up as if he's been wringing his fingers through it. This plan of hers tonight has to pan out.

"Thanks for looking after the little fella while we're gone, Holly. If anything happens, you have our cells. Don't answer the door after dark," he adds.

"She's twenty-two, Daniel, not fifteen," Sarah says.

He laughs, but it sounds fake. "I know. But you never know who might be out there." He locks eyes with Holly.

"Dan, stop scaring her." Sarah playfully shoves his arm.

Holly holds his stare. He's warning her not to take any action without consulting him. Men. They always think they know the right thing to do. But he's wrong in this case. And Holly is so sick of being underestimated.

"We'd better get on the road." Sarah points to the list of numbers stuck to the fridge. "We'll be reachable, of course, but Nathan's and my mom's numbers are here, hospital, Jacob's pediatrician, and poison control."

Daniel puts his hand on Sarah's back and steers her out of the kitchen. "Holly's got it covered," he says before heading to Jacob, who's been in the living room organizing all the board games he wants to play with Holly tonight. "Bye, buddy. Be good for Holly." He ruffles Jacob's hair.

Sarah joins them. "Bye, Jake. We love you and we'll only be gone one night." She hugs him tightly.

"Bye," Jacob says, pulling away from Sarah and turning immediately to Holly. "Candy Land first? Hedbanz? That one's really fun. Or Twister? You can spin the wheel for me."

Sarah laughs. "Well, it looks like you two are all set." She kisses Jacob while Daniel drags their bags to the front door, where Holly follows them.

"Have fun!" Holly calls when Sarah and Daniel finally exit the house and get in Daniel's car. She doesn't close the door until she's sure they've driven off.

Then she locks it and focuses solely on Jacob until his bedtime. He's so wired, though, from the games and excitement of staying overnight alone with Holly that it takes ages to calm him down enough to get him in pajamas. At 9:00 p.m. Holly finally tucks him in.

"Stay until I'm sleeping, Holly?"

The soft, sweet way he says her name evokes a flood of love. "Of course! Close your eyes, and I'll be right here."

She cuddles up next to him, his little body firm against hers, Mr. Blinkers in his arms. She watches his eyelids jump until his breathing is steady and he's fast asleep. She's going to help him grow up to be a decent man who cares more about family than money.

Once he's soundly asleep, she goes downstairs to the living room. She stands in the center of it, her eyes tracking the nanny cam in the black vase on the mantel. She doesn't know if Sarah even watches the feed, but whatever Sarah might see on this camera, she wants it to look totally normal. Which means she has to move the vase. She walks normally around the room, but then gets beside the vase where she can't be filmed. She crouches so she's under the little eye, reaches up her hand, and turns the vase around so the camera faces toward the wall instead of into the room.

Satisfied, she straightens and looks at the framed photo of Sarah, Daniel, and Jacob in front of the Stanley Park Seawall, hanging next to the sliding doors to the pool. They're such a beautiful family, grinning at the camera, Sarah and Daniel with one hand each on Jacob's shoulder, probably trying to hold him in place for the shot. On closer inspection, though, Sarah doesn't look happy. Her eyes are clouded with the same insecurity Holly saw after Sarah came home with her new hairstyle.

"I've got you, Sarah," Holly whispers to the photo, imagining that the next shot will have her in it. And Sarah's smile will be genuine.

Glancing quickly at the time on the round, silver clock on the wall, she gets busy finding the best spot for her phone to both record and be inobtrusive enough that Charlie won't notice it. She smiles when she sees the small plant on the teal table just behind the couch, between the living room and kitchen. She props her phone against the black pot, runs back to the middle of the room, and lays on the floor with only her hips lifted above the hardwood. She tests it. Perfect. Her face won't be visible, but the camera will catch Charlie in all his glory.

She sends a text.

> Holly: I'm alone at Daniel Goldman's house.
> No one will be here all night. I can't stop
> thinking about you. Come over.

Thirty minutes later, it's done. She has exactly what she wanted—Charlie on film doing what disgusting, basic men like him can't seem to resist. This is precisely what she needs. He will forgive all of Daniel's debts and set him free. He will do it, or else.

CHAPTER TWENTY-FIVE

SARAH

Now

I'm relieved Daniel and Jacob are outside playing in the sandbox and can't see me staring at the red triangle on the video I've been sent by a private caller. My heart is beating so fast, and yet I can't press play. I don't know what fresh hell I'm on the verge of witnessing. I walk to the powder room to the right of the front hall, lock the door, and sit on the closed toilet seat.

Then, finally, my hands sweaty with trepidation, I press my finger to the screen.

Immediately, trepidation turns to confusion. The setting is our living room on Cliffside. I've watched this horrifying scene with Holly play out before; I never want to watch it again. It was the moment I knew that I couldn't trust her at all, that I should have trusted only the feeling in my gut that told me all along: Holly is unhinged and dangerous.

I recorded the video on one of my two nanny cams in the living room, the sole time Daniel and I left Jacob and Holly alone overnight and stayed at a hotel for a romantic getaway. When we came home, giddy and connected for the first time in months, Holly was pure innocence, so happy to see me, telling me how great the night had gone with Jacob. She lied right to my face, and I never suspected a thing until later, when I checked the nanny cam apps on my phone.

I had set up two cameras—one in the black vase on the mantel; the other in the round silver clock mounted on the wall to the right of the television. Strangely, the one in the black vase got moved and recorded only the white wall behind the mantel, but the camera in the clock filmed everything that went down in my living room that night.

I expected to see Holly eating ice cream on the couch and watching a movie after Jacob was in bed. Instead, I saw her screwing some old man on my living room floor while my son was asleep upstairs.

I didn't recognize the man, maybe in his fifties, kneeling behind Holly, pumping with grotesque force. His craggy face was a primal growl, wedding ring glinting in the light and gold Rolex banging against her skin as he dug his fingers into her slim hips. Holly's face was off-screen, but I could clearly see her reflection in the sliding doors to our pool. And I knew the lines and angles of her body, because I'd photographed them, coveted them.

It wasn't just the fact that Holly was having sex in my house with a man even older than her father that disgusted and enraged me. It was the look on her face—satisfied, victorious, and smug. Like someone whose plan is coming together.

After that, I had dark thoughts, darker than I could ever have imagined. Is that what she did, wending her way into people's hearts and families only to tear them apart? It didn't seem far-fetched.

I called Daniel right after watching the footage. I pulled him from his golf game, telling him we had to talk. Holly was out grocery shopping, with my car, which I'd lent her, like the clueless moron I am. Jacob was home with me. Daniel said he'd come meet me right away, and I asked our neighbor Nora to babysit Jacob for a little while, which he was desperately unhappy about.

I met Daniel at Capilano River park. We sat on a bench, and I admitted that I'd placed two nanny cams in the living room before Holly came for her interview and had kept them on the whole summer.

"You were keeping tabs on her with nanny cams?" He looked shocked, maybe a little appalled at my behavior. There was no way I would ever tell him about the photos I took of Holly in her bedroom. Until I saw the video, I didn't know that my photos probably captured a young woman with a man who was old enough to be her father, maybe even older.

"It's normal, Dan, to put in nanny cams. Tons of parents do it," I explained. Then I showed him the video.

He watched a few seconds, then pushed the phone away. "I don't want to see that," he said.

But I told him he had to look because I wanted to know who the man was. He took the phone back and focused on the man's face.

"I don't recognize him," he said. "Thank god."

He then sloughed the video off as the thoughtless act of a young woman who had a whole house to herself for the night. He went so far as to compare it to when we first started dating.

"Don't you remember when my parents caught us having sex in their garage?"

"Are you kidding me? This man is her father's age. And this was in our house! Our son was right upstairs!"

"I admit it was stupid, but she's young and foolish. People make mistakes. There's no point rubbing it in her face."

"Fine. But we can't have her in our house anymore. I don't trust her. I can't believe she'd do this, but here it is—the proof."

"I just don't think it's the end of the world."

I couldn't believe my ears. Was he actually fine with the babysitter fucking an old man in our living room while our son was upstairs? Who was this man I'd married? That's when I decided to question him outright. "Are you fucking her, too?" I asked, seething and scared of the answer.

Daniel's eyes practically popped out of his head. "Are you seriously asking me that? Are you insane?"

"Are you stalling instead of answering me? I've seen the way you two talk to each other and stop the second I come into the room. I'm not stupid, Dan."

He looked horrified, and his hands went up and tore through his hair the way they always do when he's nervous. "I'm not sleeping with our babysitter, Sarah."

I yanked his hands down and gripped them in mine. "Do you want to? Do you want to fuck Holly? Has she propositioned you yet? Tell me the truth."

"No! God, of course she hasn't. And I only want you. How could you possibly think otherwise?"

I wanted to believe him. I still want to. He then said that maybe Holly had some kind of schoolgirl crush or something, but even that he thought was a stretch.

"Holly isn't a schoolgirl. She's a twenty-two-year-old puppet master," I said. Then I made a decision I never thought I'd make. "Let's do it. Let's move to Toronto. I want to start again." I was petrified that maybe Dan was lying to me, that even if he and Holly hadn't done anything, that this young vixen might find her way to sleeping with my husband, something that would be very hard to do if we lived halfway across the country.

He looked at me, shocked by the change of subject but very happy about it. "Really? You're up for it? A whole new start in a new city?"

"I'm up for it," I said. "I hate this place. There's nothing here for me anyway." It wasn't exactly true. My family was here, and I'd painstakingly made our house into a home. But in that moment, all I could think about was cleaning the slate, a brand-new start with my husband and my child, away from Vancouver, and the stupid Canyon Club, the pressures of Daniel's work, and the claustrophobic house that I barely ever left. And also, Holly. The farther away, the better.

After that discussion, the whole plan was put into place. Daniel secured a private buyer so quickly, I couldn't believe it. Then it was a matter of deciding when and how to tell people—our son especially, Holly, too, and our families. Just two weeks later, we were on a plane bound for Toronto and a whole new life.

But I haven't escaped Holly. And now, as I hold this phone in my hand and watch the horrible video that I'm responsible for recording, that some weird fuck is taunting me with, I realize it's not what I think it is. Something about this video is off. I watch it again and realize what's bothering me. The man's face isn't in profile like it was in the recording I caught on the nanny cam in the silver clock on my living room wall. This video was taken straight-on, directly facing the camera, up close and personal. I can even see the wrinkles fanning the man's almost-black eyes, and the large watch face on his Rolex. But I still have no clue who he is.

And this time, Holly's face isn't visible in any way. There's no reflection of her in the sliding doors to the pool deck. I can't see the doors at all because the video appears to be taken from behind our couch, which faced the mantel and television.

This video was not shot on my hidden camera. So who shot it, and why send it to me now?

My teeth chatter. There are only two possibilities I can think of to explain this. Holly has unfinished business with me—or the man in the video knows I've seen him and is coming for me.

I no longer know if Holly is acting alone or how much danger we might be in. The property manager told me a man was in our house before we moved in. The door was open when we arrived. It wasn't even locked.

I'm going to break if I don't tell Daniel everything—the nights I watched Holly through her bedroom window, the photos I locked away in my darkroom, the other texts I've received, and now this recording.

So, when my husband and son walk through the sliding doors from the backyard, both covered in sand, I hand Jacob a pad of construction paper and some markers.

"Jake, honey, Daddy and I have to talk in private for a bit. Can you go up to your room and make Cody a feel-better-soon card?"

"Are we going to see him?"

"Soon, I hope."

Concern creases Daniel's forehead. "Come on, Jake. I'll get you set up in your room with the paper and markers. What color is Cody's favorite, do you think?"

They leave the room, and my chest tightens. I'm scared Daniel's never going to look at me the same way again.

A few minutes later, after I've bitten off all my fingernails on the living room couch, he finds me and sits down beside me. "What's going on, Sarah?"

I take my phone from my pocket and angle it toward him. "Someone sent me this today. You have to watch it." I press play.

Daniel looks revolted. Tiny beads of sweat have appeared at his temples. I make him watch right to the end. Then I explain that it's not from the nanny cam, that it's shot from a different angle and position in the living room on Cliffside.

"An anonymous texter sent this to me, Daniel. Why?"

He shakes his head. "I . . . I have no idea. Do you think Holly filmed this herself?"

"I do." I play the video again, pausing on the man's smug face, salt-and-pepper hair brushed back from a wide forehead. I shudder. "I know you didn't recognize him in the first video. But do you recognize him now?"

Daniel examines the still and shakes his head. "I can't place him."

"He's wealthy, judging by the Rolex on his wrist. A member of the Canyon Club, maybe? Is there a directory with photos?"

"No. Memberships are private."

I slump. I was hoping Daniel would finally realize who this man is. I can't bear this constant dread, the feeling of hiding something from Daniel. It's time to come clean.

"I have to tell you something," I say. And with my voice cracking, I pour out everything, from my late nights taking photos of Holly through her window, hiding them in a drawer in my darkroom, all the menacing texts I've received. I also tell him about angling the camera into Tara's window, the discovery that she's Cody's aunt, not his mother, and my worry about what crime Cody's father, Nick Conroy, committed. Whether Conroy is really Nick's last name and if he's even Cody's father at all.

Daniel's silent, his face slack with disbelief, and maybe disgust.

"Please say something," I implore him.

"You photographed our babysitter without her consent?" he says.

"They weren't illicit shots. Not like these videos. They were tasteful and discreet. You couldn't even tell who was in her window."

"But she didn't consent, Sarah. She never said you could take those pictures."

I rub my stomach, which is tied in a knot. "You're right," I say. "It was so wrong of me. But the pictures are gone. I destroyed them all, every last one."

Daniel looks at me, his face a mask of confusion. "I just can't believe you would do that." Then he takes my hand. "Sarah, I'm sorry I haven't been the husband you want me to be." His eyes film. "But that's no excuse for the photos. Or the nanny cams."

He's looking at me so intently that I lay it all on the line. "When I realized I could see into Holly's window with my camera and caught this young, attractive woman with a man I assumed was around her age, I couldn't look away. Not because of the sex. I wanted to capture that electricity, the endless possibilities in front of her. The audacity she had to sneak him into her room in her parents' mansion. I didn't know then that I was taking pictures of an older man with a younger woman. It was only when I saw the nanny cam video that I linked the two events together."

I hesitate, but I've come too far to stop now. "I guess I started watching her out of a kind of curiosity and envy for everything she was. I thought I was watching a young woman with her boyfriend. And then when she was living with us, I watched her because of you."

"Because you thought I was sleeping with her?"

I take my hand from his and cover my face. "Yes. I saw how you were together. Secretive, standing close and whispering, and then when I found her in your cabana alone, I thought maybe she was waiting for you in there." I start to cry, all my fears, guilt, and regret bubbling to the surface and spilling out.

Daniel's voice is low and hard when he asks, "When did you find her in my cabana?"

"That night we went to Nathan's and she stayed behind. Then you both surprised me with the hotel trip—" I stop because something has just occurred to me. "It was her idea for the hotel trip, right?"

Daniel's so quiet I can hear him breathe, staccato and sharp.

"Dan?"

"I wish I'd thought of it." His eyes are watery, too.

I brace myself. I'm scared, so scared that I was right all along.

He looks me straight in the eye. "I didn't sleep with Holly." He clenches and unclenches his jaw. "But she did come on to me. And when you showed me that video and wanted to move, I decided not to tell you, because what was the point? We were leaving her—everything—behind."

"I asked you so many times! You made me think I was crazy!" I'm yelling now. "I let her stay with Jacob the day she left him all alone in the house because you convinced me I was overreacting about how vicious she is!"

He winces. "Because I didn't want to upset you."

"Daniel, Holly is *terrorizing* me. Can't you see that she sent the video to show me you're still her next conquest? She's watching us, maybe has access to our house. She might even be getting our neighbors to watch us for her. You still don't seem to get how treacherous and devious she is."

He holds up his hands. "You're right. I don't. I don't really get it."

He looks exhausted and drawn, but there's something else on his face that I don't like, that I can't read.

"You're old enough to be her father, Daniel," I say.

"We never had an affair, okay? Nothing's quite so simple."

He's right about that. Nothing with Holly was ever simple.

"She's trying to tell me something, Dan, with her texts." I scroll through the three I've received from the private caller.

I see you.

Missing something?

I know everything. Do you?

Then I inform him of what Jacob told me in the kitchen before Daniel got home. "She said, *Tell your mommy to watch out for herself.* That's what she said, Dan."

Daniel closes his eyes, then opens them a few seconds later, drilling a look into mine. "Did you put cameras inside this house, Sarah?"

"What? No! Of course not. Why would you think that?"

"Because you've done it before. I think it's a reasonable question."

I fiddle with my engagement ring. "I made a huge mistake photographing Holly. I know that."

He glances at my ring, then says, "I made a huge mistake not telling you that Holly came on to me. I'm sorry."

My phone buzzes in my hand. Daniel and I exchange a frightened look. I can't take much more of this.

But this time it is Tara.

Tara: We'll be home in twenty minutes.
You can come over then.

And then another text from her comes through.

We need to talk.

CHAPTER TWENTY-SIX

HOLLY

Before

Charlie left fifteen minutes ago. Holly listened as his car drove away, then she peeked in on Jacob, who was sound asleep, curled around Mr. Blinkers. She walked quietly back downstairs, got her phone from the small table behind the couch, and watched the video of herself. It was perfect. Her face wasn't in the frame, but his was. Totally distinguishable. Watching the video, though, makes her want to heave. The way he grabbed her, pushed into her like an animal. It suddenly makes her so angry. He thinks he controls the narrative, just like her father and Lisette think they control her. Well, not anymore. She makes a few edits to the clip to erase a strand of her auburn hair that flashes across the frame. She doesn't want anyone but him to see this, and she's not going to send it to Charlie yet. She can't make any rash moves without thinking it all through first.

Wired with nervous energy, she paces back and forth in the basement, past Sarah's darkroom. No light bleeds from under it, and Sarah and Daniel aren't home to catch her. Alexis isn't coming until after 10:30 p.m. because she's having dinner with John and Lisette at the Canopy Crescent house. Holly has about twenty minutes to poke around.

Still, she hesitates before turning the knob. But she has to see what Sarah's working on.

Holly enters quickly and quietly, closing the door behind her. The space is so dark. She pulls the string on the bulb, filling the room with a red glow, then taps her phone flashlight, thankful no photos hang from the white clips above the sink.

All the drawers on the metal filing cabinet at the back of the room are locked, but there's nothing to interrupt her as she tries to open them. The nail file slides easily into the lock on the top drawer. Nervous and excited, Holly slides the drawer open to find stacks of black binders, lined up in rows. Holly pulls out the binder to the far right and flips to the first sleeve. Film negatives are encased in little plastic squares. She sits cross-legged on the concrete floor, lays her phone next to her, and holds the negatives close to her eyes. They're all of Jacob diving into the pool; the haunting shadow of his body in contrast to the sunlight beaming down on him is remarkable.

The next binder holds gorgeous photos of Capilano River park. Holly takes out the smallest binder, tucked right at the back of the drawer. She expects negatives in the sleeves, but these are developed photos. Developed photos of her.

The first few, of Holly on the pool deck and in the water, are innocent. But the rest make Holly gasp out loud. There's Holly's house, the floodlights bright under an eerie orange moon. Another photo of Holly's bedroom window, the curtains drawn together, but they're so thin she can see her pale pink headboard, recognizes her own shape on the bed framed by the window. In yet another, through the gauzy material that acts as more of a filter than a shield, she sees herself, naked, leaning against her pillows, looking at a man, also naked—Luke—blurry and inconsequential, at the foot of her bed. Neither of their faces can be seen, and even their bodies are obscured, but she remembers the moment exactly.

Sarah's been photographing her since the day they met. This photo was taken the same night she'd started working for the Goldmans, when she'd invited Luke over as a final thank-you for hiring Alexis, even though she didn't want him in her bed anymore.

There are other photos, too, taken through the window well in the Goldmans' basement, of Holly asleep in the bedroom she's claimed as her own. Here, she's fully clothed, again her face not visible, but there's an intimacy to the shots that's impossible to ignore, and the subject is *always* Holly.

What the fuck is going on? Why would Sarah take these without her consent? Holly covers her mouth with her hand. She feels ill, confused as to why Sarah would invade her privacy like this.

But when she looks at the photos again, really looks at them, her shock is replaced with awe. They're beautiful—simple and classic. The shots are artistic, respectful. There's nothing salacious about them, even though they're intimate. It's as if Sarah has captured her gloom, that haunting feeling that Holly carries deep inside her wherever she goes.

Like a lightning bolt, the truth hits her. This isn't an invasion of privacy—it's an homage. Sarah really does love her, has from the moment they met—and not in the usual way, not romantically, but in ways that she'd always hoped for. These photos are those of a mother mourning the fact that her daughter is growing up. They're her attempt to keep her close, forever.

She jumps when her phone rings. It's a call from an unknown number.

"Hello?" she whispers even though she knows there's no way that Jacob can hear her from his bed upstairs.

All she makes out on the other end of the line is breathing.

Holly's heart wallops against her rib cage. "Who is this?"

Click.

A second later, it rings again.

"What?" she asks as she answers.

All she hears is rustling and crackling.

"Daniel?" she says.

The call goes dead.

The darkroom suddenly feels claustrophobic. She slides everything back in the drawer, trying her best to return the binders to their original places, even though her hands are shaking. She locks the cabinet. She tiptoes out of the room, closing the door behind her, and makes her way upstairs. As she reaches the main floor, her phone rings again. She answers it. "Stop calling me!" she hisses.

"What?" It's Alexis, dumbfounded.

"Oh God. Sorry. I was getting creepy hang-ups before. I didn't check who was calling this time."

"Creepy hang-ups? From who?"

She curses herself for worrying Alexis. "Private caller. Not sure. It doesn't matter."

"Well, I'm at the front door, so you're not alone anymore at least."

Holly exhales. She's glad Alexis is here. "I'll be right there."

When she opens the door and sees her stepsister in person for the first time in weeks, Holly grabs her in a tight hug and presses her face into Alexis's brown waves. She's missed her.

Alexis holds her, then releases her to look around the warm, inviting space. She lets out a low whistle. "Wow. This place is nice. Feels homey."

"It is. I like it here." She leads Alexis into the living room and points to the couch. "Sit. Tell me everything you've been up to."

Alexis flops on the couch and leans her head back. "Well, dinner with John and Mom wasn't the same without you. No one even mentions you, but it's all we're thinking about."

Suddenly, having Alexis here, in Sarah's home, feels weird and uncomfortable. She didn't invite her here to be reminded of her mistakes and flaws.

Alexis must notice Holly's discomfort because she turns to look at her. "Sorry. Should I not mention them?"

Holly shrugs like she doesn't care. "It's fine. I have another family now."

Her stepsister sits up straight. "Huh?"

She backtracks, fast. "I mean, I'm living and working here now. Sarah and Daniel want me to be their full-time nanny."

Alexis draws back in surprise. "Is that what you want?"

"More than anything."

Alexis chews on her lip. "Holly, I have to be honest, I don't get it. I know there's a rift with your dad and my mom, but it doesn't have to be like this. Maybe you don't have to go back to medical school, and you could do sales on a more part-time basis. I could talk to them. I could say that—"

"Stop." Holly feels queasy. She can't bear to hear another word. "I'm never going back there, Alexis. Accept it or don't, but this is me now. And this is where I'm living."

Alexis visibly bristles at Holly's sharp tone. "I'm not judging you. But you haven't been yourself, not since you started working here. I—" She puts her hand on Holly's bare leg. "Are you sure you're okay? You're all jittery."

Holly stops her leg from shaking. "I'm happy, Lex. Really. You're reading into things too much." She forces out a laugh. "I'm not going to be a babysitter forever, but I'm only twenty-two. I have time to fig-ure out what I want to do with my life."

Alexis nods, but she doesn't look convinced.

"You want something to drink?" Holly offers, jumping from the couch. "Come to the kitchen with me."

She doesn't want to sit next to Alexis, to be cross-examined like this.

Alexis smiles, seeming to follow her lead and pretend everything is okay. "So, what are Sarah and Daniel like?" she asks, glancing at one of Sarah's family shots on the wall as they walk to the kitchen. "He's handsome, for an old man." She looks pointedly at Holly, who shrivels under her stepsister's watchful gaze.

"It's not like that," she snaps. "I told you, what you saw in the club parking lot? That was just dumb, okay? A one-off." She thinks of her phone sitting on the couch, the video tucked away in a folder, and she feels hot and clammy. She sticks her head in the fridge to grab them a couple of sodas, then hands one to Alexis. "I'm fine, honestly. You know, you've always been able to separate yourself from Lisette and my dad. Now I finally have the chance to do that, too."

Alexis snorts. "I didn't have much choice but to separate. I'll never be the pretty debutante."

Holly searches her stepsister's face for hurt but doesn't find any. "Trust me, you're better off," she says. She gets a bag of tortilla chips from the cupboard, fills a bowl with them, then carries everything back to the living room, Alexis trailing behind her.

Back on the couch, they both curl their legs under themselves. Holly tries to steer the conversation to safe territory. She asks Alexis about her dream of working in a medical clinic one day; Alexis asks about Jacob. Then Holly finds a rom-com and that ends the conversation. They both sink into the movie, until finally, at 1:00 a.m., when the movie's ended, and she's half-asleep, she yawns. "I'm sorry. I'm exhausted."

Alexis fiddles with her necklace. "I don't like leaving you here all alone."

"I'm a big girl. And I'm not alone. Jacob's upstairs. I really appreciate you coming over. It was nice to have your company."

Alexis gets up, and Holly walks her to the door and hugs her, holding her stepsister a beat longer than usual. They have a shared history, a family only the two of them can understand.

Right before she closes the door, Alexis turns around, the moonlight creating a halo above her head. "No one will ever love you like I do," she says. She touches her pendant.

Holly touches her back. "I love you, too."

After she slides the chain over the front door, she leans against it, relieved that Alexis is gone. She turns out all the lights then changes into pajama shorts and a white tank top, washes her face, and tiptoes up the stairs. Sarah's bedroom door is open.

Holly lies on top of Sarah's bed, careful not to muss the pretty covers. In her bedside table, among a package of tissues, a bottle of lotion, and a paperback, she finds a photo of Sarah and Daniel in front of a birthday cake with Sarah's name on it. They both look young and hopeful. This must have been before Jacob was born, before Sarah lost their daughter in a miscarriage. The light from the candles makes Sarah's face glow, and Daniel is gazing at her with adoration. She gently holds the photo in her hand. Holly will bring them back to the happy couple they once were. She'll make them a true family again.

Her phone buzzes. At first Holly's nervous it's the prank caller, but it's a text from Sarah.

Sarah: How's everything at home?

Holly: Perfect. Jacob went to bed at 9:00, and I'm going to bed in a minute. Don't worry about a thing. How's the hotel?

It takes at least a minute before Sarah responds with a smile emoji. Holly laughs. It's the first time Sarah's ever used one, and it probably took her a while to find it on her keyboard.

Holly can't resist texting back: *Love you!*

Sarah's response fills Holly with a sense of peace, of belonging, she's never experienced.

You're the best! ♥♥♥

Three heart emojis. They're silly, really, but for Holly, they're everything. Sarah loves her. Three hearts is proof. And Holly can't ever imagine her life without Sarah in it.

CHAPTER TWENTY-SEVEN

SARAH

Now

I'm not sure I'm up for more stress today after unloading all my secrets and darkest thoughts to Daniel. But for Jacob and myself, I have to face Tara.

"We can go see Cody now," I tell him, and he clomps down the stairs too fast. "Go to the bathroom and put your shoes on while I get the cookies, okay?"

Jacob runs off. Daniel and I head to the kitchen, and he puts a hand on my arm. "Before you go, I just want to say that what happened in Vancouver is over. Holly's gone. And you were right. She wasn't trustworthy, and you knew it way before I did. She left Jacob alone in the house. She tried to break up our family. But she has nothing to do with us anymore. Whoever sent that video and those texts, it doesn't matter. They can't hurt us because neither of us was involved and we're not there anymore."

I nod, but I'm still scared.

Those videos were taken in our house, and even though I destroyed the nanny cams and deleted the video apps from my phone, they could still be out there.

He laces his fingers with mine, lifting my hand to his mouth for a kiss. "I love you. We're safe here. I know it."

I exhale. He wants to take care of me. That's something. So why isn't that more satisfying?

Because I can't explain the agitated energy I feel coiling through his body. That's why.

But we can't discuss it further because Jacob yells from the front hall, "I'm ready!"

"Can you prepare dinner while we're at Tara's?" I ask Daniel.

"Sure."

He kisses me again, holding my face in his hands, then Jacob and I leave. I nervously carry the plate of cookies I made for Cody as Jacob and I cross the lawn.

When the door opens, I'm immediately sympathetic. Tara looks awful. Her hair is a mess; her normally glowing skin is dull.

"How's Cody?" I ask.

"Tired, but he's okay. The swelling might take a couple of days to go down."

"I'm so glad." I clumsily hand her the platter. "No nuts or sugar. I promise."

She gives me a wan grimace and moves out of the way so we can enter her home. When she sees how scared Jacob is, she crouches in front of him. "It's not your fault, Jacob. Cody told me that Skylar gave him the chocolate, and he knows he shouldn't have accepted it."

Jacob takes his thumb out of his mouth. "I forgot to tell him not to eat the chocolate. I'm sorry." He thrusts the card he made at her. "Can I give this to Cody?" He anxiously hops up and down, trying to peer around Tara to see where Cody is. Tara takes the red construction paper card and opens it to a very well-drawn basketball and a race car that looks more like a hot dog.

"Cody will love this beautiful card. He's in the living room."

Jacob takes off to join his friend, who's lying down on the couch. I watch Jacob give Cody the card and sit beside him. He still looks worried, which is understandable because when Cody turns his head to look at Tara, I can see how swollen his eyes and lips are.

"Can I say hello to Cody?" I ask almost as nervously as Jacob. I have no idea why Tara has been so interested in us, why she lied about her relationship to Cody, but he's a sweet boy who could have died. My heart clenches at the thought.

She nods. "I'll take this plate to the kitchen while you do that."

I walk over to the couch. Cody is puffy and exhausted, his face washed out.

"Hey, Cody. How are you feeling?" I ask softly.

He attempts a smile. "Okay. I'm happy Jacob came over."

Jacob bounces at the end of the couch, and I give him a stern look. "Cody needs quiet time, so no jumping, okay?"

Cody laughs. "Jacob doesn't know how to be quiet."

I laugh, too, because it's true.

Tara comes into the living room. "Let's go talk," she says to me, then, to the kids, "Boys, we'll be out front." She leads me through the front hall to the entrance, where we step outside onto the porch landing, just us women lingering in a strained social bubble all our own.

I shuffle uncomfortably. "I'm so sorry about Cody. God, it must have been awful to get that call from the school. Any mother would be out of her mind with fear."

We lock gazes, the shiny façade gone. "Is there anything else you want to say to me, Sarah?" she asks.

I chew the inside of my cheek then spit it out. "I know you're not Cody's mother."

She nods slowly. "I'm not sure why it's any of your business, but you're right, I'm not Cody's mother. He's my brother's son." She holds up a finger. "Cody doesn't need to hear all of this. Let me close the door, and we can sit out here."

She clicks the door shut, and we settle in her light blue Adirondack chairs. I wait for her to speak first.

"You're always looking at me, watching me like you don't trust me," she says. "Why?"

"Excuse me?" I reply. "You keep walking right into my house, calling my husband Danny, and skulking in my yard at night."

"What? I've never been in your yard uninvited."

"Well, someone was. And you lied about being Cody's mother."

She bristles. "No, not exactly. I never once said I was his mother. Haven't you noticed he calls me Tara? For someone so neurotic, you sure do miss a lot."

I scoff out loud.

She stands. "We need wine for this conversation. Rosé, right?"

She goes inside without another word, then returns a minute later with two plastic cups plus a wine bottle, which she sets on the ground. "My brother, Nick? He's a disaster."

"He's in jail," I say, since we're laying it all on the table.

"I wish he were in jail," Tara says. "That would make everything easier."

Now I'm confused. "Cody told Jacob his dad is in jail."

Tara sighs. "I'm not surprised he said that. Nick has been in and out of Cody's life since he was born, disappearing for months at a time." She reaches for the wine bottle, pours us each a cup, and hands me one. "Nick's an alcoholic and drug addict who's had every job you can imagine, never lasting long, and while he has been in jail a few times, he's not in there now. Who knows where he is? Cody's mom took off right after he was born. I'm the only stability Cody has."

"So, Cody doesn't see his dad?"

She takes a sip from her glass. "Not anymore. Nick actually got clean for a few months, but then he emptied my wallet, stole a bunch of Cody's toys and games, and disappeared. That was about six months ago." She looks over at the chimes whistling in the wind. "I have an appointment with a new custody lawyer on the twenty-third."

September twenty-third, the date marked with a red "X" on her fridge calendar. I feel terrible. And maybe Tara's right. Maybe I am paranoid, because I clearly got everything about her and Cody wrong.

"I'm really sorry about . . . watching you, about doubting you. It's just . . . there was a problem before with Jacob's former babysitter back in Vancouver, and I think she's been sending me these weird texts. Then when I saw your necklace from Unique, she had one from there, too. I guess I jumped to a few conclusions."

"I guess you did. By the way, that necklace was a gift from Nick, sent to me with an apology when he was in rehab. I should throw it away. But he's my brother, you know?"

"I get it," I say.

The window facing the front of the house is open, and from inside, I can hear the boys talking quietly. Tara and I are neighbors, and maybe we're starting to be honest with each other for the first time.

"I know this sounds crazy, but have you ever seen a young woman, twenty-two, long auburn hair, lurking around my house?" I ask.

She shakes her head. "The only weirdo I've seen around here is that dude across the street. I think he's harmless, though."

I sip my wine. "I met him. Ezra. He says he's 'neighborhood watch.'"

She huffs. "Neighborhood peeper, more like it."

I grip my cup and look Tara in the eye. "Someone hid cameras in our house," I say.

Tara's green eyes widen. "Come again?"

I nod. "I found them the first day we arrived. And that babysitter back in Vancouver? Let's just say our relationship ended very badly, and I realized things about her too late. I watched her, too. But with her, I actually saw things . . ."

Tara leans in. "What kind of things?"

"She's a sexual manipulator. I caught her on my nanny cam having sex with an old man in my house."

Tara's mouth hangs open.

"Yeah. While she was looking after Jacob overnight."

Tara shakes her head in disbelief. "But why would she be tracking you now?"

I shrug my shoulders. "I have no idea. I'm probably just overthinking and reading things wrong. Seems I have a habit of doing that."

Suddenly, Tara turns to her front window. "You don't think there could be cameras in my house, do you?"

"Don't worry. I already checked," I say.

She laughs, and so do I. "I thought you were stalking me," I admit. "I don't know why, but that's what I thought."

"It's okay. I thought you were a snoop. Turns out, I was right." She raises her cup in a toast. "We're quite the pair."

And we laugh again, but then stop to look at Ezra's house across the street. "Seriously, though, how do you know Ezra didn't put those cameras in your house? He's totally creepy. Maybe we should call the police."

"Daniel already has. They can't exactly arrest someone for looking creepy and wearing tan pants."

"True," she agrees. "This has been quite a fucking day." She places her cup on the ground and reaches out her hand. "I'm Tara Conroy. I'm Cody's aunt. It's really nice to properly get to know you."

I take her hand in mine. "I'm Sarah Goldman. And sometimes I feel like the worst mother in the world."

CHAPTER TWENTY-EIGHT

HOLLY

Before

It's midafternoon on Saturday, and Holly's had three cups of coffee. She couldn't sleep after Alexis left last night. All she could think about is how she's now in possession of a video that could ruin Charlie's life forever and fix everything for the Goldmans.

Sarah and Daniel will be back from the hotel any minute. Holly's been forcing herself to stay alert through waffles for breakfast, a morning swim race, leftover chili for lunch, and now another game of Candy Land, which has to be the most boring game ever created. But Jacob loves it, judging by the huge grin on his face every time he wins.

Just as Jacob's about to beat her for the sixth time, the front door opens.

"We're back!" Daniel calls out.

"Daddy!" Jacob runs first to Daniel, throwing himself at his father's legs.

Holly follows him to the front door, where Daniel laughs, hugging his son. Sarah's face falls when she sees her son run to his father first instead of her. But then Jacob untangles himself and throws himself at his mother's legs.

Sarah pulls him into a warm embrace. "So, everything went well?" she asks, kissing Jacob's head.

"All according to plan," Holly says to Sarah but locks eyes with Daniel. He pales immediately and quickly looks away, bending to unzip a suitcase.

"Here you go, buddy." He hands Jacob a Captain America action figure.

Jacob snatches for it. "Thank you!"

"It's from Mommy, too."

Jacob wraps his arms around Sarah's waist, kissing her.

"I missed you, Jake." She smiles at Holly.

"Did you miss me, too?" Holly asks.

"Of course," Sarah says.

Sarah is glowing. She's wearing a white dress she must have bought at the hotel. It's amazing what one night can accomplish. Sarah looks beautiful and refreshed, which is exactly what Holly hoped for.

Sarah picks up the handle of her suitcase. "I'm going to unpack our clothes and throw some laundry in the wash."

Daniel takes the handle from her. "I'll take it up for you. I actually have a golf game this afternoon. I just have to change. Do you mind, Sarah?"

They grin at each other, and Sarah says, "That's fine," before kissing Daniel. "I can take my own bag." She puts her hand on Jacob's shoulder. "Let's give Holly a break, Jake. Come and sit on my bed while I unpack and tell me everything you did while Daddy and I were gone."

Holly wonders what she and Daniel talked about while they were away. It's clear something happened here. Daniel has somehow managed to get into his wife's good graces. She seems all too happy to be treated like the hired help.

Once Sarah and Jacob are upstairs, and Daniel's left the house, Holly's alone downstairs with nothing to do. Then her phone buzzes with a text from Daniel, telling her to meet him at some dive bar on Hastings Street as soon as she can. She doesn't like his tone, how he demands her to come running when he asks.

Still, she trots upstairs to Sarah's bedroom, where Jacob's sitting inside her empty suitcase. Holly laughs and asks, "Is it okay if I go out for a bit? I have a surprise for all of you tonight."

Jacob's face lights up. "A present?"

Holly laughs again. "Sort of. I'm going to make you all dinner to thank you for including me in your family." She's not a great cook, but how hard can it be to follow a recipe? She'll go to the grocery store, buy ingredients, and come home to make a family meal. After meeting Daniel, of course.

"Dinner at six? Does that work? I'll cycle to the grocery store now."

Sarah fishes her keys out of her purse on the bed. "Take my car. You don't want to drag bags back on your handlebars."

Their fingers touch when Holly takes the keys. Holly lets hers linger for a second. Then she leaves Sarah and Jacob, slides on some flip-flops, and heads to the garage. She unlocks the car, making sure the GPS in the Highlander is turned off, and uses her phone instead to drive to Hastings, where Daniel wants to meet. She pulls up to the bar, tucked between a pawnshop and an auto repair place, and parks. She makes her way inside the dark space and spots Daniel in his white polo shirt and plaid golf pants in a booth at the back next to the jukebox, under a neon Budweiser sign.

He looks so out of place. Maybe she does, too, because as she passes the bar in her designer jeans and black fitted Lululemon tank, a trio of tattooed men ogle her. Quickly, she gets to Daniel and slides into the seat across from him. He has a beer to his lips. He sips, swallows, and places the bottle on the table.

"I did what you asked," he says with no preamble. "I got you a longer stay in my home. So from now on, you need to back off when it comes to Sarah and my personal life. No more surprise stays away. And no more meddling in my finances or my family's affairs."

Her chest pricks with nervousness. She doesn't understand what he's trying to say. "You and Sarah *are* my family."

"No, Holly, we're your employers," he says gently, but it's like he's slapped her hard across the face. "And you should be home with your dad and stepmother, in medical school or wherever you want to go, doing what your father wants."

She lays a hand on the table. "You can't stop me from helping you."

Daniel stiffens and leans forward. "What are you talking about?" he hisses.

"I am part of your family now. What you do concerns me, too." She holds his stare. "And it will definitely concern Sarah."

"What are you saying, Holly?"

"Don't fuck with me."

He slumps back against the booth and moves his wedding ring back and forth. "I'm not trying to. But I do want you to simply be Jacob's babysitter from here on. No more secret talks or threats and ultimatums. I've already figured my way out of things." He rubs his chin. "Everything is going to work out fine."

Holly looks up at him and blinks. "And what about me? Can I still live with you and Sarah?"

His eyes flick to the ceiling then back to her. "You can stay in the house with us. For now."

He's being cagey, and she doesn't know why, but if she's allowed to stay, then everything will be fine. "Okay," she says. "I'll back off. For the moment."

His phone buzzes on the table. Sarah's name flashes across the screen. Daniel looks nervous, holds up a shaky finger to his lips when he answers the call.

Holly can't hear what Sarah's saying, but Daniel responds, "Hi . . . Yes, okay. Sure . . . I'll do that." He hangs up.

"What was that about?"

"Not your business. Just a family thing." He beckons for the server to bring the bill.

Holly stands up. "I promised Sarah and Jacob that I'd make them dinner. It'll look suspicious if I'm gone too long. And I have to get to the grocery store."

Again, his eyes look shifty when he says, "I'll see you later."

Holly walks out of the bar, head held high, until she gets back in the front seat of Sarah's car, where she bursts into tears. Daniel doesn't like her; that much is obvious. He's only nice to her because he's afraid of her. Her father doesn't like her, either. And is Daniel right? Is Holly just an employee to Sarah, despite all their shared confidences and special moments? Is she nothing more than a babysitter? It can't be true. She refuses to believe it. Daniel is a liar, a criminal, a man hell-bent on not getting caught.

She wipes her eyes and opens the folder on her phone where she's placed the video of Charlie. She watches it again, then emails a copy to herself. She won't send it yet. She's raging that she's put herself at risk, that she's let another man manipulate her for his gain. She wants to turn the tables. She wants to press send on the graphic, disgusting film so that Charlie sees his own perversion land in his in-box, and yet something stops her.

She's afraid. And she's ashamed.

But she'll keep it on email, just in case.

She starts the car and heads toward the grocery store. She's going to make dinner for the family. For her family. No matter what Daniel says.

CHAPTER TWENTY-NINE

SARAH

Now

I can't believe it's already the third week in September. The leaves are just starting to change into the fiery oranges and reds of fall. This weekend, Jacob and Cody are going to rake the lawns, so they can jump in the piles with Roscoe.

It's Thursday morning, and Jacob's first week of school is almost over, and Daniel's first week at the new job is nearly over, too. A new beginning, officially underway. It's been quiet on Lilac Lane, and in our house. Daniel and I have been closer ever since our honest discussion. We're talking more. He's trying. I can feel it. It's a huge relief to have my secrets laid bare, that Daniel knows everything about the photos of Holly I never should have taken, that he never did or even wanted to sleep with her, though I still don't know who's been texting me or put hidden cameras in my home. There has to be a reasonable explanation for everything. I just haven't found it yet.

Over the last few days, there haven't been any threatening texts or other strange occurrences. I haven't heard anything from Holly or seen any proof the man in the video is close by. Though I haven't been lulled into a false sense of security, it's been comforting to have Tara next door. I feel certain now that Tara's not the one I need to worry about in Blossom Court. I've moved the camera in our shared passageway back to its original position, so I'm not peering in her windows anymore.

After our heart-to-heart, and with the lies out in the open, we're forging a real friendship. Earlier this week, I even invited her over for coffee, and we discussed hiring Emily to tutor both our boys. Starting tomorrow she'll tutor them once a week. We both have the same goal: to help and protect our kids.

"Jake, time to go!" I call up the stairs, where my son is getting dressed. He bounds down the stairs too fast as usual.

Daniel's already left for work, and Jacob and I run toward Daisy Drive to catch up to Tara and Cody, who've gone ahead with Emily and Roscoe for the walk to school. Emily might not have kids of her own, but she seems to love being with ours. She's been joining us every morning this week, and it's a lovely, comforting routine, though Jacob and I usually lag behind and have to race to catch up.

I'm panting when we reach them. Tara and Emily stop to let me catch my breath. "Thank you. In your tutoring sessions, do you ever help kids with life skills? Like getting out of the house faster?" I ask Emily.

She laughs. "I can work on that with the boys if you want me to."

"Tomorrow right after school still works, right? At my place for the first time?" Tara asks Emily.

Emily nods. "Sounds great."

Tara and I smile at each other. Finally—the beginning of a real connection with an imperfect-but-trying-her-best mom like me.

We get to the school, and Jacob and Cody race to the back of the building to line up, pushing each other and laughing all the while. I wave to their teacher, Valerie, who's calmly standing at the front of the line with her clipboard, ignoring the roughhousing. I gulp my own desire to yell out a "Be careful!" to the boys.

Once the kids are safely ushered inside, Tara and I head back to Emily, who suggests a hike in the ravine. My chest warms with the genuine bond the three of us have formed. I'm building a community here, and it almost makes me forget every creepy thing that has gone on since we arrived a week ago.

"I'd love to hike the ravine, but I owe my mom a call, and calls with her are never short," I say. "She really wanted us to go back to Vancouver for Rosh Hashanah, but it wasn't a good time this year."

Roscoe pulls Emily forward, so we start to walk away from the school. She looks over her shoulder to direct a question at me. "It must be hard to be apart from your family. Do you think you'll go back to Vancouver to visit?"

"Maybe in the spring, or my family can come here. The house is big enough for all of them, though, unless we buy our own place once the lease is up."

"Maybe buy a place in Blossom Court?" Tara asks hopefully.

I'm touched. I want to stay here in Toronto, set down roots, and finally leave the summer behind. "Daniel and I would both like that. But we'll have to wait a bit longer and see how things go."

We chat all the way back to Lilac Lane, where we separate. I watch as they head off toward the ravine, the sun beaming down on them: a blond woman, a blue-haired woman, and a scrappy little dog. I watch until they vanish into the woods.

Then I enter my house, anxious as I always am at what might have happened in my absence, who might have come in, who could be lying in wait for me—inside or outside. I only breathe properly when I do a full scan of every room, and everything seems fine.

I get myself a cup of coffee from the half-filled pot, nuke it in the microwave, then sit at the kitchen table to make a phone call I'm scared to make. It's not to my mom. Even now, I don't tell the truth—not completely. The call is to someone else entirely.

Gloria Fielding answers on the first ring. "Sarah? What a nice surprise. How's Toronto?"

"Hi, Gloria. It's good. We miss everyone in Forest View, though. How are you and Stan?"

"I'm fine. Stan's fine, too. He's at work, then golfing and dinner at the club with John Monroe as usual. I swear I barely see my own husband."

"Some things never change! But I'm glad you're both well." I take a deep breath, then put my question to her as casually as I can. "Listen, I was wondering if you know how I can reach Holly, John's daughter. I've tried calling her, but no success. Jacob misses her terribly and would love to chat with her. You know, just to say hi. Transitions are hard for young ones."

"Oh, poor little guy. I'm sure he'll settle in soon, though. As far as I know, Holly's on some 'finding herself' retreat. At least that's what John told Stan. She's taking a semester off medical school." She releases a tinkly laugh. "This generation and their 'self-care.'"

I laugh as I'm expected to. "Do you know where the retreat is, by any chance?"

"Oh, I don't know. I'm sorry. John and Lisette aren't thrilled with Holly's decision not to go right back to school, so we don't talk about her much these days. You know I don't like to intrude."

"Of course." I wait a second then ask, "And her boyfriend?"

"Boyfriend?" Gloria says. "Does Holly have one?"

"Oh, I thought she did," I say. "I thought she mentioned something."

"I don't think so, but then again, what do I know?" She pauses. "Funny, I can't imagine her father letting any boy near her. That family. The company is so important to all of them, and she's been very involved on the sales side. She is a charmer, that's for sure."

I cringe. "Yes, that's definitely the right word."

Gloria laughs again. "I mean, I think she's gotten half the men at the Canyon Club to invest in Health ProX."

Gloria might have just unknowingly given me the path through the labyrinth.

We chat for another minute, then I hang up and search the Health ProX website, this time clicking through the clinical trial pages to find a list of investors. Holly's role was to snag funding, and, according to Gloria, much of her success was through the Canyon Club, where most of the members are middle-aged men, like Daniel, and even older.

I want faces and names.

But that proves frustrating and time-consuming because I have to click through PDFs of financial reports and drug trials to find corporate sponsors for each medication they've produced or that is currently being researched. I grab an envelope off the counter and jot down the drugs and names of the investors from the last year. There are ten men listed, and I know only one: Stan Fielding. He's definitely not the man in the video.

I open the video and search Google images for each of the other names to see if I can find a match. Finally, after forty-five excruciating minutes, I find a photo of a familiar, creased, tanned face, his full head of salt-and-pepper hair, and a self-important smile. Charlie Lang, a married Vancouver-based commercial property developer with two teenagers, worth close to a billion dollars. He was the man screwing Holly in my living room.

Daniel said he didn't recognize the man from the video. It's possible Charlie Lang and Daniel haven't crossed paths. Possible, but is it likely? *Stop*, I tell myself. I'm rushing to conclusions without anything to base them on.

I go to the Canyon Club website and search every photo posted there, but it's all interior shots of the decor and the pristine golf course. I head to Google and search "Canyon Club; social events" and finally I hit on images of parties, tournaments, and charity events, scanning each one for Charlie Lang. There he is. Teeing up on the course with a local politician. Clearly, he has power and influence to match his money.

If Charlie sent me this video, if he's my stalker, what does he want from me? There's only one person who can give me the answers I need.

I need to talk to Holly. Calling her didn't work, so I'll try social media. But I can't figure out how to reactivate the Instagram account Holly made for me, and I'm afraid I'll lose my nerve. I set up an entirely new account with the same name as before: Sarah Goldman Photography. I leave my bio blank.

I follow Holly, whose last photo is still the same one of the girl doing yoga on the beach. Taking a deep breath, I create a public post that I know will make Holly take notice. No photo, just words. Woman to woman. I tag her like she taught me.

Holly,
I miss you. You belong with us. You're family, and we want to keep you close.

And it's done. I wait, sick to my stomach, but also eerily calm. It's time for all the secrets and this toxic, codependent relationship to end once and for all.

A few minutes later, my little mail icon alerts me to one new message. I click. It's from Holly.

I'm closer than you think.

CHAPTER THIRTY

HOLLY

Before

After getting tomatoes, noodles, ground beef, and even chocolate cupcakes with sprinkles for Jacob at the grocery store close to Cliffside Road, Holly drives back to the Goldmans' and parks Sarah's car in the garage. Daniel's Audi isn't there, so he's not at home yet. That's good because she's still too angry with him about their discussion at the bar to fake normalcy right now. Now that he and Sarah are in a good place, all loved up from the night away they couldn't have had without Holly, he's trying to distance her from the family. He promised to let her continue living with them, but how long will that last if he's found a way out of the grave he's dug for himself? At least Sarah and Jacob will appreciate the delicious dinner she's making for them. Or so Holly hopes.

She unlocks the front door, imagining a perfect dinner, with

Sarah sitting at the kitchen table with a glass of wine and Jacob learning to cut his food himself. Maybe Sarah will immortalize the night in a photo. And perhaps she can tell Sarah to post it on Instagram—or add it to the family photos on the wall in the living room. Humming to herself, she carries the bags toward the kitchen, passing the living room, where she sees a blond stranger sitting on the couch.

She drops the bags. "Who the hell are you?" Holly asks.

"I'm Nora. I live three houses down the road," the girl replies. "Sarah went out. She's going to meet Daniel."

Holly balks. Went out? But she's making Sarah and Jacob dinner. And Holly had Sarah's car, so where could she have gone? In her mind, she quickly replays everything she and Daniel discussed at the bar after the phone call he'd taken from Sarah. He never mentioned going anywhere.

Miss Thing sticks out a small, freckled hand, which Holly shakes, because she has no choice. The girl's fingers are sticky.

"Do you know when they'll be back? I actually live here, you know. Did they tell you that?"

"They did," she says, taking her hand back and smiling uncertainly. "They said they'd be back after Jacob's bedtime. They went out for a walk and dinner."

"Where's Jacob?"

"In the bathroom."

If Jacob weren't in the house, Holly would rage or cry. Why on earth did they suddenly hire another sitter? What's going on?

She goes to the kitchen and calls Sarah. There's no answer, and she doesn't leave a message, because she doesn't know what to say. Next, she opens her texts to find the last one Daniel sent from his secret phone and tries to call him. He doesn't pick up, either.

"Shit," she says as she decides not to leave a voice mail in case Sarah's close enough to hear Holly yell at him. Finally, she checks the tracker app on Daniel. The red dot isn't moving, which means he's turned off his phone.

Then it hits her. They're ghosting her.

"Holly? Why are you home? Mommy said you can't babysit for me tonight," Jacob says when he walks into the living room from the bathroom.

She arranges a smile on her sad face and goes to him, pulling him into a tight hug. "Hey, Jakey. I'm not going anywhere tonight. I'm making you dinner, remember?"

Jacob looks nervous. "Nora ordered pepperoni pizza for us. Mommy gave her some money."

So no fucking lasagna for dinner.

"You loved the pizza, right, Jacob? You ate three slices!" Nora chirps, obviously not picking up on Holly's frustration.

Holly kisses Jacob on the head. "Yup, pepperoni-scented hair."

He giggles, and it breaks her heart. She's going to lose it if she stays inside with them much longer. She grabs the package of chocolate cupcakes with sprinkles, hands them to Nora, and says, "I'll be out by the pool."

"Can we go swimming?" Jacob asks hopefully.

"Your parents asked me to keep you inside tonight," Nora tells Jacob, bypassing Holly completely.

"Sorry, Jakey. Maybe tomorrow." Holly swallows, then slides open the glass door and stands on the pool deck, fuming. She turns once to see Jacob and Nora devouring the special treat she bought just for Jacob.

For the next two hours, she sits on a lounge chair, glaring at the cabana. Her phone is silent. Only Alexis has texted, but Holly can't think straight enough right now to write her back.

At 8:00 p.m. Jacob comes out onto the deck and plops next to her on the lounge chair. "Are you mad, Holly?"

Instantly she feels guilty. "No. Just thinking."

He cocks his head. "Can I think with you?"

She's about to say yes when Nora steps outside and joins them. "Bedtime, Jacob." She looks at Holly, no longer trying to be nice for appearances sake. "Sarah wants him asleep by eight thirty at the latest."

Holly stands and kisses Jacob good night. Then Nora takes him inside. Before the sliding doors seal her out of the house, Jacob, clearly confused, asks, "Is Nora my new babysitter?"

"No way, Jakey. This is just for tonight," Holly says. She's near tears, but she can't let him see her cry.

Is Jacob right, though? Is Holly being replaced? With Jacob gone and with nothing else to do, Holly goes back inside and down to her basement bedroom. She crawls into bed, dejected and rejected. She hears the front door open around midnight, Sarah and Daniel whispering. "I'll walk Nora home," Daniel says, and she hears the front door close.

Sarah's light steps cross the floor above her, then she hears the sliding doors to the pool open and close. Holly debates going up to talk to Sarah alone but decides against it. Maybe if she can just get some sleep, everything will be better tomorrow. Back to normal. As though nothing ever happened. Holly waits until she hears Daniel come home, then she gets out of bed to eavesdrop through the air duct in her closet. But besides a few whispered niceties, she hears nothing. They're quiet now. And she's entirely shut out.

The worst part? She hasn't done anything wrong.

CHAPTER THIRTY-ONE

SARAH

Now

I'm closer than you think.

The Instagram message from Holly is chilling. Does she mean she's here in Blossom Court? Here at my doorstep? Here inside my house? I don't know what to do. I'm nervous to communicate with her again, but I have to find out what she wants so I can figure out how to remove her from our lives forever.

After Tara and I pick up the boys from school, I ask if Jacob can have a playdate for a couple of hours with Cody at Tara's. Once Jacob is next door, I wait alone in the house for Daniel to return from work. When the mudroom door slams shut at 5:00 p.m., I run to him.

"I know who the man in the video is."

His eyebrows shoot up, and he puts his satchel on the floor. "Who?"

"Charlie Lang." I search his face for any recognition of the name.

"I've heard of him, but I don't know him personally. How did you figure it out?" He turns to take off his leather jacket and hangs it on a hook by the door.

"I called Gloria and put some pieces together."

He fiddles with something in his jacket pocket, not looking at me.

"Dan, this is important."

He faces me. "Sorry. From what I know, Charlie is a busy man, and I highly doubt he sent you that video. Pretty gross, though, that he was involved with Holly."

I decide to drop the next bombshell. "I think Holly sent it. And I think she's here in Blossom Court."

"What?" Disbelief, confusion—and something that looks a lot like fear—suddenly cloud his face.

I fill him in on the Instagram account I made and show him the direct message Holly sent me. Daniel shakes his head. "She's a piece of work."

"Maybe a dangerous one. Remember the night we saw the video and we asked Nora to babysit? Nora was scared of her, too. She practically ran out of the house when you walked her home."

"Can I get a beer for this conversation? It's been a long day."

We go to the kitchen, where he grabs a beer from the fridge and sits at the kitchen table. I'm too wired, so I stand.

"Here's what I don't get," Daniel says. "Why would she wait until we moved to get in touch? Why not torment us from the day she was fired?"

"Why? To fuck with us. I think she knows I photographed and videoed her. And I think she's furious we sold the house, left her behind."

"How would she even get here? John and Lisette disowned her."

"She stole things. She told me she stole a really expensive bracelet from Lisette just because she could. I should have twigged then to how unstable she is. She could easily have stolen things to pay for a plane ticket. Plus, who knows how much money she had sitting in her bank account. Her father's rich after all."

Daniel takes a long sip of his beer. "So, what do you want to do?"

"Confront her. In person."

His hand jerks when he puts the bottle on the table. He's quiet, and I think he's about to tell me I'm crazy, but he nods. "I'm going to lure her here. And we'll talk to her. Here. On our turf, in our home. We just have to make sure Jacob's not around."

I swallow hard because, even though I think it's the right plan, I'm scared to even send her a message in reply. "Emily's supposed to tutor Jacob and Cody at Tara's tomorrow at four. I'm sure Tara will be okay with Jacob staying longer if we need him to."

Daniel nods. "Do it."

I open my DMs, my fingers trembling as I type to Holly:

I know you're in Blossom Court. I know everything.

My heart leaps to my throat when three dots appear then a message.

You're right about one thing. I am here.

Daniel's hovering over my shoulder. I glance at him. He looks as frightened as I feel. But I'm determined to end this. I tap out my final message:

We need to talk. Our house. Friday. 4:00 p.m.

I press send and wait.

———

It took Holly a good few hours last night to respond to the invitation, probably relishing that I'd be checking my phone constantly, jumping every time a new notification popped up. Finally, at 9:00 p.m., after Jacob was asleep and I was unbearably anxious, she agreed with a simple "yes." She never asked for our address, because somehow she knows exactly where we live.

Now, at seven on this gorgeous Friday morning, my eyes are sore and crusty from barely sleeping, but I'm alert. My body zings like I've had six cups of coffee when I haven't even sipped a drop. The air is chilly, but the rising sun is strong as I stand on the porch surveying the neighborhood. Jacob and Daniel are still asleep, but Ezra is on his own porch in his rocking chair, his eyes on me with every sway forward and back.

Everything changes today.

I'm glad I won't be alone with Holly in the house. Daniel has promised to be back from work by 3:00 p.m. so we can face her together. Tara's picking up Jacob after school and taking him to her place for his and Cody's first tutoring session with Emily. I haven't yet told Tara that Holly's coming over, but I did ask if Jacob might be able to stay at her house after tutoring. She agreed immediately without pressing for more information. And Jacob happily assented to tutoring because it's happening with his best friend and Roscoe, Emily's dog.

I'm scared to see Holly again, but I have to admit that I also feel an odd excitement buzzing through me. Who is the young woman I treated like my own daughter, and what the hell does she want from us?

"Hey."

I look behind me. Daniel holds out a cup of coffee. Grateful, I take a sip then make a face.

"Too hot?"

"No sugar."

"I forgot. Sorry." He leans over to kiss me. "You okay?"

I kiss him back. He tastes minty and sweet. "I will be after today is over. If she leaves us alone, if she goes away for good and stops tormenting our family."

Emily and Roscoe meander up Lilac Lane, stopping so the dog can pee on our lawn. I think he's marked every spot as his territory, but I don't mind. That scruffy terrier is a godsend to my son.

Daniel says hello to Emily, squeezes my shoulder, then goes to the garage for the car. I blow him a kiss as he drives away. Emily, wearing a yellow fitted trench coat over slim black dress pants, comes up to the porch with Roscoe. I put my coffee on the porch railing. "You look nice," I say.

She looks down at her outfit and grins. "Thanks. I have an interview later this morning."

"Teaching job?"

"Yes. Private school."

"That's fantastic! Let me know how it goes. Here, sit," I say as I gesture for her to join me on the steps.

"I can only stay for a sec." She sits and lengthens the leash so Roscoe can explore my lawn.

"I hope the tutoring goes well today. Don't let Jacob railroad you."

"Jacob's a sweetheart. And don't worry. I have tons of experience with energetic kids like him."

"Thanks," I say. "I know I worry too much. Listen, soon, we'll invite you for dinner. You've been so great. You and Roscoe have really helped Jacob to feel comfortable here."

Emily's eyes light up at my offer. "I'd love to come for dinner."

Roscoe barks as if on cue.

"Don't worry, Roscoe. You can come, too," I say.

"By the way, Jacob's staying at Tara's after tutoring today. Daniel and I have something to take care of."

"Sounds good," she says. "It takes a village, right?" She gets up and brushes dirt off the back of her coat. "I'd better go."

"Good luck with the interview!" I say.

She smiles, then takes off with Roscoe and is soon down the street.

I head inside to give Jacob breakfast and get him ready for school. I let him choose his own clothes and say nothing when he grabs

Mr. Blinkers for show-and-tell. Then Tara and I meet up outside the house.

The boys run up ahead, and I turn to her. "I really appreciate that you're having Jacob over today." I hesitate for only a moment because I have to share my feelings with someone other than Daniel. "Holly, our former babysitter, is coming over to talk."

Tara raises her eyebrows. "She's here? In Toronto?"

"She is," I say.

"Jacob can stay as long as you need. Just text me when you're done." She quickly squeezes my arm, then lets go.

Once we've brought the boys to their line at the back of the school, I hold Jacob extra tightly before his class goes inside.

"I love you," I tell him.

"Love you more!" he calls before disappearing through the back doors.

Tara and I walk home together, and in front of my house, she hugs me. "Good luck," she whispers in my ear. "You've got this."

Grateful, I hug her back and enter my house. The day crawls by at first with the mundane routine of laundry and the dishes. I'm so wound up that I even rearrange the fridge.

At 1:00 p.m. I head outside. The wind whistles, blowing my hair in my face. I check that all the cameras are in place should Holly come earlier than expected. I will be prepared for her. I will track her every move before I invite her into my home. I feel someone watching me when I look once more at the camera over the front door. I turn, and there's Ezra, on his porch, as usual. He gives me a thumbs-up. Creeped out, I run back inside.

At 2:00 p.m. I go upstairs and shower, then blow-dry my hair. In my bedroom, I dress carefully, choosing a pair of black leggings and a fitted orange sweater that enhances rather than hides my true shape. I don't know why, but I want to look good for Holly. Maybe to prove that I'm more capable, stronger than she thinks. I put on mascara, but it's a mess. My left eye is goopy and clumpy. I grab a tissue from the wicker box on the nightstand, yanking it with force. The tissue box falls on the floor.

"Smooth, Sarah," I say out loud as I bend to pick up the box. My hand freezes.

There's a tiny eye in the middle between the brown wicker weaves. A hidden camera. It's been there all along, watching us since the day we moved in.

Fear shoots up my spine, followed quickly by rage.

I call Daniel at work. When he doesn't answer, I leave a message. Then I text. No response. I sit on the bed, frantically jiggling my leg.

But I'm too jumpy to sit for long. I smash the tissue box with my foot and pace around our bedroom. We're scheduled to meet Holly outside on our porch in less than an hour. I'm going to confront her about this. This and everything else. I'm boiling with anger. I want to wrap my hands around her soft, delicate throat and squeeze the life out of her for torturing me like this.

At 2:30 p.m., half an hour before Daniel's supposed to be home, I hear something. I strain to pinpoint what made the sound. It wasn't a bang or footsteps, more like a distant hum.

"Dan?" I call from the upstairs landing.

Nothing.

"Is that you?" I look over the railing. The main floor is empty. I go back to my bedroom and pace because I don't know what else to do with my restless energy.

By three fifteen, Daniel still isn't home. An ominous heaviness pervades the house. I sit on the bed and check the app for the outdoor cameras again. Goose bumps cover my arms when I see they've all been deactivated. I count to ten in an attempt to calm down because I'm letting panic overrule reason. I need to talk to Daniel.

I try his cell one more time, but it goes to voice mail. "Damn it!" I say out loud. Then it occurs to me. I search on my phone for the general line of Strategic Solutions, Daniel's company. I dial the number.

"You've reached Strategic Solutions Consulting. If you know the extension of the person you'd like to reach, please enter it now. Otherwise press three for our directory."

I stab "3," and listen to the list of all employees. I listen again and again, not hearing Daniel's name. Finally, I press "0" to speak to a human, my head throbbing.

"Strategic Solutions, how can I help you?" I hear.

I'm dizzy and light-headed, like I'm in a tunnel. "I'd like to speak with Daniel Goldman, please. I'm wondering if you can page him since he's not answering his direct line?"

"I'm sorry. There's no Daniel Goldman who works here."

"What do you mean? Of course there is."

"Ma'am, I've worked here for the last ten years. We're a really small firm. And that is not one of our employees."

I drop the phone and hit the floor as my world crashes down around me.

CHAPTER THIRTY-TWO

HOLLY

Before

Holly sits on her bed, afraid to go upstairs. It's Sunday at 8:30 a.m., so she's not technically working today, but she doesn't want to stay in her room doing nothing but worrying.

She doesn't think she slept more than an hour last night. Her eyes are swollen from crying. How could Sarah treat her like this? Walking in yesterday and seeing that girl, Nora, on *her* couch, with *her* Jacob, and not even a text or call from Sarah to tell Holly what was going on? No explanation at all for the sudden freeze-out? Holly thinks of her father, how easily he let her go, as though she was worth nothing the minute she stopped doing his bidding.

Whatever the reason for this devastating exclusion, the morning noises in the house—rushing water through the pipes; Jacob and Daniel's heavy treads and the softer ones belonging to Sarah; the smell of toast and coffee—stab her in the heart. This cannot be the last morning she'll wake up to that.

Sometimes you have to hurt someone to help them, she thinks to herself.

She hears Daniel call out that he's going to the Canyon Club for a golf game, and Sarah calls back that she loves him. If he's lying, Holly will know. She'll track him on her phone.

After quickly pulling on her favorite black bathing suit—a one-piece racer-back—loose cutoffs with wide pockets, and a black tank top, she gets her phone, with the video of her and Charlie plus all the screenshots of Daniel's Monero and CoverMe apps. The tracker shows he really is heading toward the Canyon Club, goddamn it. She shoves the phone, plus the key to the house, into her jean shorts' pocket.

When she gets upstairs, she's disappointed that Sarah and Jacob aren't in the kitchen. Judging by the crumbs on the table and the dishes stacked next to the sink, breakfast is over. They never even waited for her. It's like they've forgotten she exists. They're not in the living room, and when she goes to the deck to check outside, they're not by the pool. They must be upstairs. It's a bright, sunny morning. Surely, they'll come down soon.

"Act normal," Holly says to herself as she crosses the deck to grab the skimmer that's leaning against the fence so she can clean the leaves and bugs from the pool like she and Jacob usually do before every swim. Maybe when they come outside, she and Jacob can show Sarah his diving. She's taught him a lot this summer.

She hears the sliding doors open, and Sarah steps out. Holly grins just as she would any morning and waves. Sarah doesn't wave back. She storms toward Holly, who drops the skimmer and rears back in shock.

Sarah steps right in front of her.

Holly is speechless. This isn't the Sarah she knows. She's fuming with rage, rage that's directed at her.

"What's going on?" Holly asks. "Please, I don't know what's made you so upset."

She takes a step backward, giving Sarah space. She will make everything okay, no matter what. She has to.

"You know exactly what's making me so upset," Sarah says. Her voice is seething and full of hate.

Holly fiddles with her yin necklace. Sarah looks awful. Her hair's in disarray, and she's wearing her pilled yoga pants and a T-shirt she must have pulled out of the dirty laundry.

"Honestly, Sarah, I don't know what you're talking about," Holly says.

"I want the truth. You owe me that after everything I've done for you, all the support I've given you." She comes closer and growls, "What is it you're doing here anyhow? What game are you playing?"

Holly's spent her whole life telling people what they want to hear, acting how they want her to act. Now, confronted like this, she can't think straight.

"It's not—" She can't find the right words, doesn't know where to begin. Tears spring to her eyes. "It's not *my* games you should be worried about," she says.

"Who exactly should I be pointing fingers at, then, if you're not responsible for doing what you did in my house?"

What the hell is Sarah talking about? Why is she the villain? She's not going to take the blame for Daniel.

"Ask your husband," Holly says.

Sarah gets right in Holly's face. "Stay away from my husband. Do you understand?"

"No, I don't. What are you implying?"

Sarah grits her teeth together, then snarls, "Shut up and listen. Here's what's going to happen. You'll finish the day and then you're gone. Pack your bags and don't mention anything to my son. You've found another place to live. That's it. You're moving on."

Holly feels her face crumple, and her knees buckle. She's losing Sarah, her home, her family, and there's nothing she can do to stop it.

"What did Daniel tell you?"

Sarah's eyes flash with fire. "Don't speak his name ever again."

"Why would you do this, Sarah? I've never done a single thing to hurt you."

"Except lie. Deceive. Betray my trust. You're a manipulator and a conniver, and I don't want you anywhere near us anymore. You don't belong in this family, Holly. We've sold the house. We're moving to Toronto." The last thing she says is: "I saw what you did."

There's no way Sarah could know about Charlie. Unless . . . But something in her snaps then. Sarah isn't exactly innocent herself. "And *I* saw what *you* did." She's about to reveal that she saw Sarah's photos of her, ones she never consented to, and every last bit of dirt she has on Daniel that's stored on her phone, but then Jacob walks through the sliding doors and stands behind his mother. His sweet little face is pale as he watches them with panic. "Why are you fighting?" he asks.

Holly can't hurt him. He's the best person she knows, too young to witness the breakdown of his family, too perfectly whole to tear into pieces.

Sarah quickly spins around. "We're not fighting, sweetie. Just grown-up talking. There's a difference." She smiles at her son. "I'm going for a walk, okay?" To Holly she demands, "Take care of him. Tell him exactly what we agreed to and nothing else. I'll be back soon."

As Sarah strides toward the back gate, Holly says quietly, "He won't get away with this."

Sarah doesn't turn around. She just exits to the front of the house.

Holly has completely missed her chance to get Sarah back on her side. And how can they leave this gorgeous house and Holly behind? It's all too cruel, too mind-boggling, too sudden to understand.

Jacob presses his little hand, warm and soft, to her cheek. She smiles at the little boy who has become a little brother to her. The thought of losing him cleaves her heart.

He's not smiling. The dusting of freckles on his nose scrunch together on his confused face. "Do you and my mommy hate each other?" He slips his thumb in his mouth.

Holly holds back the howl that rises to her throat. "No. You know how sometimes people think you're not paying attention and not listening, but you're trying so hard? And they don't get it?"

He nods vigorously, his narrow chest rising and falling.

"That's what happened with me and your mom. But we'll work it out. Everything will be okay."

It won't be okay, though. Holly is the problem to get rid of, just like with her father. Family sticks together and leaves her out. This truth slices her insides so much it hurts.

"Race you to the end and back?" she says to Jacob.

He cannonballs into the deep end and starts the front crawl before she even gets a toe in. "Look at you go!" His strokes have improved so much over the summer. She's made this boy strong and resilient in the water.

"Hide-and-seek, Holly?" he asks as he climbs out of the pool and shakes himself off.

"Yes. But only in the house, okay? Not the cabana."

Jacob takes Holly's palm and kisses it. "I love you."

She hugs him, holding him close for a second before letting him go. "I love you more." Her voice breaks as she says, "Hey, Jakey? If I'm not home at bedtime tonight, tell your mommy to watch out for herself, okay?"

Before Jacob can answer, Holly hears footsteps outside the gate, close to the driveway. Is Sarah home already? Maybe she wants to apologize and put things right. Hope soars in her chest.

Jacob runs off inside the house to hide, and she calls out, "Ready or not, here I come!"

A hand reaches over the fence to unlatch the gate.

It's not Sarah's. But she recognizes the hand immediately.

CHAPTER THIRTY-THREE

SARAH

Now

A shrill, repetitive beep and an explosive bang wake me from my stupor. I gag again and again, my head pounding. Why am I on the bedroom floor? "Daniel," I croak. I've lost my voice. I want to scream out, but I can't.

The wicker tissue box I smashed is a foot away from me, my phone on the floor beside me.

Suddenly, it all rushes back.

Someone was here. Someone did this. To me.

I can't move my arms and legs. "Jacob!" I try to shriek, but it's useless. Then I remember he's not home. It's okay. He's with Tara and Emily. He's safe.

I have to get out of this room, but there's no way I can stand. I don't even think I can crawl. Tears leak out of my eyes onto the hardwood.

There's a noise. Loud crashing. Someone's in the house.

"Sarah!" I hear.

I slowly move my head. Ezra is standing in front of me. He's holding an ax. I open my mouth in a silent scream.

He lifts me into his arms, and I hang limply, pushing, fighting with no power to get away from him.

"I've got you. It's okay." He carries me down the stairs and steps through the splintered wood of our front door, all the way to his house, where he gently sets me down on his lawn.

I kneel, gasping in air. "What the hell are you doing? Get the fuck away from me!" I manage to say between gasps.

He crouches beside me. "You're safe now. You have carbon monoxide poisoning. So does Daniel. An ambulance is on the way."

I can't quite understand what he's saying. "Did you poison us?"

"You're confused. It's common with carbon monoxide. Stay here." He walks to the porch and comes back with an oxygen tank and mask, which he carefully places over my nose and mouth.

It's only then that I see Daniel slumped in the chair on Ezra's porch, a mask over his face, too. I look up at Ezra. His face swims in front of me.

"I'm a retired paramedic. I heard an alarm from your house, and the car running in your garage. I found your husband unconscious on the floor. His head was bleeding at the back. I think someone hit him. I found a shovel on the garage floor, too."

I stumble to stand and make it right to the bottom porch step before crashing on my knees in front of Daniel. He's gray and haggard but alive. Ezra joins us, giving us space yet carefully watching over us. "Who did this?" I ask Daniel.

When he only shakes his head, I turn toward Ezra. "You watch us all the time." I blink over and over to clear the hazy waves in my vision. "Did you do this? Did you hurt us?" A gravelly sob releases as the reality of what's happened filters through the thick fuzziness in my brain.

"I'm trying to help," he says. "If I wasn't on neighborhood watch, I wouldn't have seen your garbage can on the sidewalk. When I dragged it up your driveway for you, I heard the alarm and the car running in your garage with the door closed. I knew you were inside the house and carbon monoxide could be leaking in through the mudroom door. I had to check on you. And then I had to get you out."

I struggle to focus as things slowly fall into place. "Have you been in the house before?"

Ezra nods. "I viewed it before you moved in."

Through the oxygen mask, Daniel's mouth moves, but it's hard to make out what he's saying. I edge closer.

"Ezra turned off the car, lifted me from the floor, and carried me outside." Tears drip out of the corners of his eyes. "I think Holly knocked me unconscious."

I look at Ezra, the blurriness in my eyes clearing a bit. "Thank you for saving us," I say tearfully. "Did you see a young woman, twenty-two, tall and slim with auburn hair around our house this afternoon?"

Ezra shakes his head. "I didn't see anyone except Tara and the boys. And that blue-haired woman with the dog."

"Did you deactivate all the outside cameras?" I ask Daniel.

"No," he says. Slowly he puts his hand on my arm. Then he takes a palm-size phone I've never seen before out of his pocket and hands it to me. "This is all my fault," he rasps, and points to the phone. "Holly found this phone in my cabana and must have put a tracker on it to follow me." He lets out a hacking cough. "I never wanted to hurt you. I have a gambling problem."

I am concentrating as hard as I can, but the words don't fully register. Nothing makes any sense. "No," I whisper.

He keeps going. "I lost everything to Charlie Lang. I was in debt. Major debt. Charlie runs an illegal gambling ring through the Canyon Club. I got in too deep. I knew he was the man."

Ezra hands me an open bottle of water. I sip greedily as the pieces start to come together in my mind. "The man in the video?"

Daniel nods, releasing a guttural sob. "Holly wanted to blackmail him. For me. For us. So he'd forgive the debts. Let me out of the ring." He bows his head, like his shame is too heavy to carry. "I gave him the house practically for free. Holly and I were never involved. Never in any way. She wanted to fix everything for our family, but I wanted her away from us."

I'm so stunned by his revelations I can't find words. "So why is she stalking us now? Why would she hurt us? Why?"

"I don't know," he says. And I can see in his eyes—it's the absolute truth.

Ezra turns his head and squints at the bottom of the cul-de-sac.

"What is it, Ezra?"

"There was someone rushing down the street earlier toward the woods. I was so fixated on the car running in your garage that I didn't connect the two until right now."

I get up carefully, but I'm steadier than I thought I'd be. I scream at Ezra to call the police.

"I'm going to the ravine!"

"No!" Daniel cries.

"Sarah, stop!" Ezra shouts.

I ignore them both to run down Lilac Lane, faster than I have ever moved in my life.

In seconds I'm at the entrance to the trail. I tap out a frantic text to Tara.

Sarah: Stay inside with Emily and the boys.
I'll explain later.

Immediately, she texts back.

Tara: Emily canceled. Family emergency.
But Roscoe's here with the boys. Everything
okay?

I don't answer her. Closing my eyes, I listen for footsteps or breathing. I hear the leaves rustling in the icy wind. I run, tripping over rocks, branches ripping into my skin as I tear past the trees down the trail. I'm about to keep running when, in the dense grove beside a steep lookout, I see a flash of yellow.

My head is still stuffy, and it takes a second for the horror to sink in. When it does, I peer into the riot of trees and choke the words out, "I see you."

CHAPTER THIRTY-FOUR

HOLLY

Before

Holly stands at the edge of the pool, mouth open in surprise at who has just entered through the gate into the backyard—her stepsister, Alexis. And she wasn't invited.

"If you've come to yell at me or lecture me, today is so not the day," Holly says.

"I know Sarah Goldman just left. I watched her leave. We should talk."

Her tone is so strangely serious, so unlike Alexis, that Holly's pulse spikes.

Alexis comes closer. "It's time you listened to reason. You're coming home with me. I keep telling you this family isn't good for you. You can't just change families like this, overnight. I'm your real family. You can't leave me behind."

"Leave you behind? I would never—"

"I heard the horrible way that woman talked to you. I was right outside the gate. And they spring the fact that they're moving on you, just like that? They don't care about you, Holly. How can you not see it?"

Holly's first instinct is to defend the Goldmans. She's about to do just that when she has another thought. "Alexis, why are you here?"

Alexis touches her yang pendant. For once, Holly doesn't touch hers back.

"I asked you a question, Alexis."

"I know everything. I know you've been stealing from my mom for years. And I saw you on Hastings yesterday. And before, at the parking lot at the Canyon Club? You're getting paid to have sex with old men. You know what that's called, right?" She looks at Holly sadly. "And you met Daniel Goldman at a strip club, the father of the kid you babysit. Holly, that's fucked up."

"What?" Holly says, too loudly. Before she can say anything more, she takes a deep breath. The last thing she needs is for Jacob to come out here right now and witness this insanity.

"Look, you have it all wrong. I can't talk about this right now. But I'll explain everything to you later, okay?"

"You won't call me. You'll ignore me, cancel on me, and give everything to this family that uses you. Don't you see it?"

Holly clenches her fists. She's furious and this is demeaning. "You are so dead wrong." She thinks back to the night at the strip club. So she did see someone in the alley outside Pinky's, someone who looked too familiar. And she saw the same figure run through the woods behind this very house the first time she snuck into Daniel's cabana. "Have you been *following* me?" Holly asks.

"For your own good," Alexis answers. "You're my little sister. It's my job to watch out for you."

Holly turns her back and takes out her phone to text Sarah, to apologize and ask her to come home so they can talk, but Alexis grabs her by the shoulder and whirls her around. She snatches the phone from her hand.

"Hey! Give that back."

Alexis holds it in the air above her head. "No. Not until you promise me you're going to come live with me. I can take care of you. I can show you how to be a better person."

"I don't need you to take care of me!" she yells. "I have another family now, and you're ruining everything!"

Alexis's face falls. Instantly, Holly feels guilt turn acidic in her stomach. "I have to go check on Jacob."

"You can pay attention to me for another minute," Alexis replies. "It's not going to kill you."

Holly gawks at her, rendered speechless.

"All I want is for you to reach your potential."

"*My* potential? What about *your* potential? I got you the job with Professor Phillips—"

"After you slept with him."

Oh my God. So she knew that all along, too. Holly looks down at her feet. "Why didn't you ever say anything to me? And how long have you been trailing me like a puppy?"

Alexis's face reddens, but still, Alexis doesn't stop. "I'm your older sister. And you're coming home with me. Right now."

Holly's voice is cold when she says it, just the one word: "Stepsister."

Alexis's arms reach out.

CHAPTER THIRTY-FIVE

SARAH

Now

"I see you," I say again, stronger this time, to the figure hiding in the grove next to the steep escarpment I'm standing on.

Emily steps out from the trees onto the rocky, uneven ledge, still wearing her bright yellow trench coat from this morning. But the light catches a glint at her neck. There's something new there hanging, a silver chain. It's too far to see exactly, but I know it's a pendant, a yang pendant with an "A" engraved on the back.

"Alexis," I say, a rough whisper.

"Alexis Emily Lawrence, because I've never been a Monroe."

What is she planning to do? We're about three feet apart on the rugged, narrow terrain. There's no fence barring the sheer drop to the shallow, rocky creek twenty feet below us. I can't get any closer to her because she's almost at the edge of the drop-off. My knees buckle a little, but I manage to stay standing.

"Is this about Holly?" I ask. "Because I've been trying to reach her. We've been in touch."

Alexis doesn't answer right away. She inhales then exhales, looking around at the dense canopy of treetops stretching for miles.

"It's pretty up here. The view's a lot like yours was in Vancouver."

My breath catches in my throat. "You were at my house?"

Alexis steps a few inches closer to the edge. "I visited. More than once."

My heart pounds in my chest as I consider what to say. "You . . . you visited your stepsister?"

"I did. Someone had to look out for her. She never had a mother, you know."

I remember the longing ache in Holly's eyes when she told me her mother had died giving birth to her. "She told me that. It's very sad," I say.

Alexis fixes her hard gaze on me, making me take a step back. "You don't know how vulnerable Holly was. Your husband used her. You're both terrible people."

I shake my head. "That's not true. We both care a lot about Holly."

"You only care about yourselves." Her hand goes to her neck, and she starts to move the pendant on her necklace back and forth across the chain. "I know everything, Sarah. Do you?"

It hits me like a punch to my stomach. "Your stepsister, she's on a retreat, right?"

"That's one way to put it," Alexis replies.

Out of nowhere, a blur of fur darts past me. It's Roscoe, and he's moving so fast that his paws struggle to get a foothold on the rocks. Then, just as quickly, my son appears behind him, following Roscoe right to the edge of the lookout, only inches from Alexis.

"Jacob, no!" I yell, but it's too late. Alexis's hand shoots out and grabs Jacob's arm.

"Don't worry," she says. "I've got him."

Roscoe jumps toward Jacob, but his back paws slip, and he falls down the edge to a narrow crevice between two boulders a few feet down.

"Mommy, he's stuck on the rocks! It's all my fault. I snuck out of Cody's house, and he followed me!" Jacob cries, pointing to Roscoe, who's balanced precariously on the only small jut-out before the rest of the steep plummet. "I have to help him."

"Please, Jake. Don't move," I plead. To Alexis I say, "Let go of my son."

"Why?" she replies. "I'm his tutor. We've been having a lovely time together. Haven't we, Jacob?" She smiles at me, but it's frightening. "Jacob and Cody are my only students, actually. I only came to Toronto for Jacob."

Jacob looks up at her and nods, his face so trusting I feel sick.

"We have to get your dog," he says.

"You're right. We do," she replies as her grip tightens on his arm, pushing him within inches of the drop-off.

"Are you really a teacher?" I ask.

Alexis shakes her head. "A nurse. I guess I'm as good a liar as you and your husband."

Jacob looks at Alexis's fingers on his arm. Then he looks at me, opens his mouth and closes it. I know he's all mixed up inside, dumbstruck by what the nice woman with the dog is saying about his mom and dad.

I need help. I need Daniel. I need the police. My body doesn't feel right. I don't know what she's capable of. Carefully, I move forward one slow step at a time. I'm terror-stricken, but I have to pretend I'm not. "Jacob, honey. Can you move back from the edge? Can you do that for me?" I ask gently.

He nods, but his eyes keep darting to Roscoe below us, and Alexis has his arm in a viselike grip.

"Everything I've done is for Holly. My whole life. Then she exchanged me for you as if I were nothing. All she cared about was you, and you destroyed her."

I swallow hard, trying to will the right words to come. "I never meant to hurt her by leaving. I want to tell her that."

"You can't." She looks at Jacob. "Did Mr. Blinkers make you happy, Jakey? I wanted you to be happy and to remember Holly," Alexis says, her voice harsh and strange. "Holly loved you."

Jacob's eyes light up. "Wait, is Holly here?" he asks.

Alexis shakes her head. "No, Jakey. She's not here anymore. And it's your parents' fault."

I watch my son's face fill with bewilderment.

It feels like everything stops. The air compresses around me. Jacob looks at me with so much confusion, but I can't explain.

Jacob is shaking hard. Alexis has nudged him right to the edge so that his feet send small pebbles flying over.

"Jake, look at me, okay? Just look at me."

"Look at *me*, Sarah!" Alexis says. "Look what you made me do. My whole family is ruined, because of you." Her face twists with sorrow, and her hand wrenches my son's arm.

"Is Holly dead?" Jacob asks, suddenly understanding what he's just heard.

Alexis frowns at him. "You're not supposed to be here, Jakey. You were supposed to be at Tara's until the police discovered your parents where I left them. Then they would have begun the search for a good and decent family to raise you."

She takes her hand off Jacob's arm and crouches so she's at eye level with him. All it would take is one shove, and my son would go over the edge.

"Do you know that you're the only good person in your family?" she says to him.

I have barely a beat to make a life-altering decision. I launch myself at her, clearing the few feet between us in a fraction of a second. It takes me only one push to separate her from my son. She flails backward, right on the edge of the cliff. I stumble on some loose gravel and land hard on my hip beside her. "Run!" I shriek at Jacob as he stands there in a state of utter shock.

Alexis scrambles, trying to find a foothold, but then I feel her hand clamp onto my ankle as she slides down the escarpment.

I'm going down with her.

"Mommy!" Jacob cries.

My stomach free-falls as I scrape down the rock face with Alexis and catch a flash of Jacob looking horrified at the edge of the cliff, Roscoe nowhere to be seen. Alexis's hand still grips my ankle, and I kick to get her off me, cracking my ankle on a boulder.

There's that small ledge between two boulders in the middle of the drop, and that's where we land. I grab a tree root sticking out of the rock face and come to a halt. I collapse, pine needles stabbing my face and arms. Next to me, Alexis smashes into a boulder with an audible thump. But she's conscious and throws herself on top of me, digging her elbow into my throat.

I can't breathe. I can no longer see my son.

Suddenly, the air whooshes back into my lungs and Alexis is pulled off me. I turn to see Ezra holding her arms above her head, while Daniel pins her legs. She writhes, but she's no match for them.

"Where's Jacob?" I croak.

"At the top with Roscoe. He's fine. Don't talk," my husband says, his voice choked with tears while he holds Alexis down with Ezra.

"Get off me!" she yells.

Footfalls and commands echo all around us.

"The police are here!" It's my son's voice, and it's the sweetest sound I've ever heard.

I look up to the top of the escarpment where a team of four police officers and two paramedics arrive on the lookout to take over.

"Quick! Down here!" Daniel shouts.

"Jacob!" I yell. I'm covered in blood and dirt, and my ankle is screaming in pain, but none of that matters.

"I've got him!" a female voice calls. Then I see Jacob next to a uniformed police officer, Roscoe held tight against him. He's safe. I start to sob.

"They're coming to get you, okay?" the brunette officer yells down to me. "Your son is unharmed!"

"We have the suspect contained!" Ezra shouts up as Alexis spits in his face. He turns and smiles at me. "Not the first time I've been spit at."

I owe this man my life.

While Daniel and Ezra keep Alexis down on the ground, three officers, two males and a different female than the one with my son, carefully scramble down the cliff until they reach us.

"I'll take it from here," one of the male officers says, pulling out handcuffs, and securing them around Alexis's wrists, allowing both my husband and Ezra to finally release their hold on her. "You're under arrest on suspicion of attempted murder."

She looks bruised and battered. The officer calls to the top of the cliff, "Stretcher!"

I look up to see two firefighters who must have just arrived. They use ropes to slowly drop a yellow stretcher vertically down the escarpment. All three officers lift Alexis onto the stretcher and click thick, black straps over her chest and legs so she can't move.

As the firefighters begin the process of pulling her to the top, I turn my head to Daniel who is crouched on the ground, spent. He looks at me and whispers, "I'm so sorry."

That's when the tears come harder.

Ezra is standing in front of us. He eyes me from head to toe, then says to the officers, "I think she probably has a broken ankle and minor contusions."

"Are you able to stand?" the female officer asks.

I try to stand, but the female officer shakes her head. "Don't move. We'll take care of you."

Ezra climbs back up the lookout on his own where he talks to the paramedics, and over the course of an hour, my husband and I are also brought to the top on stretchers. Alexis is gone.

Once I'm safely on the lookout, where a paramedic vehicle awaits to transport us out of the ravine, Jacob runs to me. "Mommy, are you okay?"

"I'm fine, baby," I say through my tears and hold his soft hand in mine. "Are you okay?"

He shakes his head. "Why was Emily so mean?" he asks.

"Because she's not who we thought she was." I want to say more, but my voice fails.

And all I can do is close my eyes.

CHAPTER THIRTY-SIX

HOLLY

Before

At first it's not clear what Alexis is trying to do. Her hands are reaching out toward Holly. Is she reaching out to apologize? To hug her? But before Holly can think further, her stepsister hits her hard on the shoulders. Holly's pushed backward suddenly, and she struggles to regain her balance on the pool deck by putting out her hands and grabbing hold of Alexis. Except she misses. Alexis's hands come toward her neck, and her fingers latch on to Holly's necklace, pulling her forward by the chain. The chain snaps. Holly loses her footing.

She trips over the pool skimmer on the pavement by her feet. She registers the shock on Alexis's face in the split second before she falls, her head slamming into the poolside concrete, her body rolling into the water with barely a splash.

Holly loves the water, but this is different. Why can't she swim?

Is she dreaming? She hears noises, muffled and far away, above the distorted surface of the water. The only thing she can hear clearly is her own heart, pulsing in her ears. There's pain somewhere, but it's so distant, so far away. Is it her head? It doesn't matter. She feels safe and warm in the water. It's the same way she feels with Sarah, like everything's going to be okay. She takes in a breath, but something's wrong. Why can't she breathe?

She extends a hand to the surface. Her stepsister's at the edge of the pool. She can see her there, shimmering and blurred. No matter what, Alexis always watches out for her. Holly's arm feels so heavy. Why can't she lift it? Her head feels like a boulder. She's sinking down, down, getting farther away from the surface. As she descends, she admires the water around her, a beautiful, vibrant turquoise, but there's a strange strand snaking above her, like a red and twisted rope.

Something glints on the bottom of the pool. Her necklace.

Then, she hears it. She hears it for the first time, so distinctly, a voice saying her name.

It isn't Alexis. No. It's someone else. It's her mother, calling her home.

CHAPTER THIRTY-SEVEN

SARAH

Nine Months Later

It's a beautiful summer day, a slight breeze tickling my bare arms as Jacob and I head home together. Today was his last day of second grade at the elementary school he's been attending since October, when we left north Toronto and moved to a two-bedroom apartment in Bloor West Village. Only a five-minute walk from us, High Park is lush and breathtaking, and our neighborhood is warm, eclectic, and diverse. I prefer this to the suburbs.

"Mommy, can you carry my backpack? It's so heavy." Jacob looks up at me with his big blue eyes, long lashes fluttering in his attempt to charm me into doing something for him he is perfectly capable of doing himself.

"It's a good thing you're so strong," I say. "Strong enough to carry it yourself."

He groans and hoists his backpack higher on his shoulders. "Daddy's taking me to Canada's Wonderland today?"

I smile. "Yup. Right after he gets home from his meeting."

I mean his Gamblers Anonymous meeting, something we don't hide from Jacob. It's important for him to see that people make mistakes, but if we admit to them, talk about them openly, and work to be better, forgiveness is possible.

It's taken a long time for me to trust Daniel again. After the York Regional police took Alexis into custody, Daniel cooperated with the Vancouver police to take down Charlie and the gambling ring he organized through the Canyon Club. Because of Daniel's help, Charlie is no longer a member of any club, as he's in custody, awaiting sentencing after being convicted of fraud, criminal organization, money laundering, and tax evasion. Daniel was never charged for his involvement in the gambling network. He got off legally, but in many other ways, his involvement took its toll, especially on our marriage.

After that day in the ravine, Tara let Jacob and me move in with her until we got our bearings—because I never wanted to step foot inside the rental house of horrors ever again. And before Daniel entered rehab, he admitted everything he'd done, his gambling addiction that had plunged us into financial ruin, how he'd hidden it all from me because he didn't want to lose me, us—his family. He lied about why we were moving to Toronto. He'd never been headhunted. There was no job waiting for him. He spent his days looking for work, trying to land legal employment for us to live on, because there was no sale of our Cliffside house. He'd gifted it to Charlie Lang to clear all his debts and buy his way out of the gambling ring. We were surviving on nothing but his credit.

Daniel spent so much time hiding his compulsions, and I, hiding mine. The whole time that strange things were happening to us in Blossom Court, he wasn't sure if it was Holly or Charlie who was terrorizing us. He was terrified that Charlie hadn't kept his word, that he'd never release him from the dangerous net he'd gotten snared in.

He, too, had received threatening texts, but on a secret phone I never knew about. A secret phone Holly had found in his cabana, which led her to sacrificing her body, her whole self, to help him get out of debt. He also secretly tried to contact Holly to stop her, but of course, it was Alexis we were both communicating with all along.

Jacob skips ahead, no thumb in his mouth, no heavy burden of sadness weighing him down. But he's still grieving Holly's death, as I am. We had to explain to him that Emily was Holly's stepsister and that she was a bad, bad lady who did a horrible thing to Holly, something that killed her. He never asked what, and thankfully, we never had to tell him it happened in our own backyard in Vancouver.

The day after Alexis tried to kill Daniel and me, the Vancouver police found Holly's body buried under mounds of dirt in the dense, tangled woods outside our home on Cliffside Road. It was the same place where I used to take photos, my camera pointing up to Holly Monroe's bedroom window. Holly was found with her broken yin necklace placed over her heart.

Whenever I think about Holly's last moments, I feel guilty. All she wanted was a family to love and accept her for who she was. She tried to save me when I didn't even know I required saving. Yet when she needed me most, I wasn't there.

The only solace is that Holly now rests next to the mother she never knew but always longed for.

Alexis was initially charged with criminal negligence causing Holly's death, but her lawyer argued that she'd pulled Holly's body from the pool and tried to resuscitate her, proving that she had no intention of drowning Holly. The autopsy showed that Holly's skull had evidence of blunt-force trauma to the side of her head caused by the cement of the pool deck; her brain suffered a subdural hematoma. The official cause of death was asphyxia from the pool water filling her lungs and cutting off her oxygen supply before her stepsister could save her.

I believe the coroner got it right when he ruled Holly's death an accident. I believe that Alexis loved Holly and didn't mean to drown her. But dragging her stepsister's body into the woods by our house, hiding it under thick clumps of dirt and wet leaves was horrifyingly intentional. And she failed to report a dead body, a crime under the Coroners Act of British Columbia. She was charged with indignity to a human body, and attempted murder of Daniel and me, forcible confinement, breaking and entering into our homes on Cliffside Road and Lilac Lane, criminal harassment, and illegal surveillance for placing hidden cameras all over the house in Blossom Court. Alexis has pled not guilty to all the charges levied against her. She's currently being held without bail because she's considered a flight risk, based on the Monroes' considerable wealth and connections. Her trial is set to begin in Vancouver in the fall. I'm relieved she's being held halfway across the country and that we're free of her—for the moment. I just hope justice is served.

Now, my son bounds up our porch steps, eager to get to Roscoe, who we can hear barking and whining inside. After Alexis was arrested, we kept the dog, which we later found out she'd bought off Craigslist to emotionally exploit my son. Roscoe's been a great comfort to Jacob, and to me and Daniel, too. I open the front door that leads to a shared hallway with the upstairs tenant, then unlock the door to our place. Jacob races inside, flings his backpack to the floor, and Roscoe covers him with kisses. I laugh as they entangle themselves in a hug of fur and skinny boy limbs.

It's still hard for me to reconcile Emily, my neighbor, with Alexis, a woman who may not have wanted her stepsister dead but who most definitely tried to kill my husband and me. Sometimes, when I think of Alexis, I think she's pure evil. Other times, I'm not so sure. Maybe it's not as basic as being good or evil.

I should never have taken photos of Holly without her consent. Daniel should never have hidden his gambling from me. Everyone has parts of themselves they're ashamed of, that they hide. Desperate people do desperate things. Not always on purpose. But sometimes.

The details of what happened after we left Vancouver became clearer over time. After she'd concealed Holly's body, Alexis took possession of Holly's phone, posting on Instagram and sending texts, making everyone—even Holly's own negligent parents—believe Holly was really at a retreat. She used that phone to track Daniel, the same way Holly did, leading her straight to us in Blossom Court. She also bought a burner phone registered to a private number to terrorize me and Daniel with texts, aware that we were scared about every secret Holly had discovered about us.

Sometimes I wonder how things might have been different if Holly had confided in me. Maybe I could have helped her. Maybe Alexis could have, too.

How many Health ProX investors did Holly sleep with just to win the love of her father? I'll never know.

Holly's relationship with Charlie never came up at his trial. We don't know if Holly followed through on her plan to blackmail him because Daniel's never spoken to Charlie again. Investigators never found Alexis's burner phone or Holly's phone. I think Alexis must have destroyed them. All of Alexis's texts to us, and the video of Holly and Charlie in my living room on Cliffside, are likely underwater or smashed to bits, and I burned all my photographic evidence long ago. Perhaps the videos exist somewhere in the ether, but I try not to think about that. I've tried to erase those recordings from my mind.

I hear a key in the lock, and the door opens. Daniel steps into the entryway, which I've painted a lovely shade of gray. Jacob flings himself at his father, much like he did with Roscoe.

Alexis was right. Only Jacob is purely good. My boy has so much strength, courage, and forgiveness inside. He never ceases to amaze me.

"Hey, buddy, how was the last day of school?" Daniel's thinner, and his black board shorts hang off his hips. He looks a bit drawn, like he always does after his meetings. I, too, have lost weight but in the wrong places. My skin is looser, my age is showing, but I'm trying to love the body I'm in, love the age I'm at. I'm grateful to be alive.

"School was awesome. There was a party on the field. Can we go to Wonderland now?"

Daniel grins at our son. "After you clean your room. You were supposed to do it yesterday."

"Aw, man," Jacob complains, and we laugh.

After Jacob runs down the hall to his room, Daniel sits on the light pink armchair Tara reupholstered for us as a housewarming gift. Tara is my friend, the first and only mom friend I've ever made. Since we moved away from Blossom Court and she and Cody remained on Lilac Lane, they drive down here a few times a month to visit. Sometimes Ezra comes with them, always wearing his favorite tan pants, which no longer seem so strange to me.

Nick still hasn't surfaced. In his absence, and because Cody's mother, who lives in Hawaii, agreed, Tara's gotten full custody of Cody, and they both seem more secure and settled. Happy even.

I catch Daniel staring at the framed photo of Jacob, Holly, and me on our pool deck, one of the only photos of her that I'm proud to display. It's on the living room wall, surrounded by other family photos I've taken. Holly's looking at me with so much love. My therapist, Priya, recommended by Ezra, who sees her for the PTSD—part of the legacy of being a frontline medical worker—told me it's good to remember her. So I do. Priya also suggested Daniel and I work extra hard to keep lines of communication open, something we've never been very good at. Whenever he returns from a meeting, I ask him how he's feeling, though I know it's hard for him to talk about.

"Today was good. Draining. We talked about why I got addicted to gambling, how the thrill of being in the big leagues at the club became all important to me." He shrugs, but it's not nonchalant or uncaring. It's an attempt to shift the weight of his guilt, which I know is painful for him to carry. "I never felt like I measured up in my family, or anywhere, I guess. I thought if I had all the money and the things and the connections, then I'd be a winner. I'd feel good enough."

I wish we'd talked about all of this when we'd met, married, and had a child. Wanting to be accepted drives so many of our actions. But eventually, we face the consequences.

"For the record, all I ever wanted was you. You and Jacob."

He brushes his hand over his hair. It's shorter and grayer these days. It suits him. He's started his own consulting business, and he deposits everything he earns, which isn't much yet, into an account that only I have access to. I control all of our finances now, and I like it.

I'm making my own way, selling new photos I'm taking—of people with their permission—on my Etsy shop, and I teach a photography class for children twice a week. Daniel's parents and my mom and Nathan have been helping us out financially, too, and I accept it when it's offered.

There's a bang from Jacob's room, across the hall from ours.

"I dropped my book. Sorry!"

Daniel and I share a smirk. "He's jumping on his bed," I say.

Daniel nods. "And hasn't cleaned a thing."

I chuckle. "Some things never change."

Being Jacob's mother is one of the greatest joys in my life. But I know that's not all I am. I'm a photographer, a citizen in a community, a friend and neighbor, and much more. I'm learning to define myself. And to find myself. If everyone understood that people need to define themselves separately from their families, maybe the tragedy that befell Holly would never have happened. Maybe she'd still be alive.

Jacob comes into the living room, sweaty and grinning. "I'm done cleaning."

I'm sure his room looks exactly the same, if not messier than before, but that's okay. Giving him responsibility is really about letting go of the reins a little bit, as far as I'm comfortable for now. It's a step.

Daniel gets up. "I'll text when we get to Wonderland."

I get up, too. "Just have fun. I trust you."

I kiss my son and husband goodbye. Jacob holds Daniel's hand, my little boy and the father he worships, as they walk together down the hall and out the front door. I wait on the porch while they climb into our used car, parked at the curb outside our new home. And they drive away from me.

I keep my eyes on them until they disappear, until I can no longer watch them.

ACKNOWLEDGMENTS

Writing is often considered a solitary endeavor, yet I was never alone while writing *Watch Out for Her*. Literally.

In March 2020, like everyone in the world, I learned that we never know what's around the corner, good and bad, beautiful and devastating. Writing a second book—during a pandemic, no less—was a cathartic, daunting, excruciating, and exhilarating experience. With two kids at home most of the time, the concepts of "juggling" and "balancing" went out the window, along with all plans for how my debut book launch would be and how life would unfold.

The book and parenting communities all pivoted and came together to support each other to get through the long days and also find joy and hope in one another's work and lives. I'm immensely grateful to all of them and for having an identity as a writer that's all my own, a place to put my fears and worries, and a career that sustains me in every way. But I absolutely do not do it on my own.

ACKNOWLEDGMENTS

My remarkable, dedicated, fearless agent, Jenny Bent, is by my side every step of the way and the very best person to have in my corner. The Bent Agency is the most wonderful, collaborative team, and I'm so lucky to work with all of them, especially Amelia Hodgson, Victoria Cappello, Claire Draper, and Nissa Cullen.

I hope every author has the magical opportunity to work with an extraordinary editor like Nita Pronovost. Her brilliant guidance, immense patience, and invaluable insights transformed this book. Draft after draft, and through epic Zoom and phone calls, Nita pulled everything out of my soul and helped me pour it onto the page. She advocates for me and has become a treasured friend and part of my author community, as well.

Simon & Schuster Canada has given me the most supportive home, with the hardest working team of people. Thank you to my phenomenal publicist, Jillian Levick; remarkable marketing leads, Alexandra Boelsterli and Rebecca Snodden; fabulous vice president of marketing and publicity, Felicia Quon; fantastic vice president and director of publicity and Canadian sales, Adria Iwasutiak; genius copy editor, Erica Ferguson; eagle-eyed proofreader, Carla Benton; superb cover designer, David Gee; and to the wonderful Kevin Hanson, Sarah St. Pierre, Jasmine Elliott, Mackenzie Croft, Karen Silva, Shara Alexa, David Miller, and Rita Sheridan for everything you do for me.

Though Google and I are very well-acquainted, I am grateful to the experts who give very generously of their time and knowledge so my work is as accurate as possible: Detective-Constable Minh Tran, Toronto Police; and Brett Cohen, Assistant Crown Attorney in North York, Ontario. Any errors are my own and/or creative license.

Thank you to Craig Bell for donating the winning bid in the CIBC United Way auction to have a character in this book named after his wife, Valerie Martin.

To the librarians and booksellers all over the world, I am so thankful for everything you do for me and other authors. I want to give a special mention to Sheila Bauman at the Kitchener Public Library; to

ACKNOWLEDGMENTS

Scott Pardon at Chapters/Indigo in Toronto, who has been so kind and supportive of me; and to Courtney Calder, Scott's wife, for being the first reader, aside from family and friends, to love my debut right after it published, and who has recommended it to so many people.

The author community is one of the most genuinely loving groups of people I have ever had the privilege of knowing. Their words inspire me, and their friendship means everything to me. Thank you Lisa Unger, Lisa Barr, Rochelle Weinstein, all of the 2020 debuts, Genevieve Graham, Hannah Mary McKinnon, Natalie Jenner, Jennifer Hillier, Bianca Marais, Daniel Kalla, Heather Chavez, Sharon Doering, Tessa Wegert, Heather Gudenkauf, Wendy Walker, Kathleen Barber, Kimberly Belle, Christina McDonald, Samantha Downing, Brad King, Meredith Jaeger, Lori Nelson Spielman, Amber Cowie, P. J. Vernon, Amina Akhtar, May Cobb, Laurie Elizabeth Flynn, Caroline Kepnes, Gilly Macmillan, Allie Reynolds, Stephanie Wrobel, Karen Hamilton, Amy McCulloch, Sheena Kamal, Lydia Laceby, Amy Stuart, Hank Phillippi Ryan, Andrea Bartz, Mary Kubica, Vanessa Lillie, Robyn Harding, Roz Nay, Marissa Stapley, Karma Brown, Rebecca Eckler, Jen Griswell, Lucie and Jesse Thistle, and Jess Skoog. There are so many others, as well.

There is also a group of women who are my soul sisters, authors who have supported and believed in me long before anyone knew my name. They are my Beach Babes, and I don't know what I'd do without them. I love you, Meredith Schorr, my trusted critique partner, roommate on every trip, and the person I email a hundred times a day; Francine LaSala, my editing partner, vault, and favorite snuggler; Eileen Goudge, master foot rubber and storyteller; Julie Valerie, a brilliant mind coupled with the warmest heart; Josie Brown, prolific and the best confidence booster; and Jen Tucker, sweet, sassy, and sharp. All incredibly talented authors and my closest confidantes.

My friends in "real life," who make sure I leave the land of make-believe once in a while, are so important to me. Miko, Michael, Nicole, Cheryl, Deb S., Lisa G., Rachel Y., Kailey, Simone, Leslie C., Lise,

ACKNOWLEDGMENTS

Laura C., Erin, Patty, Kathy D., Helen, Val, Karen J., Christine H., Jessica H., Audrey, Beth, Frances, Caroline, Luis, Maggie, Hugh, Lesley, Catherine M., Karen R., Idan, Mitch, Sylwia, Matt, Jen S., Amanda, Jon, Robynn, Pauline, Steve, Leanne, Jenny R., Adam N., and Melanie, thank you for being you.

An author can't get the word out about her work by herself. The entire book community puts enormous effort into posting, sharing, and reviewing, and I'm so grateful. I'd love to name them all, but it would take ten pages. I must give a special thank-you, though, to Andrea Peskind Katz (Great Thoughts; Great Readers), Athena Kaye, Kristy Barrett and Tonni Callan (A Novel Bee), Annie McDonnell (World of the Write Review), Tamara Welch (*Traveling with T*), Judith D. Collins, Laurie (*Books and Chinooks*), Nic Farrell (*Flirty & Dirty Book Blog*), all of the Canadian Book Enablers, Jenna (@flowers favouritefiction), Sonica Soares (@the_reading_beauty), Candice (@candice_reads/*Magnolia Reads*), Dana (@danish_mustardreads), Tina Barbieri (@bookwineclub), Jenn (@burlingtonbibliophagist), Kate Winn (@katethismomloves), Jennie Shaw, Kristin (@k2reader), Ashleigh (@teatime_with_a_book), Laurie (@bakingbookworm), Erin (@girlwellread), Eleni (@lafemmereaders620), Jamie Rosenblit (@beautyandthebook), Gare (@gareindeedreads), Emily (@emilybookedup), Jeremy Stewart (@darkthrillsandchills), Kayleigh (@2babesandabookshelf), Alex (@alexatthelake), Kaley Stewart (@kaleys23), Stephanie (@stephanielikesbooks), Joanne (@jojosbook nook), Katie (@theinstabookworm), Dany Drexler (@danythebook worm_), Jen Jumba, Suzanne Weinstein Leopold (@suzyapproved bookreviews), Kate Rock (@katerocklitchick), Melissa Amster (@chicklitcentral), Angie (@readwithangie), Olivia (@torontobiblio phile), Heather (@themaritimereader), Dawn (@dawnsworldblog), Sue (@soobooksalot), Natalie (@bookandbakeryfinds), Norma (@readinginthecountry), Aymie (@periop_bookie), Angie (@angies bookshelf), Pepper & Digger (@pugsnpages), and Carrie Shields (@carriesreadsthem_all).

ACKNOWLEDGMENTS

I know how lucky I am to have an amazing family. My parents, Celia and Michael; my brother, Jonah, sister-in-law Perlita, niece Hannah, and nephew Mikey; and the taller side of my family, Eileen, Ron, Scott, Lindsay, Todd, Lori, niece Brynna, and nephews Felix, Bassie, and Owen; I love you all so very much.

And to the people who are my whole life, the ones who have to live with a writer, which is not always easy (especially when I accidentally call them by my characters' names): I could not have finished this book without Brent, Spencer, Chloe, and Jasper. My darlings, you gave me as much space and time in my kitchen/office as you could over the last year, but most of all, you gave me laughter every day. I am in awe of all your talents and strengths. My heart can't beat without you.

Finally, to my readers across the globe, you have embraced me and my debut more than I could ever have dreamed of, sent me the most beautiful messages, and truly are the reason I write, why I leap out of bed every morning, excited to create. I hope you want to follow my voice and characters in every book I publish.

ABOUT THE AUTHOR

© Dahlia Katz Photography

SAMANTHA M. BAILEY is the *USA TODAY* and #1 national best-selling author of *Woman on the Edge*, which has sold in eleven countries to date. She is also a journalist and freelance editor; her work has appeared in *NOW Magazine*, *The Village Post*, *The Thrill Begins*, and *The Crime Hub*, among other publications. *Watch Out for Her* is her second novel. Samantha lives in Toronto, where she's currently working on her next book. Connect with her on Twitter and Instagram **@SBaileyBooks** and on her website at **SamanthaMBailey.com**.